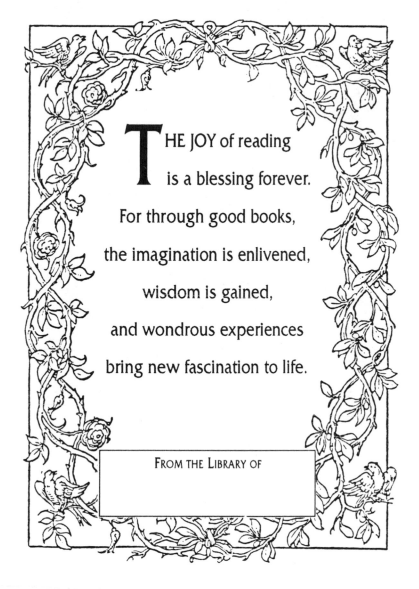

THE JOY of reading is a blessing forever. For through good books, the imagination is enlivened, wisdom is gained, and wondrous experiences bring new fascination to life.

FROM THE LIBRARY OF

THE BUCCANEERS

The Pirate and His Lady

by Linda Chaikin

COMPLETE AND UNABRIDGED

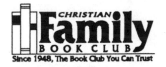

CHRISTIAN Family
BOOK CLUB
Since 1948, The Book Club You Can Trust

ISBN; 0-8024-1072-3

1 3 5 7 9 10 8 6 4 2

Printed in the United States of America

First Hardcover Edition for Christian Family Book Club: 1997

To Ella K. Lindvall,
one of the finest editors in
Christian publishing—Psalm 20:1–5

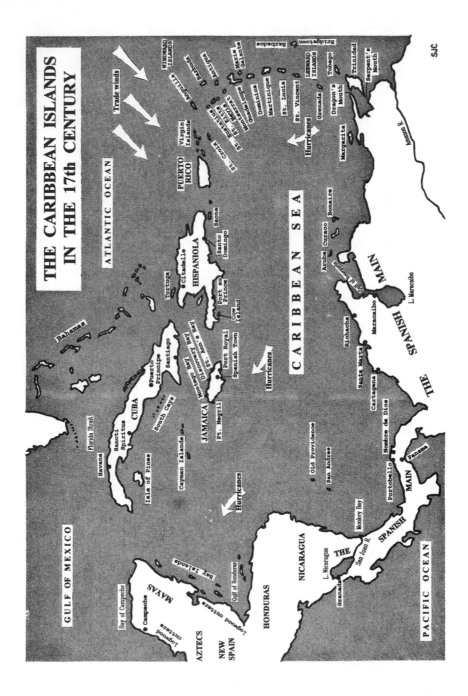

THE CARIBBEAN ISLANDS
IN THE 17th CENTURY

Trade winds

ATLANTIC OCEAN

GULF OF MEXICO

Bahamas

Florida Strait

Havana

Sancti
Spiritus

Isle of Pines

CUBA

South Caye

Cayman Islands

Puerto
Principe

Santiago

Montego Bay

Discovery Bay

St. Ann's Bay

JAMAICA

Pt. Negril

Spanish Town

Port Royal

Tortuga

Citadelle

HISPANIOLA

Cape
Nicoli

Port au
Prince

Santo
Domingo

Saona

Mona

St. Croix

PUERTO
RICO

Virgin
Islands

Anguilla

Barbuda

St. Eustatius
St. Kitts
Nevis

Antigua

Maria
Galante

Guadeloupe

Dominica

Martinique

St. Lucia

St. Vincent

Barbados

Bridgetown

Grenada

WINDWARD
ISLANDS

LEEWARD
ISLANDS

Dragon's
Mouth

Tobago

Serpent's
Mouth

Trinidad

Hurricanes

Margarita

CARIBBEAN   SEA

Hurricanes

Hurricanes

Old Providence

San Andres

Aruba   Curacao   Bonaire

Rio Hacha

Santa Marta

Cartagena

Nombre de Dios

Portobello

Panama

Monkey Bay

San Juan R.

L. Nicaragua

NICARAGUA

THE

SPANISH   MAIN

Maracaibo

L. Maracaibo

THE   SPANISH   MAIN

Amazon R.

Granada

Bay Islands

Gulf of Honduras

HONDURAS

Logwood cutters

MAYAS

Campeche

Bay of Campeche

NEW
SPAIN

AZTECS

Logwood cutters

PACIFIC OCEAN

SJC

CONTENTS

Part One

ON THE SPANISH MAIN

1

BARET BUCKINGTON'S DILEMMA

Aboard the twenty-gun buccaneering vessel the *Regale,* its enigmatic captain, Baret Foxworth—in reality Viscount Baret Buckington, grandson of Earl Nigel Buckington II—opened his desk drawer and replaced his worn, leather-bound copy of John Calvin's Institutes beneath a sheaf of drawings. The copy of Calvin's theology along with a book of Puritan prayers were contradictory evidence revealing Baret's complexity.

Included in the papers he kept at hand were several pirated maps of the West Indies, which he had gratefully confiscated from a Spanish *capitán* before happily sinking the galleon to the bottom of the blue Caribbean. There were also several of Baret's better sketches that he'd done in pencil. One of them was of Emerald Harwick. The second was of the woman he had intended to marry—until she had betrayed him by marrying his cousin.

Flaxen-haired Lavender, a future duchess, was now Lady Grayford Thaxton. He knew he should get rid of the drawing, but his emotions had not yet been able to release her. He comforted his troubled conscience by telling himself that he kept the sketch only because it was well done.

The third drawing was of his staunch Puritan tutor from Cambridge, Sir Cecil Chaderton. His sharp, sanctified gaze pierced Baret's soul with scriptural conviction of the absolute holiness of the God he read about in Calvin's Institutes.

Gazing at Sir Cecil's hawklike countenance brought an unlikely half smile to Baret's face. When Cecil discovered that Uncle Felix Buckington hoped to have Baret arrested for piracy and hanged, he would be quick to remind Captain Foxworth of his past warnings against the dubious career of buccaneering. Baret's mouth curved with bitter irony.

"Warm family affection runs as deep as the Caribbean currents," he murmured. "An uncle, in order to inherit the earldom of my father, will justify his decision to hang a nephew who stands in his way."

"*Har*, you was sayin', your lordship—I means, Cap'n Foxworth?"

Baret glanced at his serving man, Hob, seeing a grin-creased leathery face beneath a floppy hat pulled low over shaggy white hair. His cool cotton drawers were cut off calf-length, and his sun-faded red shirt was too big on his stooped shoulders. The sleeves were rolled up haphazardly and tied into place below the elbows. He carried a gleaming coffee pot in one gnarled brown hand and a spotless captain's mug of Peruvian silver in the other.

"More's the pity I can't hang Felix instead," Baret said.

Hob scratched his chin and chuckled. "Always did think ye had a shark's sense of good humor. Aye, ol' Felix would make a pert sight, says I, but better think twice. Havin' Jamie Boy danglin' on the yardarm of the *Regale* be trouble enough for ye at port. If ye go to danglin' Lord Felix too, I'll be bringin' your coffee to Gallows Point. Them rascally-mouthed judges in the Admiralty Court don't have any humor."

Hob set the coffee service on the desktop and left.

Baret snapped the heavy drawer closed and locked it, then turned to an ornate peg on the cabin wall behind the desk and removed his buccaneering regalia. He slipped the wide leather baldric, containing a pair of silver-butted French pistols, over his dark head. Unlike his Puritan beliefs and the short hairstyle generated by the Roundheads, his own hair bore quiet proof of his royal blood and was worn in the fashion of the Cavaliers of King Charles II.

Catching up his wide-brimmed black velvet hat with dashing pristine-white plume, he flecked away a speck of lint and settled it on his head with a tap. He wore a matching black velvet jacket with wide lapels and a white Holland linen buccaneer shirt with full sleeves. His appearance had earned him young feminine sighs, but the reaction to his goodly countenance brought Baret more cynical amusement than it cultivated conceit.

Sir Cecil had taken laborious pains to lecture him as a growing lad about the evils of undisciplined handsome flesh. "Good looks are the devil's playground. So is idleness. It is now time for your lesson in Greek."

12

Baret smiled at the memory of his days in France with the exiled King Charles. He took only a sip of the coffee, then turned to leave his immaculate cabin. As he did, an accidental glance at his darkly handsome reflection in the small looking glass brought a thoughtful pause, followed by a slight frown. The frown was not at the remembered words of his teacher but at what his reflection represented in the Caribbean.

His image belonged to a stranger, not the youth he remembered under the strict tutelage of Cecil. Baret hardly knew the man in the mirror. The ruthless challenge in his dark gaze might have belonged to the pirate Henry Morgan or to Pierre LaMonte. Nor did he even try to reconcile the difference between what he had been at Cambridge and what he was now.

"You make a realistic enough rogue to gather a crowd at your hanging." A crisp voice came from the cabin door.

Baret turned toward the familiar voice. Sir Cecil stood without, wearing his wry yet affectionate expression.

Surprised and genuinely pleased to see him, Baret smiled disarmingly. "Welcome home to the *Regale,* my dear Cecil. I'm soon ready to sail for an attack on Cartagena. Have a seat." He gestured to an unlikely furnishing to be found aboard a pirate ship, a luxurious velvet chair that Cecil had claimed for his own in the past.

Baret turned his head and called, "Hob! Quick! Tea for the Cambridge scholar! We have a royal guest today, the gentleman who taught me Greek and—" he doffed his hat and bowed to Sir Cecil "—Spanish. A debt I can never repay."

Sir Cecil's thin mouth went down at the corner. "My one mistake." He eased his lanky frame into the soft chair, looking about.

"Seems like old times," said Baret. "I've been wondering what to do with that odious chair."

"Old times and comfortable chairs are not as easily forgotten and packed away as books—and Bibles." He shot Baret a meaningful glance.

Baret slipped from the uneasy moment as smoothly as a live wet fish, and smiled. "I'm glad to see you've returned. Your presence graces my ship with an aura of respectability. His Majesty will find the report you will write about our venture on the Venezuelan coast of serious interest—and acceptance. In light of the trouble I'm having with Governor Modyford, we'll need your endorsement."

"I dare say. There will be no more respectable reports to the king by this Cambridge divine until you quit the life of a buccaneer. The tropics are going to your head, and the gallows are waiting for your neck."

Baret folded his arms. "Now you're sounding uncomfortably much like Earl Nigel Buckington. Did you come this dangerous distance to Tortuga to have me surrender to the High Admiralty Court—or to board a merchant ship for London like a whipped puppy?"

"Discipline your tongue, you impudent rogue. Neither the Admiralty nor Nigel knows I've risked a trip to the odious Tortuga to find you and bring you safely back to Foxemoore." He smoothed the starched white shirt at his throat. "I've come on my own—and because Jette is asking for you each night in his prayers."

Baret let out a breath, more troubled over his half brother than he could or would admit. "I can do nothing for the boy yet. I've written a letter. You can deliver it for me. Along with a wood turtle that Hob carved."

"He'll be up till midnight with delight. Look, Baret, come home! The boy needs you. Your father may be dead, and Jette is only eight. He looks on you as his father. Then there's the delightful young lady Emerald, just waiting to become Lady Buckington. I would think you'd be beating your sails back to Port Royal with the first fair wind. She's as lovely as they come. Marriage will be good for you. Sell the *Regale* to one of your pirate friends, and let's return to Foxemoore."

Baret looked at him from beneath dark lashes, resisting the pull. He managed a laugh. "I always knew there was more humor in that mind of yours than pure Calvinism would allow. I confess I'd enjoy Jette immensely. And I've missed the schoolgirl treachery that Harwick's daughter so blatantly inflicts on me. She ought to be here now, rummaging my desk and gliding about in pirate's drawers. But—"

"Pirate's pantaloons! Is that how you envision her?"

Baret concealed a smile. It wasn't, but he wouldn't admit this to Cecil.

"She's emerging into a fair and noble young woman," said Cecil.

"I've no doubt." He tapped his chin thoughtfully, pretending consideration.

"Yet you persist in calling her 'Harwick's daughter.' Do you realize how often you say that? As though you wish her to remain impersonal. Her name is Emerald."

"I know her name."

"Then use it. You might as well call her 'Harwick's brat,' like the rest of the family."

"I've never called her that!"

"And now you're furious. Why? You care for her more than you admit, yet you are still thinking of Lavender."

"I never mentioned Lavender. As for Emerald, I know she's growing up. She's sixteen—"

"Seventeen now."

He knew quite well that she was seventeen. "And three years more is fine with me."

"I'm certain it is." Cecil gave a laugh. "You'd make it ten if you could get by with it."

"You don't know what you're talking about, Cecil. I intend to marry her. In fact, I admitted I wanted her, didn't I?"

"In a small way."

"Do you call twenty thousand pieces of eight *small?* I bought her." He smiled. "She's mine."

"Indeed?"

"And it's also been quiet and peaceful even on Tortuga now that she's safely on her way to England. That's just where I want her. Out of my life for three years. I need time to breathe. She can learn under the prim and sour instruction of a schoolmistress, who will do her willful spirit wonders." He added with silky innocence, "And when I see her next, she will be donned in French gowns and wearing sugar curls. She'll be bowing and pleasing me, her dutiful master and upcoming husband!" His dark eyes danced. "'Yes, m'lord, no, m'lord. Why, anything you say, m'lord.'"

"*Hah.* You scoundrel." Cecil's eyes flared with malicious amusement. "Well, you may see your new darling much sooner than you expect, but without bowing and pleasing your conceited whims."

Baret scrutinized him with suspicion. *Much sooner than you expect.* Cecil had sounded too sure of matters. Baret glanced toward the door. "Don't tell me you've brought the little darling back to my ship? I fear I've run out of pieces of eight, and who can tell what knave will next wish to duel me for her?"

"No, no." He waved a hand airily. "I came alone. And if she heard you making light of your audacity in buying her with pirated pieces of eight, she'd relinquish your betrothal to the sharks swimming about and never shed a tear."

Baret leaned against his desk. "Your warm words cheer me. It's always cozy to have the girl you intend to marry so desperately attached."

"You could consider your own wealth of cozy warmth sadly lacking. From what I hear from Karlton, you sent Emerald away without so much as a ring of credential promising your intentions. Every girl wishes a ring to wave under the noses of jealous friends."

Baret glanced at the family ring on his hand, and his mouth curved. "And the Buckington ring would do well enough, I suppose. It would make Lavender uncomfortable, wouldn't it? She always boasted it was worth the crown jewels," he said with a touch of sarcasm. "I should send the ring to Harwick's daughter at once. After all, it's only been worn by family earls and countesses for generations."

"And pirates."

Baret winced. "I guess I deserve that."

"You do indeed. If you're not serious about your claim to her, Baret, you best play the gallant scoundrel you are and do something about it as soon as possible. She's a fair child, and I won't have her hurt any more than she has been. With your growing reputation for piracy, and Emerald known to have voyaged with you, you'll ruin any further chances she has to marry a godly man."

Baret frowned, and his dark eyes narrowed. "She'll marry no one else unless I'm good and ready to give her up."

"Such conceit. You sound the viscount, to be sure."

"And I'm not ready," he stated flatly. "Of course, I'll make good. I told her that."

"Did you? Very businesslike, I suppose."

"Not exactly business." He felt unexpected irritation as

though trapped by the huntsman. "Did she send you here to hound me?"

"Good mercy, no! I've not seen her, but I have spoken to Karlton. So has Lady Sophie."

"Then that accounts for it. Sir Karlton would want me to send the ring with blaring trumpets."

"Do you think Emerald is the kind of young lady to chain you to her even if she is not wanted?"

"If it's a ring she demands, I'll send her one—one from Porto Bello. And a trunk of gowns. That should keep her busy for a while. She can tell Lavender I proposed to her on bended knee with thudding heart."

Sir Cecil stared at him, interlacing his long fingers and tapping them with tried patience. "You would do well to bend the knee to Emerald rather than Lavender. Need I remind you it was you who dueled that odious French pirate Levasseur to claim her?"

"I remember quite well."

"I didn't see her chasing after you, begging you to stay, as I've seen the others—including Lavender."

Baret flipped the pen on his desk. The thought brought further irritation. "Never mind. As for Lavender, why do you persist in bringing her up? She's married to Grayford."

Sir Cecil's fingers fell still.

A moment slipped by. Baret, aware of the strange silence, looked up from the pen, frowning, wondering why the man had ceased his badgering. "One would think I'm yet a lad in knee pants the way you lecture. This is like that cramped chamber above the narrow streets of Paris. The only thing missing is my glass of milk."

Cecil laughed. "Ah! Those were the days . . . but in truth, I didn't come about the raven-haired Emerald *or* Lavender. You won't be so pleased when you know why I'm here. I won't be sailing with you, Baret. I've just come to ask you to come home before I must come to the grief of my old age."

Baret laughed.

"The grief," said Cecil distinctly, "of seeing your death."

Baret cocked his dark head, scanning him. "So soon?" he mocked. Cecil's grim expression convinced him that he was not jesting.

17

Baret swept an arm about his cabin. "This, beloved scholar, is 'home.'" He looked up as Hob entered with the tea. "This is our new serving man," he said. "You've not met Hob yet. He sent the turtle the night we first arrived."

"Ah, yes . . ." Sir Cecil peered down his hawk nose at Hob, taking him in from head to toe. "So this is our turtle man."

Hob's shrewd eyes danced with good humor. "Aye, I be him, says I. An' beggin' your pardon, Lord Scholar, but do ye wish a dab of sweet cream in the mix?"

Cecil's brow lifted.

"Tea it is, ye can be sure of it. An' no swish of kill-devil rum neither. Straight black tea it is."

"Well, that is something to be grateful for on this day, Hob. Have you any cream?"

"Nary a drip, ye lordship, but I be knowing of an old cow the *boucaniers* took from hereabouts. She's aboard the *Black Dragon.* If'n ye have a hankering, an' if Captain Lex Thorpe's ship ain't sailed yet, an' if the cow be in a kindly mood to give a wee bit of milk, I'll get it for ye. She ain't always so obliging."

Baret laughed.

"Thank you, no," said Cecil with bored dignity. "Black tea will suffice, Hob."

A minute later as Cecil sipped the brew, Baret watched him, again growing uneasy. "You know me well enough, Cecil. You know I won't return to Foxemoore yet. So why did you come, really, if not because Emerald sent you?"

"I told you. To convince you to hang up that baldric once for all."

"A possibility for the future. But not yet. And leave my father in chains, tormented by Spanish whips? I see no cause to give up my role as buccaneer until my father's reputation is restored and we both have audience with His Majesty. After that? I'll decide if I like the sea well enough to remain a blackguard. After all," he said lightly, "it's the one career that permits me the liberty to attack Spain. Being a pirate brings me immense advantages."

"Yes, and doubtless you'll hang for your immense advantages," his dour tutor challenged. "And I'll be below the gallows reading from the Scriptures about the due results of your sins until you cease your kicking and the vultures come to feast upon you."

Baret winced. "You always were the grandfatherly sort, Cecil. You might instead read of His grace and mercy while I twist in the tropical breeze."

Cecil arched a dignified silver brow. "You are certain of His grace and mercy, are you?"

"As certain as a man can be."

"Need I remind you there is also the truth of evidence of one's having sipped pardon from His cup?"

"You may sip if you like," said Baret with a disarming smile. "I prefer to quench my thirst with a few satisfying gulps." Turning to the mirror to straighten his hat, he saw Cecil's smile. Regardless of his pretended hardness, Baret knew the old scholar took great pleasure in Baret's having learned the doctrine well.

Sir Cecil placed his thin hands on his lap and sighed as he pushed himself to his feet, housed in shiny black shoes. He threw back his thin shoulders beneath the dark frock coat and retrieved his scholar's hat from Hob, who stood gravely as Cecil peered at him with suspicion.

"Then you're determined to sail on this new venture?"

"The *San Pedro* holds an important Spanish don, one who will answer a few questions at my insistence. Yes, I intend to sail," said Baret easily, the strength of conviction showing in his handsome face.

"Take the *San Pedro* and you will have double piracy charges on your hands," Cecil warned.

When Baret regarded him evenly, his tutor sighed. "You're as stubborn as Royce was. Then I shall leave you to your vices, Baret, and you, Hob, to your turtles."

"Aye, me lordship, an' I'll be thinkin' of ye with kindness as I makes me turtle soup."

Cecil placed his hat snugly on his head, his jaw-length silver hair hanging straight and neat. "One thing about Foxemoore, Lady Sophie sets a delectable table. I have never seen so much food. You should repent and turn to raising sugar, if only for roast capon and guava jelly, Baret."

"I will ponder your advice." And Baret smiled, amused.

"I have better hope of getting my divinity student out of little Jette than you. Though I admit you studied much harder at Greek. Jette," said Cecil with emphasis, "prefers to sing."

Emerald and her interest in a singing school and slave

chants flashed before Baret's mind. "I'm disappointed you've given me up for dead," he said smoothly. He knew his tutor caught the underlying tone of his remark, for Cecil looked at him sharply.

"I, too, have better plans for Jette," he continued, turning grave at the mention of his half brother. "I don't fancy Felix as his stepfather. Nor do I trust Jette to be left to his explicit care. Remember, Jette is next in line to the inheritance after me."

"I'm well aware. So is Nigel," he said of Baret's grandfather, the earl of Buckington. "Jette's in capable hands between us, and you mentioned you wanted the charming Emerald to become his governess. A wise decision."

"A governess is hardly the title for a young girl I am expected to marry in the future. But what is this you say? My grandfather is at Foxemoore indefinitely?"

Cecil cast him an impatient glance as though Baret had been dozing at his desk. "The war, my son Baret, the war with the Dutch! You are surely aware England is fighting Holland this very hour? The earl can hardly voyage safely across the Atlantic now, can he? The rest of us are rooted to Foxemoore as well. At least until the war ends. And that may take several years. Jette will need to have his schooling on the plantation. A wry set of circumstances, considering that the plans of so many have been turned inside out, including Emerald's schooling in London. By the by, where is she? She hasn't shown herself at Foxemoore, and I haven't seen Sir Karlton recently. If she's to help me with Jette, she ought to be brought with her trunk to the Great House."

Baret straightened from the desk where he'd been leaning. He'd been so preoccupied with his planned expedition that the possibility of a delay in Emerald's voyage to England hadn't occurred to him.

"They sailed for Barbados," he told Cecil. "By now she's on a ship for London."

The long-range effect of the war could be disastrous to his plans, thought Baret, considering what it might mean to have the earl in Jamaica while he attacked the Spanish Main with Henry Morgan.

"The war means a good deal of trouble all the way around," Baret told him with a frown, remembering he had promised his grandfather he'd fight for the king against Holland.

Sir Cecil appeared to follow his concerns. "So I thought myself. At least the three years or more in England for Emerald will settle the Jamaican dust as far as this marriage is concerned."

Baret scowled under his probing gaze. "Don't look at me like that. I intend to keep my word to Karlton, though he played the game cheaply."

"You did little better by her. Twenty thousand pieces of eight! Well, she won't need to move into the Great House for who knows how many years until this war is over and you redeem her honor. A fine mess of pottage that would be."

Baret's eyes narrowed, and he leaned back against the desk.

"Stubbornness is written in your countenance," said Cecil.

"I said I'd keep my promise."

"Saying so to the girl in that tone isn't likely to send her into titters over donning a wedding dress. You look as though a matchlock were barreled into your back."

"Never mind. I got us both into this, and I'll defend her before the hounds." In a gesture of frustration over more than Emerald, he doffed his hat and dropped it with boredom on his desk. He thought of Lavender.

"I suppose Grayford will now be called on to fight the Dutch here in the Indies," he said thoughtfully, looking over at Cecil curiously, for as yet his mentor hadn't mentioned Lavender and his cousin Grayford's unexpected marriage at Foxemoore.

"I suppose he will," was all he said.

"You don't sound enthusiastic," said Baret dryly. "What's the matter? Do you think he's not up to commanding the H.M.S. *Royale?*"

Sir Cecil brushed his sleeve, avoiding Baret's gaze. This wasn't like Cecil. What was he trying to hide?

"I'm not jealous of his commanding the king's ship, if that's what troubles you," said Baret flatly. He snatched up the silver Peruvian cup of fresh coffee that Hob swiftly poured him. "I wouldn't trade the *Regale* for two of the Royal Navy's ships!"

Cecil cast him a glance. "I must be going," he said. "The knave whose sloop brought me here will be wanting to set sail for Port Royal. In the meantime, if you won't redeem your reputation on the Caribbean to save your own neck, do think of the rest of us. You should, if you would listen to my advice, return to

Jamaica to make peace with Governor Modyford and your grand-father. Wed the girl and settle down to grow cane."

Baret's mouth turned into a bored half smile. "Thank you, no. Not while my father drags Spanish chains on his ankles at Porto Bello. Forget the Dutch and French! It's Spain that England needs to blast off the Caribbean map!"

"Temper, temper. Do you also wish to forget Emerald as well as the Dutch?"

Baret caught up his hat. "I've no time now to consider her or anyone else," he said easily.

"I suggest you have time and not the inclination. Forget Henry Morgan. You'd do better to write a letter of appeal to King Charles."

Baret ignored him. "Morgan's getting the expedition ready for Porto Bello, and the *Regale* is itching to unloose her cannon on any Spanish galleons who try to stop us."

"Attack the Main when England has signed a peace treaty with Madrid and you *will* hang," said Cecil gravely. "There is no question in my mind. It's the Dutch colonies that His Majesty has sent word to Modyford to attack."

"If His *Majesty* wishes me to attack fellow Protestant brothers in favor of the inquisitors who marched across Dutch soil, he may do better in appealing to his brothers in Madrid."

Sir Cecil winced. "Softly, lad—treason will be added to piracy."

"I can only hang once. Hob! Here—fill it." And he held out his cup.

Minutes later, Baret led the way to the open cabin door, ducked his head, and stepped out.

The tropical sun was blazing. The water of Cayona Bay was a glassy green-blue. The warm breeze did little to cool him as he stood, hands on hips, looking across the cove to the other vessels at anchor, all belonging to the Brotherhood.

He took the quarterdeck steps up. What Cecil didn't know was that he wasn't going to sail with Morgan just now. He was sailing with Erik Farrow to attack the Main.

Sir Cecil stood looking up at him. "As I said, Baret, I leave you to your vices. My conscience will stubbornly retain you in daily intercession to our gracious Lord. In the meantime, if you need me I shall be found at Foxemoore."

22

Baret smiled down at him. In spite of the man's gruffness, he was deeply attached to his divinity master. "Take care, and speak also fair words on my behalf to my grandfather. With Felix at Foxemoore, I will need someone who can define to the earl the difference between a buccaneer and a pirate."

"I shall try. Nigel sees little difference, and I begin to think he is right."

Baret watched him depart the ship for the cockboat. Cecil's words continued to plow through his mind as the small craft was rowed toward a waiting sloop on its way to Jamaica. His warning of certain trouble was not lost on a rebellious spirit.

Baret knew his plight. He had taken his share of Spanish ships and had won more than his share of fencing duels. His sword was stained with Spanish blood; he insisted it had all been done in war and not for personal vengeance.

Cecil was wrong about one thing, though. Even without his warnings, Baret's conscience was alive and smarted with more pain than he would ever admit. Hatred for Madrid and anything Romish was the reason he had taken to privately studying Calvin's theology and the worn Geneva Bible. There were two natures within him that were at war with each other. Perhaps neither would emerge as total victor yet.

It was not a trivial matter to him to simply forgive and forget those responsible for the torturous death of his mother. They had buried her alive for refusing to recant her Reformational beliefs. Now his father, too, was a prisoner and suffering.

He watched Sir Cecil until the boat was but a dot. Cecil wanted the youth he remembered, but it was too late to return to his Cambridge innocence, Baret thought. The young viscount who had once been was forever gone, changed by the cruelty of the West Indies and life on Tortuga.

He wondered that he felt such little concern at the possibility of premature death. He had not meant it to be this way, but little by little the hardness had set in. It had been Lavender's gentleness that he depended on to restore tenderness to his heart. Then she had betrayed him. Now there was only Emerald. Could she ever take the place of the idealistic girl he had seen in Lavender and whom he had expected all these years to make his own?

Perhaps he would never return to England. Perhaps he

would remain in the West Indies. Perhaps he would one day settle down to build his own plantation, not in Jamaica, not even in Barbados, but in the Carolinas. It was a thought. Not more than that. He had thought of the Carolinas because of Emerald. She wouldn't need to be a countess there, enduring the gossip and cheap innuendoes that would surely plague her steps for the rest of her life. No matter that he married her. The tale of the infamous duel would endure a lifetime. No, it would last for generations if he married her.

If he married Emerald. It was curious, even to himself, that he could look back and wonder just why he had relented to Karlton.

Had he been dazed? Had it been anger at Lavender? He had felt reckless, ruthless, and, yes, even impulsive! A trait that was not like him at all. Why, then, had he agreed to the marriage? Was it possible he felt more strongly about Emerald than he understood? That made little sense, unless his mind could not relinquish the illusion of a young woman whom it had been easy to love from afar without truly testing his affection.

Marriage could not be entered into with frivolity. He knew that. And, yes, he still felt attached to Lavender, despite her marriage to his cousin. Emerald had entered his life suddenly; dramatically, and she had left her indelible imprint on his mind, but there had been no leisure to consider what it meant. Her appearance stirred his passions—she was alluring, willful, sometimes sweetly innocent—but did he know her well enough to love her, to pledge his undying devotion, his utter faithfulness before God in a marriage ceremony officiated by Sir Cecil?

He would not need to think about it now. The painful process of that emotional decision was years away. She was safely packed off to England, he told himself. His emotions, too, were securely locked away, where he intended to keep them for an indefinite period of time.

The Spanish Main waited. A dangerous path lay between him and any future in the king's court, and liberating his father would take all his energy and skills. Emerald was out of his life now. He was free to attack Cartagena, Coro, Cumaná, Margarita! And a certain Spanish galleon, the *San Pedro*, leaving Cartagena, awaited boarding by his buccaneers.

Baret was still musing over his contradictory thoughts as he strolled the quarterdeck, feeling the warm wind tug at his hat. He noticed a small cockboat being rowed from the beach toward the *Regale*. Carib slaves dipped their oars while the one passenger picked up a telescope and fixed it upon Baret. After a moment, Baret lowered his own glass.

"If it be Cap'n Farrow," suggested Hob, coming up from behind, "a piece of eight says he comes 'bout Morgan."

Baret watched the cockboat come alongside. The slave knelt in the prow to grab the rope and steady the boat against the *Regale's* side. A moment later Captain Erik Farrow came nimbly up the awkward rope ladder.

Baret stood on the quarterdeck looking down at him.

Erik doffed his hat in response to Baret's similar buccaneer salutation. He climbed to meet him.

Erik Farrow, in keeping with his style, revealed little emotion. He joined Baret at the railing, the breeze tossing his golden hair. His lean, tanned face was elegantly chiseled of fine bone, both somber and arresting, sometimes reminding Baret of a Michelangelo statue of an archangel that he'd seen as a boy, although he would never say so to Erik.

He'd told Baret he was born on the island of St. Kitts. He'd never known who his parents were and grew up as a mistreated cabin boy aboard a slave ship, trading out of Africa into the Spanish Main. Slaving was a part of his early youth that he would not discuss with Baret, however, except to tell him how he had loathed his captain and eventually set out as a buccaneer on his own. Later he became a soldier in the first Dutch War. They met while Erik convalesced in London and Baret was a youth at Cambridge. A shared hatred for the religious politics of Madrid bound them together in silent agreement to sink any galleon they came upon.

Baret had soon discovered that title and social position meant much to Erik. There had been a time in the recent past when Erik had even seemed willing to betray him to Felix for a comfortable life of nobility in London—with Lavender. Felix had hired him to spy on Baret and in return for his services had knighted him. Since then, he'd broken pact with Felix and was now loosely aligned with Baret. For how long? With Erik he was never quite sure.

Erik removed his hat. "Did Sir Cecil come about Emerald?"

Baret turned his head and gave him a measuring glance. He called her by her first name, as though he had the right.

"Yes, why do you inquire?"

Erik shrugged. "Emerald is a noble woman at heart."

"You have deduced this, I suppose, from lengthy musing about the rarity of Harwick's daughter?"

"I try not to think."

He now had Baret's full attention. "You try."

"Yes."

Baret's gaze narrowed. "But you've noticed her."

Erik shrugged lazily. "I confess I haven't had much time. I was foolishly enamored with Lady Thaxton. Then there's that cousin of hers—Minette. A bold little wench, that one."

Baret's irritation prickled under the hot, tropical sun that was making his dark hair stick uncomfortably to the back of his neck. His eyes turned hard. "It seems, Sir Erik, that you are destined to unwisely allow yourself to become enamored with the same women as I. First Lavender," he said too calmly, "now, Harwick's daughter. I confess I'm beginning to find it irksome."

Erik lifted a fair brow. "So it seems, your lordship."

Baret's gaze narrowed. He waited in vain. "Is that all you have to say about it?"

Erik contemplated calmly. After a long moment he said, "Yes, your lordship."

"Call me by title one more time," gritted Baret, "and I vow I'll draw sword over it."

"As you wish, my captain." Erik's gray eyes sparkled like sun on the snow.

Baret pulled his hat an inch lower and leaned back against the rail, crossing his boots at his ankles.

"Tell me, Erik, for the question begins to plague me, how long before I knew did you vainly make plans to steal Lavender from me?"

Erik scowled. "You behave the typical offended viscount, impatient and irritated."

Baret laughed. "Never underestimate the tantrums of nobility. If we were in London I'd have you arrested and tossed in the Tower."

Erik's lips tightened into silence.

Baret's smile was dangerous. "I should, even at this late

26

date, turn you into gallows bait for having tried to take her. However, since our precious Lavender has already become Lady Grayford, it won't be necessary." He turned, as though now bored, picking up his telescope again and fixing it on a ship. "Stay far afield from Emerald. You may have her little French cousin. And now! Let us forget the fairer sex, who make men's lives miserable. Any word from Morgan?"

Erik cast his gaze skyward to watch a soaring gull. "We both waste time on memories." He held his hat under his arm and glanced toward a ship making for Tortuga's harbor. "No word. And we waste time waiting. We have two of the best ships on the Caribbean. We can make an expedition of our own."

Baret tapped his chin. "You'd risk the Venezuelan Main alone?"

"Why not?"

"We'd need at least a ship or two more."

"Pierre LaMonte wishes to join us. He's steady and cool."

"We'll talk to him, but let's be discreet. Even here there are few I trust. The French buccaneers may have cheered my defeat of Levasseur in the duel; nevertheless, they are first loyal to their own blood. And with England now at war with Holland *and* France, they will be sure to side with them."

Erik went down the quarterdeck steps with him. "This venture of our own would get us both out of Tortuga for a seasonable time," he said. "Need I remind you there is the unresolved matter of the treasure of the *Prince Philip*?"

"You need not remind me. I remember well. So does Levasseur. He's been prowling about recently. Last night he met with Lex Thorpe of the *Black Dragon*."

Erik glanced at him, troubled. "You should have run Levasseur through when you had fair opportunity—or let me do it."

"There was no need. And I will take care of my own enemies. If I had killed him, Harwick's daughter would have mourned him."

Erik looked surprised. "She dislikes him!"

Baret's dark eyes flashed. "She only pretends to."

"There is something between them still, you think?"

Baret wasn't certain. There was much about Emerald he didn't know. "No matter, she'd have held his death to my account. I won't give her the opportunity. She's already offended with me over the duel." He smiled. "It goads her that I bought her."

Erik's fair brow shot up. "A woman's pride is a curious thing, my lord viscount. One must rarely trifle with it."

Baret said thoughtfully, "I've a notion she's more fond of Rafael than she admits even to herself."

Erik shrugged. "She was willing to run away to Massachusetts with Maynerd's brother."

"Yes. So she was." Baret flicked a sand fly off his wrist. It was surprising how remembering added to his ill humor caused by the heat and the stinging insects. "Ah. Dear, sweet, and gentle Jamie Boy."

"Jamie was soft all right. But Levasseur is dangerous. You've not seen the last of him. He despises you even more because you spared his life."

Baret sighed. "The world is full of ingrates."

"And you injured his pride with the rapier when you defeated him before his crew."

"Yes, a palatable experience."

"Perhaps—to save yourself from further trouble—you should let it be known you are no longer interested in Emerald."

Baret paused on the steps and stroked his thin black mustache. "A possibility," he mused with mock seriousness, "but after I paid twenty thousand pieces of eight?"

Erik replaced his hat too carefully. "For some women a man would pay more then that."

Baret affected consideration. "Would they now, do you think? Maybe—fifty thousand?"

Erik gave a gesture with his hand. "I suppose all things are possible."

With a cool smile Baret suggested, "Next, even you will be wishing to duel me for her."

The breeze blew between them. Erik went on down the steps and waited for him at the ladder.

Baret watched him for a moment with a smirk. He thought back to the duel. His own words sounded in his memory: "I have every intention of making good. A bargain is a bargain," he had told her when she suggested he need not keep his vow of marriage, and that she understood it had been forced upon him by her conniving father.

28

He remembered her words exactly, for he had not expected them, and they had irritated him. Why they irritated him, he didn't exactly know, but they still did: *I would not marry a man because of a bargain.*

"You have very little to say about it," he had replied.

He might have behaved the rakish viscount, free to do with her as he wished. Still—even with his heart fuming over Lavender's betrayal—when he had held Emerald and kissed her goodbye, she had captured his entire vision of all that was noble and beautiful. His own reaction had surprised him, and still did. He frowned. *A mere lark,* he thought. She was still little more than a fledgling.

The vision of the woman who came to mind, however, was anything except a child emerging into womanhood. Stubbornly he shut her from his mind. No one, including Sir Cecil, would rush him into marriage. Emerald wasn't emotionally ready, and neither was he. Marriage would change his entire life! Instead of only himself to consider, he must make decisions that were best for her, for both of them, for if two became one flesh, so also did marriage ask that they think as one, sacrificially giving for the best of the other.

He frowned. Strangely, that seemed an easier task with Emerald than with Lavender. He wondered rather maliciously how Grayford was getting along with his delicate little rosebud. If he remembered right, the rosebud had a way of pricking sharply enough to bring blood.

He saw Erik watching him, waiting to row with him ashore. He continued on down the quarterdeck steps and swung his muscled frame over the ship's side. Then he went lithely down the ladder to the waiting longboat to parley with Pierre LaMonte, captain of the *Bonaventure.*

2

DESTINATION: PIRATE'S COVE

Fire exploded from the guns of the pirate ship *Black Dragon*. In response, the *Madeleine* quaked and groaned from a broadside impact.

Emerald gasped, clutching the corner of her father's desk.

With a shriek, Minette toppled backward onto the bunk. "Scads of horror, Emerald! Those blackguards will claim us for booty, for sure!"

Or the Spaniards will, thought Emerald. With a prayer in her heart, she hid the satchel containing the precious translation notes on the African slave chants that her uncle had accumulated while on Foxemoore sugar plantation. Then she took the small pistol that Captain Baret Buckington had given her and maneuvered through the fallen baggage and tipped chairs of the cramped cabin out onto the poop deck of her father's ship. Grasping the carved taffrail with one hand, she peered below.

In contrast to the horrors presently going on around her, Emerald's appearance better suited the sheltered veneer of an arriving daughter of the governor-general. Her pale blue camlet dress, with its belled, elbow-length sleeves and soft flounces trimmed with white lace and ribbon, spilled becomingly about her cloth slippers. Her thick, dark tresses were arranged in a serene chignon at the back of her neck, and a silver cross embedded with pearls glimmered at her slender throat. In the wild and dangerous atmosphere that burst about her with smoking culverins, her cinnamon-brown eyes glowed as warmly as did the tropics themselves, while her ivory skin bore little evidence of having experienced the burning equatorial sun.

In truth, she had not come from England but from the pirate stronghold of Tortuga, where she had sailed from Cayona Bay three weeks ago for Barbados aboard the *Madeleine*. At Barbados she was to have boarded a merchant ship for London. But alas! Dark fortunes! Three weeks of turmoil and plans were now scattered like ashes of the dead upon the Caribbean Sea.

Her gaze narrowed, anxiously searching the quarterdeck below for a glimpse of her beloved father, Sir Karlton Harwick. How could he have brought them to this fate instead of going on to Barbados as planned?

All because of the treasure of the Prince Philip, she thought, frustrated.

The decks of the *Madeleine* stared back at her sullenly, littered with broken woodwork, mizzen, and sagging sail. The sharp reek of gun powder stung her nostrils. Hellish sallow smoke began to settle over the vessel like a shroud. This was it, she told herself with resignation. They were going down into the dark green waters to be met by hungry sharks. Even now the vicious creatures could be seen cruising the shoreline, just waiting for the smell of blood.

If she survived, she and Minette would be left to the evil appetites not of sharks but of Captain Lex Thorpe and his pirates—or they would be taken as heretic prisoners of Spain!

Her father stood grim and formidable in sea-splattered leather jerkin and a round black castor, under which his head was swathed with a red scarf. Tenaciously he shouted orders to his scrambling crew to prepare for the pirates' boarding. Her stomach lurched when he whipped his cutlass from his baldric.

"Musketeers to the prow!"

Emerald gripped her pistol. She could shoot Minette first, then herself, but that would certainly show no faith in her heavenly Father. No, whatever came must be endured with trust.

Her troubled gaze lifted to stare across the glittering waters. She believed them to be somewhere in the Lesser Antilles between the Dutch island of Curaçao and heavily reinforced Porto Bello. *Porto Bello!* Her heart surged with expectation. Had Baret sailed there yet with Henry Morgan?

But no . . . it was too soon, she thought, her hopes sinking again. Baret would still be held up at Tortuga, preparing for the war with the Dutch. And yet, Curaçao was in this area of the Caribbean, as was English-held Barbados, often called "Little England" because of its staunch loyalty to King Charles in the days of Cromwell.

Ahead, the distant coastline of the Spanish island of Margarita, the "isle of pearls," stood shrouded in a green aura in the brilliant sunlight. It was a mysterious island, which had been her father's point of rendezvous with an unknown partner—or so he had said. *Who was that partner?*

Her heart pounded in her ears. The sleek *Black Dragon,* once believed by her father to be friendly, had recently sailed from the Tortuga Brotherhood on a pirate expedition of its own. It now hoisted its real colors. Her eyes riveted upon the *joli rouge*—"pretty red"—an ironic French description of the blood-red banner flown by early privateers, featuring skeletons, cutlasses, or bleeding hearts. The *Black Dragon* flew a red flag showing a white cutlass and a yellow skull over crossbones. It seemed to grin at her as the banner snapped devilishly in the warm wind.

Panic seized Emerald at the sight of the dread pirate ship bearing down on the *Madeleine.* She held the rail, dazed, watching flashes of fire and smoke belch from its guns.

Minette had come up beside her and now gripped Emerald's arm. "I knew we shouldn't have sailed here," she groaned. "Whatever made Uncle Karlton do it?"

"Treasure," murmured Emerald, her gaze fastened on the *joli rouge.*

"There's no treasure," moaned Minette. "Don't they know that? It was all a tale. Oh, why didn't we voyage straight to Barbados?"

Emerald stared ahead. Because there were pearls on Margarita, her father had said. But explaining all this to Minette would do no good now. They were trapped, just as hopelessly as a hungry barracuda on a baited hook!

The *Black Dragon* was presenting her larboard guns and loosing her second broadside. Emerald pulled Minette back. A projectile ripped through the rigging overhead, and they held their ears. Another parted the water, sending white spray across the deck.

"Uncle K-Karlton's been w-wounded!"

Emerald rushed to the rail again, looking below to see him holding a bloodied hand to his shoulder. "Father!"

He squinted up at the sound of her voice, his rugged face troubled but resolute, then turned and barked an order.

A tall and gaunt man garbed in a faded blue coat with tarnished gold lace managed to climb his way up the steps. As always, Zeddie carried his two big boarding pistols. In his younger years he had been a crack shot, as he always liked to boast, and had fought in the English Civil War, where he had lost an eye. He was sent to Barbados as a political prisoner in the days of Cromwell, and her father, who had known him in England, had found him on Governor Modyford's sugar plantation and arranged to buy his freedom. Zeddie ever remained a strong ally and was a bodyguard to Emerald.

Now he came tramping onto the high deck, his golden periwig in disarray.

Emerald rushed to meet him, her eyes reflecting a surprising calmness though her voice was breathless. "Will they board?"

A rumble came from his throat. "Aye, m'gal. Them bloodthirsty sharks be comin', to be sure. Your father bids you and Minette be brave."

"Brave!" wailed Minette, nervously running her fingers through her waist-length amber hair. "Oh, no-o, Emerald! What'll we do?" and she began to rush about frantically.

Zeddie's one good eye gleamed like a rooster's, while a tattered dark patch covered the other. He drew a calico scarf from his bulging jacket pocket and dabbed his brow. "Sink me sails, but your father is a shrewd fellow. He has a rare plan. Sure now, you'll see! Why, he's already sent a message during the night to the viscount."

Emerald's breath caught, her eyes searching his. "Baret? How?"

His eye twinkled, and he cocked his head toward Minette, who ceased her nervous flitting and perked up. "And that handsome Captain Erik Farrow too. So happens they both be prowling the waters near Margarita."

Bewildered, but much too excited over the possibility of help to worry about details, Emerald grabbed Zeddie's arm. "Margarita is under strict control of the dons. Why would Baret and the *Regale* be near by?"

"It may be he has a mind for the treasure his father stored."

"You mean *it's* on Margarita?"

"That much I don't know, m'gal, but 'tis my guess it is or he wouldn't be here. Farrow neither."

She wondered, growing more uneasy at the thought of piracy. Baret Buckington "Foxworth" was already in serious trouble

33

with the High Admiralty for venturing into Maracaibo. If he also entered Margarita . . .

"Could a longboat get past the *Black Dragon* to reach the *Regale?*"

"Your father be as shrewd as Captain Lex Thorpe, when he's under the cannon. Nae fear otherwise, m'gal!" And he cleared his raspy throat. "Nevertheless, ye both best take to your prayers —just . . . er . . . in case."

Emerald wondered if she could fully believe him, or if he were only saying this to give them hope. How could Baret be near by? She didn't think that possible, but she restrained herself from asking questions.

Minette's smile vanished like summer dew. "Are you sure, Zeddie? It's a long way in a longboat to shore—and sharks and Spaniards are everywhere. You can be sure they've heard the battle and seen it, too, through a telescope."

"She's right, Zeddie."

He fingered his baldric.

Minette's eyes widened. "Vapors, no one can save us now but God!"

Emerald was quick. "Then we have reason for cheer. If God is for us, who can be against us?"

"Oh, Emerald—are you *sure* He's for us?"

The wail almost brought a rueful smile to Emerald's lips. She took Minette's arm, propelling her back into the cabin. She went straight to the desk and removed the Authorized Version of the Bible that had belonged to their Great-uncle Mathias. She placed it carefully in her cousin's shaking hands, hoping to strengthen her wavering faith.

"Here, you hold to this and pray while Zeddie and I make plans of what to do when they board. And it may be that Zeddie's telling the truth after all. Baret and Erik *may* be nigh at hand. If the Spaniards can see the smoke from the cannon and hear the battle, maybe they will too."

"If they're really near," Minette whispered. "Zeddie could be trying to give us a false hope—like a bloated frog facing his enemies."

Zeddie now followed them inside and closed the door. "Stab me, lassies, if'n Sir Karlton knew the *Black Dragon* was in these waters, he would not've come here. He'd have sailed on to

Barbados as planned. It was that rascally-mouthed pirate cousin of yours who lied to him."

Surprised, Emerald faced him for explanation. "You mean Rafael Levasseur?"

"There ain't many as dark-hearted as he."

Cautious, she watched him. "What business did Rafael have with my father?"

Zeddie scowled uneasily, as though wondering if he should say anything. "Treasure business. They're both seeking what was hidden from the Spanish galleon, along with Captain Foxworth and that too-quiet Sir Erik Farrow. And I say *he's* a rogue to be watching."

Minette frowned. "Captain Farrow is a perfect gentleman."

"I'll not argue now—we need him."

"Yes, yes, what about the *Prince Philip?*" asked Emerald impatiently. "What has it to do with my father?"

He cleared his throat. "More'n we realized, is my guess. Just how much, only Captain Foxworth and Levasseur knows. Levasseur was to meet your father in these parts and go to Margarita."

"After the duel on Tortuga with Captain Foxworth, why would Rafael be friendly with my father? He blames Papa for that duel just as much as he does Baret."

"Treasure makes strange fellows sign pirate articles, m'gal. An' it may be Levasseur thinks he can get you back from the viscount. Anyway, it ain't a *friendly* agreement between him and your father, I'm thinkin'. Now that the *Black Dragon* showed up suddenlike, your father is agreein' with me about Levasseur's treachery."

Emerald paced. "Treachery doesn't surprise me. How could my father have trusted him!"

"He didn't, and so he's wisely sent the longboat to alert Captain Foxworth of his plans. But the presence of the *Black Dragon* complicates things, to be sure." He frowned and shook his head. "Her captain be worse than Levasseur."

Emerald drew in a breath to steady her nerves, realizing she knew very little of all that was going on. But she lifted her head bravely. "Does my father know Lex Thorpe?"

Zeddie scowled. "Aye, he knows the captain of the *Black Dragon*, all right. A cur, that one."

Emerald's knees weakened. She went to the open port and

turned her gaze seaward. "They're coming!" Emerald stared at the great black hull moving toward them, the sun slanting across its billowing canvas. The *Black Dragon* shortened its sails and crept steadily forward to overtake its prey, like a cat stalking a young bird unable to wing its way to safety.

Zeddie came to stand beside her. "Thorpe'll be holdin' his fire now, wanting to board. He wants no more damage to the ship."

Emerald's throat turned dry. From where she stood, she could see the odious pirates on the *Dragon's* bowsprit.

"They're readying the gaskets of her spritsail," murmured Zeddie. "An' them men in the fore-chains are holding their grapnels ready." He checked his pistols.

Fear wrapped about her heart, but she managed to retain her dignity. *Please God, help Baret to get here in time. If not, there's no one to rescue us.*

The cabin door burst open. Emerald whirled, and Minette jumped to her feet from her prayers, leaving the Bible open on the bunk.

Zeddie stepped forward, hand on a pistol.

She was surprised to see her father enter.

Though a privateer, Sir Karlton Harwick could display, when he wished to, as much dignity as an earl. In this situation he was a master at calm. Beneath silvery-blue eyes, his robust face was besmirched with a mixture of sweat and gun smoke. He towered a good six feet, had broad shoulders, and showed a weaving of gray in his auburn hair and in the short beard that curled upward. His brows were straight and slashed across a sea-roughened face.

Emerald ran to him, her alarmed gaze searching his.

He managed a grim smile and took firm hold of her arm.

"So much for the pearls I wanted to send you to London wearing."

Her eyes moistened. "Oh, Papa, as if I wanted them. The viscount would hardly be impressed." Her tone was mildly scolding but soft with pride in him nevertheless, for love covered weakness. She held him tightly, her cheek against his arm.

"Aye, lass." He patted her shoulder and sighed, as though agreeing. "But it's not too late yet."

The tone of his voice brought her head up, and she scanned his expression. His eyes glittered like silvery stone.

"That pirate scum of the sea wants my *Madeleine*. He's going to board, and there's no stopping the pack of sea rats now. Still, we've hope. Flynn got away last night. If the Almighty aids us, he'll contact Baret, who's known to be prowling the area." He turned his head. "Zeddie, get my dueling weapons!"

Zeddie rushed to oblige him, and Emerald's heart contracted with alarm.

Her father peered down at her gravely, taking hold of her shoulders with both strong hands and giving her a mild shake for emphasis. "You've always been a steady girl and no flighty thing, so I'll tell you the truth. There's no chance of escaping them now—they'll take us. But if my plan works, we'll get out of this the richer for it. Now, it's important to go along with whatever I say to Captain Thorpe. That goes for you too, Minette."

"Yes, of course, Papa." Emerald clamped her jaw to keep her teeth from chattering.

"We've a few minutes," he said with a heavy sigh. "'Tis my fault it's come to this, daughter. No doubt I'll live to regret my folly and greed in coming here, but I had good and ample reason for doing so. It wasn't for pearls alone, but the treasure of the *Prince Philip* is near at hand. And Baret and Farrow are clued in."

She thought again of the treasure ship from Cartagena that Baret's father, Captain Royce Buckington, had been accused of pirating several years earlier. If that treasure was located in these parts, how did her father know?

"You mean the treasure is real—it's near here?" she whispered.

"Aye, it's real enough, and it's the reason Thorpe is prowling these waters too. He was warned by Levasseur that I was coming here. There's no hope now but to bait Thorpe and stall for time." He must have seen her trepidation, for he looked sheepish. "I'm sorry, lass, it's the only way now. I must work with Thorpe to see you safely delivered to the viscount."

His gravity convinced her.

Her mind turned to the curious decision he had made several days ago. The *Madeleine* should have sailed to Barbados. Instead they turned toward the Gulf of Venezuela, coming close to Maracaibo, where Emerald had once sailed with Baret, searching for his father. It had taken her several days to realize they

37

were in Spanish waters. She questioned her father about the change.

"We're off the coast of the Main near Margarita," he had explained. "Don't be overly alarmed. Friendly ships belonging to the Brethren of the Coast are in the coves and inlets nearby. Any attack by the *guarda costa* will bring me all the help I may need. Yet I expect no trouble. I've already been in touch with the Spanish governor. He's assured me he's prepared for a friendly meeting."

"With a Spanish governor? Can you trust him?"

"He's interested in trade," was all he had said. "I've been here before. More important, so has the viscount."

Her interest was piqued at learning of Baret's visit, but her father would give no more information despite her probing.

And there had been little time, for word was brought him that a friendly buccaneering ship of a fellow Brother from Tortuga had been sighted. Soon, however, that "friendly rendezvous" with a fellow buccaneer had turned into the surprising and terrible roar of two brass culverins and the news from the bosun that the ship was the *Black Dragon*.

Now the black vessel was inching closer, and she could read the regret in her father's eyes over his decision to bring her with him to these waters.

"I should have taken you to Barbados first. It was a mistake to risk coming here without Baret and the *Regale*." He walked briskly to the port opening and looked out. "I should have told Baret at Tortuga," he muttered to himself.

Emerald took hold of his arm. "Told him what? About the treasure?"

Whatever it was, Karlton had no intention of discussing the matter now, and he turned toward Zeddie. "You're to keep your pistols in your baldric when they enter the cabin. Do nothing. If anything happens to me, insist that the viscount's expecting Emerald. Is that clear?"

"I have me story down well enough." Zeddie handed him his weapons.

Sir Karlton strapped them on while Emerald tried to keep from trembling and Minette hovered in the back of the cabin. Then he turned to Emerald. "If the worst comes to me, Thorpe may be baited enough by greed to spare you. He will, if my plan works."

"What plan?" she whispered. "Is there anything I should know, Papa?"

"Aye, make certain you keep Viscount Baret Buckington a bulwark between you and Thorpe. At the moment, daughter, Baret's your only shield."

"The Lord is our protector," she reminded her father, holding to him.

He nodded gravely. "Aye. Now wait here, you and Minette both, and say nothing. You will need to play this hour by hour. I'll need to go on deck."

He left the cabin, and she and Minette stood together, waiting, while Zeddie took his place, facing the door.

Her father was a buccaneer and could handle himself with pirates such as Lex Thorpe, she soothed herself. He knew the West Indies and the mind-set of the other freebooters.

It was reported that Tortuga buccaneers did not attack or plunder other buccaneers. But Thorpe was no buccaneer. He was a pirate, the vilest of the vile, with few, if any, scruples. Still, circumstances were never so dark that the sovereign God could not come to their aid.

And yet . . . what was this greed that her father had just confessed to as having been the provocation for their dreadful dilemma? Had he been pursuing some cause in this area of the Caribbean that could not be defended? And if so, was this end to be their chastening?

Emerald felt the gloom of the fading daylight pass over her soul as the *Black Dragon* came astern on their larboard quarter, overshadowing the *Madeleine,* as if Jonah's sea monster prepared to swallow them whole.

Minette's amber eyes widened with horror. "They're boarding now." She clutched Emerald's arm. "Hear the drums?"

The throb of pirate drums caused Emerald's skin to crawl. Then frantic shouting filled the air, followed by the crack of muskets. The deck beneath her feet shook with the sound of breaking timbers, the ring of the grapnels landing and hooking into timber, the scuffle of many feet climbing over the ship's side and landing with a thud equal to the drumbeat. Pistol shots exploded.

A herd of feet rumbled across the deck. Captain Lex Thorpe

and his crew were aboard. Shouts merged with more gunfire, the clang of cutlasses, and the brutal sounds of hand-to-hand fighting enveloped the ship.

Minette drew back against the cabin bulkhead, watching the door.

Emerald winced at the yells. She visualized men struck with the blade and then flung overboard into the shark-infested water. Her ears caught the dreaded sound of the fighting coming ever nearer.

Zeddie stationed himself in front of her and Minette. "Be brave, m'gals. The crewmen serving your father are hearty buccaneers themselves. Be sure Thorpe won't be wasting his crew o' cutthroats unless he has to. He'll want to bargain with your father."

Along the deck came the rush of boot steps, and lewd, shouting voices became still louder.

Emerald's gaze was riveted on the door. She gripped Baret's pistol, concealed behind a layer of skirted crinolines, and waited.

The sounds of battle were diminishing. In their place came a sound Emerald found even more ominous—triumphant laughter and the shooting of muskets to announce victory. Thorpe's pirates had outnumbered her father's crew. Swarming across the deck of the *Madeleine,* they had cut down all resistance. The approaching footsteps warned her of those who came to claim the captain's booty and to kill any who might resist.

She blinked as the cabin door crashed open and struck against the bulkhead. She saw pirates in the passageway, their tanned faces menacing and without mercy, their heads swathed in faded scarves of black, yellow, or blue. They held gleaming cutlasses coated with blood in one hand and pistols in the other.

Zeddie's feet were firmly grounded to the cabin floor in front of her. Beholding him, the pirates stopped, but then, at the sight of Emerald and Minette, they let out a low chortle and surged forward.

Zeddie, never more courageous despite his years, kept himself directly in their path. His hands rested on his pistols in the baldric, but the fact that he did not trouble to draw them, as Sir Karlton had ordered, lent him an added authority.

"Step back, you sulfurous scum! One step more, and I'll empty the brains of the first sea rat who gapes on the betrothed of Viscount Baret Buckington!"

Carrying cutlass and cocked pistol, one growled, "Blow me, get a parrot's eye of 'im! Viscount, 'e says!"

Another, in blood-soaked garments, hooked his thumbs under a belt stuffed with pistols and surveyed Zeddie. "You poke wi' one eye, wot's your masquerade, eh?"

"He's King Charlie."

"Ho! A piece o' shark bait, that's wot!"

Zeddie emitted a growl. "Be it known, ye vermin-infested curs, that I'm in service to his lordship. An' if ye have your wits intact, ye'll know that the viscount is none other than the pirate Captain Foxworth of the *Regale!* So beware! Now—" he nodded sagely "—go an' fetch your murderous Captain Thorpe."

3

THE BLACK DRAGON

Emerald held her breath, watching, wondering how the pirates would regard Zeddie's challenge. Captain Foxworth was well known on Tortuga, perhaps better respected there than among the blooded nobility.

The men stood primed for action. Each hand gripped either machete or cutlass or pistol. For a terrifying moment her heart throbbed in her throat lest she see Zeddie cut down before her eyes.

Then their shrewd consideration of his warning appeared to take hold. Their ruthless stare fused with suspicion. Because they knew the name of Captain Foxworth or because they were already weighing the possibility of the high price they might gain through ransom, Zeddie's warning had a quieting effect upon them.

"Foxworth's not a man I'd cross," mumbled one.

Then there was a stir as someone approached. The pirates moved aside to allow a man broad of shoulder and chest to thrust his way past them. Captain Lex Thorpe surveyed his prize.

His blood-smeared shirt hung open from neck to waist. His chest glistened with sweat. He was breeched in leather, and a tangle of red-brown curls clustered about a thick neck, where veins protruded. Quick-darting eyes took in the scene, then whipped their way past Zeddie with indifference and settled with satisfaction on Emerald. A flash of teeth showed beneath a rat-tailed mustache. Fingering the leather *bandero* over his shoulder housing six pistols, he entered the cabin reeking of old sweat and rum.

"So this is the wench."

"Says she's Foxworth's."

"Aye," growled Zeddie. "Sink me, Captain Thorpe, if ye ain't heard about the fancy duel between Foxworth and Levasseur on Tortuga."

Thorpe gave Emerald full attention, his bold eyes measuring her from ankle to eyebrow. "Who ain't heard of Foxworth's highborn wench? Levasseur's still squawking." A laugh rumbled in his deep chest.

Emerald stood her ground, meeting the leering stare as though unafraid and confident of Baret's soon appearance. "Where's my father, Sir Karlton Harwick?" she demanded.

Thorpe called out to the others behind him, who stood gaping at her with evil grins. "Well, brethren, we have us the bride of his lordship the captain of the *Regale!*"

There was further movement at the door, and Sir Karlton pushed his way past, a hand on his blood-soaked sleeve. His silver-hued eyes reflected cool anger. "Not for long, you won't. Foxworth will cut your gizzard out and hang it up to dry if you as much as lay a hand on her, Lex. Like his father before him, he's one man of the titled blood who can out-buccaneer any scoundrel on Tortuga!"

Emerald knew his wound was serious, for she saw the whiteness of his face, the sweat prickling his brow. She winced as her gaze dropped to the front of his shirt where blood soaked the cloth.

"Zeddie, bring me the medical satchel!" she told him calmly, aware of Thorpe's narrowing gaze.

Zeddie moved to do as she ordered, and Captain Thorpe's eyes followed him, then fixed on Sir Karlton with obvious suspicion. He stroked the skinny tail of his reddish mustache. "The wench be your daughter, Karlton?"

"Aye, and a lady. An' you'll not be forgetting it, Lex, or it'll mean your death. You know Foxworth as well as I do."

"I knows him all right, and ye better not be wily with me, Harwick. You always was a sly one—it's why you're in these waters—but you ain't as privy as me, an' I'm knowing the bait bringin' you. If you be lying about her—"

"I've no cause to lie. She's my daughter, and Foxworth fought a duel to win her. Everyone knows it, including you. Levasseur warned you we were coming here. He would have told you about his duel with the viscount. And of my daughter being aboard."

Thorpe pretended ignorance. "Levasseur told me? Why, I ain't seen him since the last campaign to Gran Grenada."

Her father's eyes sparked with contempt. "No use lying to me, Lex. If you're wise, you'll call off your stinking crew so you and I can talk treasure of the *Prince Philip*. 'Tis a small matter of two hundred thousand pieces of eight."

Emerald glanced at Captain Thorpe to judge his response, believing her father was trying to beguile the man into thinking they could work together.

"There may be more if we play it right, Lex." Karlton sat down at the table, looking confident.

With Zeddie at her elbow, Emerald worked to stop her father's bleeding.

As she did, he continued to talk. "If you weren't a fool, Thorpe, the two of us could be as rich as King Charlie. You're the one freebooter with enough men and wit to join me on the enterprise I'm set upon."

Thorpe advanced a step, wiping his long fingers on the open front of his shirt. "Maybe. If ye be fooling me, though, they'll soon be mopping up your innards to throw over the side."

Her father's eyes narrowed. "We'll talk, all right, but not with your crew gaping like baboons."

There was a flash of interest in Thorpe's eyes. "We'll talk. An' if ye bore me with empty words, I'll end it plainly enough." He gestured for his men to leave. Then Thorpe came to the table and pulled out a chair. Turning it around, he sank down, arms resting on the back, chin on his hand.

Emerald's skin crawled, and she glanced at her father as she added the finishing touches to her treatment of his injury.

Behind Thorpe, his henchman lieutenant, Vane, stood with his cutlass. He was a wiry man with long arms and skin charred brown by the sun. Blond curls poked out from beneath a faded blue scarf. His prominent eyes under bleached brows watched Emerald and Minette. He wore a torn canvas shirt of salt-faded red, and breeches of rawhide, so soiled with everything from caked blood to fish oil that Emerald believed they could stand on their own.

"Zeddie," her father said, "bring rum to the captain and his lieutenant. We've much to discuss, and our time hastens from us."

Zeddie went to the carved cupboard set against the forward bulkhead.

Emerald stood beside her father's chair, one hand on his shoulder, pretending not to feel the stare of either Thorpe or his foul lieutenant. Her father amazed her. He was behaving as one of the Brotherhood and, though she could see he was in pain, offered courage and authority.

Zeddie set on the table a tray holding a jar of rum, another containing Spanish tobacco, long narrow pipes, a tinderbox, and three drinking mugs.

They poured for themselves.

Vane came to sit at the table beside his captain. Taking a pipe, he stuffed it with tobacco leaves.

"What's the enterprise, Karlton?" Thorpe asked.

"As if you didn't know what was on my mind. Surely it's why you were lying in wait for me."

Emerald looked on, trying to pick up information.

Thorpe measured him narrowly. "I didn't know it was your ship, Karlton. Thought it was the *Warspite.*"

At the mention of Erik Farrow's ship, Emerald glanced across the cabin to where Minette purposely stayed back in the flickering shadows of the lantern. She saw the girl's interest peak. Evidently Thorpe was not on friendly terms with Baret's ally, Farrow.

"The devil's luck be good enough for me. I'm glad it was your ship, Harwick, an' this here enterprise ye speak of, along with Foxworth's woman, be prize enough for the likes of ol' Lex Thorpe. Speak on." He stretched back in the chair, drinking his rum and staring boldly at her.

Despite the heat, Emerald now wished that she had worn a cloak.

Karlton, too, leaned back, as though he didn't notice Thorpe's straying gaze. "I speak of the treasure of the *Prince Philip*. What else, lad? The treasure be as big as any you'll likely to see on the Main. There's gold worth over two hundred thousand pieces of eight, and while we wait for Foxworth on Santa Margarita, bushels of pearls are there for the taking."

Was he speaking the truth, she wondered, or baiting the pirate captain?

Neither Thorpe nor Vane appeared to consider it a bluff. They sat watching him, and, at the mention of the *Prince Philip*, their eyes burned with greed.

Emerald recalled how Maynerd, just before he'd been hanged in Port Royal, also claimed there was treasure. And on the *Regale,* Baret Buckington had spoken of it to Levasseur. If what they said was true, there would be enough treasure to go around to satisfy them all, but would they be satisfied to share it?

She refused to believe her father was involved. *He's only trying to hold off the hungry dogs,* she thought. *It's a ruse. One used by Baret with Levasseur on the voyage to Maracaibo.*

"An' how much does Foxworth know of the treasure of the Spanish galleon?" demanded Thorpe. His eyes were cold and suspicious, reminding her of a cobra weaving to its charmer's music.

Her father lit his pipe calmly. "He knows more than either of us. Foxworth's own father took the Spanish ship. Maynerd was with him."

"So?" snarled Thorpe, as if her father were making an excuse to cut him out of the booty. "We all knows the talk among the Brotherhood about Royce Buckington being alive—and of Foxworth seeking him. And Levasseur is hot to find where Buckington stored it. He says you and Farrow know its place. As for Maynerd, he's corpsing away, so as I'm hearing, hung by Foxworth's own uncle."

"Aye," said Sir Karlton darkly. "He was hanged all right. There's more than pirates seeking the whereabouts of the treasure, and of Royce. Felix searches also."

"Levasseur says he expected to find out from Maynerd where Royce buried it, but was crossed."

"Levasseur won't find it, because there's only one man left who knows where Royce stashed it."

Emerald looked at her father, masking her incredulity.

Thorpe stared at him, tapping his grimy fingernails on the back of the chair. "An how'd ye be knowing where to find it?" He added menacingly, "I don't believe ye, Karlton."

"Neither does I," said Vane. "He's trying to keep the women from us." He gestured with his head. "There's another one back there."

Emerald glared at him. "She's my cousin. And Captain Foxworth will have your head if you so much as lay a finger on her."

Sir Karlton touched his wound. "If you think I don't know where the treasure is being held, Lex, then you're both bigger fools than I thought you were. I would've been on my way now to find it, then bring my daughter to England, if you hadn't come swooping down upon me like a black vulture."

The pirates exchanged interested glances, then watched him as though afraid they might be wrong after all. Thorpe drummed his fingers on the table now, his evil eyes fixed on her father.

"All right, Karlton, seeing as how ye've a name on Tortuga. An' you're a friend of Foxworth too. Suppose ye be telling me just what you know."

"I learned of it easy enough, seeing that my daughter is to marry Foxworth. He tells me everything, and why shouldn't he? He's to be my son-in-law. And there's not a buccaneer on Tortuga or Port Royal who won't back me up on the fact as how Baret dueled Levasseur for Emerald. All the Brotherhood are witnesses."

Emerald stirred uneasily, remembering that frightening and embarrassing hour when Baret had agreed to marry her. She listened as her father told the two pirates his smooth, convincing tale. She carefully masked her shock when he stated easily, "No one knows I sailed with Royce on that last voyage. Aye, I was there when we took the *Prince Philip.*"

He had been there?

Sir Karlton continued his tale as Emerald watched him, riveted. They had been cruising for Oliver Cromwell off the coast of Hispaniola soon after Admiral Venerable and William Penn took Jamaica for England. Captain Royce Buckington had successfully attacked a Spanish ship off the southern side of Santo Domingo, and Sir Karlton was in command of one of the frigates that accompanied Royce's flagship. After successfully removing the cargo—of which there were more than 300,000 pieces of eight—they were caught in a hurricane and became so battered by wind and sea that they not only had to lighten Royce's ship of part of the booty but were hurled off course for weeks. When the storm abated, they were far from Hispaniola and Tortuga. They were forced onto "a certain island in the area, of which I'll not be telling you now."

"Santa Margarita," snapped Thorpe. "We all knows as much now."

"There on the island, the remaining treasure was safely

stashed away and now waits fair and sweet distribution among the brothers signing the articles. The rest of what happened to Royce is known to all the Brotherhood. The crew came down with sickness. The weakest died or were killed by the Spaniards. The strongest, including Royce himself, were taken as slaves and sold to Spanish colonists up and down the Main—compliments of Sir Jasper. The treasure remains securely stored."

Emerald looked across the cabin at Minette. Their gazes met in the wordless suggestion that *they* were convinced.

"An' what makes me fool enough to believe *you* escaped death or slavery?" Thorpe snarled.

"I was wise enough to sleep away from the crew the night the Spaniards attacked. I managed to hide. I might have given my life a sacrifice, but one more sword would not have turned back the Spaniards. After they left, I managed to walk across the island to friendly Indians who helped me make it to Barbados. I caught an English merchant ship to Jamaica."

Vane glared. "An' you ain't gone back for the treasure all these years? You expect us to believe that?"

Sir Karlton shrugged. "I was a friend of Royce. I've spent time searching for his whereabouts, even as Foxworth has."

"And you didn't bother to tell Foxworth you knew where the treasure was? How come the two of ye didn't work together to find it, eh?"

Emerald shifted cautiously, certain now that they had caught her father in the ruse, but he merely smoked his pipe and looked into their swarthy faces with a calmness that reminded her of Baret. "I did tell him—on Tortuga before I sailed here. After all, he's soon to be my son-in-law. One can't keep such secrets from his son. Now, can he?"

They exchanged glances. "Maybe not," said Thorpe.

"Aye, Foxworth knows all about it now," her father said again. "Just like Levasseur discovered my point of rendezvous and notified you, Lex. I notified Foxworth before I set sail from Tortuga. I have big plans where my daughter is concerned. And then there was my portion of Foxemoore plantation in Jamaica. I have debts to pay, or I'll lose her inheritance. I first intended to sail with Henry Morgan, but I learned secretly that Morgan isn't sailing yet."

"Clever, ain't he, Vane? As sly as a rum-drinking fox. An' of course ye need us to help you find and disperse the treasure."

Sir Karlton touched his shoulder again. "More than ever, 'tis a fact. On one condition."

Thorpe stirred in his seat and looked at his lieutenant. Vane reached for the rum.

"An' the location?" Thorpe demanded . "Where's the three hundred thousand pieces of eight?"

"Two hundred thousand," Sir Karlton corrected. "We lost some in the storm."

"An' where is it?"

"Do you take me for a blubbering idiot, Thorpe? There'll be no more information until my daughter and her cousin are safely in the hand of Captain Foxworth on the *Regale.* "

"Ye jackanapes!" Thorpe jumped to his feet and snatched up his cutlass. "I would as soon 'ave your head as put up with ye. D'ye thinks I'm idiot enough to send for Foxworth?"

Emerald trembled, her eyes on the cutlass, a prayer in her heart, but her father seemed to pay no attention to the cutlass or to Thorpe's rage.

"Sure now, Thorpe, you're no fool, but a pirate who smells treasure when it's dangled before your nose. Of course, we need Foxworth! An' I've already sent for him. He's not far from here. Farrow, too."

Thorpe's eyes squeezed into slits. "You're lying."

"I speak the truth."

"Why do we need him? I'd sooner face a shark!"

"Because," said Sir Karlton calmly, drawing in on the pipe and watching him evenly, "Foxworth has the map to the treasure."

Thorpe's breath sucked in with a curse. He banged his fist on the table, sending the cups bouncing. "He has the *map!* You say he has it?"

"Sure now. He does. He doesn't know which island, though. So you see, we need one another. And we'll all be signing articles. Now, captain, shall we talk of terms, like sensible men?"

Thorpe scowled. "You take me for a fool."

"I take you for a clever fellow who knows a bargain when he sees one. With your share of the treasure and pearls to boot, you can retire with ease wheresoever your yearnings take you."

Vane, at least, seemed to be satisfied, thought Emerald, glancing nervously at the gangling blond giant.

He wet his lips and said to his captain, "We need Foxworth, Lex. An' seeing as 'ow you have his pert wench here with you, he's sure to come with the first wind." Vane smiled. "Ye've forgot the price of ransom we can get too. A viscount, even one sportin' as a buccaneer, has hisself riches even without the treasure his father pirated. He'll pay for her too."

A breath escaped Emerald's lips as she silently looked from Vane to Thorpe.

Thorpe's eyes slitted with interest. "She looks the kind o' baggage a daw cock like Foxworth would pay plenty for. Now I knows why I keeps you around, Vane."

Emerald's heart raced over the prospect that Baret would be sent for, but was he as close by as her father and Zeddie insisted? She stole a quick glance at her father and saw his subdued spark of satisfaction. She knew matters had proceeded as he had hoped.

"Now you're thinking as the pirate ye are, Thorpe," said Sir Karlton. "A double booty. If Foxworth paid twenty thousand pieces of eight to Levasseur, what will he pay you?"

"Fifty thousand pieces." Thorpe's eager gaze ran over Emerald. "And so worthy a prize stays in my cabin till Foxworth pays."

Emerald stepped away, her hand again clutching the pistol hidden in the pocket of her skirts. "Never. Captain Buckington won't pay you a single piece of eight if you insist."

"She stays with me, her father. If not, there's no signing articles, Thorpe. No matter my willingness to play you against Foxworth when it comes to the treasure, there's no compromise when it comes to my daughter."

Thorpe sat back down and laid his cutlass across his lap, no longer watching Emerald but Karlton. "We'll call your bluff, Karlton. Keep your daughter, but I'll send Foxworth the terms I want."

"I'd have it no other way," came the smooth reply, and Karlton stretched his legs before him, appearing entirely at his leisure. "You'll need send that message to Margarita tonight, and we'll all sign it—including Emerald."

"That's right smart of you, seeing as how you know I can't write, nor can Vane." He gestured his head of curls toward Emer-

50

ald. "I 'spect the wench can put pretty words to paper. She'll write it, and she'll bid him to come save her, if she's as smart as she is pert."

"I'll write the letter," Emerald agreed, surprised that her voice did not shake. "But just how do you expect to get it to him? If he's waiting on Margarita, won't the Spanish governor arrest you? Perhaps we should sail first to Barbados—"

A rude laugh interrupted. "We ain't that rum-sodden, sweetheart." He looked at Karlton. "An' just how *do* ye expect to get a message to Foxworth?"

"The Spanish governor is a friend of mine. And Foxworth's."

"A friend! Blow me over, Vane! They 'ave papist friends, so they says. Look here, Harwick. Maybe ye do, an' again maybe ye don't. To protect our own hides in case ye've got double-crossin' plans to turn us over to the *guarda costa,* we'll take to land to wait for Foxworth. There's a cove nearby where we can hole up so the papists can't see us. I'll send three of my men, and you can send three of your own to bring Foxworth and Farrow."

"Fair enough. And now, shall we sign articles?"

"Aye, we'll sign 'em."

Her father gestured to Zeddie, who went for paper and writing quill.

"Seeing as how ye say Foxworth has the map, he'll be signin' 'em too, or maybe your lying tongue will see you dead and floating with the seaweed before it's over."

Emerald looked on as Thorpe and Vane dipped the quill to ink and scratched their names on the articles of agreement, followed by her father.

Then Thorpe stood, Vane with him, and both pirates left the cabin.

Emerald knelt beside his chair, grabbing his hand and pressing it to her cheek. "Papa . . ."

He leaned toward her, his eyes pained, and held her with his good arm. "It will be all right, lass," he whispered. "We'll make it, you'll see. Baret will come."

Zeddie came now with paper for Emerald to write the letter.

She sat down and wrote swiftly, then handed it to her father. "What will we do when Thorpe discovers there is no treasure?"

Her father sank back in his chair and frowned, looking from Emerald to Zeddie. "It's not Thorpe I'm worried about when it comes to the treasure of the *Prince Philip,*" he confessed in a low voice. "It's Baret."

Emerald grew uneasy. "What do you mean? Why should you be concerned about Baret?"

"Because what I told Thorpe and Vane is true, lass. I *was* with Baret's father. And Margarita *is* the island where the treasure is stored. I was with Royce, Maynerd, and Lucca that wild, rainy night we staggered ashore with the chest."

Emerald's breathing paused, and she stared at him, shocked, stricken. "Papa! And you didn't tell him all these years?" she whispered.

"No," he confessed, "I had plans of my own to come for it. It was to be the treasure I came home with after pretending to sail with Morgan." He sighed. "My wicked way, lass, has turned against me—but far worse, it has come against you. If I hadn't come here . . ."

"But—why did you wait so long to try to locate the treasure again?"

"Because of where it's kept. I'll say no more until Baret arrives. It is best for your sakes that I don't. And now, the letter must be delivered in case my man didn't get through on the longboat."

4

MAROONED

Emerald removed her slippers, lifted the hem of her full skirt, and stepped from the longboat. The warm, wet sand sank beneath her feet, pulling away again as a tiny wavelet withdrew to the water's edge. Another rolled in, splashing her ankles.

Glancing about the isolated cove of white beach and palm trees, she had no notion of where Captain Lex Thorpe had brought them, but Zeddie concluded it was somewhere along the coast of the Arya Peninsula. To the northeast, the smaller islands near Margarita, like giant purple sleeping turtles, sat in the twilight near the Gulf of Venezuela.

The day's sultry heat clung to her skin, causing her deliberately chosen, modest cotton frock with its high neck to stick uncomfortably. Behind her, the evening horizon began to speckle over with gold dust, and ahead in the thickly vegetated interior, indigo shadows draped the trees like netting.

Minette crowded close to her elbow, whispering nervously, "Do you expect the viscount and Captain Farrow will come?"

Emerald's hopes were anchored in the memory that Baret Buckington, though often a rogue, had proven himself on several occasions to be extremely gallant.

"He'll come if the message reaches him." She glanced about at the pirates. Their presence evoked an unflattering comparison in her mind to a pack of wary foxes sniffing cautiously about a hen house guarded by traps. "You can be sure of trouble when he does come. Stay close, and don't look eye-to-eye at any of them."

She was as worried about her father as she was about herself and Minette. His injury had left him weaker than he had let on in the cabin, and she took his arm.

Minette followed them up the wooded beach, and Zeddie came just behind her, carrying his pistols and occasionally eyeing

Thorpe and Vane, who prowled still farther behind, keeping them all under surveillance.

"Things are going better than I hoped," Sir Karlton murmured. "That he decided to come here to wait for Baret is to our advantage. I was afraid he'd decide to hole up nearer Margarita."

His reasoning confused her. "Isn't Baret on this island?"

"He's more likely to be anchored not far from here, off Cumaná."

That encouraging thought lent her new bravery to endure the unpleasant situation of setting up camp for the night.

Emerald, who knew the trials of the West Indies as well as its lush beauty, was spared a hungry night. Guarded by Zeddie, she sat on the beach with Minette while the pirates and her father and their crewmen scavenged about before sunset to come up with their supper. She had recognized the trees called *carmetia,* on which grew small edible fruit like plums. They also dined on bunches of cabbagelike leaves, red-brown plantain, oranges, and stone crabs, which Zeddie roasted in the fire.

As the night deepened over the cove, she watched Thorpe and Vane gulping rum with their cutthroat crew, sprawled on the sand a distance away. Emerald avoided being seen looking in their direction. She sat with Minette on a log bleached white by years of sun and surf. Her father rested close at hand, and his drawn face, pale in the flickering firelight, reminded her of how uncertain was their predicament. What if he was wrong and Baret was *not* anchored near Cumaná? What if for some reason he had remained at Tortuga to await Henry Morgan and Mansfield?

Thorpe was volatile, dangerous, and his mood had changed into one of sullen discontent as he guzzled Barbados rum. Her pistol was still concealed within reach, and both her father and Zeddie kept their weapons at hand, but with every stir of the trade wind that ruffled the strands of hair against the back of her neck, she felt her skin prickle with unease.

Please, Lord, she prayed, *see us safely through this evil night. Send Baret soon to deliver us.*

Even before the stars blinked through a rose-colored sky left by the setting sun, Thorpe ordered his crew to kick out the fire.

Karlton stirred. "There'll be no darkness tonight."

"Stow your sauce, Harwick. Do you take me for a rum-sodden fool? The sight of fire will draw filthy, sneaking Caribs or Spaniards. An' ye know it as well as I."

"Aye, I know it, and we'll tread warily and set up a guard on the beach, but you and your crew will sleep on the other side of that rock. An' the first bloke we find prowling anywhere near here will find their brains splattered in the sand come sunrise."

Thorpe stood and spat. "Ye needn't threaten me nor me men over your highborn wench and her cousin. Foxworth's woman be worth more as ransom then booty."

He snatched up his rum and said something to Vane and the others, who struggled to their bare feet and strode away into the shadows.

Emerald was not satisfied, for there was more than Thorpe to worry about. Just how efficiently did the pirate captain rein in his crew? Too much rum could provoke any one of them to come creeping about when the moon set. She heard her father speaking quietly to Zeddie about their safety and realized he knew that as well.

The water in the cove became a glassy purple-black beneath white stars. The wind grew cooler, but the warmth of the sand, still heated from the day's sun, seeped through to her fingers and toes. She smelled the odd fragrance of sea and flowers stirring together as she listened to the mournful breaking of the waves onto the deserted beach.

She leaned over to where Minette huddled and whispered a verse from the Psalms, "I will both lay me down in peace, and sleep: for thou, Lord, only makest me dwell in safety."

Emerald's confidence was too soon tested by the fires of fear. After lapsing into a restless slumber, she awoke, alarmed by the heart-stilling silence. She sat up trembling, blinking into the dark night, listening hard.

Minette clutched her wrist, whispering, "Uncle Karlton and Zeddie are gone!"

"Gone! They'd never leave us willingly!"

For a moment, raw panic reigned, but then, before she could answer Minette, Zeddie crawled up from the direction of a sheltered gully.

"Never thought I'd be glad for rum, but Thorpe an' Vane's crew is dead out. Quick, follow me, m'gal."

"Follow to where? Where's my father?"

"He's waitin' in the trees. He didn't want to say anything, not sure if that Barbados rum would work on the innards of a tough old gizzard like Thorpe, but Foxworth is anchored about six miles from here."

The thought that Baret could be a mere six miles away sent joyous expectation rippling through her heart.

"Can Father walk that far? He's terribly wounded. And what of the message already sent to Baret—was it delivered to Cumaná?"

"That's the ill news. It was sent to Margarita."

"Then," she said in a small voice barely above a whisper, "Baret doesn't know we're here yet."

"No, but we've our chance now. We'll make it, m'gal, if I have to carry him." In the starlight Zeddie grinned. "Your father was always a shrewd one. That particular cask of rum from the *Madeleine* was kept on board for just such an emergency. It had a hefty dose of drugs in it, straight from the Carib Indians. It'll put most any man to sleep. He learned that bit o' trick from Foxworth."

"But if our message was sent to Margarita, then how does he know Baret is anchored near Cumaná?"

"A friendly *boucan* hunter sent word tonight through a Carib. The Carib says the Spaniards caught Flynn. Come along, now. Two crewmen is on guard till we get a head start, then they'll cover our trail."

Emerald groped for her shoes and the cloak she'd used for a pillow, then followed Zeddie across the warm, soft sand. She could just make him out ahead, crouching beneath dew-drenched aloe branches. She glanced back.

Minette, with shoes in hand, was circling the small area where they had made their bed of dried ferns, perhaps searching for the canvas bag so precious to them both, since it contained personal items not easily replaced.

"It's gone!" she hissed.

Emerald heard the despair in her voice. And what was that other sound? Voices? Zeddie had said the pirates were sleeping! Had they already stirred awake?

She tensed, hearing men talking in some foreign tongue. These were not Thorpe's rogues! A quiver raced along her skin. *Spaniards!*

The thought froze her with terror as accounts of devilish torture flashed across her mind. The *guarda costa* must have spotted the *Black Dragon* and the *Madeleine*. Maybe someone had been sent to warn the governor of the two ships fighting. The voices seemed to come from a circle of darkness surrounding the encampment. She knew that any strangers daring to penetrate the Spanish Main were routed and ofttimes massacred. Perspiration burst out along her brow.

"Minette, run! Minette!"

Emerald started back, but Zeddie latched hold of her so tightly she winced.

"No time! Run!"

Terror gripped her throat. "I can't leave her!"

In the semidarkness she glimpsed leather-and-steel-clad figures surging forward from among the trees, swords brandished and glinting silver in the moonlight.

"*¡Santiago! ¡Muerto a las piratas! ¡Las heréticos!*"

She glimpsed pirates staggering awake beyond the rock, calling out in a daze. Others groped to get to their feet, shaking rum-crazed heads. They fumbled for pistols, swords, daggers.

More Spanish soldiers came running up the moonlit beach. There was the shivering clash of steel, and the roar of firearms crackled in the hot night.

"Come then, ye murderin' papists!" She heard Vane's voice. "I'll carve out yer innards for the buzzards!"

Zeddie, leading Emerald, struggled deeper into the thicket. She tripped in the sand, scrambled to her feet again, stumbled forward for cover. Minette, where *was* she? Minette, and her father? The dread baying of a hound sent chills down her back. The dog would pick up the trail of any who sought to flee or hide. And then she heard Minette scream.

Emerald's blood ran cold. "Oh, God, help us," she sobbed, even as Zeddie relentlessly pulled her forward.

They didn't get far. Thorny vines caught at her ankles. Branches raked across her face. She lost her footing, and a sharp pain skewered her ankle. She had tripped on something sticking up from the ground.

Zeddie pulled her to her feet, but Emerald gasped, "There's no use—they'll find us—the dogs—"

"Faith, m'gal! We got to try."

57

Wet with sweat, she broke into a sob. "Go—without me—"

"Never, lass!" His grip on her arm tightened.

"It's no use, Zeddie. My ankle . . . I can't—" She sank to her knees, gasping.

"Sink me if'n I didn't think of it sooner—up that tree—!"

"The dogs will pick up our scent—"

"It's worth a try. If them Spaniards stay in the camp, the dogs won't come either. Look! It's a *ycoa* tree! Easy to climb!"

The hope the tree offered was slender at best.

Zeddie hobbled her toward it. "Ye can do it—up with ye!"

As Emerald stared at the low, spreading branches above her head, Zeddie cast a backward glance. Then he stooped, interlaced the fingers of both hands, and formed a stirrup. "Come, m'gal, an' don't break the bark," he whispered. "God speed ye!"

She held to the trunk with one trembling hand, carefully balancing her good foot on his palms, and with her other hand lay hold of an overhead branch. She pulled herself upward as he steadied her, until her foot was mounted on his shoulder. Then she agonized to work her way up the tree trunk, feeling the pain in her ankle and the creepers scratching her arms and neck. A branch snagged her hair. She struggled to free it, nearly losing her hold.

Trying to hurry, she worked her way higher until she was able to straddle a large branch and catch her breath.

Zeddie climbed after her as though he were climbing a ship's rigging and perched on the branch below.

Her heart still pounding in her ears, Emerald realized that up here, if it were light, she could see the encampment as well as the beach and sea. The sounds of conflict raged, and the barking dogs terrorized the night. She covered her ears at the sounds of torture and wept silently, crying out to the Lord for strength and mercy.

Her father, had he gotten away? And Minette, had she been able to hide in the darkness?

When the sky brightened, Emerald looked with horror upon the scene below. Bodies lay strewn across the encampment, some with unspeakable atrocities done to them. She understood now more clearly that this expedition by the Spaniards had been dispatched to exterminate trespassers, not take prisoners.

She watched the soldiers, wearing their traditional brimless conical steel caps, gather from all directions to their captain, who stood pointing down the beach and calling orders.

Beyond the beach, she saw a Spanish *barca longa*, manned by chained slaves, dropping anchor. She stared as a Spaniard in a striped red-and-white shirt stepped to the sand, shouting commands. An important visitor seemed to be arriving.

The newcomer, wearing a gray monastic robe belted by cords, was assisted down from the *barca longa*. He strode up the beach toward the encampment, escorted by a Spanish officer donned in a scarlet cloak worn over a steel corselet.

Emerald's breath caught sharply. Here came the *capitán*, dragging Minette. He flung her down before the friar's sandaled feet.

The hooded figure produced a rosary. "You kiss crucifix?"

"I—I can't. My—my Great-uncle Mathias taught me that it's i-idol worship!"

A circle of soldiers in steel headpieces and breastplates moved forward threateningly.

The friar again offered the glinting silver.

Emerald's heart surged with such overwhelming pain and horror that she thought it would burst. For a moment, in mindless emotion, she stirred on the branch, thinking to climb down and rush to Minette's aid.

But Zeddie whispered harshly, "We can do nothing, lass! Pray! Pray! Only Christ can save her!"

Emerald shut her eyes so tightly that her pounding heart sent pulse waves. Tears wet her face, and her sore and stiff fingers clutched the tree limb.

"Praise God," murmured Zeddie, "at least the friar's taking her. Those devils won't touch her now."

Emerald opened her eyes and blinked hard, trying to see what was happening on the beach. *Taking her?*

She watched Minette being escorted back down the beach toward the *barca longa*. Dazed, Emerald stared after her.

Minette! Oh, Minette!

When the *barca longa* bore the Spaniards out to sea, Emerald climbed down from the branches. Despairing, she sank to a rotting tree trunk, head in hand. "I must find her again," she sobbed. "There must be a way!"

Zeddie awkwardly patted her shoulder, sniffing back his own tears. "Sure now, if there's a way, we will. We will. God is good, an' we will. Your father will know what to do, and then there's the viscount ye can turn to. Sink me! Captain Foxworth will be riled aplenty is my guess!"

Yes, she thought, with a fresh surge of hope that brought strength. If there was any man who might be able to help her rescue Minette, it would be Baret Buckington.

The first thing they did, by unanimous consent, was to kneel and pray for Minette and for her father and to thank Him for their own safety.

Then, while Emerald satisfied her thirst from Zeddie's water skin, he looked back in the direction of the encampment. "If anyone's yet alive, they will need help. And I will look for your father."

Was her father alive? Had he been able to conceal himself in time? What if he'd gone back when Minette screamed, thinking to deliver her from the clutches of the Spaniards? She feared to even consider what Zeddie might find.

"I can walk some . . . you mustn't go alone." She stood, masking her apprehension.

"Nay, m'gal, you don't know these devils of the *guarda costa.* The dead are not a sight I'd wish you to see. Wait here. If your father managed to save himself, he'll be out looking for us too. Not that I expect to find any of the others alive." Grimly he set off on the grotesque task before him.

Emerald's anxious thoughts returned to Baret. If it was true that his ship was anchored out of sight somewhere near Cumaná, could they locate him? Would he have heard the gun battle between the *Madeleine* and the *Black Dragon?*

The day grew hotter as the sun climbed in the morning sky. And then Zeddie returned, sooner than she had expected, shaking his head and mopping his brow.

"There's no sign of your father. Maybe he was able to hide same as we. Or he may have gone on for help to the *boucan* hunters—or toward the cove where Captain Foxworth is expected. We can't stay here, m'gal—we best follow on."

She swallowed. "Then the crewmen from the *Madeleine* are also dead?"

"There's not an Englishman could live through what took

60

place during the wee hours. Lex Thorpe and his pirates is all dead too, what's left of 'em. Pirates or no, I wouldn't wish the fate of fallin' to the hands of Spaniards on any man, not even Thorpe."

Emerald swallowed, a sick taste in her mouth.

"But they'll treat Minette well. Sure they will."

Her eyes moistened. "There's no use, Zeddie. They won't. Why should they? They'll make her a slave, I know that. Or worse." She stood and gazed out toward the sea, troubled. "And I told her before we went to sleep last night that the Lord was our safety, our only bulwark."

He straightened his leather baldric, scowling, as though uneasy with the direction of the conversation. "And so He is. Nary a thing can change that. Not death, not life, not suffering, not witless trouncing."

Her bruised faith stirred to the trumpet call only briefly, then sank again into hopelessness. "Yes, but He's permitted the enemy to break through our wall of defense."

"So it looks, m'gal." He sighed with resignation, then brightened. "Then sink me! If'n that's so, then He allowed it for a goodly purpose, now didn't He? Ye have to admit that much! He's the God He says He is, good and wise and faithful."

"Mathias would say so." She agreed but found that admitting what her godly Puritan great-uncle had taught her while she was growing up on Foxemoore did not end her struggle with emotional exhaustion and disappointment. Furthermore, her ankle had swollen, and she wondered how she could walk six miles to a cove where the hope of finding Baret's ship was merely a possibility. And if it wasn't there, then what?

Remembering again how the Lord had taken her beloved great-uncle away from her through the doorway of death increased the loss she felt now over Minette and her father. Yet, through it all, lodged within her soul, faith in all that she knew to be true of God and His Word remained untouched by the attacks of the devil's hordes. *For my faith is founded upon a Rock. I may shake and tremble, but the Rock on which I stand remains firm and steadfast beneath me.*

The trustworthiness of God was based upon His character. The trials, the unexplainable tragedies of life, must wait in faith, not in sight, for understanding. It was enough now to trust the wisdom and purpose of God for good to all who trusted Christ.

Zeddie cleared his throat and cocked an eye at her. "Anyway, she'll be all right, because she pleased the friar."

She looked at him for explanation.

"I wasn't going to say, but maybe I should, so ye won't worry as much. She kissed the crucifix."

Emerald remained silent. For Minette to have done so, in light of the religious wars raging in Europe, was tantamount to committing idolatry in the minds of those so recently embarking on the journey of the Protestant Reformation. Multitudes adopting the Reformed faith were being put to the horrors of the Inquisition rather than submit to religious ritual and tradition imposed by Rome. And refusing to show allegiance to the Church by kissing the crucifix or a statue of Mary had already sent many of the Reformers to horrible deaths.

But she could not bring herself to be disappointed with Minette. At least there was hope for her safety until they could find her. Emerald's heart was solaced. She avoided Zeddie's eyes and brushed the sand flies from her face.

He must have guessed her reaction, and he cleared his throat again. "She's only a child, I'm thinking. We best be moving on, m'gal," and he took her arm, turning her toward the foothills.

Emerald glanced behind her toward the encampment, shuddering. "What of the *Madeleine*?"

"The *guarda costa* took both ships. I heard 'em saying as much to that jackanapes *capitán* when we was up the tree."

The Spaniards had taken the ship, and they were marooned in Spanish territory, which gave no friendly quarter to intruders. Baret and the *Regale* were their one chance of escape.

"M'gal, there's no going back to anything. What hope we have lies ahead."

"Would my father have left a trail?" she asked hopefully.

"Nay, never. Thinking something might go wrong and Thorpe might find him gone and follow. He'd be as careful as I must be."

He was right, of course, and she said nothing more.

Zeddie went on to reassure her that he, too, was acquainted with the ways of the wild cow hunters and that the route they now traveled would bring them into contact. The hunters usually hunted beyond the foothills, where many savannas ran near the shore. He and Karlton had spotted their smoke.

It was in the meadows, Zeddie explained, that the small red cattle and swine multiplied, feasting on the grasses, lemons, and yams that were in full supply. They had been brought many years earlier by Spanish colonists and then abandoned. The animals had increased into free-ranging herds and had become a food source for the island's Protestants, driven out of France by persecution. But Spain allowed for no heretics in any domain she claimed as her own, and she often sent raiders here to hunt and kill them.

"'Tis my guess the hunters already know what's happened here last night," Zeddie said.

"You mean they may have seen the Spanish ship arrive?"

"And also leave, is my guess. Aye, the hunters are a rough sort—an' clever. Many have already abandoned these parts because the Spaniards wouldn't let 'em hunt in peace. Along with the *boucaniers* from Hispaniola, they formed the Brotherhood on Tortuga. Those who are left here are always on the watch for the *guarda costa*. Thorpe should've known better—but he had a folly for rum. A man's appetite for his favorite sins is usually the bait the devil will use to trap him."

Then he looked at her ankle and shook his head. "You can't go a-walkin' with a swollen ankle like that."

She tried, venturing several painful steps that soon frustrated her progress. "Oh, Zeddie, there's no use! I'll never make it. It would take days at this pace."

"I can carry you."

"And wear yourself out? No, the only wise thing to do is for me to hide myself here until you get through to Captain Foxworth."

"Aye, or I could make a walkin' stick to aid you."

"You'll travel twice as fast without me. And should my father return, I'll be waiting for him. We'll both be here when you get back." She wondered that her voice was steady, showing none of her doubt.

"The Spaniards are as thick as locusts! We're nigh Porto Bello!"

"Leave me you must. It's our best chance to find Baret. It's not likely the *guarda costa* will come again soon. They were satisfied, or they wouldn't have set sail."

He still frowned at the idea of leaving her behind. "Ye have the pistol Foxworth gave you?"

"Yes. Don't worry. Did we not just agree our faith looks to God? We have prayed and trusted our way to Him. Whatever befalls us must first pass through His sovereign will."

The frown did not lessen, but he nodded. "Aye, then with that we part, m'gal. And may God speed me on my way. Let us hope your father was right when he said Captain Foxworth was to set in at Cumaná, lest I walk into a nest of Spanish cockleburs!"

Emerald listened to his footsteps diminish through the dense vegetation until silence surrounded her. Her heart thudded, and fear settled in like fog. She was alone, just like Minette. Minette must face the ordeals that would await her at whatever her destination on the Main.

And I must listen to the buzzards! She covered her ears with both hands, shutting her eyes. *I must be brave. I'm not really alone.*

She glanced then toward the distant foothills. Between them lay dense vegetation. The wooded area nearby was thick with cedar, oak, mahogany, and gri-gri trees. Had she not been so despondent, she would have enjoyed the scenery and the myriad lovely birds that flew among the branches. Thrushes, warblers, quail, and ground doves joined green-and-yellow flocks of squawking parrots. Carpenter birds left off their boring at the trunks of *ceiba* and *ycao* trees when they saw her, and fled.

The temperature turned hotter and more humid. Emotionally exhausted, she slapped at the insects and peered at the glaring sun. Longingly she remembered her hat aboard the *Madeleine.*

Unfortunately, something far more precious was aboard her father's ship—the satchel containing Uncle Mathias's translation of the African chants. Like Minette, his work too had slipped through her fingers. If only they had sailed for Barbados to catch a merchant ship for England.

Even now, Baret must think her safely embarked, never thinking her father would bring her with him on the Main. If Baret could see her now! Her dress torn and soiled, her hair unbound and most of the pins lost, her skin becoming sunburned—

Her thoughts collided with the sound of vegetation crunching beneath someone's feet. Thorpe's crew of pirates were all dead—her eyes darted toward her pistol. She had set it down beneath her cloak under a tree only a few feet away, yet if she made any move to retrieve it, the twigs would snap.

The footsteps slowed, hesitated. Anyone could find the trampled path they had carelessly taken in their flight last night. She'd been unwise to remain here. Not even Zeddie had expected anyone to remain alive. Could it be her father? Yes! Of course! She took a step. The leaves crackled. She wavered.

Her anxious gaze darted about, and her heart lurched as a man stepped out from the thick vegetation, moving warily as a tiger. She stared, dismayed.

"Ye take me for a fool?" Thorpe said. "Do ye think I'd drink that foul rum? If Vane wasn't such a daw cock, he'd be alive now too. I can't watch him every moment, now, can I? While I was trailin' your father, Vane was guzzlin'. 'Tis no matter to me, seein' there'll be more out of this enterprise for meself." An evil grin turned his mouth. "Now move, gal. It's you and me."

He had trailed her father! Did this mean he'd found him? Killed him? There was still the hope of Zeddie's getting through to Baret.

As if he were reading her thoughts, his eyes turned cold. "An' don't pin your anchor on that one-eyed nape. I've sent a man after him. He'll be food for buzzards come this afternoon."

She made a brave effort to reach her cloak, the pistol, but her ankle throbbed, and Thorpe sprang, catching hold of her roughly.

"Traitorous wench!" Ignoring her cry, he dragged her back in the direction of the encampment and the beach. "Shut ye'r tongue, now, lest I give ye a heap more to yowl about. We'll be making for Margarita soon as Levasseur gets here. D'ye thinks I didn't know your yellow-livered father stole off to Cumaná lookin' for Foxworth?"

She struggled to jerk away. "You fiend! What did you do to my father!"

He gave a vicious laugh. "He's tied, keepin' comp'ny in the sweet sun with the buzzards feastin' on Vane."

She let out a cry of rage, but his grip was like an iron trap. "A tigress, eh? I'd flay your bones if ye weren't a temptin' morsel for Foxworth to pay me for!" With a vicious flourish, he shoved her ahead violently. Her sprained ankle gave way, and she landed on the ground, scratching her face.

He came up behind her and gently placed a boot on her hand as though he would grind it into the dirt. "More sass an' ye'll be wishin' the filthy papists took ye like your wench cousin. Now get up!"

"You can't just leave my father tied in the sun. He'll die!"

"An' why not, I ask? I can tell Foxworth the Spaniards got him wi' the others. Wot's Harwick good for, eh?" He grinned at her.

"You'll never get out of here without a ship! I don't believe you have my father. You're lying."

"Don't try me patience." He stood. "I 'ave him. An' he'll be playing things my way now. He played the traitor, an' for that he'll suffer. As for how I get a ship, don't ye be botherin' your head about it. Levasseur will be showin' soon, and we'll sail on the *Venture*. An' if it's the last deed I do, I'll get the *Black Dragon* back too."

"I—I can't walk. I hurt my ankle."

"Ye'll walk all right, an' be quick aboot it too."

When they arrived back at the encampment, Emerald turned her head away, sickened by the sight of buzzards hopping and quarreling among the carcasses. Then she stifled a cry when she saw her father tied to a tree in the sweltering sun.

Thorpe didn't stop her when she struggled toward him, grimacing from the pain in her ankle.

"Father . . ."

His swollen eyes opened and showed signs of life when he recognized her. "Untie him!" she told Thorpe. "Can't you see neither one of us can get far in our condition? If anything happens to him through your neglect, I'll tell Captain Foxworth. You'll never get any of the treasure your soul covets."

"Stop squawkin.'" He turned to a half-dozen survivors who came up from the beach, scowling—presumably at the loss of the *Black Dragon* and their fellow pirates.

"Levasseur's ship ain't nowheres in sight, cap'n. Suppose he don't come? We're marooned."

"He'll come. The *Venture's* due tonight. He's watchful of the Spaniards is all." He gestured with his head toward Emerald and

66

Karlton. "Take 'em down to the water's edge. No need to tie 'em. They's both in a bad way. The smell in camp is gettin' to me."

One of the pirates loitered, gesturing to the dead. "What about them?"

"D'ye think we got time for burial? Don't be a bloke, Wooton."

"Who's talkin' burial? We ain't divvied up their belongin's."

Thorpe spat. "Divvy 'em up, then. Vane's pistol is mine—so's his ring."

"It don't come off."

"Then cut it off, ye cur, an' be quick wi' ye."

Emerald picked up a half-empty water skin and brought it to her father. Kneeling, she tipped it to his cracked lips.

"Where's Zeddie?" he rasped.

"He escaped," she whispered. "He's gone to Cumaná to find Baret."

A sigh escaped his lips. "Thank God. Lass, I'm sorry . . . Thorpe . . . more clever than I thought. I . . . came back when Minette screamed . . . thought they had both of you . . . couldn't get away again . . ."

She leaned her forehead against his shoulder and held back her sobs.

Karlton's hand came weakly to console her. "Baret . . . will come yet."

5

ENCOUNTER
ON THE BEACH

The evening stars paraded forth on a battlefield of black sky. In stained jerkins and leather breeches, the captain and remaining crew of the *Black Dragon* gathered on the beach where white waves rolled in from the bay and scattered foam like tiny bubbling pearls.

Thorpe sat on an empty cask, his telescope turned upon the sea, growing more impatient as the late hours dragged by and the *Venture* did not appear.

Even the arrival of her French cousin Rafael offered more encouraging possibilities than being left alone with Thorpe, Emerald thought. She sat next to her father, who lay propped against a bleached sand dune. By moonrise, she had become so exhausted that soon not even her fears could keep her alert.

Karlton's head moved, and he seemed to tense, looking past her into the night. Emerald's love and pity stirred her to action; she knew he needed water. But Thorpe had already confiscated the skin when Levasseur did not show as expected.

"Any w-water?" he whispered through parched lips.

Offering a prayer for help, Emerald struggled to her feet. Every movement brought discomfort to her swollen ankle. She was unable to stand her father's suffering and was forced to confront Thorpe. She looked across the sand at him, still seated on the cask with the telescope, now and then cursing under his breath and muttering, "If we don't get outa here soon, the Spaniards may come again."

Thorpe saw her edging across the stretch of sand to where the water skin lay near the cask. He snatched it up, stood, and walked toward her. He stopped, uncorked the skin, and drank long and deep, then wiped his mouth on the back of his hand with a satisfied sigh. He dangled the skin just out of her reach. "Lookin' for this?"

68

Emerald closed her eyes in frustration.

"Is that any way to wait on a future countess, Thorpe?"

Emerald's breath sucked in and held. The voice coming from the darkness behind them was wonderfully familiar. It sounded too pleasant just now, tinged with danger.

Startled, Thorpe and his diminished crew looked back toward the opposite end of the beach.

In sharp silhouette against the glassy bay, where brilliant moonlight fell as from a lantern in the sky, stood a rugged form scrupulously dressed in white, ruffled buccaneer shirt and black breeches. An ostrich plume curled about the broad rim of his hat. His hair was held back from a suntanned face that was devastatingly striking and comely. Yet the expression he wore now was dark and ruthless.

"Foxworth!" Thorpe threw down the water skin with an oath.

Emerald's heart pounded, but she remained utterly silent, uncertain whether or not Thorpe would unsheathe his sword.

The pirate crew gathered cautiously around him, eying Baret uneasily, as if wondering how his appearance were possible when they hadn't seen his ship.

Captain Foxworth walked toward them, his black leather boots sinking into the dry sand. Then out of the shadows came his officers, ranging themselves for swordplay if it came to that.

Emerald crept back toward her father, silent as a kitten.

Baret's gaze evidently was quick to note her injury. He walked toward her, caught her beneath her arms, and lifted her to her feet. She covered a wince, but he noticed, and his dark eyes flashed with anger. Turning her toward the moonlight, he cupped her chin and studied the bruises and cuts on her face.

His finger gently touched her cheek. "Who did this?"

Having longed for Thorpe to be brought to justice, she now held back. She feared justice would come too brutally at Baret's hand, adding to his difficulties with the Jamaican authorities.

When she said nothing, he looked down at her ankle.

"Did he do this to you?"

"She tripped," Thorpe said coldly. "We was runnin' from the Spaniards. Tell him. Tell him how I tried to help you."

Baret waited for a truthful answer, but her eyes faltered.

"It doesn't matter anymore," she whispered. "You're here now. I'm all right."

He turned his head and looked at Thorpe.

Among the buccaneers who had arrived with Baret was another captain that she recognized, the fair-haired and handsomely somber Erik Farrow. At his side stood his lieutenant, a massive African with shaven head glinting in the moonlight. A large gold hoop ring dangled from his left earlobe.

Baret handed her to his officer Yorke, then doffed his hat in mockery to Thorpe. "Good evening, my captain. You've been awaiting my arrival anxiously, I see. My apology for the delay. We watched the gun battle between the *Black Dragon* and the *Madeleine* with grave interest."

"Did ye, now? An' how could ye 'ave watched when your ship was nowheres about, I ask? Are ye tryin' to cozy up to me, Foxworth?"

"Would I so presume, Lex? You, a captain of honor and worthy esteem among the Brotherhood?"

"Honor, he says! Esteemed, he says! That's a good play! An' what've ye got on your mind, Foxworth? Ye know why *I'm* here. So if ye've come to sign articles, where's your ship? And why d'ye come on cats' paws like Spaniards?"

"Yes, I know why you're here. It was necessary to put into a cove across the islet. We've walked across to pay you our fairest greetings." And he gestured a hand flashing with gold toward his officers and Captain Farrow. "I've brought the best of honorable captains just to greet you—of course, I had no idea most of your crew would be dead so quickly. It proves a grievous disappointment to us, doesn't it, gentlemen?"

"Aye, captain, we're sorely aggrieved."

Thorpe's bulging eyes darted from Baret to Erik, then skimmed over the buccaneers with them. "Are ye now? Fife! Ye're all a glad cockle of rotting fish bait! I say ye're pleased me men are dead!"

"Lex, your suggestion is indeed provocative!"

"Provocative, he says."

"I also came to give you a message from our warmhearted Frenchman Captain Levasseur." Baret lifted a folded white paper from his shirt and held it up. "He's returned to Tortuga without a share in the treasure of the *Prince Philip.*"

"That ain't possible. We left Tortuga together."

"He decided to return—at my orders."

70

"Whaaa . . . at *your* orders? Now I've heard everything, Fox-worth!"

"Yes, at my orders. It was either beat a path back to Cayona Bay or find the *Venture* sinking to the bottom of the Caribbean, the Frenchman with it. He took my threat seriously, Lex. A pity you are not as clever as Rafael."

Thorpe stared at him in sheer amazement. "It's lying ye are, ye fancy daw cock!"

Baret pretended offense, then gestured toward Emerald and Karlton. "I am disappointed to arrive and find you've neglected your manners. Why are my friend Karlton and his charming daughter in such foul condition? Is this any way to treat honorable guests?"

Thorpe said nothing but eyed him cunningly. "So ye've not come peaceably after all."

"You attacked the *Madeleine*, the ship of a fellow buccaneer. You know the Brotherhood Articles, Lex. There is honor among the Brotherhood. And how is it I arrive to find that the Spaniards have taken Karlton's ship? He is wounded and his daughter mishandled. Did you think I would take this lightly? Now, what do you think I ought to do about it?"

In comparison to the unkempt pirate and his crewmen, Baret stood out as the image of excellence, however arrogant, and his disposition suggested that beneath his affected calm lived a man every whit as dangerous.

Thorpe's eyes narrowed. "It was a mistake, Foxworth. As captain of the *Black Dragon*, I didn't know it was Harwick's ship."

"You thought it was the *Regale?*"

Thorpe glowered, then shrugged. "What if I did?"

"A pity we didn't meet."

"It were Levasseur's idea to take Harwick on. He had a notion of learnin' from his uncle where the treasure was. Things got a mite outa hand was all."

"So it appears."

"Harwick drugged the rum, but I was too clever for him. Then them filthy Spaniards attacked us. He tried to escape to find ye at Cumaná, but I fooled him and was waitin'."

"You're indeed clever. It's fortunate your devious ways must come to an end."

71

"An end, he says! An' what have ye in mind? D'ye think to kill me? I'll carve your hide first."

"Kill you, Lex? There's no need to bloody my sword. I intend to leave you and your brilliant crew to face the Spaniards again."

Thorpe's color changed, and he chewed his lip as his eyes ran over Baret. "Surely ye're makin' sport, Captain Foxworth. Ye wouldn't leave me here. It ain't human. Ye seen what them fiends did to Vane and the others?"

"I'm well acquainted with the creativity of the soldiers of the king of Spain."

"They skinned 'em alive and rubbed 'em with pepper!"

"Gentlemen, all. You'll make fit company for the *guarda costa,* my captain. They may even learn a thing or two, should you share some of your own tactics with them."

"Now wait a minute—" Thorpe began. "Ye can't do this, Foxworth! Some o' that treasure is mine!"

"Is that so? Now this is uncanny! Since when have you sailed with Captain Royce Buckington under commission from Cromwell?"

"Cromwell! Let him rot. I'm cuttin' meself in this booty by sheer cunning."

"Then I advise you to begin to build yourself a canoe, Lex. And when you've paddled up the coast of Venezuela, dodging Spanish galleons, we can discuss it again on Tortuga."

"The devil take ye, Foxworth! I'll kill ye first and spill your innards on the sand!"

"I was hoping you would suggest that."

Thorpe hesitated, then decided against whipping out his sword. "I won't duel ye, seein' as how ye've an uncanny way about ye. I'll survive, Foxworth. An' I'll come after ye, ship to ship!"

"A wishful thought." Baret looked briefly at the other members of Thorpe's crew.

They turned their backs and walked away to slump sullenly onto the sand.

"Your men," said Baret flatly, "wait for your company."

Thorpe's lip curled like a snarling dog's, forced to retreat. When he was far enough away to guard against a sudden attack, Baret turned to Yorke, a huge, burly man, and gestured that he should carry Karlton.

72

Emerald looked on, totally taken with the incident. She held to an empty cask to keep her balance, becoming aware that he had turned to her. Self-consciously she looked away, brushing the hair from her cheek as he walked up to her.

"We met Zeddie on the way. He's all right and waiting with Hob. And you? Other than cuts and bruises, you're all right?"

"Yes, but my father—"

"Yorke will take care of him. He's brought along medical supplies. Better let me treat that ankle—"

"No . . . it can wait."

"You're sure? I'll carry you back."

"My pistol and cloak—I'd rather not leave them. They're ahead in those trees."

"It's too dark to find them tonight. I'll see that you have another weapon." His mouth curved up. "Next time, use it." He turned as one of his buccaneers approached.

"Sorry, captain. Jeremy's come to report a Spanish galleon. Looks to be heading toward Margarita. And what do you think the illustrious *capitán* is hauling in her wake? The wounded *Madeleine.*"

"Ah! What of the *Black Dragon?*"

"No sign of her. Maybe she's headed with the *barca longa* for Porto Bello. Sweet pickings, captain."

"Sweet pickings at Porto Bello must wait till we sail with Morgan. We'll settle for the pearl islands," he said. "The galleon towing Karlton's ship is booty enough."

"Aye, captain. When do we move out? Our skin's beginnin' to crawl with the thought of Spaniards. Yorke had us make a hammock to carry Captain Harwick."

"Start out now. I'll join you in a minute. I've one last thing to do." He turned. "Erik?"

Captain Farrow sauntered up, and Baret said casually, "Her ankle is sprained. See to her safety, will you? I'll catch up."

Emerald glanced at Baret, wondering why he wished to remain behind. She looked uneasily toward Thorpe, who hadn't budged from the sand.

Erik seemed to know, but something more appeared to be on his mind. She had noticed earlier, during the discourse between Baret and Thorpe, that Captain Farrow took a brief stroll around the immediate site as though casually curious

73

about something. Now Erik glanced about again. His ice-cool gray eyes flickered as the wind moved his fair hair away from his chiseled face.

"Your flighty French cousin—the one with all the hair—did she not board with you at Tortuga? I thought she was going with you to London?"

"Thank God you and Baret have come, but if—if only you'd come last night—" Her voice failed.

Erik seemed to be more interested now, and anger sparked in his eyes. "What did they do with her—Thorpe, I mean?"

She hastened to assure him. "They did nothing. My father made certain of that. But the Spaniards took her away with them. I must find her! You and Captain Foxworth will help me?"

His hand tightened on his belt. "The soldiers took her?"

"No, the Franciscan. She was under his protection. I am thankful for that. They sailed on the *barca longa.*"

Was she mistaken, or was there a restrained look of relief on his face? What Minette would give to know of Erik's strong reaction to her abduction!

"I won't offer more hope than what's reasonable. We're on our way to rendezvous at Margarita and should locate them on the way. The viscount's friend Captain Pierre LaMonte is already in those waters. Knowing the condition of the three ships involved, including the *Warspite,*" he said of his own vessel, "I don't think your cousin will remain a prisoner for long. You've given me even more reason to intercept the Spanish ship."

"Then you'll help rescue Minette?"

He looked at her, and for a moment she thought she had misread his concern, since his face was calm. His words, however, assured her.

"If Pierre has not taken the ship by the time we arrive, then I will. I'll return your cousin."

Her fear relieved, she could even smile, though wearily.

"At the viscount's request—" And he picked her up in his arms and walked toward the beach.

Emerald glanced over her shoulder to try to see where Baret was, but the trees blocked her view.

"Do you think he'll kill Thorpe?" she asked quietly, tensely.

"No."

She was silent, still uneasy. "Then why did he remain behind?"

"You'll need to ask him that."

Baret approached Thorpe, and the pirate stood.

"I've had a change of heart where your crew is concerned, Thorpe."

Thorpe looked at him cautiously. "You'll let us board the *Regale*?"

Baret looked at Thorpe's few men, who likewise anxiously scrambled to their feet.

"Aye, Cap'n Foxworth," one said. "We swear we 'ad nothing to do with the debacle where Harwick and his lass was concerned."

"I'll take you as far Pierre LaMonte's vessel."

"A deal, Foxworth! And we ain't be forgettin' your kindness!"

"Then get on with you. I'll join you soon. Not you, Lex."

As the pirates ran ahead through the sand, Baret turned to Thorpe, who was gnawing his lip.

"What d'ye have in mind?"

"You're a foul and worthless coward, Lex."

"If ye 'ave a mind to duel me, then draw your cursed blade!"

"For those cuts on her face—and your little game with the water skin—"

Baret's fist landed a vicious blow to Thorpe's face and another to his belly. When the pirate doubled, he struck a hammer blow to his neck. Thorpe jarred to his knees with a curse hissing between his teeth.

Baret looked down upon him. "An end far too kind for you, Lex. *Adiós!*"

Captain Erik Farrow and the buccaneers brought Emerald to a deserted inlet, one among many other cays along the Venezuelan Main. Miles of deserted beach shielded by thick palms and protected by barrier reefs made havens for the buccaneers to rendezvous with less chance of detection.

Here at this unknown cay, as dawn arrived, flooding pink and gold above turquoise water, the *Regale* and the *Warspite* were anchored, safely camouflaged from the patrolling *guarda costa*, which Captain Farrow informed her sailed regularly in and out of their headquarters farther west at Caracas on the lookout for trespassers.

She learned that another buccaneer captain from Tortuga, a Frenchman named Pierre LaMonte, was a few miles down the coast, also out of sight and waiting to spy a certain Spanish ship from Cartagena on its way to Margarita. The three captains with their combined crews of a hundred men had come with plans previously made at Tortuga to seize the Spanish ship.

Just when Emerald thought she understood him, the captain of the *Regale* portrayed himself more enigmatic than she had supposed. That he was a fine seaman, she knew, but was the viscount-turned-buccaneer capable of becoming an outright pirate as well? She came to the conclusion that he could quite easily merge into the role of pirate—and do so without apparent qualm.

Emerald minimized her shock upon learning of the planned attack, for the unnecessarily cruel horrors she had witnessed by the Spaniards at the cove were still fresh upon her mind. An attack also appeared to be the answer to her prayers for Minette's rescue. A lookout from Farrow's crew, hiding on the beach, had reported that a priest and a young woman captive had been transported from the *guarda costa's barca longa* onto the Spanish ship. Whereas the *barca longa* was returning to Caracas, the ship from Cartagena was on its way either to Cumaná, Margarita, or on to Trinidad.

Emerald thought the young woman had to be Minette.

Captain Farrow was convinced as well. As soon as he arrived at the beach, he left Emerald with Yorke and ordered his crewmen to board a longboat and row out to the *Warspite* to set sail.

Baret had not yet arrived when Yorke and another crewman prepared a smaller pinnace to row her to the *Regale*. She wondered what was delaying him. Yorke did not seem concerned, however, even when the remaining crew from the *Black Dragon* came scrambling up the beach, hailing them.

"Foxworth is taking us as far as Pierre's *Bonaventure,*" one announced.

Lex Thorpe was nowhere to be seen, and Emerald turned to Yorke uneasily. "Shouldn't your captain have returned by now?"

He grinned. "You don't need to worry about him, Miss

Emerald. It's Thorpe who best worry. The captain will return later tonight. He knows some *boucaniers* in these parts he wants to meet with first."

"But aren't the *boucaniers* mainly on Hispaniola?"

"Aye, sometimes called Cow Island. You know of the hunters, miss?"

"My father spoke of them when I was growing up in Jamaica. He had friends among them also. He spoke in glowing terms of their hunting abilities. He used to anchor off northern Hispaniola, and the men would row out to barter with him for their dried beef, *boucan*. It's an Arawak Indian name, isn't it— 'green willow branch'?"

He looked at her, obviously admiring her insight into their ways. "Aye, and my grandfather was one of them early colonists." His ruddy face darkened with memory. "Then an edict came down from the Spanish colonial government in Madrid to kill off the heretics migrating to the West Indies." He leaned over and spat onto the sand. "Some of us stayed alive in the woods by hunting the wild cows there. So we learned the Arawak's ways of smoking and curing raw meat. Most of us at Tortuga come from grandparents who fled persecution against Protestants in France, Holland, and England."

He looked suddenly sheepish. "Looks like we've forgotten the faith of our fathers. Most of us drifted from Hispaniola to Tortuga and became what we are now, the Brotherhood. The *boucaniers* have become the Buccaneers—or worse, pirates like the captain of the *Black Dragon*. It's a fact, miss, even old Thorpe's grandparents came from Scotland. They was some of the finest Presbyterians you'd ever keep company with on Sunday. But all of us, seeing atrocity after atrocity done by the Spaniards, was soon raised not on the Bible but on vengeance and hate. Well— I'm not making excuses, miss. It's the way of things. Not much of our grandparents remains in us now 'cept a burning hatred for the ways of the inquisitors."

She had heard this before from her father, but Yorke put a face on the history. "Your captain also despises Spain," she said quietly. "His mother died in Holland."

His eyes turned granite blue. "With good cause he hates 'em. He knows better than me how the Spanish government works in the Indies. The presidents, the captains-general, the royal governors are all bound by orders issued through the Holy Office of the Inquisition. That means there's no place for us in the Caribbean, an' there isn't a cruelty that isn't blessed by heaven to be used on us. So they say to the soldiers."

Yorke smiled suddenly, but it was a brittle smile without mercy. "When we're through with their fancy galleons and treasure ships, ol' King Philip will be absent his silver, and his army in Europe will be broke. Then let's see how them devils can war against us and Protestant Holland!"

He turned abruptly to Thorpe's crew, hanging back apprehensively. "Wait here for Foxworth. Dugan—guard these men till the captain comes!"

He took Emerald to a smaller boat and sat her on a low seat toward the back. Then Yorke and his comrade shoved off, quickly hopped aboard, and took up their oars.

As the pinnace pulled away from the beach, she felt the unsteady movement of the water beneath them and heard the oars slicing through the quiet blue water of the cay.

She looked back. A dozen men waited on the beach with the bigger longboat that would return their captain to the *Regale*. She wondered why Baret wanted to meet with the *boucaniers*, but Yorke had not seemed eager to explain.

As they neared the *Regale*, Emerald looked up the tall side of the ship to a young lad with a thatch of chestnut hair and unusually tender brown eyes.

"Jeremy, my lad, how goes it?" Yorke called up in friendly fashion.

The young man, perhaps eighteen, smiled. "I'm still disappointed the captain made me stay behind, Yorke. You leave with a crew of buccaneers and return with a lady!"

"The captain's lady, my lad. You best remember that!"

"Aye, how could I forget? There isn't many of us who hasn't seen that drawing!"

The exchange made no sense to Emerald, who was completely absorbed in the task before her—climbing the rope ladder up the side of the ship. She remembered the first time she climbed it with Zeddie, thinking the *Regale* belonged to her pirate cousin, Rafael Levasseur. What a surprise greeted her when Baret had found her rummaging through his belongings!

"Make haste! Get the lady aboard!" called up Yorke. "She's got a bad sprain in her ankle."

She set her good foot onto a swaying rung and, with the help of Yorke, cautiously began the steep ascent, gripping the rough rope. When she neared the top, Jeremy carefully hauled her over the side, and she felt her feet touch the deck. She took hold of the rail to steady her balance.

Jeremy smiled shyly. "Morning, miss. You sure do justice to that drawing the captain keeps."

"What drawing?"

"Later, me lad," said Yorke. "Tell Hob to bring tea and something to eat. Is the cabin ready?"

Jeremy cast him a cautious glance. "The captain's cabin is already borrowed, remember?"

"I know as much. What of the cabin below?"

"I did my best." Jeremy looked at Emerald, obviously anxious to please. "I hope you'll be comfortable, miss."

"I'm sure I will, thank you. Is my father in the captain's cabin?"

Jeremy looked at Yorke, saying nothing.

"First, I'll get you settled," said Yorke evasively.

Wondering, she said no more and found herself being carried down the steps to the lower deck. Unlike the last time she'd sailed on Baret's ship, she wasn't taken to the main cabin. Finding herself in smaller quarters, she supposed it was because her father was taken there to have his injuries cared for.

"Is my father all right?" she repeated anxiously.

It came as a surprise when Yorke explained that both Sir Karlton and Zeddie had been transported to Captain Farrow's ship.

"My father's on the *Warspite*? Why?"

"It was by his own asking," Yorke said.

This puzzled her. She had naturally thought that he would sail on the *Regale* with her. As she mulled over his request to be brought to Erik's vessel instead, a dark intuition of trouble arising between him and Baret settled over her soul. Her father would have a good deal of explaining to do to Baret about how he knew where to locate the treasure of the *Prince Philip*. And obviously he would not feel prepared to take him on now. She believed that Baret was in no fraternal mood either, though he had risked much to rescue them from Lex Thorpe.

She became curious about the plans that Baret had already made with Captains Farrow and LaMonte, and why they had rendezvoused off Venezuela, contrary to earlier plans to join Henry Morgan in a raid against Porto Bello. Had the Dutch war intervened, cutting short their plans? Even now they were close to Dutch-held Curaçao, and north from Spanish Margarita were other Dutch holdings: St. Eustatius, Saba, and St. Martin. Did they plan to aid the Dutch against England? When last she had seen Baret on Tortuga, he had implied that he'd promised his grandfather that he would fight for England to please King Charles.

Hob, the old turtler from Chocolata Hole who was now Baret's serving man, entered with tea and something to eat. The familiar sight of the short, grizzled man in canvas breeches and a faded red scarf tied over his thick, white locks brought a smile to Emerald's face. His shrewd blue eyes were bright with wry humor beneath walruslike brows. He chuckled and glanced at Yorke.

"Tea, Miss Emerald. Be a kind hour to see ye aboard his lordship's pert ship again."

She thanked him, taking the hot, sweet drink gratefully. Then, as Hob sliced meat from a roasted wild hen to serve her, she questioned Yorke about Baret's plans.

Yorke remained vague, saying only that they were to weigh anchor to voyage in the direction of Margarita to trade.

"*Trade?* Will the Spanish governor allow it? The laws of Madrid forbid her colonists to buy or sell with privateers from England, France, or Holland."

Yorke rubbed his chin and smiled a little. "Well, miss, the captain don't always abide by the laws of Madrid."

Hob chuckled.

"I'm aware of that," she said, "but isn't it dangerous to sail to Margarita? What if they open fire when the *Regale* nears port?"

"The captain has his friendly ways," Yorke said.

To Emerald that was no explanation at all, and she could see he was deliberately avoiding giving a plain answer. Her curiosity grew even stronger to know what Baret was about.

"The royal governor of Madrid isn't likely to be won over by his friendly ways," she said with a crooked smile.

"Aye, but what the captain has to trade will make him a mite more friendly."

She wondered at his underlying tone. Just what did Baret have that the governor of Margarita was likely to want badly enough to allow the *Regale* to do business there? And what manner of business did Baret have on Margarita that would cause him to risk going into the heart of Spanish territory? She remembered what her father had said about the treasure of the *Prince Philip*. Could it really be hidden on Margarita?

As she rested, drinking tea and nibbling on the succulent slice of fowl, she felt safe and secure among trusted men for the first time in a week. She settled comfortably back into her chair and watched Hob and Yorke, trying to read their guarded expressions. They were on their best behavior but seemed determined to remain mute about anything the captain was up to.

"The governor won't be friendly once he learns Captain Foxworth helped seize that ship from Cartagena," she suggested. "Is it . . . um . . . a treasure ship, by any chance?"

Treasure galleons often carried as much as one million pieces of eight, plus emeralds, pearls, bars of silver from the Peruvian mines, and all manner of silk, spices, and other rich commodities.

Hob looked slyly at Yorke, who cleared his throat.

"You best wait for the captain to answer your questions, miss," Yorke said. "Now, excuse me—I best be getting back to the beach. Foxworth will be arriving soon, an' he may have more fightin' men with him if the *boucaniers* be joining us, as he hopes. They're some of the best fightin' men in these parts. They know all the ways and customs of the Spaniards."

She tensed, and Yorke, as though he had already said too much, murmured something about not wanting to keep Baret waiting. He ducked his head under the door frame and departed.

Hob remained, turning his attention to her injured ankle, clucking his tongue as he gently inspected it. "Thorpe be a cullion, says I. Ought to be strung out for what he done to ye and Sir Karlton. That ankle—" he shook his head sadly "—ye not be walkin' on that foot for a few days. A mite o' turtle rum soaked in rawhide be helpin'. *Har*, a good thing Cap'n Foxworth be in these waters."

Emerald agreed and guided the conversation back to Baret's plans, thinking she might get more out of Hob, who loved to talk, than she had from the more cautious Officer Yorke.

"Why are you so certain the governor of Margarita will be friendly with Captain Foxworth?"

He glanced at her, then toward the door that stood open allowing the breeze to enter, then back again. "Because his lordship—I means, Cap'n Foxworth—be holding the governor's niece as ransom to bargain with. He done moved out of the great cabin and loaned it to her." He grinned. "He'll be surprised to find ye in this one, seein' as how this was to be his new quarters. He told Yorke to take ye to Farrow's ship. Maybe Yorke misheard. Cap'n Foxworth didn't want ye to know he's plannin' to teach the Spaniards a hard lesson. He has himself plans to attack Cumaná, Puerto Cabello, and Coro."

She stared at him.

The governor's niece!

Baret was accustomed to seeing rough-looking scoundrels in Tortuga and Port Royal as well, but he had never seen anything that approached the friendly *boucanier* hunters. They smoked odd-looking pipes, wore round, rawhide hats, and their stiff leather breeches and sandals still bristled with animal hair. Strips of leather bound their chests in crisscross fashion, and cowskin pouches hung from belts bulging with leaden balls that were eighteen to the pound.

They carried a host of weapons: long-barreled muskets that Baret knew to be supremely accurate, firelocks, snaphauches, arquebuses, and broad-bladed cutlasses. Accompanying them were large mastiffs, used to flush out wild pigs and cattle from the tropical underbrush. The men spoke mostly French, mingled with English and Dutch.

The remaining *boucan* hunters were dwindling in favor of life on the sea. Those who remained to hunt and sell their dried meat instead of joining the Brotherhood of the Coast were a hearty group.

Baret lounged near the glowing firestones, where a favorite delicacy of the men—heaps of marrow bones—splattered and sizzled. Barbados rum was hauled out from somewhere and passed around in halved coconut shells.

Marquet, their spokesman, described with a flourish how

the process of curing the *boucan* took place. Strips of meat three or four feet long and half an inch thick were laid across strong racks fashioned of thick green branches. The strips, heavily salted and lashed around green wooden rods, were rotated from time to time, some two feet above a thick bed of hot coals upon which the hunters cast bones and offal, creating a thick greasy smoke.

Marquet then spilled out horror tales of past persecutions by the *guarda costa*. "Nevair have we seen such cruelties, *ma foi*, and out of decency I would not speak of zem even now. You know well enough zair ways. Ze Spaniards have no pity. Nor have we pity for ze likes of papists. Our brethren on Tortuga will sink every ship zey come across. And we, monsieur? Ah! We will slay every Spaniard we shall find!"

Baret knew the sad history of the French, Dutch, and English who had come out of desperation to the West Indies, escaping the religious wars in Europe. With wives and children killed, the remaining male colonists had banded together to survive. They sold their dried jerky to passing merchant ships by rowing out to them in their canoes, *barca longas,* or *piraguas.*

As Spanish expeditions persisted, the *boucaniers* discovered they could turn their canoes and small barks into raiding vessels. They were able to row quietly up to the side of an unsuspecting larger vessel at night, board silently, and actually take over the ship. Eventually, the wild cow hunters began to use bigger vessels, which in turn were able to attack still the larger and more prosperous Spanish ships called treasure galleons. Their success became a growing and frightening reality all along the Main.

Though they were first called *boucaniers* because of their smoked *boucan,* the word eventually came to mean any freebooter who preyed on Spain's shipping. Most of the early *boucaniers* had already left northern Hispaniola for Tortuga, where the Confederacy continued to grow, drawing ruffians and pirates as well and creating a force that Baret estimated to be near 700 men. A common cause bound them: intense hatred for Spain and a passion for booty, all the more dear because it was taken from the Spanish throne.

The first admiral of this nationless group of freebooters had been a fiery old Hollander by the name of Edward Mansfield, but as he grew older there was talk of following Henry Morgan instead.

"You have us the smaller vessel we need?" Marquet asked.

"She's a ketch, a mere fifty feet in length at her waterline. Like Morgan's *Free Guift*, I've had a blunderbuss mounted in the main crosstrees. At that height, we'll have a clean shot of the *San Pedro*'s deck if needed."

Baret and Marquet looked at each other, pleased.

The small-sized ketch forbade carrying heavy cannon, and the shot of the smaller demi-culverin was no larger than a man's hand. But the brass guns called "murdering pieces," the big blunderbusses mounted on swivels, could shoot everything from musket balls and rocks to glass. A single well-aimed blast across an enemy's deck was frightfully effective.

"Monsieur, we will join you," Marquet said. "There is no more place for us as hunters. First we left Hispaniola, now we leave zese parts. Zis idea of yours to take ze *San Pedro* in ze old way of ze *boucaniers* will be a mission most dear to our hearts. When do we leave, *mon foi?*"

Smiling, Baret gestured to the sizzling strips of smoking meat. "As soon as we eat."

They laughed, and Marquet leaned over and heaped Baret's hollowed-out coconut plate with barbecued beef.

6

THE PIRATE'S
SAVAGE VIRTUE

Boot steps sounded firmly on the companionway of the *Regale,* and from her small cabin Emerald heard Baret's resonant voice speaking to Yorke.

"I *told* you to bring her to the *Warspite.* You know why I didn't want her aboard. This is a war voyage. We'll be attacking by sea and land. We'll soon be in battle! Where is she?"

Yorke cleared his throat. "In there, sir."

"My cabin! *Again?* Where's that wily future father-in-law of mine?"

"I did my best, captain, but Captain Harwick insisted on being brought to the *Warspite.* An' Farrow upped anchor. He's making his way now to join the *Bonaventure.*"

She heard Baret draw in a breath with exasperation.

"Harwick! So he's avoiding me, is he? Wait until I see him alone. He has a lot to answer for!"

"Aye, captain, but maybe his daughter can answer a few of 'em."

"She has questions to answer all right. Weigh anchor— we're already behind schedule. If I miss the *San Pedro,* my plans are ruined. Sound the orders!"

"Aye, captain!"

Emerald winced, tensing for the ordeal ahead as the door was thrown open and Baret entered, his disconcerting gaze locking with hers.

She offered a sweet smile. "Why, Baret, hello . . . um . . . how kind of you to loan me your cabin . . . again. If I'd known the other cabin was already occupied by a female passenger, I'd have insisted Mr. Yorke bring me to my father. I thought he was aboard."

"So did I!" He folded his arms and regarded her through dark lashes, a sardonic smile on his mouth. "I wonder where he went so quickly. And why."

She plucked at her sleeve, still smiling. "I'm sure he'll be able to explain everything to your satisfaction."

"You're quite certain about that, madam?"

She wasn't but dare not admit it. She was as much in the dark over her father's behavior as Baret.

He gestured to his belongings piled on a makeshift captain's desk. "Strange," he mused, "I could almost be certain we've lived through this before. Another time, another voyage. All that's missing is Levasseur and Jamie Boy."

Her eyes flickered with restrained temper.

"However, madam, this time I've no other cabin to retreat to since I've already been turned out of the great cabin."

"You forget the sailroom, captain," she said innocently.

"Ah yes, the sailroom . . ." he said. "Housing my buccaneers and their hunting hounds. I can see this is going to be a very pleasant voyage." His gaze hinted of malicious teasing. "But then, come to think of it, there is a way out of my dilemma. I could call for the chaplain. He could marry us here and now. Then we wouldn't need to worry about it, would we? Think how cozy we'd be."

She stared at him, her heart jumping to her throat. He was teasing. Of course, he was. Wasn't he?

He must have read her fluster for his mouth turned. "That's what I thought."

He didn't mean any of this, she was sure of it. He was an impossible rogue at times, but how could he make light of anything so serious? Obviously because he had no intention of ever following through, and they both knew it.

"I believe," she said airily, "it was also your plan that there be a very long betrothal, your lordship."

"So it was. I wouldn't want to rush so serious a matter until we both find out where we truly stand. In a very few weeks I've discovered a good deal more about you."

Why did that make her uneasy? Her eyes swerved to his, watching her with thoughtful irritation. She lifted her head with a suggestion of dignity that opposed his allusion to shortcomings. "Well, that goes both ways, Captain."

He touched his thin mustache, studying her thoughtfully, his dark eyes unreadable.

She flushed. "Why is it you make me feel guilty?"

86

A smile appeared. "Because you are, perhaps?"

"May I ask what it is, sir, you've discovered that you didn't already know when you made a spectacle of me at Tortuga?"

"A spectacle!" He gave a laugh. "Your father did a fairly decent job of it himself, didn't he?"

"Yes, and that doesn't mean I approved, which I didn't, and I've no foolish dream of either of us ever following through on—"

"Dream? Ah—something for me to contemplate. Does that mean you nourish sweet dreams about becoming mine?"

She stood quickly, then winced, clutching the arm of the chair.

He caught her, frowning. "Did Hob look after your ankle?"

"Yes, it's only a sprain—let go of me. I'm fine! Let go, I said!"

His eyes narrowed. "Before dreams there was the matter of your schooling in London, if I recall. And that brings me to one of the questions at hand." He sat her back in the chair and stood looking down at her.

Now it was coming, she thought, all the impossible questions she couldn't answer about her father and the treasure of the *Prince Philip*.

"Would you mind explaining just what you were doing here, sailing with Karlton along the dangerous coast of Venezuela? Do you realize how many Spanish garrisons there are up and down this Main? How many pirates like Thorpe? You're blessed he knew I was here. The greed of ransom was the one thing that spared you."

He removed his hat and flung it on the scarred table. "If I recall our sweet good-bye on Tortuga, you were on your way to English Barbados—to board a merchant ship for dear Mother England. A few weeks later and—behold! I find you in grave peril. My dear," he said silkily, "is that any way for a future countess to behave?"

Future countess. She could swoon. As if he meant it!

"And in *my* fondest dreams," he said lightly, "I ignorantly imagined you safe aboard some English ship on your way to Buckington House, nibbling sweet dainties and sipping lemon water, with your sprightly French cousin for company. Instead, she's captive to a priest of the Holy Office of Inquisition, and you fell into the clutches of Lex Thorpe."

Yes, possibly the most horrid experience in my life, she wanted to say, but her loyalty rallied to her beloved father. To blame him would add substance to Baret's argument that her father was willing to betray him for the treasure. Her conclusions about her father's motives were hazy and bringing more discomfort by the hour, but she could not tell Baret for fear he'd turn completely against him.

"Be fair—it wasn't my father's fault."

"Then whose was it? Yours? Do you yearn, madam, for yet another adventure on the Main aboard the *Regale,* is that it?"

Her irritation began to kindle. "If I weren't here, it would have made it easier for you, wouldn't it? What of the poor senorita you hold a prisoner for ransom!"

"Ah, yes. The poor senorita. How ill and cruel her fate!"

"You hold her a prisoner in your cabin. I know. Hob told me."

"Hob talks too much. Suppose I state she's not a prisoner but is my cousin? And that she is helping me locate my father?"

"Oh, come, captain."

"As I thought. You dismiss my honesty without consideration."

"Carefully considered, sir. Yes, quite carefully. A cousin from *Spain?*" She laughed softly.

"Half Spanish."

"From Cartagena? A treasure city? The nobility is known to sip Madeira with English heretics, of course. A cousin. Yes, I see."

"There are those in the family with sympathy for Spain and ties to the families of the dons. They do more than sip wine."

"With your wrath so readily outpoured against anything hinting of Madrid, you really have a cousin with Spanish blood?"

"Did I say I was pleased about it?"

"I don't believe she's a cousin. She's a prisoner. The royal governor's niece. And you've locked her in your cabin. Just the way you locked me in when you sailed to Maracaibo."

"Not quite the same."

She took him in briefly, dubiously. "I can't keep myself from wondering how you captured her."

He smiled. "She came to me begging for assistance." He spread his hands innocently. "What could I do? She was like a ripe plum falling into my hand!"

She didn't like his vision of a ripe plum. "Do you expect to use her so you can attack and loot the island of Margarita? Perhaps I was wrong about Morgan—maybe he'll rendezvous with you and Captain Farrow, after all. And your French buccaneer friend—what was his name?—Pierre LaMonte?"

"Ah, the Frenchman. He brings me to the second topic we need to discuss, and I am not speaking of Pierre and his *Bonaventure* but of Levasseur!"

She turned her head away. "I will not discuss Levasseur. And if I'm to be on my way to England, what of you? I bade you farewell on Tortuga while you were waiting for your scoundrel friend Henry Morgan. Is he here also?"

Baret's dark eyes warmed, and his expression was anything but placating. "I'm asking the questions."

"Oh! I see. That changes matters considerably, my lord Buckington." She smiled again, too sweetly. "It's quite all right for a viscount to blame me for reckless behavior, while at the same time risking being hanged at Port Royal by turning pirate."

"Cheer up. If anything happens to me, you'll be my heir. You can return to Foxemoore, where you may subdue all those who tossed you out onto the Caribbean."

"Do be serious. You could hang—you know that."

He gestured as though that were of no import. "It's you I'm worried about. It was enough that the Admiralty officials may wish to ask you questions about your involvement with me at Maracaibo, but this is a far more serious voyage. I intend to attack the Spaniards and take the *San Pedro.*"

How casual he made it all sound!

"With you aboard again, we may both face the gallows."

She sucked in her breath, drawing back in the chair.

He laughed unpleasantly. "You've your father to thank for bringing you here. Rest—I will amend all. I've no intention of getting caught. And if they arrest you, I promise to take Port Royal and break you out of the gaol. Your neck is much too attractive for a necklace of rough hemp."

"How can you!"

"The truth must be spoken," he said airily. "You might as well know you're betrothed to a blackguard. I suppose you wish to cancel the engagement?"

She sat up stiffly. "You're saying this to frighten me. Well, sir! I have no intention of marrying a blackguard. What do you think of that?"

He smiled. "You'd have preferred James Maynerd, if I recall —or was it dear Rafael, smelling of French perfume and waving silver lace? Ah, mademoiselle, you grieve me."

She stood, carefully this time, and said with dignity: "I shall leave this ship at once."

"Will you? And where do you expect to go? Back to the captain of the *Black Dragon*? I fear he's in a worse mood now. Do sit down, dear foundling. I promise to behave myself. And now— where were we?"

"I've no wish to burden you—"

"It's your safety that burdens. If your father hadn't signed articles with Levasseur and Thorpe, I wouldn't have had to delay plans to sail into Margarita—the best opportunity I've had in three years to clear my father of the charge of piracy."

Her mood changed to one of astonishment. "You don't actually think the treasure is on Margarita, do you?"

He regarded her evenly, a brow lifting as though questioning her motive for interest.

"My father didn't betray you," she rushed on, embarrassed. "And he had no mind to cooperate with that sordid captain of the *Black Dragon.*"

"I'm certain of that much, yet he did have plans to rendezvous with Levasseur."

"Never. You saw what happened on Tortuga. You know what happened there. He was angry with Rafael. How can you think they were planning to work together? Oh, I know my father said as much to Thorpe, but he had to say those things to trick him. Father wouldn't betray you. Why, you even came to see him at Foxemoore about the map and journal because you trusted him."

"So I did. Little did I know that he'd sailed with my father on that fateful voyage and kept it from me these three years. Just how much does he know that he still hasn't told me? Trust him? Yes, I suppose I still do, but you have to admit he wasn't completely truthful with me."

She swallowed, feeling horribly upset, for deep in her heart she reasoned the same. But how could she deal with it? Had he indeed withheld these three years information that might have aided Baret in rescuing his father from torment?

"I can't bring myself to believe he'd deliberately deceive you or keep back anything crucial. I know my father too well. He has his faults, yes, and he's not always . . . well . . . completely Christian in his schemes. But he's not vicious, nor is he so selfish that he'd allow either of you to suffer on behalf of some personal dream."

He tapped his chin, musing. "Maybe. He still has to answer about what he was doing with my father's pistol, and why he never told me about it."

She lapsed into silence, also wondering.

His mood altered perceptibly. "By the way, did you send a message to Levasseur on Tortuga before you left, informing him of your father's plans to come here?"

Startled, she wondered how he could even suggest that. "I had no idea we were *coming* here. I only learned where we were a few days ago. Even if I had known, why would I inform Rafael?"

"The one answer I can come up with at the moment is that you did so to aid your charming cousin. Why is it I somehow think you've entertained more feelings for him in the past than you will admit?"

"Rafael? You're jesting. If you think so, then you don't know me as well as you thought."

"Perhaps," he said quietly.

"My father can explain everything to your satisfaction if you'll only give him a chance."

"Is that why he insisted on sailing with Erik? Because he's so anxious to explain?"

She hesitated. "I'm sure he will. Give him a chance. He thinks well of you."

"He thinks well of me, indeed. And I know why."

She flushed, reading between his words the suggestion that it was his wealth and position that had caused him to arrange the duel on Tortuga between himself and Baret. She wanted to tell him she would not hold him to the betrothal agreement, but the words stuck in her throat. "He told Thorpe he was working with Rafael because he was concerned for our safety."

"I would accept that if it were true, but it isn't."

"Not true, what do you mean?"

"Karlton came here to rendezvous with Levasseur. If he told Lex anything false, it was that he was also working with me." His

91

mood was challenging, sardonic. "Unless he wishes to help pirate the *San Pedro.*"

"I don't suppose you'll tell me why you'll risk pirating a Spanish galleon?"

"Not yet. The less you know, the safer you'll be. And now—" he snatched up his belongings "—I've no more time. I've a rendezvous with Farrow and LaMonte to keep." He looked back from the door and smiled lopsidedly. "I hope you'll be comfortable. If you need anything, call for Hob."

Holding to the desk, Emerald stood looking after him.

She tried to shake the qualms from her mind. Would her father be able to satisfy Baret's questions and why he'd said nothing to him until now?

Uneasily, her mind went back to that night two months ago at the bungalow. Baret had arrived to speak with her father about a journal belonging to Captain Royce Buckington, which he believed held information to help him exonerate his father of the piracy charge. If that were true, how did the treasure taken from the Spanish galleon fit in? A thought churned in her mind but was too disturbing to bring to the light. It was Felix who had confiscated that journal, she told herself. Perhaps by now he would have destroyed it.

She thought of something else. Her father claimed that on his deathbed the old earl—Great-grandfather Esmond Stuart Buckington—had left a double portion of the sugar not to grandsons Royce and Felix but to Karlton Harwick. Felix claimed the change in Esmond's will had been due to the unethical practice of a London barrister. Her father heartily denied this. Now, her father's shares in Foxemoore were at risk because of debt incurred by the loss of family merchant ships and loans from merchants who had invested in his voyages.

Felix would show no leniency. His marriage to Geneva placed him in a position to force Karlton to either pay up or relinquish his shares. If her father knew anything about the treasure of the *Prince Philip,* might not he want to claim a hefty portion in order to settle his accounts?

Her mind stole backward to consider anew the reasons for her father's moodiness on Foxemoore. He had said it was over a Spanish man-of-war that had sunk his ship. He had often threatened taking to the Main alone on a mission of revenge. Might those dark moods have had something to do with the treasure?

What if—she thought, troubled—what if it hadn't been revenge at all that had burdened him but a desire to return to the territory where the treasure was located?

The idea was too upsetting for her to accept, since it would mean her father was a pirate. And had he indeed withheld crucial information from Baret that might have permitted him to find his father? This new face of her father did not fit the memories she held of him, nor did it explain his concern for the whereabouts of Royce or his wish to help Baret locate him. Or did it?

All that day she nursed her ankle and recuperated from the ordeal at the cove with Thorpe and his pirates. She hoped Baret would return at supper to explain matters more thoroughly. Hob arrived at sundown with a tray. "Roasted crab, mussels cooked in black butter and garlic. An' his lordship's favorite—chicken fried crisp brown and tender with slices o' plantains."

"Thank you, Hob. It looks very tasty, and I'm starving. Will . . . um . . . the captain be joining me?"

He grinned. "He be eatin' with Miss Carlotta tonight on deck. Moon be as big as a melon, says I, and just as ripe too. Sea be smooth, wind warm, and—"

"Yes, I get the picture, Hob. Thank you."

"I don't think ye do, miss. He don't care a turtle's wink for her. It's information he's learning—all about the ways of the treasure ship and the goings-on in Porto Bello."

Her suspicions grew. "I thought she came from Cartagena."

"She do, but the captain-general she were supposed to marry be from Porto Bello."

"Oh." Taken completely off guard, she said nothing for a moment. Then she inquired cautiously, "You mean her plans have changed?"

"She don't love the Spaniard, she says. Says she's in love with a better rogue."

Emerald lapsed into further meditative silence. So. The senorita was in love with someone else . . .

"How be your ankle? Better? 'Twas the turtle rum. Best brew for curin' ills that be in the Indies."

When he left, Emerald sat staring at her supper. She took a bite of the chicken and imagined the moon as ripe as a sweet melon.

93

She had no idea when Baret arrived back on the *Regale,* but she realized sometime during the night that the ship was moving. They were sailing toward Margarita.

The dawn was peeking in through the window, but it wasn't the brightening sunlight that awakened her. It was the sound of commotion on the deck overhead—rushing feet, the dragging of tackle, boisterous activity in the gun room underneath her where cannon, culverins, powder, matches, and ammunition were kept. The big guns were being run out. She sensed that the *Regale* was no longer moving.

The pitch of readying for battle was familiar. She'd heard the same dreadful sounds aboard her father's ship just before the *Black Dragon* had attacked. But this situation seemed different. The *Regale* appeared to be the challenger, but why?

Emerald sat up, heart racing. Her first thought was that he was about to attack the *San Pedro,* on which Minette was held, then realized that something far different was taking place.

She listened intently to the movements of the crew above and the gunners below. What Zeddie called "the leaden aprons" were being removed from the guns. She envisioned the touch-holes being primed, all ready to be ignited by the linstocks as the gunners waited for Captain Foxworth to give the word to fire.

Using table and chairs for support, she moved to the window as swiftly as her sprain would permit.

Across the blue-green water of a bay, the sun broke bright and hot. She made out the shoreline and a curving white beach. What looked to be a fort was under construction but not yet completed. Farther inland, thick vegetation and fringed palms stood green against the soft blue morning sky. Spanish soldiers were scurrying about as though aware of imminent attack from an accursed ship belonging to *piratous hereticos!*

Emerald attained new understanding of Baret's keen instinct for seizing unexpected opportunities to harass the Spaniards, for she didn't think this present action had been planned until coming upon the soldiers. He enjoyed a sharp appetite for adventure and perhaps Spanish treasure as well, she decided, especially when it offered a hard blow to the coffers of Madrid.

There came a bulge of white smoke, followed by the ear-splitting thunder of cannon. Since the *Regale* had twenty guns,

94

the nerve-shattering noise continued. The vessel shuddered beneath her bare feet, and she struggled to keep her balance while trying to cover her ears. When she looked again, showers of spray exploded upward on the beach. Smoke loomed above the fort, and, although she could not see them, she knew Spanish soldiers lay sprawled on the sand, while others ran to mount their defenses.

To Emerald, the cannon booms lasted forever. When they finally ceased, a deathly still hovered over the ship. She held her breath, waiting for return fire that she remembered too well from the attack of the *Black Dragon,* but the silence held. Could the Spaniards not return fire? Had they been caught before the fort's cannons were installed?

Longboats bumped alongside, as they were lowered into the water. Firm voices and the dip of oars followed, as boats filled with buccaneers pulled away toward shore. Captain Foxworth was taking the attack to land.

Sporadic gunfire sounded from shore. The longboats were being bombarded by the soldiers. Her tension mounted as she envisioned Baret shot or soon run through with a sword.

No more could be seen through the window, and she finally gave up, hoping Hob might come to fill her in. But as minutes dragged into hours, even Hob didn't appear with his usual tea and cheery words. She considered hobbling onto the deck to find out from some crewman what was happening. She might even dare to go to the captain's cabin and inquire of the senorita.

But Emerald restrained herself. If Baret had wished her to know more, he would have informed her before the attack. And if he found out she had sought out the young woman, he might think she was spying on him. It hurt—but was true nevertheless, she told herself—Baret wanted to avoid her. The betrothal embarrassed him, made him feel trapped into complying.

The long day wore on, a day in which she knew nothing of what was happening except for the message coming to her ears in the distant sound of gunfire. The *Regale* was ghostly quiet. She heard only the squeak of the windlass, the creaking of timbers at rest as the ship lolled in the still waters off the bay, safe from harm's reach.

A thousand questions paraded through her mind, and not

even Hob, who loved to talk, had time to answer them all when at last he appeared.

He came to the cabin after sunset with her supper. "Be ashamed of meself, I am, Miss Emerald. Done got too busy to take care o' ye like his lordship ordered. A mere bowl o' turtle soup is all there be tonight, seein' as how I was busy all day in yon wardroom, cleaning guns. I done told Hogan to bring ye tea this mornin', but the bloke forgot."

"It's all right, Hob. What happened! Is the captain well? Has he returned? And his crew?"

"All safe, except Jeremy. The lad took a musket ball in his leg, an' it were so bad the cap'n had no choice but to cut it off above the knee."

"He'll live?" she whispered.

"Oh, aye, he will, says I. An' he ain't weepin' neither. Says half a leg is more'n them papists left his father on Hispaniola. They was *boucaniers* there until a raid from the *guarda costa* caught 'em. They was all killed or made slaves. Young Jeremy has himself a brother who's a galley slave on the *San Pedro*. He be waitin' anxiously for the ship to be taken, I can tell ye that. And Cap'n Foxworth keeps tellin' him to be patient."

Emerald, alert, hung on his every word. "Is that why they plan to attack the ship from Cartagena? Protestant prisoners?"

He rubbed his chin. "Aye, it is, and more. The cap'n best tell ye 'stead of me. I got meself in a kettle o' trouble last time for talkin' to ye too much about Miss Carlotta."

The tale of horror surrounding prisoners was growing all too familiar to Emerald. Until recently, she had never fully realized just how strong was the hatred between Spain and the European colonists on the sugar islands. Since she had spent most of her life on Foxemoore, her own trials had come from family rejection and the plight of the slaves from Africa. True, her father had spoken of the Inquisition, and so had Great-uncle Mathias, but the tales had been secondhand. That is, until she had met Baret and learned of his mother's martyrdom in Holland and the capture of his father.

Wherever she moved among buccaneers and pirates alike, she found extreme loathing for Spain and what they scurrilously called "papists." Not that there weren't Catholics among the buccaneers and pirates. Her father said there were many. But since the Church of Spain often failed to recognize them as true communicants, the Catholic buccaneers joined in shouting, "Death to all papists!" as fervently when taking a galleon as did those of the Reformed faith.

"Har!" Hob continued. "It were a gloatin' eyeful, seein' fancy soldiers of King Philip scamperin' to hide like wailin' mice." And with glee he rubbed his gnarled hands together.

"Did the captain plan to attack? Is that why he sailed here?"

"Warn't expectin' 'em at all as we come up on the coast. An' then we learned how ships was here earlier from Cumaná, unloadin' cannon, but the guns warn't in place yet."

"Oh? How did he learn that?"

"Miss Carlotta tells him."

"The supper under the 'sweet melon moon' paid off, I see."

Hob's eyes twinkled. "Ye don't need to be jealous of her, Miss Emerald."

She offered a too casual shrug. "It never entered my mind, Hob."

His grin gave away her pretense.

"The viscount is still in love with Lady Thaxton—we both know that," she told him quietly, for there was no reason to pretend with Hob.

"Is he, miss? Ain't be so sure meself. I got a drawing to show ye one o' these days—if'n I can borrow it from his desk without him knowin'. And now—I be sayin' too much again. He'll stew me in a pot like me turtles if'n I don't watch me tongue."

That was yet another reference to a drawing, and she wondered curiously which one Hob could have in mind. She knew Baret often relaxed his tensions by sketching, and he was quite good at it. Still, how could a drawing suggest, as Hob hinted, that Baret was not in love with her cousin Lavender.

"An' then, when I comes upon his lordship at dawn to bring 'im his coffee, what's he doing but peering through his telescope at the Main, and he laughs. 'Look, Hob,' he says to me. 'Did you ever see anything so ripe for picking?' An then I looks and sees all these Spanish soldiers bunched together like plantains, instead of spreading out for cover. He says the thing be too sweet to ignore. So he attacks. Then he goes after 'em, and the Spanish captain took off for the trees. So we routed 'em all. They left all their weapons and boxes of ammunition, and their clothes too—

well, ye knows what I mean, miss. Then there's talk of how we can take all them cannon back to the Dutch islands to use in the war with England, but Foxworth says that were impossible. So they pushes 'em into the bay to rust. *Har!* A pert sight it was, says I."

As Emerald contemplated, interested in Baret's reasoning about aiding the Dutch, Hob grinned. "And now we be headin' for Cumaná."

"But why?" she asked nervously.

"Sure now. Cumaná be a star center for Spanish pearl fisheries. His lordship be interested in collectin' a few. Soon we'll be loadin' the innards of the ship with pearls aplenty." He crowed with laughter.

So Baret Buckington from Cambridge Divinity College was not above donning the garb of an outright pirate. To show mute disapproval, she refused to smile.

Hob cleared his throat and grew serious. "Aye, I be knowin' what you're thinking, but his lordship is for anything that pains them Spaniards. An' the more pain, the more pleased he be. He'd loot Cartagena if he could. An' he wouldn't blink an eye over it, nor apologize to Madrid, neither."

"Nor to King Charles, I'm thinking," she said wryly. "He'll hang if Lord Felix can catch him."

Hob rubbed his wrinkled neck. "Aye, we all will be twistin', says I. An' that be the rusty side of the piece o' eight. But his lordship has his reasons, and he thinks he can outsmart his Uncle Felix. Knowin' Foxworth, I'm wagering he will."

Emerald was not as certain. Her concerns for Baret grew as she thought of the upcoming attack on the *San Pedro*. Even though Minette was aboard, and she wished her cousin's safe return, how much better it would be for Baret and Erik Farrow as well if they could somehow simply trail the ship to its destination, learn where Minette would be taken, then arrange for her freedom through the governor or even the friar. Perhaps she could mention this option to Baret, though he was not an easy man to convince of anything.

She slept fitfully that night but awoke to a tropical breeze filling the cabin with the pleasant smell of the sea. The *Regale* was racing with the wind in her sails. She took this to mean Baret was in a hurry to rendezvous with Captains Farrow and LaMonte.

Hob came to tell her that plans had been arranged beforehand and there would be a parley at sea that night. "The cap'n will sup with 'em aboard the *Warspite*. He says if'n ye still have a hankerin' to join your father, now be your opportunity. Ye can row across with him. Says he'll send Yorke to carry ye up when he's ready."

"Tell him I won't need Mr. Yorke. My ankle is stronger, and I can walk." She smiled. "Thanks to your turtle oil."

"I'll tell him ye've made up your mind."

Emerald waited anxiously throughout the day. That night the ship dropped anchor, and she supposed that they had arrived at the designated spot for the parley. Was there still a hope of convincing him to avoid attacking the *San Pedro*?

She took a last look in the mirror. Deftly twisting her thick braid of dark hair, she pinned it, then smoothed the lace at the high neck of her plain, full-skirted muslin dress. Carefully she put on her shoe and found it only a little snug. At least she could walk. Minutes later she started up the flight of steps to the deck.

The trade wind felt wonderful after Emerald's several days inside the cabin, and the white moon reminded her of a smooth giant pearl on black velvet. She came slowly up the steps to the quarterdeck, and halted.

Ahead, leaning against the bulkhead was the young Spanish senorita called Carlotta. Her dark hair blew freely in the wind, and she wore an expensive red silk mantilla. Jewels flashed at her earlobes and about her throat. She was speaking anxiously and quietly to Baret, who stood before her in his usual stance, arms folded, listening.

It was distracting to Emerald that his masculine good looks were so easily and unpretentiously displayed without his trying. The breeze tugged at the full sleeves of his white shirt, gathered at the wrists but loosely laced with a crisscross cord at the neck.

I'm hopelessly in love with him, she thought with a pang of realization. *If only I were the lady that Cousin Lavender is—or nobility like this Spanish senorita. Or is she?*

Doubtless, Baret had wanted these last moments alone with Carlotta. Hob had said there was nothing between them, but was that true?

The senorita's head turned. Seeing Emerald, she said something to him, then proudly walked away as he gazed after her.

99

The girl came down the steps with head high, not giving Emerald another glance of her flashing eyes. Emerald caught a whiff of strong perfume, felt the red silk float against her hand.

She looked suspiciously up the steps at Baret.

He left the rail and crossed the quarterdeck, watching her with a countenance that told her absolutely nothing. It was maddening! *He* must *find Carlotta attractive,* she thought.

Emerald reluctantly met his potent dark eyes. They had a way of making her heart beat too fast. She felt the plainness of her frock. The dress was modest, with bell sleeves at the elbows, over a longer sleeve of white lace that encircled her wrists.

He swept her with one brief glance, taking in the braid. "Looks as though you're recovering well enough. Are you ready to go?"

Her frustration bubbled over despite self-lectures that she would say nothing. "Is that all you're going to say?" she breathed.

He glanced about at the sea, the sky. "There's nothing like the Caribbean for a romantic evening—the sea teeming with pirates and sharks. The longboat waits. And," he added wryly, "I'm hungry."

Her hands clenched. She brushed past him toward the ship's side. "You didn't appear as anxious to leave for Captain Farrow's fish stew when bidding the senorita good-bye."

Now why had she let that come out!

"Am I to believe this flare of jealousy means you care? Rather, perhaps you are disappointed I haven't greeted you with the ardency of Rafael? How often have you lingered in the moonlight with him?"

His suggestion about Levasseur came as a whiplash. She floundered, then, *"Rafael?"*

"Yes, Captain Rafael Levasseur. Pirate without honor."

"Are you daring to still suggest there is anything between us when I've already denied it?"

"I asked you in the cabin if you sent a message to him on Tortuga giving away my plans, alerting him I would be here. You denied that."

"Yes, I denied it. I deny it still!"

"Then what, madam, is *this?*" His voice grated. "Read it. Perhaps it will help awaken your conscience."

She stared at a folded note he had taken from his shirt, and she recoiled slightly. Rafael, skunk that he was, could not be trusted, and she wondered if some trap awaited her. Some undefinable pain appeared to trouble Baret, and because it did, she was all the more afraid. She reached for the paper he held out, knowing she was innocent of any misdoing, yet somehow feeling a sense of guilt. "Is it from Rafael?" she asked meekly.

A half smile touched his mouth. "How innocent you look. Your sweet face deceives me again. Refresh your faulty memory, please. Or should I read it to you?"

She snatched the paper with cold hands and opened it, turning the writing toward the bright moonlight.

Darling Rafael,
Our plans are working better than we anticipated. Neither my father nor Captain Foxworth suspects anything between us. As planned, I shall meet you at the point of their rendezvous near the smaller islands close to Margarita. The treasure is there. Once the Spanish governor is alerted, they will arrest Baret, and we can make our escape. Be sure my father is spared.

Emerald

She looked at him, embarrassed. "You don't believe this of me?"

"I admit I had difficulty."

She turned cold as he stared hard into her eyes. "This is absurd," she whispered.

"Is it?"

"How can you think I wrote this?"

"You deny it?"

"Yes! Yes! I deny it! Where did you get it?"

"Actually, I happened upon it by chance in his cabin when we met a week ago."

Tears stung her eyes. "I have never been in the arms of Rafael," she choked, throwing the letter at him. "Nor in Jamie's either, if you must know."

"Then explain how this came to be on the desk aboard darling Rafael's *Venture*. What I told Lex was true. I did meet Levasseur. And I would have sunk his ship had he not capitulated. I met him in his cabin to talk terms. He agreed to return to Tortu-

101

ga. And when he left to call for his lieutenant, I found this on his desk."

"If you 'found it,' I suggest he placed the bait there for that purpose—which you snapped up like a hungry shark."

"Do you think I'm that gullible?"

"You must believe me, Baret. He intended you should find it! It is like Rafael to do something like this. He despises you—and me. He once asked my father to marry me, and I refused him. He's never forgiven me for that. Nor will he forgive what happened on Tortuga. His pride is diabolical. Oh, don't you see? He wants nothing more than to plant suspicion between us. I'd never betray you."

He stared at her, weighing her response, and his gaze momentarily softened, but she was not sure he believed her. And more than anything else, she wanted his love, his respect, his wholehearted trust.

Slowly he retrieved the note and then, while holding her gaze, ripped it in two and tossed it overboard.

"We'll let the matter go. If you deny it, I've no choice but to accept your word."

No choice? She wanted him to believe her because he *knew* he could depend on her loyalty.

"I'm grieved you'd think so low of me," she murmured, her eyes smarting.

He let out a breath. "What was I supposed to think!"

"That when I make a vow to faithfulness, sir, I'm a woman of honor—and purity. I don't go chasing after every rogue who sails the Caribbean!" She turned her head so that he wouldn't see the trail of tears forming on her cheeks. "You've been suspicious and angry with me since before I boarded your ship. I suppose you think I came here to spy on you! I'm surprised you even came to save me from Thorpe—"Her voice broke with a sob.

In a moment he was beside her, his voice soothing, his touch gentle. "I'm sorry, Emerald. Please—you mustn't cry."

She wondered at the sudden change. This was a Baret Buckington she hadn't met before. One thing was growing all the more clear—neither knew the other well enough for marriage yet. They were both uncertain, suspicious. She had doubted him because of Carlotta, and he thought her capable of making plans with Rafael. His mood change pleased her and made him all the more intriguing. *But just what is he truly like?*

"There, now," he said softly, "we won't talk about it anymore."

"But you still think I wrote that letter . . ."

"I cry pardon. I was too quick to accuse. If you say you did not, then likely you are right—I did take the bait."

Silence held them, and she enjoyed the stroke of his hand on her hair. She laid her cheek against his chest, shyly fingering the cord on his shirt.

It was time to pull away. "You don't think I betrayed you, then?"

"No."

"You trust me? You don't think I'm the kind of girl that would be—" she hesitated, unable to say the word.

"Unfaithful?"

"Yes, you don't think that about me, do you? Perhaps all the gossip in Port Royal has actually influenced you even more than you realize."

He was quiet for a moment as if considering. He cupped her chin, raising her face toward his. The look in his eyes turned her weak.

"No," he said softly. His lips took hers, and the heavy thudding of her heart snatched her breath away. He spoke of everything that was strong, secure, and decent in a man, and she loved him.

"We'd better go," he said quietly.

"Captain?" came a shout from the longboat waiting below. "Captain Farrow is signaling us to row over."

Baret drew her to the railing and looked down. "Prepare to receive the lady."

"Aye, captain!"

The lady! She looked up at him, her eyes moistening.

He smiled as he swept her up into his arms. "Can you make it with your ankle?"

"I think so."

"Hold tight to the ladder rope." And he handed her over the side to the waiting crewman.

7

TREASURE

Aboard the *Warspite,* in a small cabin adjoining the Round Room, Emerald could hear the heated discussion between Baret and her father.

"Despite all that's gone wrong, better that you fell prey to Thorpe than to the Spaniards at Margarita. Not even Levasseur could have handled them. It was madness to have risked coming to these waters alone, least of all with your daughter! By now, all of you would be prisoners of the inquisitors at Cádiz!"

At that instant, Emerald decided to enter the cabin. "Do consider, Captain Foxworth, that my father is much too ill to engage in this kind of discussion."

Baret turned toward her, his dark eyes flickering.

Her father, too, scowled, but he appeared more miserable than anything else.

"It won't wait. We'll have this out, Karlton, before you're on your feet again and in command of the *Madeleine.*"

Karlton looked at him sharply, raising himself on an elbow. "The *Madeleine?* You've news about my ship?"

Baret smiled. "She'll be waiting for us near Margarita. If that doesn't ignite a healing flame in your bones, nothing will. We're going to blast the Spaniards clear out of the water."

Her father threw aside his blanket, grimacing as he placed both feet on the cabin floor. *"Hah!* A sight to behold, me lad, and I'm going to be boarding myself!"

"Papa, you mustn't get up yet," said Emerald, rushing to restrain him. Trying to bridle his emotions, however, proved impossible.

"Nay, daughter, your father is well enough, to be sure. I've taken worse shots in my life."

Emerald looked at Baret and saw his crooked smile. He

seemed to have known just the right medicine to return him to his old self.

"I thought the news would inspire you," said Baret. "About as much as the thought of the treasure of the *Prince Philip*," he added evenly. "But you've questions to answer, Karlton. We'll not proceed with anything else until you do."

"Baret, please," began Emerald, but her father held up a hand for her silence.

"He has a right, lass. Keep silent." He looked from her pleading gaze across the cabin to Baret, who stood unrelenting, watching him.

"I've nothing to hide. I knew you were coming here, and I made a change in plans in order to rendezvous with you, Farrow, and LaMonte!"

"And Levasseur."

"No, he was in on it with Thorpe."

"How did you know my plans? How did *they?*"

"The same way Levasseur knew. Then he contacted Thorpe —you know how word gets around Tortuga. All the Brethren were baited with your tale of two hundred thousand pieces of eight!"

"The tale was for a purpose—to discover what they knew of my father. I had no idea you'd sailed with him. Nor did I actually know where the treasure was until I found a small drawing Lucca had left in my father's Bible. I wasn't certain treasure even existed."

Karlton eyed him shrewdly. "So now you know its odd hiding place. Royce was clever."

"Yes."

Emerald watched them nervously. She knew that the High Admiralty had already condemned Royce Buckington for piracy, and that the report saying he had stowed the treasure was widely believed—notably by Baret's uncle, Lord Felix. She knew, too, that Baret had deliberately boasted of his father's treasure as he moved among the buccaneers at Tortuga, hoping someone would come forward who knew his father's fate. He had been planting bait, knowing that others would begin asking questions on their own. The shoals, bays, reefs, and tricky channels in and around the Caribbean strongholds were safe quarters for pirates, who were likely to hear things.

"Now Baret, I had every good intention of explaining to you what I knew of the treasure. It's the reason I came. My conscience wouldn't let me keep silent any longer."

Baret laughed, and Emerald, embarrassed, gave him a reproving glance, which he ignored.

"Your conscience, Karlton, has never troubled you until now."

Emerald turned her back.

Karlton ran a strong hand across his short beard. "It's not the way you think. I knew nothing of your father's actual whereabouts after the Spaniards took him away. What I told Thorpe was a true account."

She glanced over her shoulder at Baret to see if he believed him. He was inscrutable as he removed the familiar pistol from his belt and handed it to Karlton. A glance at her father's face convinced her of his genuine pain at seeing the Buckington coat of arms.

"Aye," he murmured, "I recognize it. 'Twas your father's, all right."

"How did it come into your possession?" came Baret's too quiet voice.

Emerald moved closer to beside her father, her face warm with tension.

"I found it where he hid it before the Spaniards came upon him. He knew there was no chance, you see. Most of the crew of both our ships was already dead. We'd put up a grand fight, Baret. You'd have been proud of him. They outnumbered us ten to one. They thought they killed us all. There was one Spaniard who saw him hiding, but didn't know about me, Lucca, and Maynerd."

"Don Miguel Vasquez?"

"Aye, the man."

Emerald caught the venom in Baret's voice and wondered how he knew the soldier's name.

"Royce stashed the pistol where we'd find it, and before we could stop him, he surrendered. He was a valiant man, Baret. I've thought many times that I should have followed him into slavery out of honor."

Baret was silent a moment. "It would not have done you nor my father any good, and certainly not Emerald. Somehow I believe you, Karlton, but that doesn't account for the fact you've kept the truth from me these three years."

"I kept nothing from you except the fact I had sailed on that ill-fated mission. Do you think I *knew* he was in Porto Bello? Why, I'd have told you so at once. Nay, I didn't know. Like you, I thought he was in Maracaibo with Lucca. It wasn't until you told me what Lucca so cleverly inscribed in that Bible that I knew about Porto Bello. Before that, I did some searching on my own. Each time I sold contraband to the Spanish colonists at Santo Domingo and San Juan, I bribed and baited them for information, but no one knew anything. And I had to work secretly because of Felix. You know he's thick into smuggling. If word from the dons reached him that I was asking about Royce, well— you know what your uncle would have done."

"Yes, I know quite well. And now, with both Maynerd and Lucca dead, you are the one remaining witness who can testify to the king. You have become extremely important to me. And that's why you won't go on the voyage to Porto Bello—or to Margarita."

Emerald smiled at her father and looped her arm through his. "You heard him, Papa. He's a viscount, you know—you must do what he says."

"*Bah!* I'll be hoodwinked if I will. Now, look here, Buckington! Viscount or no, am I an old codger that you think you can order me about? I'll be goin' on that voyage to Porto Bello, aye, and not even you will stop me!"

"I'll stop you, even if I need to shanghai both you and Emerald on a ship to England. If Felix learns you sailed with my father on that mission for Cromwell, he'll end your life just as surely as he has Lucca's and Maynerd's. Think about that, if not for yourself, then for your daughter. Until I clear my father's name—and my own—there's not much I can do for either of you at Jamaica. If I dock at Port Royal, Felix would be on me in a moment. Then everything we've worked for will be lost."

"He's right," she insisted. "You mustn't do anything that may give Lord Felix opportunity."

"Aye, I've known the danger from Felix all along, and 'twas the reason I kept my sailing with your father to myself."

"I'll accept that much, but you haven't explained all to my satisfaction. The treasure—you've known of its whereabouts these years and said nothing to me?"

"Aye, I'll admit my sin there. But I was on my way here to rendezvous with you and explain. Royce himself swore a portion of the *Prince Philip* to each of us. We all fought in that battle, and we took both the *Prince Philip* and the *Isabella* fair and square. I needed my share of that treasure for Emerald."

"I don't want it, Papa."

"Silence. I'm above my neck in debt, Baret. And I'll die first before giving up what's mine in Foxemoore. Certain shares belong to her."

"I don't want it at the cost of piracy," she insisted, but neither he nor Baret appeared to pay her any mind.

"Granted, Karlton, and you'll get your share of the treasure and more—on one condition," Baret told him. "After repairs on the *Madeleine,* Emerald is to sail for England according to the bargain we made on Tortuga. And I want to make sure you keep yourself healthy and alive."

"Aye, a bargain it 'tis, but you'll need help with that crypt."

"Crypt?" Emerald repeated with distaste.

Baret looked at her. "They sealed the treasure chest in a crypt at a mission near shore."

"It won't be an easy matter to convince the head Franciscan we've come on business for Spain."

"Simple, indeed," Baret told him, "since I've come prepared with a friar's habit—and a letter from Madrid ordering the mission to turn over the contents of the crypt. You forget I speak fluent Castilian."

Emerald gave him a reproving glance. "One slip, and they'll deliver you to the inquisitors."

"Now behave yourself, daughter. You're among gentlemen, so no need to get uppity about this."

"I'm among *pirates,* so it seems!"

Baret offered her a lazy smile, then said to Karlton: "I suggest a few pearls from Margarita will go a long way to please and mellow Governor Modyford next time you see him."

"Aye, I wouldn't think of disappointing him."

Emerald looked at Baret, but he turned and left the cabin.

"He's a rogue if there ever was one."

"Aye, but an honorable rogue, indeed. You've a good future ahead of you, lass."

She went after Baret then, following him down the quarterdeck steps. "Your attack on the garrison yesterday will have every Spanish don on the Main after you, not to mention Lord Felix. And after the ship—"

"After the *San Pedro*," he smoothly interrupted, "it will be Cumaná, Margarita, Puerto Cabello, and Coro. We expect to leave them with fond memories and bring back enough booty to weaken the resources of King Philip's armies substantially."

She scanned him dubiously, lifting one brow. "You didn't tell me at Tortuga that you were a pirate."

He looked not at all intimidated or ashamed. He smiled. "On the contrary, you have a short memory. I told you aboard the *Regale*. Have you forgotten so soon?"

She recalled vaguely an exchange between them just before Levasseur and Jamie boarded. "Then you *are* a pirate," she had said, upon learning he would sign articles with her cousin. "You may say that I am," he had replied casually.

"You may rescue your father's reputation," she said now, "but what of your own?"

"By the time Felix arranges my hanging, I will have found my father, and the two of us will return to London to pledge our loyalties anew to His Majesty."

"You're also putting yourself at great risk! Even if you locate the treasure, your actions won't be sanctioned by the king. You yourself said the Spanish sympathizers in the Peace Party have much sway over him. After terrorizing the Main and infuriating King Philip's ambassador, he may put you in the Tower."

"Charles will see us both, since we will have the treasure. The charges against my father will be dismissed if I can prove that he sailed to the West Indies under a commission from Cromwell to establish English colonies. He was a legal agent, not a pirate."

She looked at him cautiously. "Is that how you see yourself—as an agent of England and the king?"

He tapped his chin, musing. "I can only say that if Spain is defeated, it won't be on the battlefields of Europe but here in the Indies. Each time we take a treasure galleon heading for Madrid, they lose a year's income. Bankers in Genoa, Milan, Venice wait in vain to be paid their interest—and some, their principal as well. The Spanish army in the Netherlands goes without cash to pay for provisions. Her army is defaulting on loans, something which the international bankers never forgive.

Spain is learning that their slave-labor silver and gold mines are only as secure as the galleons that carry it home. We intend to destroy their ships and confiscate their wealth. Call it piracy if you wish; to me it is war. And before it's over, we'll have them at the peace table on our terms. That means a right to trade in the Caribbean."

Emerald had no argument she wished to raise. Though she wouldn't admit it, she still could not bring herself to think of him as a pirate but as a privateer, serving the better cause of England and Holland.

"Then you really think it's possible?"

"I wish King Charles did. He underestimates the buccaneers. Men like Sir Christopher Mings have done more to defeat the Inquisition army than anyone in Europe. By the time we've sacked Porto Bello, Cartagena, and Panama, Madrid will be broke. Even now they run dangerously short on galleons to patrol these waters. And that commission from Cromwell—if I could find *that*—it would exonerate my father."

"Since his ship was sunk, what hope is there of that?"

"There is one—that he was careful enough to store it with the treasure of the *Prince Philip*. We may be able to locate both. You see why I had to question your father's motive for working with Levasseur. No one must find that important information except me. I wouldn't trust anyone else with it, not when Felix would pay anything to have it destroyed."

A silence came between them.

"Emerald, there's someone on the *San Pedro* who can tell me where I can find my father. And," he said evenly, "he will, if he wishes to live."

She looked at him quickly, searching his face. "Is that why you've come here to take this galleon?"

"Yes, and it's the reason Carlotta is aboard my ship. What I told you was true. She *is* my cousin. She has done much to help me recently. She's from Cartagena and was on her way to Margarita to marry *Capitán* Don Miguel Vasquez."

The name immediately caught her attention. "The man my father mentioned?"

"No, his son. His father is the wealthy planter in Porto Bello who bought my father as a slave. From his son I will learn where he's being held. He could be anywhere in Porto Bello. The information Vasquez holds is crucial. Carlotta wishes to escape marriage to him and sail to Jamaica—to a certain hacienda that I cannot tell you about now. She offered to help me if I would help her escape."

So . . .

"What if he refuses to tell you?"

His smile was dangerous. "He will talk. And I have Carlotta for ransom. What he does not know is that it was she who told me of him and the ship. She wishes to marry another man in Spanish Town—a scoundrel, a man I would not find worthy to keep company with, but that is her concern, not mine."

A swell of relief filled her heart, yet fear gripped her as well since what Baret was about to do with the *San Pedro* and *Capitán* Vasquez would bring even more to the attention of those who wished his downfall.

"The victory will be hard won," she warned softly. "Anything could go wrong." *And you might be killed,* she wanted to say.

"Hard won, yes, but it's something I must do."

She noticed that Captains Farrow and Pierre LaMonte had come on deck and were waiting for him below.

"I must go," he said quietly.

She looked at him for a long moment. "Then I wish you success and God's protection."

His eyes were warm and intense. "So you're willing to be a pirate's lady, are you? I shall cherish your trust in me."

She watched from the ship's side as they boarded a longboat and were rowed to a craft she had not seen before. Already there were buccaneers aboard, and she wondered with amazement and new alarm why they would use such a craft and leave the *Regale* anchored with the *Warspite* and the *Bonaventure*.

How could they even think they could take a galleon in what looked to her to be a fifty-foot vessel? What of cannon? What of the hundred men they had between them? What could they possibly have in mind?

8

THE *SAN PEDRO*

The fifty-foot ketch slipped through the Caribbean, her sails filled and on steady course. Erik Farrow, stripped to a pair of leather breeches and pistol belt, and wearing a black head kerchief, climbed the main shrouds and braced himself there, his toes hooked securely over the ratlines. The late afternoon wind surged against his muscular chest, and his golden hair whipped behind him. With one hand he held the brass bound spyglass steady as he swayed with the movement of the craft.

His heart leaped. *There she is.* A huge, sun-gilded Spanish galleon loomed against the horizon, moving slowly and clumsily through the water, her canvas sighing, the bold red and yellow banner of Castile snapping proudly.

"Sail ho!"

Baret had been sleeping aft under the small cover, and he came out at once, strapping on his belt with its sword and pair of French pistols. Pierre LaMonte breathed something in French and was on his bare feet, tossing his half-eaten breakfast to the porpoises frolicking behind the boat.

"The *San Pedro!*" Erik called, sliding down the backstay.

A resounding cheer went up.

Erik turned to his officer, the huge African. "Take over the helm and sail, Jeb."

"Aye, captain!"

"Leon! Hoist the cursed Spanish colors!" Erik ordered.

The French *boucanier* boatswain rushed to a locker and pulled out a new red and yellow flag with disdain, then hoisted it to snap in the wind.

"There the filthy rag blows!" commented Yorke.

Erik watched Baret climb into the main crosstree, where he removed his own spyglass from his belt and fixed it upon the *San Pedro*. Then Erik again went over in his mind each step of his

112

well-laid plan to find Minette. Glancing up at Baret, he knew the viscount was doing the same concerning *Capitán* Don Miguel Vasquez. Both he and Baret felt confident in letting Pierre lead the main body of buccaneers in the open assault on the galleon. The French captain of the *Bonaventure* was a calm, relentless, and ferocious fighter.

Erik watched the men haul up shot from among the ballast and pile it near the small demi-culverin. They all knew the maneuver was essentially meaningless, for shot the size of a man's hand would have little effect against the proud galleon.

But it was not an exchange of firepower that the small ketch was embarking upon, else they would have employed their ships instead. The manner in which they hoped to take the *San Pedro* had been developed when the three captains met to discuss tactics.

The idea had been the viscount's. He had heard a tale from old Hob about the cheeky pirate Le Grande, who had lived in the 1630s. With twenty-eight *boucaniers* he seized a Spanish treasure ship, using a mere pinnace. Scorned by the galleon that had paid Le Grande no mind, the Frenchman had been able to pull off an audacious deed.

The advantage of following Le Grande's daring, as the viscount saw it, was in taking the *San Pedro* off guard, while at the same time masking their own identity to the Admiralty Officials by keeping their ships concealed. News of who was involved would eventually get back to Port Royal, London, and Madrid, but, for the present, time would be on their side.

Baret, clad in worn breeches, came down the shrouds and landed steadily. Erik watched him snatch a cool cotton shirt from where it hung and slip into it. Then he readied himself for battle, checking the priming of his long-barreled pistols.

"If things go as planned, we'll soon have the Spanish *capitán* by his arrogant pointed beard," commented Baret. He offered Erik a smile of confidence as he accepted a black scarf from his hand and tied it around his head. "The little French waif will be forever in your debt, Erik."

Erik saw the teasing flicker in the viscount's eyes and remained outwardly impassive. "I'm doing this deed of valor out of gallantry," he stated coolly. "I'd do the same for any English woman held captive by an inquisitor."

Baret smiled easily. "I never doubted for a moment, Captain Farrow."

Erik's mouth curved. "We're all ready," he stated, with a gesture of his head. "About twenty more minutes and she'll be on us."

Baret looked out across the sea at the approaching ship. "A very long twenty minutes."

The two vessels, which to each other had been but dots on the Caribbean, moved steadily along on intercepting courses but, as the helmsman Jeb had carefully planned, out of cannon range.

"Steady as she goes, captain," he called to Erik.

Erik watched the Spanish vessel's giltwork gleam like gold in the afternoon sunlight.

Baret stood by him with hands on hips. "Look at that forecastle and poop," he said of the intricately carved structure. "A curse in the heavy wind and sea. Yet the dons persist in building their wooden castles high fore and aft."

"All the better to blow them to pieces, *mon ami,*" said Pierre with a vicious twinkle in his bold black eyes. "Come then, you slow-moving behemoth," he muttered between his white teeth. "Come to the arms of Pierre!"

Aboard the *San Pedro* was Don Miguel Vasquez, a handsome dark Spaniard, newly appointed captain-general at Margarita, who had come to marry Senorita Carlotta Maria Alvarez. He decided to join the captain of the galleon on deck, having heard a report that an unknown vessel appeared to be heading boldly toward them.

Miguel's eyes flashed with disdain. *More filthy pirate dogs! Fit for nothing but to become our galley slaves!* He strode up beside the robust Captain Hector Gavali.

"Trouble, *capitán?*"

The captain took one look at the approaching craft and turned away from the crew members who had alerted him. "You bother me with *this* pitiable thing?"

The men looked embarrassed and shifted their glances away.

Captain Gavali shook his head and turned to Miguel. *"Una*

114

Pulgita—a little flea, Don Miguel, a single-masted craft with small guns!"

Miguel smiled thinly in response.

"With many cannons and a large crew, Miguel, this magnificent ship has few to fear." Nonetheless, Don Miguel walked to the rail to peer at the coming vessel, his polished black boots clicking on the newly swabbed deck. The fine Castilian ecru lace at his neck and sleeves blew gently in the warm twilight breeze. His gaze narrowing thoughtfully, the don's alert black eyes continued to watch. He heard *Capitán* Gavali snap orders to hoist the banner of Castile and steer steadily down on the humble ketch, riding low and contrite in the blue Caribbean.

Above where Miguel stood, the trumpeter in crimson and black blasted the air with the Spanish tribute, the notes resounding across the water.

In quick response, the small craft humbly dipped its colors in a low bow to Spain. Miguel saw the yellow and red colors flutter. Then as the mighty *San Pedro* slipped past proudly, Miguel heard the fishermen in the ketch shouting enthusiastically, *"¡Viva¡ !Viva! ¡Viva!"*

Miguel turned from the rail as *Capitán* Gavali came up with a wide smile. "There was no need to be concerned for so pitiable a thing, Senor Miguel. Come, let us get back to our card game!" He shouted an order. "Gustavo! More Peruvian wine for our honored guest!"

Don Miguel, though he descended to the cabin with Gavali, gave the matter more thought. "It is known, Senor Hector, that these heretic dogs are often bent upon astonishing impertinence. They are desperados, and as such, they are as daring as the *Diablo* himself."

"Trouble yourself not, my good Miguel. These are Spanish waters, close to Caracas. Except for the heretic hunters on Hispaniola, we have little to worry about. And the *guarda costa* is making a swift end to them." He snatched up his cards in one hand and his Peruvian silver wine goblet in the other. "The ships and soldiers of our Most Christian Majesty Philip are ever alert and capable! *¡Viva!*" he declared cheerfully. "I have the winning match! You owe me ten pieces of eight, Don Miguel!"

Dwarfed by the *San Pedro*, looming like a great winged fowl ready to devour its victim, the buccaneers' ketch closed with the galleon. So maneuverable and swift was the small vessel that she could slip in under the guns of a galleon and achieve boarding position before the victim could fire an effective shot in defense.

As the sun declined, the buccaneers rowed in unison, adding to the thrust of the sails. The ketch sliced cleanly through the darkening swells and came alongside the Spanish ship. Jeb nimbly nosed her in under the bow. Baret and Erik skillfully tossed two grappling irons into the galleon's fore chain.

"Now!" Baret said.

Erik turned to the silent men, all handpicked from the best of the well-disciplined crews. "Board and board!"

Cutlasses gripped between teeth, the men latched hold, vigorously scrambling up the tall side of the ship where gilded lanterns ornamenting the stern gazed down upon them.

Baret and Erik came over the side of the *San Pedro* at the same time, followed by barefoot Pierre LaMonte and the buccaneers.

The startled Spaniards froze, then yelled wildly. Unleashing their blades, the soldiers raced forward to confront the invaders.

Erik dropped to the deck, sword in hand, but Baret paused long enough to steady himself. Then, with pistols in both hands he blasted into the soldiers surging toward Erik. Unstoppable, the buccaneers surged across the broad deck. Amid the frenzy of clashing steel and pistol shots, the swell of raging voices merged into an undistinguishable cacophony of Castilian, English, and French.

"The gun room!" ordered Baret, and men fought their way below to seize the small munitions and overwhelm the soldiers who met them with a frenzy of swords.

Amid the flurry of glittering blades and the smell of powder, Baret emerged from the chaos to gain the companionway. He hesitated a moment, foot on the bottom step, and looked up. *The captain's cabin,* he thought. *Don Miguel would be there.*

Erik was with him now, and Yorke, with a handful of buccaneers coming behind.

Baret bounded up the steps, his blade smashing a ringing blow against the opposing thrust of a soldier who thought to halt his progress. The soldier toppled, and Baret stepped over him and continued on. The cabin he sought was ahead, its door flung

116

open, and the captain of the *San Pedro* stood wild-eyed, one hand gripping a sword limply at his side.

"Mary, bless us!" he gasped in stunned disbelief. "Surely these are *diablos!*"

"For your answer, senor, we are liberators of heretic galley slaves."

"Liberators!"

"And collectors of taxes from the king of Spain!"

"Taxes!" He breathed a curse, his eyes spitting temper.

"And—" Baret bowed elegantly "—we are also wedding escorts, sent to summon the merry groom, *Capitán* Don Miguel Vasquez! He is here, yes?"

The captain of the *San Pedro* drew in a chest-swelling gust of air.

Baret gestured with his head to Yorke, who walked up and leveled his pistol at the captain's heart.

"Surrender the *San Pedro, Capitán,*" ordered Baret evenly.

The captain's sword clattered to the deck. "I am in your hand, senor."

Baret motioned him aside, and as Yorke took him away to bid his crew cease their resistance, Baret stepped into the elegant cabin.

Two men were there, an older man without weapons and Don Miguel. The don stood straight and looked on impassively. "You might as well kill me, senor. I have none of the 'taxes' you wish to collect from the noble king of Spain."

A thin smile touched Baret's lips. "The taxes can wait, *Capitán* Vasquez. I have Senorita Carlotta Maria Alvarez aboard my ship."

Startled, Miguel stared at him, then as Baret's smile deepened, the Spaniard let out a breath. "You foul dog! What price your ransom?"

"Information."

Miguel's lips tightened, and his hands formed fists. "You will receive no information from me!"

"Alas! What romantic groom is this? You would permit the lovely senorita to languish aboard my ship? Where are your gallantry and valor, Senor Miguel? Seeing as how it is not information on your military post I care for but information on a mere slave, an English heretic dog."

117

Miguel's demeanor changed to suspicion, then to curiosity as his glittering black eyes raked him.

"A slave? An Englishman?"

"You will come with me, *Capitán*. Cooperate, and I will spare you and the senorita. If not, you will swim."

Miguel stood rigid until the older Spaniard said softly, "Do as he says, Miguel. If he did not have Carlotta in his grasp, how would he have learned about you? Release your pride and spare the governor's niece!"

Miguel achieved a bow. "I surrender, senor."

"Yes, *Capitán*—to your advantage."

Captain Erik Farrow ordered his men aside and entered one of the staterooms.

A man of the Franciscan order sat in a high-backed chair by a table, darkly cowled, a silver cross glinting against the cloth of his habit, an amber rosary in hand. Stark brown eyes like pools stared at him from a strong-boned face that revealed no emotion. He did not rise.

A small gasp sounded from a corner of the room, and Erik looked there. A young woman of lustrous hair confined beneath a gold net, and wearing a gown of burgundy silk that lent her cream skin a golden glow, stared back at him. She moved swiftly behind the Franciscan.

Erik's handsome face showed nothing as his gaze left her and glanced about at the fine rugs, vessels, and velvet furnishings.

"The girl you abducted from the cove after your fellows tortured and massacred to your heart's content," he stated. "Where is she?"

The Franciscan's eyes responded with a flicker, and the woman exchanged low words with him in Castilian.

"She is a serving maid of the senora."

"Bring her."

The Franciscan stood slowly and crossed to another carved wooden door and opened it. "Minette?"

A moment later Minette Levasseur came out, cautiously. She glanced about as if wondering what to expect. Then her eyes fell on Erik.

Minette's heart leaped. "It can't be! Not Captain Farrow!"

But it was. Her eyes drifted over the thoroughly masculine buccaneer, her stomach and heart both aflutter. For the first time since she had laid eyes on Captain Farrow, he was out of immaculate fashion—he wore a torn sweat-stained shirt, leather breeches, and a black pirate scarf about his head—but his rugged stance only set her heart pounding. His golden hair fell damp across his tanned forehead and muscled neck. His cool gray eyes swept her, then he bowed.

"Your servant, madam."

Minette felt her knees weaken, and she backed against the bulkhead, hands resting on the carved wood paneling.

Erik looked across the cabin at the Franciscan and the senora. In fright, she was swiftly removing her earbobs and a jeweled pendant about her neck. She laid them on the table.

"Keep your jewels, senora. I have what I came for." He held out a hand toward Minette. "Come, sweeting, we best get out of here."

Minette simply stared, certain she must be dreaming.

He quickly crossed the room, snatched her up as though she were as light as cotton fluff, and edged from the room, while two of his men kept an eye on the Franciscan.

"Cap'n," breathed one, sweat standing out on his face. "Lemme kill the papist!"

"No! He has not harmed her. Out!"

They obeyed his terse command, and Erik strode off with Minette in his arms.

She remained speechless, aware of the strength of the arm that bore her. His silence intrigued her, and she glanced up, blushing, noting that up close his face was as handsome as from afar.

He carried her down the companion onto the deck, where the buccaneers were gathering ingots of gold and bars of silver. He went to the bulwarks where a long rope ladder had been tossed over the side and secured at the bottom "Jeb!" he called down. "Prepare to receive the girl!"

She looked into his eyes and saw restrained amusement in their gray depths.

"Well, have you nothing to say?"

Minette swallowed, gripping the rough rope, knowing her

cheeks had turned a hot pink. "I—I'm in your debt, Captain Far-row."

His eyes drifted over her face, and a smile softened his otherwise hard expression. "Your cousin will be pleased to see you again."

"Emerald is safe? And Uncle Karlton?"

"Both safe aboard the *Warspite*. You'll be there in the morning."

She didn't know what to say. So great was her relief and joy that tears turned her wide amber eyes into sparkling gems.

He looked down at her, his smile fading. "How old are you?" he asked quietly.

Under his gaze the answer stuck in her dry throat. *Almost sixteen,* she wanted to say truthfully, but she heard herself speaking as if listening to a stranger. "Seventeen."

He studied her for a moment, as if measuring the truth of her confession. Slowly one hand took hold of her waist-length hair, shimmering like warm honey in the last rays of the setting Caribbean sun. Minette felt his firm embrace and his lips on hers.

The encounter lasted only a moment, and he turned her loose, a thoughtful look on his chiseled face. He leaned over the rail, grasping the rope ladder that fell to the small craft below. "Can you climb down?" he asked her. "Jeb! Come up and help the damsel!"

When she was safely in the ketch and set on her feet, Minette looked up again to Erik. Their gazes caught before he turned and walked away.

Dazed, Minette followed Jeb to a cushion at the back of the vessel. There she sat, staring at the last vestige of scarlet sunset fading into the sea and hearing the distant shouts of the buccaneers.

He actually kissed me. She raised trembling fingers to touch her lips. The tears came again, and this time wouldn't cease. Did God have good plans for her after all? The Lord had rescued her from captivity, even though she had surely betrayed Him by kissing the crucifix.

And Captain Farrow had noticed her, noticed her as a woman and not as a mere half-caste.

Part Two

ON JAMAICA

9

IN THE NIGHT HIS SONG SHALL BE WITH ME

Facing windward, Port Royal Bay shimmered and glittered jade green beneath the noontide sun, but Emerald felt no pleasure in being home on Jamaica. She swallowed back the uncertainty that wanted to tighten her throat. She had dreaded the return ever since they had set sail, but never more than now as the possibility loomed that she must face the Harwick family after all.

Emerald, her father, and Minette had parted company with the buccaneers three weeks earlier. They sailed home without further contact with the *guarda costa,* even though voyaging alone through the Gulf of Venezuela had been dangerous. They had arrived in Port Royal the evening before on the recovered *Madeleine* after completing repairs on Curaçao.

Emerald now anxiously awaited her father's return from his business in town, where he had gone to report to Governor Modyford as well as to arrange for her and Minette's passage to England aboard a civilian merchant ship. If only she could board the ship without the necessity of meeting the family!

Her trunk was packed, and the small satchel containing her precious music notes sat close beside her crossed ankles. Before his death in the slave uprising the night of the dreadful fire on Foxemoore, Great-uncle Mathias had labored long and hard, meticulously gathering the musical chants of the African slaves brought to the West Indies from Guinea. He'd entrusted his work to her before his death, and she kept it close beside her to be hand-carried. During her upcoming schooling years in England, beside learning social graces, she expected to devote private time to continuing her uncle's creation of an African hymnbook to be used to teach Christianity to the slaves on Foxemoore and—if the Lord blessed—to all Jamaica.

The concept of teaching Africans about Christ was not accepted by the Europeans in Jamaica—*nor elsewhere in the English, French, or Dutch colonies,* she thought. The laws of the Jamaican Council forbade this, and the reason seemed obvious to Emerald. From the beginning of slavery throughout the West Indies, the planters had realized that educating slaves might soon require that they be treated as brothers, and how could one in good conscience enslave his own brother? Laws also were enacted forbidding teaching slaves to read and write. And, of course, they were not permitted to attend the churches.

What an evil thing is this, she thought angrily. With the help of God these laws must be changed, and a good place to begin would be on Foxemoore, the sugar plantation belonging to the Harwick and Buckington families.

But even though her father owned shares in the estate and had some say in its business, she knew that those shares were at risk because of debt he had incurred several years earlier when losing a family merchant ship. Whether or not her father had gone with Baret to Margarita to locate the treasure of the *Prince Philip,* with the hope of paying off those debts, remained a mystery to her. Nor had the numerous questions she asked her father about the island of Margarita received satisfying answers.

She had not seen Baret since he sailed on the ketch with Farrow and LaMonte to take the *San Pedro.* Erik had returned Minette to the *Warspite* and the *Madeleine* to Karlton, but Baret had gone on to the *Regale* with the prisoner he had taken from the Spanish galleon.

It's as if the entire matter has suddenly become shrouded in dark secrecy! she thought.

As for Foxemoore and the debts, her father took joyous pains to point out that her marriage one day to the viscount-turned-pirate would place them both in an attractive situation financially, since Baret was heir to an earldom. Besides, he held a good amount of treasure of his own, acquired from his buccaneering ventures.

Emerald carefully replaced into her satchel the notes on the chant she'd been looking at, again thanking the Lord that the soldiers of the *guarda costa* had not troubled to ransack the cabin where she'd hidden them.

Restive, she sat on a squeaking rattan ottoman beneath a faded sailcloth awning on the uppermost deck. She mused over all that had happened to her and Minette, while tapping her blue-and-yellow parrots' feather fan against her chin. She was dressed for her voyage in a pale green linen dress, trimmed with lacy ribbon at the bodice. A silver Huguenot cross glimmered at her throat.

She was anxious to embark on a respectable merchant ship and sail for England. *If it weren't for the lovingkindness of the Lord, I should soon give up all hope,* she thought. *But I'll not turn a cowardly goose—not after what we've been through. My future is resting upon the Rock.*

"He endured, as seeing Him who is invisible." The verse in the faith chapter of Hebrews came winging to her mind. *I too can endure by fixing my focus on Him who is sovereign and who is always with me.* Drawing in a breath, she glanced at the sapphire blue sky as though she saw *Him.*

Thinking of Baret did little to cool her runaway emotions. After all that had transpired, she knew him to be as bold and daring a buccaneer as any she had yet to encounter. That knowledge only served to remind her once again of her dilemma, for in spite of their romantic encounter aboard his ship, Emerald remained convinced the marriage was impossible.

What's more, Baret knew this as well. That realization brought a flutter to her stomach as she considered his motive in allowing the betrothal to linger on. He would not, could not, go through with it. If his plans went well, his reputation would one day be restored when he met with King Charles. One day Baret would be an earl. Why then the continued pretense where marriage to her was concerned?

It was all unfortunate and certain to end badly, she thought, not to mention the risk to her heart.

Tortuga! She thought scornfully of the place and what had happened there. She whisked her fan. The very memory raised its mocking head to laugh at her romantic ambitions.

How could her blustery father have dared to demand a duel! And from Baret Buckington, a viscount, a man known to be dangerously skilled in the use of the blade. Her father was blessed that Baret had opted for the gallant role, lest he find himself buried on Tortuga beside her mother. But then, he had counted on Baret's honor.

She reminded herself that if it hadn't been her misfortune

to be born on Tortuga with French pirates as family, she would now fare better when it came to her reputation. Could any voyage to London erase the past that dogged her steps?

My reputation was a matter of festering chatter long before any of this happened to me, she thought, for her mother was said to have been the daughter of the notorious French pirate Marcel Levasseur. *But now I face worse scandal. What of the matter concerning the* Black Dragon, *the attack on the Main, and the* San Pedro?

Her spirit shuddered at the conclusions the family would come to when they heard the tales surrounding her absence from Jamaica. Far worse than confronting Great-aunt Lady Sophie Harwick, or her father's cousin Geneva Harwick Buckington, was facing young, flaxen-haired Lady Lavender Thaxton. Lavender was heiress to the title of duchess and had been contemplating marriage to the viscount for years. What innuendos Lavender would delight to let drop from her honeyed lips—what barbed accusations she would make about Emerald's scheme to steal Baret by way of a duel!

She stirred uncomfortably. Lavender would never believe the truth about her abduction from the wharf. She would imagine the worst. So would the rest of the family. And what of the Earl of Buckington, Baret's grandfather? Remembering back to that night at the ball when she had seen Earl Nigel so coldly aristocratic, she shuddered.

"Not that Papa is likely to worry much about what they think as long as I become Lady Buckington."

The situation had all the distressing ingredients necessary to overwhelm her if she let it. It made her feel shamelessly brazen.

But maybe I won't need to face any of them, she thought, swishing the fan furiously. "In a few days, at most, I'll be sailing for England."

Still, as the wife of a viscount from the West Indies, she was likely to face a future of whispers and innuendoes in England, as well as a good deal of morbid curiosity at Court. "So this is the pretty tart that the earl's grandson picked up for countess among the pirates' brothels."

Emerald's fingers touched the cross she wore. The Father accepted her in the Beloved, and she had Him to depend upon to face each tomorrow.

And if I am afraid of gossip that is not even true, she told herself, *how will I ever be able to face the opposition that will surely come over teaching Christianity to the slaves? I must not be cowardly, but brave.*

Despite her call for courage, Emerald felt anything but victorious.

Her frown tightened as a strange pain, one she dare not consider for long, pinched her heart. *I won't be a fool and entertain the silly thought that Baret could actually care about me, even if he did kiss me.*

In England, matters would ease between Baret and her father. The years would also give her and Baret both the time and distance needed to quietly back out of the betrothal.

Emerald grimaced, swallowing a small resentment that she refused to admit even to herself that she had hoped Baret would have chosen of his own will to give her a piece of Buckington family jewelry before she sailed. Doing so would have spoken loudly enough of his intentions. Instead, he had returned to Tortuga to meet with Henry Morgan without even seeing her again after the *San Pedro* incident.

The Dutch War loomed, Captain Farrow had told her politely, and it demanded the viscount's full attention. But she suspected he intended to use the war as a cover for his other upcoming raids on the Main.

Emerald did not wish to contemplate the outcome of her dilemma, and she took out her frustration on the stinging sand flies that pestered her.

"The sooner we're aboard ship, the less chance there'll be of confronting the family," she said aloud.

She stood up from the ottoman and walked from under the sailcloth to the taffrail. Shading her eyes, she looked across the bay.

The day would be scorching. She gave an upward glance toward the topaz sky, then out across the greenish water, hoping to see her father's cockboat returning. What was keeping him? His absence ashore set new concerns on edge. What could possibly be keeping him? Might something have gone wrong in his meeting with Governor Modyford?

Sir Karlton had been gone since they had shared a breakfast of cassava melon and fried plantain in the Round Room. Did his delay have anything to do with her betrothal to Baret Buckington? Perhaps her father had taken time to speak to the family about it. The idea that he might have done so did little to ease her reservation over his absence.

She paced the walkway facing the bay, seeing the masts of brigantines and sloops at anchor. She noticed that there were fewer vessels than usual. The Caribbean sun continued to beat upon the sugar-fine sand on the beach, while her gaze swept the seven-thousand-foot Blue Mountain range far in the island's distance, said to be furrowed by deep gullies and rivers cascading through steamy jungle. The mountains rimmed the horizon, and seeing their strength and beauty, she thought momentarily of her cousin Ty, who had escaped there after the slave uprising.

Her cousin was in the mountains now, waiting, expecting to one day join a buccaneering ship to sail the Caribbean and attack the Spanish Main. She wondered how Ty was faring during her absence from Port Royal and whether or not the evil overseer Mr. Pitt had given up searching for him.

Minette Levasseur approached and sat moodily on a cushion under the sailcloth, a look of concern on her fine-featured face. She was a striking girl, with wavy honey-colored hair and amber eyes that complemented her moonstruck infatuation with the handsome but ruthless buccaneer Sir Erik Farrow—who, she had told Emerald too many times recently, "now thinks me a lady. He even kissed me!"

"I wouldn't take his kiss to mean very much," Emerald had warned softly, thinking the same of Baret's behavior. She suspected that Captains Foxworth and Farrow were equally ruthless, equally pirates, and—beneath their suave demeanor—looked upon a moonlight kiss as light payment for rescuing them from danger.

Minette, wearing a breezy cotton chemise that reached to just above her ankles, seemed to lounge amid gloomy thoughts of her own. "You're right about one thing—Captain Farrow didn't seem to think the kiss meant anything once we was back aboard the *Warspite*. Why, he didn't even come to tell me good-bye when we boarded the *Madeleine* for Curaçao."

Emerald glanced at her cousin. She was about to tell Minette that she shouldn't have permitted the rogue to kiss her, but then she recalled her own behavior with Baret. At least they had a betrothal, even if little would come of it. Still, a girl didn't go about allowing men to kiss her until the relationship progressed toward a commitment to marriage. Emerald frowned and swished her fan, pacing.

"The sooner we both leave here, the better off we'll be— and the wiser for it," she murmured.

"At least you have a chance to be a real lady in England," Minette complained again.

"Will I?" challenged Emerald dubiously. "My bloodline is considered of little more respectability than your own."

Minette showed no relief from her melancholy thoughts. "Maybe. Do you think Captain Farrow is in love with me?"

Emerald cast her a worried glance that Minette didn't seem to notice. "You best forget him," she warned in a quiet voice. "He's a rake, even if he was gallant enough to rescue you. And he's man enough to break any woman's heart, especially a young girl like you. There's small chance of winning *his* love, Minette."

She hastened on when she saw Minette's misery. "The Lord has someone else for you. I'm sure of it. And he'll come along when your feet reach the place on the path where the crossroad turns."

Minette scowled. "What if there isn't anyone, ever?"

Emerald's skirts rustled softly as she stirred. "Then, if it's His purpose, what would have been better? He loves you too much to deny what's good, Minette."

"Well, maybe. I'm not sure sometimes . . ."

Emerald squelched the rising doubt in her own heart. "Someday we'll know the truth about all of life's mysterious denials and see He was there all the time. Why," she said brightly, "I'll wager angels guard our very steps!"

Minette cast her a skeptical glance. "Is that why I was captured at the cove?"

"You're safe, aren't you? And wiser for your bitter experiences."

"You're right." Minette sighed. "I've been doing a lot of thinking about that. Are you sure the Lord's forgiven me? Didn't I betray Him by doing what the Franciscan demanded?"

"Yes, and there are far worse things you could have done. But you've asked His forgiveness, and the Lord's grace and mercy overflow to all His stumbling children. He's willing to forgive all our sins. As for Captain Farrow, he's not a marrying man.

That's a danger signal for any girl. When a man says, 'I'm not ready yet,' watch out."

Minette avoided her gaze. "How do you know Captain Farrow doesn't want to get married?"

Emerald hesitated, feeling the hot sun beat upon her head. She picked up her hat and tied the ribbons firmly beneath her chin. "He would have married by now."

Minette glumly rested her chin on her palm. "You're probably right. And anyway, he wouldn't marry *me.*"

Emerald changed the subject and looked across the bay, now gently ruffled by the breeze. "Papa's been gone all morning. I wonder what's keeping him. He should have reported to Governor Modyford by now—and bought us passage to England too."

Minette joined her at the rail. "Look—that's Zeddie coming in the cockboat now."

Emerald squinted against the sunlight. "It is, but my father's not with him." She could not mask the concern in her voice.

Minette's eyes widened. "Vapors! Ye don't think he was arrested?"

"Arrested! On what charge?" But Emerald's voice was sharp, because the same fear clamped like irons about her heart. "He's no pirate. We don't even know if he went to Margarita with Captain Foxworth. And he had nothing to do with the *San Pedro.*"

Minette added quickly, "You're right, and Lady Geneva wouldn't let the governor do such a thing to her cousin anyway."

Emerald dare not say what she thought—that Felix, who had married Geneva, was a man of independent power who would do as he wished.

"We'll soon find out," said Emerald and left the taffrail to hurry down to the main deck.

The cockboat came alongside the *Madeleine,* and at the foot of the ladder the Carib Indian reached to tie the rope. A minute later, Zeddie stepped into the waist of the ship. He turned as Emerald rushed up to him, anxious for news.

"Where's Father? Is there trouble?"

"Aye, he's to appear at the Bailey to answer a question or two."

"About the *Prince Philip*?"

"That snake-mouthed Levasseur testified to Lord Felix that your father was involved."

Fear sprang to flame as she remembered Baret's warning.

"Levasseur's also talked about Thorpe and the *Black Dragon*. He claims Captain Foxworth was workin' with Thorpe."

Rafael was in Port Royal!

"That treacherous, lying blackguard! Why hasn't he been arrested? He's a worse pirate than any who sail the Caribbean."

"An interestin' question, if you go askin' me, an' I've no answer yet except he seems to be hobnobbing with Lord Felix—who isn't anxious to arrest him. Levasseur's bitter enough over losin' you in the duel to have included you in the doings. Do you think he has the humility to lose to Captain Foxworth? Especially when his lordship made him dance the sword's edge? Har! Levasseur lost your hand in marriage, an' he ain't a good loser. An' it didn't help things when Foxworth threatened to sink his ship over the *Black Dragon*.

"Aye, m'gal, Levasseur snapped at the opportunity to do evil to him by comin' to Felix. Anyway, Levasseur has upped anchor, but the French dandy may dangle yet, and more with him. Now m'gal, try not to fret. Sir Karlton is a good man to be sure, an' he'll ride this out is my guess. So will the viscount. He'll outsmart his uncle, you'll see. Your father's given me orders to bring you to the lookout house. Says to wait for him there. Seems we'll be in Port Royal a few days more is all."

"A few days?" she inquired anxiously, her hopes faltering. "Then . . . they're holding him?"

He straightened his periwig. "This mite of trouble is causin' a minor delay. He'll be there only till the matter at the Bailey is swept clean of misunderstandin's."

Misunderstandings . . .

She remembered how Baret had signed articles with Rafael when they had sailed to Maracaibo to locate Lucca. There'd been two deaths aboard Baret's ship, even before he entered Spanish territorial waters: Jamie Bradford and a crewman of Rafael's named Sloane. Baret told her the dreadful pirate Sloane was killed in Maracaibo when Baret sought the whereabouts of the scholar named Lucca. She wasn't certain who had killed him, Baret or Captain Farrow, but if Baret was ever asked to explain to the Jamaican governor, it would mean admitting his illegal entry onto the Spanish Main.

There had been some trouble with the Spanish soldiers

guarding Lucca as well. Now there'd been the attacks on the Main of the Venezuelan coast and the *San Pedro*. All this was disturbing news for Baret, but what of her father? He had been involved in his own way.

"Then the Admiralty officials know that he sailed with Baret's father when the *Prince Philip* was taken?"

Zeddie mopped his brow with a calico cloth, looking worried. "He'll manage to convince 'em otherwise."

She couldn't help but worry. Returning to Port Royal had been a dreadful mistake. "Oh, Zeddie, we should have sailed to England from Curaço."

"It's too late now, m'gal."

Too late . . . The cold, dark words sounded a death knell to her hopes. Perhaps it was also too late for Baret, despite his plans to save his father and salvage their reputations. It seemed too late for them all, including herself and Minette. They had unwisely returned to a trap.

Port Royal remained, as Great-uncle Mathias had called it, "a cockatrice den of cutthroats, whores, and covetous merchants." Port Royal's citizens turned a deaf ear to the rumbling beneath her foundations of silt. Barrels of kill-devil rum, that hot, hellish liquor that was the main drink of Port Royal, continued to flow in place of the water that was mostly undrinkable.

Which I will once again need to boil, Emerald thought as she made large jugs of weak tea to quench their thirst.

Not that Jamaica produced only buccaneers. Those colonists who settled the island had been a hardy people, restless, energetic, greedy, and determined. Some had come for religious freedom. Many of the early buccaneers were French Huguenots and Dutch Protestants, angry at Spain for her Inquisition. Attacking their galleons and hauling off their treasure was pure delight. Others, like her father, a maverick in the respectable Harwick family of London, had arrived years earlier when the Civil War broke out in England.

Land and accumulated wealth clothed the newcomers with power, and with power was granted the nod of acceptance and respectability by others who were more powerful. Marriages unthought of in England were arranged in the rich West Indies, and the blood of the Harwicks, Morgans, and Thaxtons was joined.

132

The nobility scooped up land for sugar and traded in Spanish gold. And so Earl Nigel Buckington, Baret's grandfather, had married Mary Harwick. And now Lord Felix Buckington had married a Harwick heiress, Geneva, a cousin of Sir Karlton. The dynasty buying into King Sugar expanded and became even more powerful.

Still others came. They came with enthusiasm and built their shops and churches. They constructed brick houses with goods hauled in from Europe, but they recklessly built on Port Royal—its foundation being a cay of silt and sand—in order to be close to the water, close to the five hundred ships that called each year with their silk, spices, calico, wine, horses, pigs, and French chocolates. They built their taverns and alehouses all across Port Royal and welcomed the buccaneers and pirates to safeguard the island from attack by Spain.

And despite Sunday preaching, Port Royal would not turn from its ways. Gambling, drinking, and whoring went on all night. Uncle Mathias had always reminded her, after returning to Foxemoore from St. Paul's Church, that his friend the rector warned from the pulpit of judgment "soon to come."

Emerald had taken a special interest in what was said to be a future "fire and brimstone" calamity coming upon Port Royal, "the most sinful city in the world, as dangerous as a plague and as wicked as the devil." When growing up, she had often trembled whenever an earthquake occurred, or a hurricane struck with devastating winds, or even when she rode from Foxemoore to the edge of town to look upon the pirates of Chocolata Hole. She had never said anything to Mathias, but Emerald would wonder afterward if she too might not die along with everyone else when the looming catastrophe struck. As a child, she had told the Lord she needed His mercy and forgiveness as much as anyone else in Jamaica.

As Emerald matured, she discovered that Mathias's summation of Port Royal's notorious reputation was only too accurate. Although there were sugar planters all over the island—including Spanish Town—Jamaica's second largest settlement—people flocked to Port Royal because the wealth was there.

From the beginning, the buccaneer stronghold had overflowed with looted gold, silver, pearls, and emeralds, all of it from pirated plunder of Spanish galleons or from raids on

Spain's colonies of Porto Bello, Cartegena, and Panama. Even with Governor Modyford withholding marques from the buccaneers to legally attack Spanish shipping, Port Royal remained the "Treasury House of the West Indies."

On Jamaica's southern coast, overshadowed by the lush Blue Mountains, a long, low sandspit curved south and then west away from the island. Once called the Palisadoes, it now formed Port Royal Harbor, where deep waters and the absence of shoals made it the ideal natural port and lured hundreds of ships a year. The Spanish had used the old harbor, Spanish Town, as their chief port, and Point Caguay—site of Port Royal—had been unoccupied during the Spanish rule save for a careenage where ships were refitted.

Lying off the western tip of this sandspit was a cay separated from it by a marshy area of mangrove trees. Through the efforts of the merchants, the cay had been filled in and connected to the main island. The enterprising merchants and colonists first called it "The Point," but when Charles II was reinstated as king of England, the loyalists in Jamaica officially renamed it Port Royal.

"It's the most flourishing seaport in the West Indies," they announced. "And the privateers will find this town to offer them a most warm welcome in exchange for protection against Spain."

And so it was. Situated at the center of the Caribbean, Port Royal was ideally located for trading and privateering voyages all over the West Indies. It became a cove for buccaneers, pirates, smugglers, and all manner of adventurers, including gamblers and harlots. Port Royal became a boomtown, where pirates' gold, silver, and precious gems flowed in a steady stream across the gaming tables of the Red Goose and the Spanish Galleon. More than one fortune was gained—or lost—in a single night.

"Looks unusually quiet," commented Emerald curiously, as her eyes ran along King Street and Fishers Row, fronting the wharves, warehouses, and grog shops where buccaneers and pirates once sauntered with cutlass and pistol. A few sea rogues remained, but the dangerous throng of rum-drinking pirates she was accustomed to seeing there was strangely missing.

"Perhaps sowing to the wind and reaping the whirlwind is a lesson Port Royal has finally learned," she told Minette.

Her cousin looked doubtful, glancing about as she opened

the small yellow parasol that Emerald had given to her for a birthday gift two years ago. Its inch of battenburg lace was now soiled. She cast limpid amber eyes toward a lean, tough pirate who loitered on the wharf. His shoulder-length black hair lay in oiled waves.

"I doubt the villains will ever learn, Emerald. They're born with a crooked bent to their ways, but *'tis* quiet. I wonder why. We was only gone two months, so why should things change?"

She followed Minette's uneasy stare at the swarthy pirate, who watched them with keen interest. And Emerald's imagination envisioned his bold, tanned face turning into the pale and haughty countenance of Lady Sophie Harwick. Great-aunt Sophie was demanding answers as to why Emerald had shamed herself and the Harwick name by running away like a common piece of baggage with the first handsome rogue who looked her way— "just like her mother."

Minette was right about Port Royal's godless lifestyle not easily changing. "Can a leopard change his spots?" the prophet had asked. It would take more than ridding Port Royal of the worst pirates to bring change to Jamaica. The island needed more than reform; its citizens needed a reformation of the heart.

As far as she knew, the well-delivered sermons were continuing to be preached by the rector at St. Paul's, but except for the regular Sunday attenders, who was paying heed?

The crashing boom of a cannon in the Fort Charles battery startled her from her musings. It was followed by two more loud shots to signal an approaching vessel that it had permission to enter the harbor.

Minette snatched in her breath, and Emerald felt her cousin's fingers tighten about her arm.

"Emerald, *look!*"

10

TO TRAP A PIRATE

Emerald didn't like the shocked tone of her cousin's voice and with reluctance followed her gaze down the warped wharf. At first she saw nothing unusual. Her eyes skimmed over some new, roughly constructed buildings and more warehouses along the cay that were being built to house the king's generous proceeds from any raids upcoming on the Main. With the withdrawal of commissions, however, these were likely to stand empty upon completion, and Tortuga and the French king would gain the bounty instead.

As she scanned the area to which Minette gestured, she saw the normal amount of slaves going about their work. Half-castes, Caribs, and Africans were emerging from their huts and kennels to haul in the cargo that was evidently expected on a newly arriving gray merchant ship that bore no flag.

"I don't see anything," said Emerald, as Minette continued to clutch her arm.

"Oh, Emerald! *There!*"

Emerald lifted her eyes and focused on the large carrion birds sitting expectantly on the cross arm of a gallows on the Point. She recoiled, offended by the stark brutality made more suggestive now that her father was being held on questions of piracy.

Was it not here that Jamie's brother, Captain Maynerd, had been hanged—he who had sailed as a crewman aboard Viscount Royce Buckington's ship?

Her throat felt the iron fingers of fear grip her jugular. Six bodies hung from the newly erected execution dock, each one in various degrees of decomposition under the tropical sun. A nightmarish fear arose in her mind. "Your father," it cackled. "Go take a look—you'll see him!"

"No," she choked and broke into a cold sweat. "No!"

"Emerald," whispered Minette worriedly, "it's not Uncle Karlton. Don't be afraid. I—I shouldn't have said anything. Come on, let's get out of here." She took Emerald's arm and tried to propel her across the narrow, cobbled street, but Emerald stood unable to move. The birds seemed to be waiting for the neck of a corpse to rot through, allowing the body to fall onto the ground where it could be feasted upon.

She noticed a ladder leaning against a support, suggesting that the authorities expected another pirate to be led there for hanging soon. She struggled to concentrate on some words from Scripture: *"Fear thou not; for I am with thee: be not dismayed; for I am thy God!"*

She swallowed, and slowly her overwhelming fear began to subside like ebbing waves rolling over pure white sand. "Lord Felix is anxious to appease the Lords of Trade and Plantation in London," she murmured. "That pirate aggressors attacking Spanish shipping are being harshly dealt with in Jamaica looks good for his own position before His Majesty."

Emerald snatched up the hem of her skirts. "Come, let's cross the street," and she and Minette stepped out amid the slow traffic of horse-drawn buggies and wagons.

Minette pointed out the fine carriages belonging to the wealthy sugar and cacao planters. It was no wonder, thought Emerald, for one block inland from King Street were Queen Street and High Street, where the gentry built fashionable town houses and occupied them for at least half the year. She recalled that before Geneva's marriage to Felix, there was talk about his constructing a house as Geneva's wedding present. Emerald supposed that Felix had a supply of rich pieces of furniture to decorate with, many of them taken from the Spanish Main. *He's a fine one to hang pirates,* she thought with cynicism.

She wondered whether or not that house was completed and whether Geneva might be there. *Not that I'd ever be accepted there,* she thought. *Nor would I impose.*

For herself and Minette, and Zeddie too, they had best do as her father said and make their temporary living quarters his lookout house on the quay itself, its stilts driven deep into sand and water. Soon he would be released and putting her and Minette onboard a ship to England. Zeddie would stay on the *Madeleine* with her father, as would old Drummond, who had been his attendant at the bungalow on Foxemoore for many years. The three of them would sail with the buccaneers.

Emerald heard the brisk trot of hooves behind them. A horse and buggy were coming. She and Minette moved to the edge of the cobbled street to avoid the overtaking vehicle.

"It's Zeddie!" Minette called with relief. "He's hired a buggy."

Emerald turned to watch until Zeddie came abreast, hauled on the reins, and clambered down to assist them.

Once seated on the torn leather seat between Zeddie and Minette and on their way to the house, Emerald noticed that he was oddly quiet. Her own emotions felt frazzled, and she didn't mind the silence. Rather, she used it to recoup for what might wait ahead for them all. Oh, for a cup of sweet tea and time to take her slippers off! Carefully, she avoided a last glance toward the hideous sight at Gallows Point as they trotted past the wharf in reflective silence.

"Things are unusually quiet in town," said Emerald at last, glancing at him to see what he might know that he wasn't telling.

Zeddie flicked the reins. "'Tis the Governor's new hangin's I'm hearing. The arrival of his lordship Felix Buckington to marry Lady Geneva is seen more as the scheme of them Spanish sympathizers in London's Parliament. The Peace Party rascals intend to appease Spain by runnin' out the Brotherhood, even if it means hangin' them all."

Zeddie turned the buggy down Fishers Row, and the wooden buildings became more typically rough. With a frown, he informed them that they had not been mistaken about the bizarre silence in town. Most of the Brethren of the Coast had quietly boarded their vessels and slipped away past the big guns of Fort Charles, planning to set up their stronghold at French-held Tortuga.

Emerald stirred uneasily, unsure whether she wished the streets to be prowling with cutlass-and-pistol-toting pirates or risk cannon fire from a Spanish galleon instead. One thing *was* sure—she'd had enough of pirates like Lex Thorpe. But she reminded herself she needn't be concerned, since she and Minette would soon be sailing for the sweet civility of London.

Zeddie told her the fleet of buccaneers had left because the governor was under strict orders from His Majesty to refuse them commissions. Since the buccaneers were not about to cease pursuing their livelihood, they resorted to what they were always inclined to do under such unfavorable circumstances. When denied legal commissions, which made them privateers, many became pirates by displaying no national flag.

"They'll sail under some private color of their own, more'n likely the Jolly Roger. So they left for a warmer welcome at Tortuga, not wantin' to risk his lordship Felix's Gallows Point. Looks like trouble to be sure, m'gal. And it's you we're worried about."

Thinking that the worst was facing the family before sailing, her gaze darted to his. "No need for either you or my father to worry. I don't plan to go to Foxemoore. I'll stay at the lookout house until he buys passage."

"Stab me, lass, it ain't them blooded foxes we're thinkin' about. Governor Modyford is going to call *you* before the officials as well as your father! He wants to know what you have to say about Captain Foxworth. The *Regale* entered Maracaibo, an' there's some say about the Spanish ambassador going to protest to His Majesty about it. There's also questions aplenty about the murder of Jamie Bradford—and suddenly no one's calling the rascal 'Maynerd' anymore. And soon I expect news to come tricklin' in from Margarita and Cumaná."

Emerald watched the sweat trickle down the side of his creased face, bearing witness to his alarm. All at once dread enclosed her like a spider's sticky web. Her father was in far worse trouble than she had allowed herself to believe, and she was not much better off. Neither the governor nor members of the Admiralty Court would think much of the social status of Emerald Harwick. She was not Lavender, nor a delicately born daughter of a council member, nor even the daughter of a rich planter. She was the illegitimate offspring of a pirate's daughter and would be looked upon as a strumpet who had run away on Baret Buckington's ship.

Zeddie appeared to understand her thoughts. Unlike other times, when he sought to soothe her alarms, he looked genuinely frightened.

Her heart thudded against her rib cage. Was it possible they would arrest her and put her in Brideswell? Hang her? She recalled Baret's half-teasing suggestion that she might be arrested. What if it were true?

"Lord Felix is lookin' for blood to be had, m'gal, sure as I'm sittin' here. An' he has his plans all neat and tidy, stab me if'n he don't. A clever fox, to be sure. I'm thinking it ain't you nor even Sir Karlton he's after."

Her mind flashed back to Gallows Point, and memory of the carrion sitting patiently on the crossbeam made her shudder. She thought she knew. *Baret must not return to Port Royal.*

"Zeddie, did the viscount go to Margarita to look for the treasure?"

"That, lass, I don't have the answer to. An' your father isn't talkin'. My guess is that he hasn't gone there yet. He'd be busy with that Spanish don he took from the *San Pedro.* I have me a suspicion that your father intended to return to Tortuga and join the viscount there just as soon as he saw you and Minette on that ship safe for England."

Emerald's anxiety heightened. "When will I be brought to the officials?"

"That I'm not knowing. I'm thinking your father will do anything to spare you. He'll tell everything he knows to keep you out of this, m'gal, but is that what Lord Felix wants?"

"You think he hopes to lure Baret here, using us as bait? They're wrong—he won't risk it." Yet, he had come to save her and her father from Captain Thorpe . . .

"This is a wretched day, m'gal. Especially when I'm rememberin' that Jamie Bradford was hanged from the yardarm of the *Regale.*"

"Rafael Levasseur did that!" Minette broke in furiously. "And that pirate named Sloane! Emerald told me all about him."

"Aye, but whose word do they wish to believe for their own purposes? Your cousin Levasseur is sayin' it was Captain Foxworth."

"That's absurd." Emerald fumed.

"To be sure, Lord Felix don't care about nothing except arrestin' his troublesome nephew." Zeddie shifted on the seat, flipping the reins. "I don't need remindin' ye how Captain Foxworth's death will leave his uncle the earl's one remaining heir."

Emerald's thoughts turned a troubling corner. "No," she murmured. "There is another if Baret dies." She looked at him. "His half brother, Jette."

An ominous silence descended. Because of Felix's marriage to Cousin Geneva Harwick two months ago, eight-year-old Jette, for all practical purposes, was the stepchild of Felix.

There was only one in the family strong enough to thwart any plan Felix might entertain about Baret and Jette. "What about Earl Nigel?" she asked. "Is he still at Foxemoore?"

"I've not heard. To be sure, he's the big barracuda to appeal to about his son Felix. And Baret too, for that matter."

Emerald's alarm smoldered beneath a facade of calm, for she knew that showing how afraid she was would upset Minette and Zeddie even more.

What would she say to the Admiralty officials? What *could* she say to protect her father and Baret?

Baret was convinced his father had been betrayed and sold as a slave, perhaps into the silver mines in Peru. She now suspected something she had not had time to discuss with him on the *Regale*. Felix had questionable plans when it came to his recent marriage. And those plans would include Jette. That Felix wanted the family title of earl was no secret to anyone in the family except, perhaps, to Geneva and Baret's grandfather Nigel Buckington, who was in Jamaica to convince Baret to return with him to England.

For some reason, Emerald recalled the suspicious words she'd heard at Foxemoore when Great-aunt Sophie warned Geneva about Felix the night before the wedding. *"The letter says she died quite suddenly. And without a physician . . . he may have deliberately eliminated his first wife in order to marry you."*

As Zeddie drove the buggy toward the lookout house, Emerald lapsed into silence. No more would be known until her father was released and he arrived with news. For he must be released, she thought. They couldn't possibly hold him. Life couldn't be that cruel to her. If anything happened to her beloved father, what would she do? *I won't think about it now. I can't.*

She glanced about uneasily at the sights she knew so well, sights that now seemed far more depressing than formerly, and she noted with thankfulness that the spires of St. Paul's Church rose dominantly above red roofs like prayerful hands of intercession entreating the throne of grace.

The brilliant sunlight reflecting on the blue Caribbean caused the ripples to appear like a school of darting silver fish. As Emerald gazed out across the azure waters, war was the last thing on her mind and the last thing seemingly on the minds of those in the busy Port Royal harbor. She scrutinized curiously the gray merchant ship that she had seen earlier when the cannon had signaled the incoming vessel to dock.

"Zeddie, that ship—it isn't the vessel my father bought us passage on, is it?"

He squinted his good eye in its direction. Then, as though he had been already aware of its presence, settled his periwig. "It ain't English, lass. I'm thinkin' it's secretly Dutch."

"Dutch!" Startled, she wondered what made him think so.

"They say Sir Erik Farrow is from Holland." Minette sighed, wrapping a honey-colored ringlet of hair around her finger.

Emerald glanced at Zeddie for an explanation. "If you know it's a Dutch merchant ship, then the militia manning the big guns must know too. What if they attack us?"

He offered a scornful snort. "The Hollanders won't go attackin', m'gal, nor will our militia. 'Tis naught except a slave ship, bringin' human cargo from what used to be Dutch forts along the Gold Coast of Africa."

"A slave ship," echoed Emerald with dismay. She shielded her gaze to look toward the glittering green waters.

"And Jamaica planters are anxious to buy." Zeddie looked thoughtful as he flicked the leather reins and frowned at the horse. "I'm thinkin' that ship might belong to some in the Jamaican Council who'd wish to keep their nefarious involvement a secret."

She remembered the odious Sir Jasper, who had tried to accost her outside the Red Goose gambling den before Baret had intervened. Jasper was a pirate at heart even though he was received in the best parlors. Both his wealth and his seat on the council had opened doors for him to court the best planters' daughters on the island. What was worse than piracy to Emerald was her suspicion that Sir Jasper smuggled slaves on the Spanish Main.

"If you're speaking of Sir Jasper, then the governor and his officials should be told he's befriending an enemy ship," she said stiffly.

"'Tis my suspicion some on the council has dipped hands with Jasper in the slavin' pot. An' they'd be swifter than a viper to cover their slimy tracks if called on it by the governor."

142

"It's unthinkable the governor's own council would secretly cover expenses for a Dutch slave ship!"

He scratched under his periwig. "Sink me, gal, all things ain't as breezy as they first appear 'neath the fine taffetas of the Parliament gents. Why, Captain Foxworth thinks it was the slavers in the London Parliament pressured King Charlie to go to war with Holland."

She looked at him, scandalized. "Baret said that?"

"Sure now, he did indeed. I heard him speakin' so to your father on Tortuga. What's more, your father be agreein'. Captain Foxworth says some in the royal family itself wanted this war."

"The royal family!"

"Some are up to their jewels in the muck 'n mire of slavin'. The merchants want the African trade routes and forts, and they pressured the king to deliberately send an English vessel to attack the Dutch in Africa."

The idea was astounding and so totally unrighteous that Emerald could only stare at him indignantly, as though Zeddie himself were involved. She frowned. "Deliberately attack the Dutch? When Holland has been through the horrors of the Spanish Inquisition—and still is in some places? How could the king ever agree to turn on a friendly nation who shares the same zeal for the Reformation?"

His birdlike eye blinked rapidly in her direction. "Maybe 'cause some has the zeal for the wealth of this world more'n they have for the Lord's truth. Slavin' brings the English merchants filthy lucre galore, m'gal. If they boot the Dutch out of the tradin' forts in Africa, then the English merchants and fancy lords in Parliament can monopolize the slave traffic themselves. According to your father, it's the reason Lord Felix came to Port Royal. He's a Spanish sympathizer for one cause—filthy lucre. Just like the secretary of state, Lord Arlington, who's a force behind the Peace Party in London. An' here in Jamaica, Sir Jasper with his fancy taffetas and his ruby ring."

She looked toward the gray ship without a flag.

Zeddie cocked his head in its direction. "I'm thinkin' they expect to sell them slaves to the Spaniards. They're always in want of more to replace them who die of the sweating sickness on the tobacco farms and silver mines."

Now that Zeddie had brought up the possibility, Emerald

found herself in agreement with his conclusions. "So that's why the sentry at Fort Charles didn't seem concerned about letting in a ship that doesn't fly its national flag. They'd already been told to let her pass."

He snorted. "It's plain to see the Jamaican Council is lookin' the other way."

Minette folded her arms stubbornly and leaned back against the buggy seat, her limpid eyes sparking. "I'm feeling no sympathy for either side, be they English or Dutch, seein' as how I'm not forgettin' my mother was a chieftain's daughter and hunted down in Guinea and brought here. Not that France is any better when it comes to selling slaves."

When it came to the greed of the unregenerate heart, Minette was correct, thought Emerald sadly. The sin of selling men like beasts was shared by most of the European nations, and it went beyond the European to include the African himself, as difficult as that was to comprehend. Her father had told her that many chieftains, brutal as the white man who brought the chains, worked with the slavers to betray other tribes with whom they were at war, in order to gain tribal supremacy themselves.

Tears welled in her eyes. Men were blind enough in their own sin to willingly hunt down those Christ had died to save, and chain them like beasts in the filthy holds of slave ships to sell as work animals.

She would bring them the liberating words of the gospel. *If I love Him, I will do all I can to bring them to worship Him*, she promised with renewed determination.

The sky was a warm wash of turquoise against which the palm trees cut green patterns, and from somewhere high among their fronds wild parrots were squawking. The familiar houses and shops crowded tightly together along the edge of town, rising so perilously near the water's edge that their pilings, though driven deep into sand, would shift at the first tremor of an earthquake.

"Zeddie, look—over in the square!" And dismay showed in Emerald's eyes at the scene that confronted them.

Minette anxiously leaned forward for a better look. "Slavers!"

"Aye, not a pretty sight to behold," warned Zeddie. "We best get from here," and he flicked the reins to speed their horse to a faster trot.

Emerald caught his arm. "No, stop the buggy." And a look of both anger and pity was etched on her face. "I want to see and know, so I will never forget. So I will never lose my determination to one day fight such evil on Foxemoore. You too, Minette," she said softly. "Remember, it was here that Ty was branded just two months ago."

"I haven't forgotten what they did to my brother," said Minette darkly. "I've seen it happen again many times in my nightmares."

"M'gal," Zeddie pleaded, "don't look. What good will it do ye both to see such odious happenings?"

But Emerald took hold of Minette's arm and directed her gaze. "See that African woman, Minette? She might have been your mother when she first arrived."

Minette's breath caught with a broken sob at the sight, and she jerked her head away.

The black woman was naked from the waist up. Beside her, a naked boy child stood staring blankly at the buying audience in the square. He wrapped his fingers around his mother's knee and began to wail as the slaver approached with a rope.

"You!" he shouted at the woman. "Get down. There's a planter bought you and the boy! Take 'em away! Come, move!"

Zeddie had reluctantly stopped the buggy on a wide, cobbled space facing the sea. Emerald's gaze swept the guard of red-coated militia drawn up to keep order in the crowd of planters and merchants. She tensed on the buggy seat when she saw a tall man in a Panama hat, a *seegar* between his teeth. Red hair curled about wrestlerlike shoulders beneath a sweat-stained canvas shirt. His long brown arms were bare and swelled with hard muscle.

"Zeddie, isn't that Mr. Pitt?"

Zeddie followed her troubled gaze. "Aye, it's the rat-toothed overseer to be sure, m'gal."

"I wonder what *he's* doing here," said Emerald uneasily, drawing her skirts toward her. She watched Lady Sophie Harwick's overseer move like a stalking tiger up and down the line of African men for sale.

It had been Mr. Pitt who had arranged for Ty to be branded as a runaway slave and then placed in the town pillory. Emerald recalled the payoff of jewels that Pitt had demanded from her in order to save her cousin from the fate that had trapped him in the end. Now her eyes reflected the righteous anger she felt at the sight of the big supervisor. The family decision to make Pitt overseer had tasted doubly bitter to Emerald because the man had replaced her father on Foxemoore.

Minette too watched Pitt with flashing eyes. "He'll need to buy 'em all if he expects to replace the men he had hung after the uprising."

Emerald remembered

The day before the uprising had begun, Lord Felix Buckington had married Cousin Geneva and thus gained a double share in the sugar plantation. Felix would be a strong voice on Foxemoore as well as in the governor's Council for Jamaican Affairs, and according to what she knew of Baret's uncle, he held no sympathy for slaves. As Zeddie had said, Lord Felix was involved with men in London who wished to expand slave trade on the Main.

She watched Mr. Pitt inspect the lineup of slaves, and her skin crawled with disgust. "Judgment from God will visit us," she murmured. "How can it be otherwise?"

"Aye," Zeddie's voice rumbled in his throat. "An' I'm thinkin' the slave uprising on Foxemoore was only the beginning."

"He's seen us," whispered Minette.

Emerald tensed as Mr. Pitt shouldered his muscled frame through the crowd on the square. She gripped her parasol. "He has the bitter gall to try to speak to me?!" She turned to look straight ahead. "Ride on, Zeddie."

But Pitt intercepted them by stepping out in front of the buggy. He seized the harness and bit and held the horse's head steady. A whinny sounded.

Emerald winced at the pain in the horse's cry and leaned forward on the seat. She snatched up the whip and threatened Pitt with it. "Let go of my horse!"

The overseer grinned, his leathery-brown face amused, as his pale eyes boldly took her in. He patted the horse. "Say now, it's a right pretty afternoon, Miss Emerald, an' a fine day for hobnobbing. Calm your ruffled feathers. You and me are old friends."

"Since when did my father or any of us ever consider you a friend? Step aside!"

"Still high and mighty, ain't you? Heard all about your cozy little voyage aboard the *Regale* with Cap'n Foxworth."

Her heart sank at the veiled suggestion in his tone, but she wouldn't give him the satisfaction of seeing her wince.

"Heard you slept nigh a month in his cabin."

Zeddie's big dueling pistol slipped from the purple leather baldric over his chest and glinted bold and silver-barreled in the sunlight as he aimed it straight at the overseer.

"Out of the way, ye jackanapes, before your innards splatter like ripe melon seeds on the cobbles!"

Pitt's malevolent eyes darted from Emerald to fix on the steady pistol.

"You heard him," she said.

"You won't stay so high and mighty for long," Pitt said, but he stepped back in the direction of the square.

Zeddie flicked the whip, and the horse started with a jump, causing the buggy to lurch. She caught herself on the seat and looked over her shoulder at Pitt, who stood watching them resentfully.

So the spiteful gossip was already stirring. If Pitt knew, then so did everyone else on Foxemoore and everyone in Port Royal, including Cousin Lavender and her friends.

"Don't pay him any mind, Emerald," soothed Minette. "Pitt has an evil imagination. He'll need to eat his words when your betrothal to the viscount is announced."

Zeddie slowed the buggy. "Aye, I wish to see his face when he learns ye'll be a countess."

Emerald said nothing. A sick feeling stirred in her stomach. Neither Minette nor Zeddie's confidence matched her own.

"'Twill please Sir Karlton no end should you go and marry his lordship sooner than first bargained. Say, before England, is my guess. With his lordship's shares of Foxemoore added to what ye'll receive from your father, ye'll be crackin' the whip as the true overseer of Foxemoore." Zeddie chuckled over his thoughts and didn't appear to notice her gravity. "I'd like to see his face when ye send him out to cut cane with the same slaves he's whipped for his pleasure!"

His words slowly warmed her dull and frozen spirits. "When *I* send him?" she repeated dazedly.

Zeddie's eye twinkled under the periwig. "Ye'll be ridin'

high, m'gal. It's as plain as can be, I'm thinkin'. Seems to me that Captain Foxworth is bound to own a hefty portion of Foxemoore, seein' as how he's the earl's full-blooded grandson. Together, ye and Baret will own more'n Lord Felix and Lady Geneva put together!" He looked at her. "Says to me that will put you in position to do on Foxemoore much what you want."

She stared at him.

He winked. "An' with the arrogant and testy Captain Foxworth backin' ye up—who is stoppin' you?"

"Oooh," moaned Minette and held her arms tightly against her as though awesome thoughts gave her goose bumps. "He's right, Emerald. If his lordship decides to stand behind you, why—why, we both can walk about in silk with our heads high."

Caution restrained Emerald, and she was swift to dampen their excitement. "I'm not Lady Buckington yet. And Baret has the opposition of Lord Felix to contend with. I don't think I'll be telling Lady Sophie to send Pitt packing to the cane fields any time soon, though the idea of firing him brings joy."

Until now Emerald hadn't wasted time even thinking of what her share of Foxemoore would possibly allow her to do if she did marry Baret. Now the contemplation of how much they would own was staggering. She picked up her fan and cooled her face.

Zeddie seemed certain Baret owned a good deal more than he had ever mentioned. Did he still own it after displeasing his grandfather? True, he was heir to the earldom, but Baret had intimated that his grandfather was close to disinheriting him. Lavender had told her the same thing. Yet Baret must own much if Lavender wished to marry him.

The family had been adamantly against his taking to the Caribbean as a buccaneer. She didn't think matters had changed recently. If anything, Baret was in more difficulty with his grandfather than ever. And if Baret's suspicions about his uncle were true, Felix would surely be scheming to turn the earl against Baret in order to assume title and inheritance.

She glanced at Zeddie from under the shade of her parasol. "I don't know how much of Foxemoore Baret owns. Nor is he likely to get it as long as he insists on remaining a pirate."

And, she thought, *there are few things important enough to Baret for him to give up the Caribbean in order to win.*

11

LADY LAVENDER THAXTON, ADVERSARY

Her father's abandoned lookout house faced the Caribbean. Resembling an old lighthouse, it awaited her homecoming with a foreboding silence that Emerald was certain she could feel within its high, narrow walls. The structure's plank flooring creaked beneath the floral rug under her feet, while the one overriding sound was the slapping water against its foundational pilings, sunk deep in sand.

As sunlight invaded through the door she had left standing open for fresh air, a wharf rat lumbered away to safety in a dark cranny next to the steep wood steps that led up to the top chamber. Emerald grimaced her loathing for the furry creature, and her eyes scanned the front room in search of more lurking about.

Things certainly clashed here, she thought. A cheap rattan chair, with one leg lopsided from nibbling insects, sat beside an intricately carved mahogany desk taken from a cabin on some Spanish treasure galleon. She laid her pretty silk parasol on the desktop, then jumped as Minette squealed and retreated toward the door.

Her cousin pointed disdainfully to the floor. A two-inch-long cockroach sped across the planks and disappeared between the cracks. "There's a thousand, if I'd waste time counting," said Minette with a mouth that quivered. "You know how I hate 'em, and I won't go into the cookhouse to make tea."

Troubled by her own load of burdens, Emerald tore off her bonnet and tossed it on the desk beside the parasol. "Then call Zeddie. He simply flicks them aside."

Minette rubbed her arms and returned to the door to look down the outside flight of steps. "He's taking the buggy to Queen Street to see if Miss Geneva is at the new town house like you said. And if she is, do you think she'll appeal to the governor?"

Emerald couldn't bring herself to believe Geneva would turn completely against Karlton.

"For all Geneva's indifference toward me, she does have affection for my father. So does Lady Sophie. Oh, Minette, I'm too weary to think now. I'm famished for a strong cup of tea. And raid the jelly cabinet too, will you? There should still be a tin of honey there, and flour too. We can fry those good cakes Jonah used to make for our afternoon supper. And make them crispy, the way I like them."

Minette folded her arms and drew back. "That old sack of flour is sure to be full 'em by now."

"Never mind—I'll do it," Emerald suggested with a bravery she didn't feel and, with a sacrificial attitude born from weariness, started toward the back of the house. She paused after a few steps and looked over her shoulder, hoping to see Minette's expression of guilt. But her cousin had turned her head and was looking below.

Emerald's mouth turned ruefully, and she'd once again started for the tiny cookhouse that Jonah had built on the wharf, when Minette called, "Wait—someone's coming. A fancy carriage stopped below."

Emerald sped back to Minette's side, heart in her throat. "Oh, no! The officials?"

A vision of the filthy jail teeming with lice sent her heart pounding. *Please, Lord,* she prayed urgently, *Don't let them lock me up there! Please!*

"It's Lavender," whispered Minette, shocked.

"Lavender!" Emerald's fear washed away to surprise, then to a mounting concern all its own.

"I wonder what Miss Fancy Hairdo wants, comin' here," said Minette, watching the woman who had stepped from the pretty carriage and stood looking toward the porch.

Emerald drew in a silent breath, and her fingers brushed a dark curl from her cheek where the wind had blown it. She thought she knew the reason that brought her spoiled and beautiful cousin to see her, and the notion was not a pleasant one.

"Lavender will never help me now," she said thoughtfully.

"When did she *ever* help? She didn't help Ty none, and she's jealous of you because you're prettier than she is."

Vain thoughts of appearance were the last thing on Emerald's mind now.

"I wonder why she's come," Minette said grudgingly.

"Baret Buckington. What else?" Emerald sighed. "How could she have heard about the duel already? Surely Papa didn't mention it on his arrival in town this morning. He'd be so taken up with the charges of the Admiralty, he'd hardly have time."

Minette glanced at her, as though some memory arose unexpectedly to trouble her.

"Uncle Karlton would be as quick as a parrot after a June fly to defend your reputation. An' you know how proud he is of the betrothal. If anyone was to say anything, he would have had time all right."

"Proud?" Emerald scoffed. "Do you call threatening Baret with a duel to force him to marry me something I can lift my head about?"

Minette looked anxiously toward Lavender's carriage. "Something happened between his lordship and Miss Lavender before the duel that—that I forgot to tell you about."

Emerald's gaze swerved from Lavender, walking toward the lookout house, to confront Minette's wide eyes. A strange lurch came to her stomach. "Something happened between Baret and Lavender. Something you didn't tell me about."

Minette cast a quick glance below.

"Vapors! She's got a madder look on her snobby face than two wharf cats bickerin' over a fish."

Emerald caught her arm and pulled her into the room.

"Ouch, Emerald—"

"Quickly, tell me before she comes."

"She—she went and married another of your cousins. You remember that lord named Grayford?"

Emerald stared at her. *"What?* You're certain? She married the stepson of Felix?"

Minette swallowed and nodded firmly, her lustrous tangle of ringlets bouncing.

The silence enclosed Emerald like an iron casing. A hundred thoughts rampaged through her mind. "But why?" she whispered. "Why?"

Minette opened her mouth, then looked toward the door as Lavender's slippers sounded on the flight of outer steps.

Emerald's hands dropped from Minette's arm, and they both stepped back, drawing in breaths, when a moment later Lady Lavender Thaxton's poised and elegant form stood framed in the doorway. Her flaxen hair was arranged in coquettish curls. Her blue eyes regarded Emerald with icy scorn.

Emerald lifted her head slightly, trying to muster her own fleeing poise. *I'm a daughter of the King,* she reminded herself. *I've no reason to feel inferior.* Nevertheless, she did, and she felt frustrated with herself as her dignity seemed to abandon her.

Minette turned and started for the back. "I'll—I'll make some Dutch tea," she said breathlessly and disappeared, as though cockroaches were preferred to the overwhelming shadow of the future duchess.

Emerald stood there, her eyes locked with Lavender's chilling gaze. The trade wind, which arose each afternoon, gripped the siding facing the bay and gave it a jerk, as if to say, "I can easily shake you into a bundle of sticks to float away on the waves."

"You've heard about your father's arrest?"

"Yes. And he's innocent. I must speak at once to Geneva—or even Aunt Sophie."

"I doubt that will be possible. And Karlton is no more innocent of piracy then you are of being 'abducted' by Baret. It would be laughable, if I didn't pity you. The whole of the better families in Port Royal and Saint Jago are talking."

"They would. More's the pity they don't have more valuable things to do with their lives than to gossip about me and my father."

Lavender smiled condescendingly. "They do. The planters are getting ready for the war and yowling to Governor Modyford about the need to bring the buccaneers back to protect Jamaica."

"They'd be a bunch of fools to risk your stepfather's gallows."

"Oh—" she gave a wave of her hand "—you mean Felix. That's what I came about, but it can wait a few minutes." Lavender's limpid blue eyes ran over her, taking in the lovely folds of satin and lace. "Why, Emerald, dear," came the now poisonously sweet voice, "at least no one in Jamaica—or London—could accuse you of not *looking* like a real lady. Alas, appearances aren't everything." Her cold eyes met Emerald's.

Emerald winced before she could hide her reaction to the verbal slap.

Lavender saw and smiled, satisfied. She brushed through the door and past her, glancing about with disdain. "What a filthy place to call a home. You should have stayed on Karlton's boat."

Emerald's anger flared like a live coal. "You might have waited in the family carriage and sent your *slave* to call me."

"What I want to say is best spoken alone." She glanced in the direction where Minette had slipped away. "Is that half-caste cousin of yours gone?"

"Yes, my *cousin* went to make tea."

"I can't stay for tea."

"How'd you know I was here?"

A golden brow arched. "Why—your father has made quite sure everyone knows his precious, darling daughter has returned to Jamaica."

"I didn't know my presence would be greeted with any stir," she said too casually. "Few in the past have paid any notice to the offspring of 'that daughter of a French pirate.'"

Lavender smiled coolly. "You're right. They didn't. There was no cause until now. But you've returned boasting a star feather in your cap. Everyone will soon be talking about how you and your father managed quite cleverly to steal a marriage proposal better suited a daughter of the noble blood."

So she did know.

Emerald struggled to keep her composure, hoping against hope that a blush would not warm her cheeks. "I assure you, Lavender, I didn't try to steal anything from you. If you're speaking of the viscount—"

Lavender interrupted with an impatient lift of her chin. "You're right. You did not 'steal' Baret Buckington from me. There isn't a woman in the West Indies or London could have done that unless I allowed it to happen."

Emerald's feminine pride was stung, and she tried to keep her gaze from Lavender's left hand, where Grayford's wedding ring would glisten if Minette had been right.

"Imagine," said Lavender with a cool laugh, "your father forcing a duel on the grandson of the Earl Nigel Buckington. Why, it's laughable—if it weren't so foolish and tragic. You know, don't you, that neither the earl nor any of the Buckingtons in London will allow you to marry Baret?"

Emerald's heart thudded. "I suppose his lordship can and will marry any woman he chooses."

"What you mean, dear, is that Baret is gallant enough to take pity on you and marry you to save you from the street. You know what they do to little tarts in Massachusetts, don't you?" And her blue eyes turned into icy sapphires. "They brand an 'A' for adultery on their foreheads. Just like your half-caste cousin Ty was branded as a runaway slave."

Emerald sucked in her breath and stared at her, unable to speak.

Lavender's pretty face hardened as she looked pointedly at Emerald's small waist. "I suppose you're expecting his child?"

Emerald stepped backward. "How dare you, Lavender? Nothing has happened between me and Captain Foxworth—"

Lavender shrugged her pale shoulders. "You needn't look so stricken, like some half-sick rabbit. My little question was merely meant to help you."

"Help me! You despise me, although I once thought you were my friend. How little did I realize then that you are only a friend to those you can manipulate to do the things you want."

"Theatrics." She fanned herself with a white silk fan. "I *am* your friend, in spite of all the shameful treachery you heaped against me."

"I've done no wrong. To you or anyone else. I can explain everything, but I know neither you nor the family would listen if I did."

Lavender paced, her silken skirts fluttering. "It's dreadful what you did to me, to *yourself.* Do you think I'm the only one who thinks something happened?"

"Nothing happened, I swear it didn't. Does my Christian faith all these years mean nothing? Do you think I played a game of hypocrisy when I helped Great-uncle Mathias in the singing school? You know above everyone else what Jesus means to me—"

"Oh, do stop such silly chatter. I know nothing of the sort. I suppose you hung about that school because you had nothing finer to do. As soon as a good-looking man came about, you were ready to leave it all, hoping to trap him. That's why you sneaked aboard his ship. I suppose he was quite shocked when he came to his cabin and found you in his bed."

"It wasn't like that. What have I ever done to make you think so cheaply of me?"

"Never mind—I don't care to hear the lurid details. Aunt Sophie and Geneva are fit to be tied, and of course all the girls have their minds made up."

"It is the way of evil, suspicious minds!" said Emerald, her face hot.

"What do you expect them to think?" Lavender scoffed. "As you said, we know what your mother was. And there's only one reason why Baret would ever promise to marry you. And that's to save you from scandal."

Emerald could have cringed under her appraisal.

"He doesn't love you."

Her confident words were spoken quietly, but they couldn't have hurt Emerald more if she had shouted them. *No, he doesn't love me,* she found herself thinking and was suddenly as angry toward Baret as she was toward Lavender.

"He loves me," said Lavender calmly. "He always has, and he always will."

Emerald desperately wished she could say otherwise.

Lavender smiled a little. "He took pity on you is all. You and Karlton will privately be the laughingstock of all Jamaica and London. A duel! Imagine Karlton threatening him to save your *honor.* Poor Baret! Wherever he'd go when he returns to his title, people in London would look at him with pity."

Emerald's hands closed tightly into fists behind her back. "You're wrong," she said stiffly and lifted her chin at an attempt at dignity. "He wants to marry me. He said so."

Instead of getting angry, Lavender gave a small laugh. "Did he say that? Darling Baret—how unnecessarily cruel I've been to him. And I shouldn't have. After all, he could have just about any woman he wanted in England." She sighed.

Emerald came alert and scanned her. "At what are you hinting?"

Lavender looked innocent. "You mean you don't know?"

Emerald wanted to squirm under the victorious gaze.

"Baret was dreadful not to tell you."

The suggestion was cutting. There was something important he hadn't thought enough of her to explain.

"Tell me what?"

155

Lavender held out her left hand. In the sunlight streaming from the open doorway, diamonds and red rubies sprang up like blended fire.

Emerald stared at the engagement ring. *Not from Baret?* she thought, with a sick feeling.

"I'm engaged to marry Grayford," said Lavender in a grave voice. "I would have married him a month ago, except that this miserable war with the Dutch had to happen now. Grayford is assigned duty with Lieutenant-governor Edward Morgan to attack Curaço. So the marriage was delayed."

Emerald's eyes rushed to her cousin's for an explanation.

Lavender looked suddenly weary, as though the trials of life were dreadfully heavy for her magnolia-white shoulders. "I was angry at Baret. I sent a letter to him through Sir Erik Farrow, telling him I had already married Grayford. Of course, at the time, I had thought I *would* marry him, immediately, but . . ." Her sapphire eyes gleamed as they fixed on Emerald's face. "Now I may see things differently after all," she said with a little bite to her voice.

Emerald shook her head, stunned. "Are you saying you broke your engagement with the viscount?"

"Yes. And naturally, I hurt him. Perhaps I was too hasty. It seems he turned to you on the rebound. A dreadful mistake for both of you. He doesn't love you," she repeated. "And while you may be an attractive girl, you're certainly wrong for Baret. You'd never make a countess! It's silly and foolish of you and him to even contemplate such a thing."

Emerald's self-esteem lay in rags about her feet. The words spoken so casually and yet so bluntly stung her as painfully as any made by a whip to her flesh.

So Baret had already known Lavender was to marry Lord Grayford. No—he thought she had *already* married him. So that was why he was willing to accept her father's demands in place of a duel. *Baret had been hurt and had stepped out recklessly in his anger and grief to get back at Lavender by agreeing to marry me.*

Emerald's nails dug into her palms. He had treated her as carelessly as a man could treat a woman. He had left her on stage alone to face the jeering crowd and to feel the stones they hurled against her. Lavender was right. He didn't care anything about her.

156

I've been a fool, she thought. *I should have known better.* As though to mock her, some words spoken by Baret aboard the *Regale* came back with underlining clarity. In suggesting she'd been foolish to trust Jamie Bradford, Baret had perhaps suggested his own thoughts as well. He had said, "A word of advice—never believe a man's vow until you've known him long enough to see he means it. A rogue will promise anything."

Lavender was watching, her eyes sparkling with satisfaction. "If I were you," she said more gently, "I wouldn't show my face at Foxemoore just yet. All Karlton's talk about your marrying a viscount—in the end the words will turn and bite you, leaving you more pain and shame."

Emerald could not believe she was hearing herself say firmly, "He meant every word he spoke to me. And I will marry him."

Lavender seemed taken aback. For a moment she said nothing and simply scanned her, as though judging the danger of an opponent.

"I've done nothing to be ashamed of," said Emerald, "and I won't cringe about with my head hung low. The Lord knows I'm innocent, and He'll give me the courage to face all the chatterboxes who love to hear gossip, even when they know what they're saying is lies."

"All your Bible reading won't convince anyone." Lavender swept past her to the door, then turned back. "I won't give Baret up, Emerald. I was rash and made a mistake when I sent him that angry letter. Somehow I'll make him understand."

Emerald tensed, her anger rising. "It means nothing to you to hurt someone. What will you do—reject Grayford with another terse note? You're quite good at writing them, I suppose."

"How I tell Grayford is no concern of yours. I'll work it out and explain everything to both of them." Her eyes softened. "I don't want to hurt him—or you. But you must understand, Emerald, Baret and I are meant for each other. We always were. And he couldn't have meant the outcome of that duel on Tortuga any more than I meant the letter I sent to him. I was hurt and angry. And Baret must have been feeling the same when he agreed to your father's outlandish blackmail."

"And I suppose you also don't take seriously the breaking of your vow to Lord Grayford. Or the engagement ring you wear," said Emerald a little bitterly.

157

"I shall return it at the appropriate time. Baret will understand."

"You're so confident he'll listen."

"And I can't believe you seriously think to hold him to a vow he didn't mean or to a marriage he doesn't want with a woman he doesn't love. I would expect you to have more pride then that. Unless having Karlton hold a pistol on Baret all the way to the wedding is of value to you?"

Emerald flushed. "You needn't worry, Cousin Lavender. I've more respect for the seriousness of a marriage vow before God then to hold a dueling pistol to my husband-to-be's head. If Baret does not wish to marry me—then—then he can tell me so."

Lavender seemed satisfied. "I'm pleased you're mature enough to see it that way. I'm certain Baret will. And both of us will see to it you're well taken care of, if it comes to your reputation. We'll pay your upkeep, either in London or here in Port Royal."

Emerald's heart thudded, heavy with pain. "I want nothing from you or Baret Buckington. I can take care of myself, thank you. And don't forget, I've naught to be ashamed of, either here or in England. My father owns a share in Foxemoore, and the bungalow belongs to me and Minette."

"Of course. I was only thinking you might wish for a new start somewhere else. If not England, then the American colonies."

How easily she dismissed her. Like some shameful relative to be packed off and hidden from scrutiny!

"My life's plans are not so easily redirected. Whatever God has for me, it won't be cloaked with the appearance of evil. I intend to serve Him one day, and my reputation will be free of whispers. I'll go to England to school as planned—and after that I intend to come home to Foxemoore to carry on the work of Uncle Mathias."

Lavender looked offended. "I should think after the uprising and the death of my mother and Mathias, you wouldn't even consider stirring up the fires of rebellion again. But we won't discuss that now. Look, Emerald, I've no more time to talk. I wanted you to know where things stood, and now you know. So I'll be returning to Government House. There's talk of Governor Modyford recalling the buccaneers from Tortuga for the war.

There'll be a ball next week, and I expect Baret to be there to work for the good of England with Grayford. If you are wise, you won't show at Government House. You'll save face and be on that ship for London."

"That's exactly what I intend to do. And if you think Baret will show himself at a ball, you don't know the half of things. Lord Felix is bent on Baret's arrest for piracy. What do you expect to do about that? Or are you willing to risk your own reputation to marry a pirate?"

She took perverse enjoyment in seeing the flash of alarm on Lavender's face. So then! Lavender hadn't realized what a rogue Baret really was—or how much risk he was in!

Emerald smiled crookedly. "You want Baret Buckington Foxworth, Cousin Lavender? It may be that in breaking your engagement to Lord Grayford, you'll end up with a roguish buccaneer for a husband instead of a future earl. Then what will you do?"

Lavender's eyes narrowed. "I don't care what Baret is. If having him back means marrying a buccaneer—then I'll do it. Anything to keep—" She stopped as though she had nearly said too much.

Emerald folded her arms. "Anything to keep me from having him?"

Lavender tilted her head, her golden hair shining in the sunlight. "There aren't many women who'd care if he did have a somewhat unsavory reputation. He's still got the blood of the earl of Essex, and Baret will yet inherit everything from his grandfather, despite the wishes of his uncle."

Emerald looked at her, alert. "So you know about Lord Felix's schemes."

"That he wishes to inherit title and wealth? Yes, I know. He's not very casual about keeping it masked, is he? No matter. I'm as clever as he, and I have something even Felix doesn't have." She smiled whimsically. "Earl Nigel Buckington thinks especially well of me. He happens to think well of the title of duchess I'm to inherit when my grandmother dies. That, my dear Emerald, is something you will never have to offer. And in the Buckington family it happens to mean more than a sweet face."

Emerald said nothing to that, for she knew the earl would look upon her with horror should his grandson ever truly wish to marry her. "What will the earl say when you break your engagement to Grayford? I don't suppose he'll be pleased. And unless Baret salvages his reputation soon, the earl won't want you to marry him is my guess."

In seeing Lavender's response, Emerald sensed she had touched a raw nerve.

"No," she admitted dully, "Earl Nigel doesn't want me to marry Baret. And that's why I won't simply break the engagement to Grayford right now, though I'd like to do so. I will need time to work matters out. Baret, of course, will help me."

"You're certain of that?"

"I will make certain of it."

"If he comes here, he'll be arrested for piracy and hang."

"I will see that he doesn't hang."

"It doesn't matter that my father may meet such a fate?"

"Karlton won't hang either," she said and, turning away, walked out onto the porch.

Emerald listened to her cousin's footsteps die away as she descended the wooden steps to her waiting carriage. She became aware of how exhausted emotionally she was and how dull her hopes and spirits. She walked to the stairs that led to her father's upper chamber and sank to the lower step, mindless of the rat she had seen earlier.

Whether moments or minutes passed she did not know, but she stirred when she realized that Minette was standing beside her, a hand on the railing. Minette's eyes reflected sympathy. She had probably overheard part of the conversation.

"I'm sorry, Emerald. She was mean and hateful. Pay her no mind. Captain Foxworth has a mind of his own. An' I feel sure he isn't the poor, brokenhearted lover she tries to make out. If he hadn't wanted to accept Uncle Karlton's ultimatum, he isn't the kind of man who would have done it."

Emerald rejected the pain festering in her heart. "Maybe," she said with an attempt at indifference. "But he's as much to blame for my embarrassment as Lavender. He knew all along she had broken her engagement. And he was under the belief she had already gone ahead and married Lord Grayford. Baret's a scoundrel! And I won't forgive him easily."

Minette winced. "It's my fault too, 'cause I knew about the letter back then."

Emerald looked up at her. "You *what*? You knew, and you didn't tell me while we were at Tortuga?"

Minette squirmed. "I'm sorry. I heard the gossip, but I guess I was so wrapped up with my own problems with Sir Erik that it slipped my mind."

Emerald stood and faced her. Then, seeing Minette's unhappiness, she sighed. "It doesn't matter. Baret didn't forget, you can be certain of that. Oh, Minette! I almost convinced myself he did care for me."

"He does, I can tell. Maybe even he doesn't know just how much himself—yet. But he will. You'll see. Why, I'll wager he turns Lady Thaxton down as smoothly as warm honey. He'll tell her he loves you and is going to marry you as planned."

Emerald, in frustration, walked to the open doorway and looked out toward the glittering green bay. Her eyes filled with tears, and she blinked them back quickly before Minette saw them. "No. He loves her, though why is a mystery to me. She's as mean-spirited a woman as I've ever met. And conceited too."

"He doesn't know what she's really like."

"Love, they say, is blind," murmured Emerald, leaning against the doorjamb wearily. "He won't see it unless he wants to. And there isn't a woman in Port Royal who can behave as sweet and helpless and Christian-spirited, when she wants to, as Lady Lavender Thaxton! It wouldn't surprise me if she doesn't pretend to become suddenly deathly ill just to gain his sympathy. She's done it before, and Baret has fallen for it. She wraps him around her dainty finger when she wants to. Oh—" her hands knotted into fists "—what I wouldn't tell him if I could."

"If you get mad at him, you'll only drive him into her arms," said Minette sagely. "What you need do, Emerald, is show yourself twice the Christian girl Lavender isn't. And you are, too. She brags about being a duchess someday. So what? is my answer. She doesn't care about the slaves or the singing school. She wouldn't do a thing for any of them if she were mistress." Her eyes reflected pain. "I heard her call me 'that half-caste.'"

Emerald lingered at the door, her face drawn with weariness. At the moment, there seemed little to say that would salve her cousin's concerns, or her own. "She thinks no better of me. It hurts when those we wish to esteem us as valuable do not. We can remember how God's Son willingly paid an infinite price to buy us from the slave market of sin. Let's seek to find our sense of worth in His estimation."

Minette's eyes moistened. "You know, Emerald, when there ain't anyone else and I feel all alone, I find a joy floods my heart when I think of Jesus. Maybe—maybe things will work out after all. About Uncle Karlton, about us, about everything. D'ye suppose it will?"

Emerald tried to smile, even while her wounded heart fought against the optimism. "Sure it will."

There came a strained moment of silence between them, and each looked away as if by mutual agreement.

"The first thing we'll do is pray and trust," said Emerald. "And you know the next thing I'm going to do?"

"Unpack Uncle Mathias's Bible?" asked Minette hopefully.

"Yes, that too." Emerald's eyes unexpectedly glimmered with humor. "However, the next thing is to win a great battle."

When Minette looked bewildered, Emerald managed a laugh. "I won't allow a rat or a cockroach to keep me from enjoying that cup of tea."

Minette laughed too. "After all we've been through, we deserve it."

12

AT THE TOWN HOUSE
ON QUEEN STREET

The afternoon trade wind flooded in through the open front door of the lookout house and lifted the hem of Emerald's skirts, showing the cream-lace crinoline border. But the cooling wind did not soothe her fevered emotions. She sat wearily on the steps facing the door, her head resting against the rail, her musings causing upheaval.

Her father wasn't the only man on Tortuga who took unfair advantage of a situation. So did Baret Buckington, she thought. He was willing to place her emotions at risk because he thought Lavender had jilted him and married his cousin. He was angry and acted on the rebound. *At my expense.*

She held her cup of tea between both palms, feeling its warmth, thinking that she shouldn't allow herself to be hurt by this turn of events. She should have been realistic enough to know that nothing could come of a betrothal forced by dueling pistols! How could it be otherwise? Did God honor duels or a vow that was forced from a man?

"I won't let this make me bitter," she murmured to Minette. "If anything, I had it coming to me. If I hadn't deceived my father, if I hadn't sought to run away with Jamie, I wouldn't have ended up on Baret's ship. None of this would have happened."

While she had already confessed her willfulness and knew the Lord had forgiven her folly, she must endure the painful consequences. Bad decisions yielded an unhappy harvest. Her one hope was in a God who was good, who could use even her mistakes to benefit her maturity. Again, she committed herself anew to His purposes. She would choose to believe that the best would yet come her way.

The dream had been her father's, and it was he who had wrangled the marriage commitment from Baret. And yet, when she had told Baret so, he had seemed to dismiss it. The notion

163

that Baret would allow himself to be drawn back so quickly to Lavender's arms hurt much more than she had anticipated.

I should be thankful this sad situation will be brought to a swift end, she lectured herself bravely. What if it had been allowed to linger on through her years of schooling in London?

"I don't love Baret." And she took a drink of tea to swallow back the iron fingers that pinched her throat. "I don't love him," she repeated firmly. "I won't allow it. Now I can go to England with my mind set on one thing. To become all I can be in order to carry on the work of Uncle Mathias."

Shutting the door to her awakened emotions was not easily done, however. She closed her eyes, tried to dismiss his memory, to refuse the thought of his past embrace, his kiss.

I told him not to do it, she thought in a moment of anger.

"He's a rogue anyway," she said to Minette. "Let Lavender have him."

Minette wore a dismal expression as she sat in the wicker chair, her feet drawn up beneath her calico skirts while she dully munched on English tea biscuits that she had found in a tin in the jelly cabinet.

Emerald could see that her cousin wasn't convinced. Finishing her tea, she looked toward the open doorway.

"I feel sorry for Lord Grayford," said Minette. "That's the third man Lavender's dug her feline claws into."

"What do you mean?"

"Sir Erik," said Minette shortly. "He was expecting to marry her too."

Emerald fixed her with a searching gaze, for the idea of the buccaneer Farrow in love with Lavender came as a total surprise. Captain Farrow seemed to be a man who guarded his emotions more carefully than did even Baret Buckington.

"Hoped to marry her?" Emerald repeated, her voice suggesting the absurdity of that notion. "That's about as farfetched an idea as my marriage to the earl's grandson. Whatever gave you the idea that he thought Lavender might marry *him?* You know how she'll inherit her grandmother's title."

Minette swatted at a sand fly. "It's only her title and money they all want. I don't see what any of 'em see in her, she's so spoiled and ill-tempered."

"How could Captain Farrow expect to get anywhere with Lavender?" Emerald pursued curiously.

Minette shrugged, frowning. "The viscount's uncle promised."

"Felix? Why would he promise such a thing?"

"He hired Sir Erik to discover the plans of the viscount and report them back to Lord Felix."

"How is it you knew all this and didn't tell me?"

Minette looked as if she were about to defend herself but instead unexpectedly lapsed into silence by biting into the shortbread. Under Emerald's gaze, she looked away.

Suspicious now, Emerald grew more uneasy. "Who told you Captain Farrow expected to marry Lavender?"

"I learned it aboard Sir Erik's ship. Before we rendezvoused at Monkey Bay. I was aboard when Captain Buckington arrived with Rafael. They had a big meeting that night about the treasure of the *Prince Philip*. And they signed articles together to share in the booty. When I was leaving Captain Farrow's ship, his slave told me there was only one woman who had ever turned the head of his captain and that was Lavender. In the longboat he told me about the letter she sent to Captain Buckington through Sir Erik."

"You mean the letter telling him that she had married Lord Grayford?"

Minette nodded. "Lavender was mean and hateful to Captain Buckington. She accused him of running off with you. She'd married his cousin, so she said, to get even. Captain Buckington crumpled up the letter and threw it away. The slave found it."

Emerald stiffened. It was as Lavender had said. *And then he decided to marry me at my father's insistence.*

Minette stood, frowning. "I'm sorry, Emerald. I didn't mean to forget to tell you. Even Uncle Karlton didn't know, but maybe he's found out now."

Emerald didn't think it would make much difference to her father. It was marriage to the viscount he wanted, regardless of the means. She inspected the open doorway, hoping her expression did not betray her. It was true that her father had taken advantage of him, but why hadn't Baret told her about Lavender's marriage?

She recalled their last moments together on Tortuga at the Sweet Turtle.

"Have you forgotten your vow to Lavender?" she had asked and had seen his jaw tighten. At that response, she should have been more cautious.

"I have not forgotten," he had stated. "We'll not discuss that now."

Emerald's eyes flickered. She rose from her seat on the step and set her empty cup on the desk. No wonder he hadn't wanted to discuss Lavender. *He didn't want me to know he was agreeing to marry me because he thought she was now Lady Grayford.* How easily he dismissed me, she thought. *"We won't discuss that now. You'll be sent to England as I agreed upon with your father. I have a war to fight. A few years growing up will benefit you."*

Emerald envisioned Baret's surprised pleasure when he should learn that Lavender hadn't gone through with the wedding after all. What would he do when he realized she was available again? Would he come rushing back and risk arrest?

Lavender was the one woman who could get by with rashly breaking her engagement to Baret in order to marry Lord Grayford, then admit her mistake and ask for Baret's forgiveness! Naturally, he'd wish to pursue her again. He might feel obligated to Emerald for a time, she decided, but departing for England would soon change that.

He'll wonder how he might gently inform me he's changed his mind. Well, if Baret Buckington thinks I'll insist he go through with the marriage, he's wrong. Does he think because my mother was the daughter of a pirate that I have no self-respect? I don't want a man who wants another woman. And I won't let my father force me into such a marriage either.

Thunder rumbled, and the wind from the Caribbean struck the outside wall. The pilings moaned beneath the floorboards, and Emerald listened to the unpleasant sucking sound of water. Light weaved as she carried a half-burned candlestick on a saucer to the topmost room her father amusingly called the crow's nest.

The evening was warm and humid, and she had piled her waist-length hair onto her head to keep the heavy, dark strands from sticking to the back of her neck. She stood looking about.

At the wing chair her father had loved to lose himself in, the too-fine, tall secretary reaching toward the ceiling—how had he ever managed to get it up the steps?—the sea trunk stuffed with old clothing and papers from past voyages. Everything appeared just as she had left it two months ago, but her beloved father was not here, her father with the smell of the sea about him and the strong, warm arms that comforted her in her aloneness.

Emerald felt the familiar cramp in her throat. *Please, Lord, don't let the authorities try my father for piracy. He's all I have, all Minette has. If You take his protection away from us, what will we do? What will become of us? Don't leave us orphans.*

"Emerald?"

The voice calling up the steps was Minette's, and Emerald ducked through the small door and stepped out into the tiny alcove to peer over the handrail.

Minette looked up. "Zeddie's come—from going to see Miss Geneva."

Hope leaped into life. "I'll be down!"

Then Geneva *was* at the town house that Lord Felix had built for her. Would Geneva help her in this desperate hour?

When she came down the steps, Zeddie was removing his wet jacket retained from the days he had fought Cromwell. It was faded and patched, yet retained its past dignity. He looked to be in an ill mood.

"Did you leave my letter with the maid?" she asked with breathless expectation.

He snorted. "Sink me! The gal was as sour as lukewarm vinegar. Took one look at me and wouldn't give me a second more to explain things." Impatiently he hung his wet periwig on the peg to dry beside his pistol belt. "Sent me off the porch steps like I was peddling turpentine for his lordship's table!"

Emerald restrained her disappointment. "Did you tell her that the letter was from me—Geneva's niece?"

"Sure now, I tried to hand her the letter, but she was quick to slam the door."

Minette sank onto the hardback chair. "Now what?"

Emerald seized her cloak. "We'll try again. If Geneva is in the house, then I'll go there myself. I'll get in to see her somehow. She must be told about my father."

"You're going there tonight? It's pouring outside. What if she won't see you?"

"I must. If there's anyone who may be able to do something, it's Geneva. Zeddie, you'll need to bring me in the buggy again. Minette, stay here. There's nothing you can do."

"There's no lock on the door anymore. Any rogue could come creepin' about."

Emerald told herself she'd think about the lock tomorrow. Right now, Geneva and her father's dilemma filled her mind.

"I'll stay, but you're going to get drowned in that cloudburst."

Most of the town houses on Queen Street belonged to the largest sugar and cacao magnates. They served Governor Modyford either as royal officers in the militia or on a council seat. It didn't surprise Emerald that Felix would spend as much time here as he did on Foxemoore. His work with the governor and the High Admiralty would normally keep him busy going between Spanish Town, where the inland seat of government was located, and Port Royal, near the opulent Merchant's Exchange.

Emerald had always enjoyed viewing the Exchange from the buggy when coming into town to attend Sunday worship. The building was perhaps the finest in Port Royal. It had a stone gallery adjoining the parish church, which was graced by Doric pillars and a twisted balustrade. There, elegantly shaded from the blazing sun, well-to-do merchants made rich by the merchandise of the buccaneers met to drink rum punch and transact their affairs.

With space a rare commodity, Emerald saw few houses having large front yards or English-style gardens. The streets were all narrow, and even Queen Street, paved with ships' ballast, was no less so. What gardens there were consisted of a few flowering vines and palm trees. Giant red, yellow, and orange five-petaled vine flowers made up for quantity and variety. And even here in town, tiny harmless fruit bats flew about looking for insects.

The Jamaican planters often built their town houses more elaborately than they did the great houses on their inland plantations. Because they could not build wide, they built tall. As Zeddie stopped the buggy by Felix's Spanish-style iron gate, Emerald looked upon a four-story brick house with red tile roof and glazed sashed windows. There seemed to be a number of rooms on each floor, and a cellar. There was also a fine cook room set off by itself in the back. She was certain that the house would be sumptuously furnished. It looked to be one of the finest on Queen Street.

It was still pouring rain, and she was drenched running for cover beneath the porch roof. She knocked loudly while Zeddie found refuge in a swing chair beneath the canopy. When no one answered her knocking, she feared the inhabitants had all retired, but Zeddie pointed out a lantern's glow in an upper window. Bracing herself against the wind, Emerald continued her pounding until she heard a key turn in the lock and the bolt slide back.

A moment later, a young African serving girl, holding a softly glowing lantern and looking as though she were prepared to parrot the refusal that Zeddie had experienced earlier, peered out at her.

But before she could be refused, Emerald, desperate, pushed past her.

"What's you doin', you high-flung—"

"I'm sorry, but it's very important. Please, I must see my father's cousin, Lady Geneva Harwick Buckington."

The girl dubiously eyed her. "Cousin?"

A voice interrupted from the hall shadows near a flight of narrow stairs. "Emerald, is that you?"

That voice!

Emerald turned hopefully as an older woman came forward into the lantern light. Emerald stared into a dignified face with tawny skin drawn taut over well-formed cheekbones. Deep-set brown eyes beneath straight black brows stared back at her. Her blue turban was neatly tied, and several parrot feathers were artfully arranged with colorful beads.

"Zunsia," Emerald said with relief.

She knew that this woman of Carib and French blood had served Geneva loyally for years as personal maid. She had traveled with her to France and England to bring Jette to Jamaica. She had later served in the nursery, looking after Jette. Did this mean the child was here?

A sudden smile drew the woman's lips back from even white teeth. "Miss Emerald, why—was that Zeddie who came earlier? Yasmin turned him away. Gracious, come in. You're soaked. Yas-

169

min, take Miss Emerald's cloak and parasol an' bring a towel an' hot punch too. Then bring Zeddie to the back an' take care of him."

"Yes, ma'am." The girl hastened and took Emerald's wet things, looking apologetic. "I'm sorry, miss. I didn't know who you was."

Zunsia brought her into a room off the small hall and went about lighting candles. "I heard you was back, but I didn't expect you to come."

"Nor did I expect to. I must speak with Geneva tonight. You'll tell her I'm here? Tell her it's about my father."

Zunsia's dark eyes appeared to assess the situation with keen understanding. "I'll tell her. I'll go straight up. She's awake an' reading. You sit an' unload your heart a minute. Yasmin will come with that punch an' a towel to dry you with. I wish I had a suitable change of clothing for you."

Emerald smiled her relief to be among friends. "I'll be all right."

She took brief solace in the comfortable room. When the girl came and poured a cup of sweet citrus tea, she removed her sopping slippers and used the soft towel to dry with. She smoothed her windblown dark curls back into the hair net at the nape of her neck and dried herself as best she could for her audience with Geneva.

Then she absently drank the tea and looked around her with cautious interest. The receiving room appeared to be the lived-in section of a grand chamber, divided by two amber brocaded drapes of heavy fabric edged with silver thread. It was an imposing and lordly house, just as she imagined its master to be, and she felt her heart begin to beat faster.

The walls were paneled mahogany, adorned with tapestries of forest scenes. Heavy furniture was placed in a semicircle, and various tables and stools were intricately carved with hunting hounds and foxes inlaid with silver. Thick cushions were upholstered with black velvet, and the floor was covered with equally plush rugs.

When Zunsia returned, her expression revealed that the matter had not gone well. "You might as well know, child. Miss Geneva's ill. She took sick at Foxemoore a month ago."

170

"It's serious?" said Emerald uneasily, thinking of Felix's first wife.

"I wish we knew. She has these terrible spells of weakness where she can hardly get herself about. Doctor doesn't know its cause, an' his lordship were going to take her to see a specialist in London, then the war stopped their plans to travel. It's the reason that brought us here to the town house. We was leaving with little Jette, an' Miss Lavender too was coming, just as soon as she married Lord Grayford. That too was put in waiting."

Emerald said quickly, hoping her alarm didn't show to Zunsia, "Is Lavender *here?*"

"She's upstairs with Miss Geneva, keeping her company."

"Then—Geneva won't see me?"

"I didn't get opportunity to speak to her. Miss Lavender said she were sleeping."

Naturally Lavender would not wish Geneva to see Emerald.

"I told Miss Lavender it was important about Sir Karlton, but she say it must wait. Geneva's health came first."

Emerald turned away and caught a glimpse of Yasmin eying her curiously.

"You go now," Zunsia told the girl with a look of rebuke.

"Yes, ma'am."

"Did you see to Zeddie's comfort? It's pouring out."

"I'll do it now."

"No, don't bother," said Emerald wearily, turning toward them. "I won't stay if I'm not allowed to see Geneva. I must get back to Minette."

Yasmin bustled out with the tray, and Zunsia showed her concern. "I'm sorry, child. It's that Miss Lavender." Her low voice had taken on veiled dislike. "She has her way with everyone in the family, including Miss Geneva. Lavender can do no wrong, an' it's worse now than it used to be."

Emerald swallowed her disappointment. She entertained a sudden impulse to climb the steps and force her way past Lavender, but she didn't wish to upset Geneva if she was ill.

Zunsia was quick to see her dilemma. "I'll bring Miss Geneva's breakfast while Miss Lavender's asleep. I'll tell her that you came to see her. Do you have a place for the night?"

She told Zunsia about the lookout house, and Zunsia shook

her head. "An unsafe place to be alone with Sir Karlton in the gaol."

"Then you've heard about my father?" she asked uncertainly.

"Everyone's heard."

Emerald didn't see any critical expression and wondered if Zunsia had also heard about her running away to meet Jamie. She decided that she would have heard that gossip also.

"There's smuggling in the area of the lookout house. I heard his lordship talking about it to Sir Jasper. Maybe I can find a place for you with Yasmin if you wouldn't mind—"

"Smuggling?" Emerald came alert, thinking of when Zeddie had told her about Lord Felix and Sir Jasper. "What did you hear them say?"

"Not much. They stopped talking when they saw me. It was something about a Dutch ship."

The door opened, and Emerald turned.

Geneva herself stood there, looking pale but otherwise well in an ivory dressing gown. Her red hair was smoothly drawn into a chignon, and her silvery eyes, much like her cousin Karlton's, revealed her surprise over Emerald's presence. She took in her wet clothing and what must have been, thought Emerald, the unmistakable alarm on her face.

Geneva said, "Leave us now, Zunsia."

Before Emerald could rally, Geneva walked into the room.

"Lavender thought I was asleep. I'm taken aback to see you here, Emerald. After your shameful behavior, I'm surprised you'd have the gall to come to me."

Emerald searched her face for some hopeful sign. "I had no one else," she admitted quietly.

Geneva wavered. "I suppose you think I shall shield you from the scandal you've created, but there's little I can do now. I admit that after the slave uprising I was impressed with your maturity. I had even entertained thoughts of speaking to Sophie about you and seeing well to your future." She walked to a large velvet chair and sank into it. "Needless to say, I was shocked and disappointed when I'd learned you'd run away with an indentured servant. A common thief," she added. "I've since learned he was the brother of the *pirate* they hanged a few months ago."

Emerald could not deny her folly about Jamie. Geneva's words hit hard, but she wondered why Geneva was bringing that

172

up now when it was her father she'd come about. Surely Geneva had heard?

"I made a grave error, and I've paid."

"Indeed? Hardly. Not yet. You will bear your reputation until you're an old woman. And then the young girls will speak of the sprightly old lady who once ran away with a pirate."

Emerald's lips tightened against the pain that pricked her heart. "Then I hope God gives me the grace to not hear them. My reputation, madam, was ruined long before I left Port Royal with the hopes of marrying James Bradford."

"You hoped to marry him? An indentured servant! A pirate?"

"I did not know he was a pirate, madam. Nor did I know his real name was Maynerd."

"Yet you knew he was an indentured servant."

"Who else was I to marry? Did I have opportunity for anything more?"

Geneva waved a hand and sighed, then rested her brow against her hand as though her head ached. "I'm quite aware what your situation was. I had hoped to do something to better things, when you brought ruin to yourself by running away. I don't see what I can do now. You did know the man was wanted for involvement in the slave uprising."

"He was innocent of that. I vow he was."

"It's too late to consider whether he was or not. I suppose he's escaped? I gather you've come to me now to tell me how wrong you were and you wish me to send you home to Foxemoore until Karlton arrives."

Emerald stared at her, confused. She didn't know.

"Perhaps I can speak to Karlton about having you sent to Massachusetts for schooling. At least you'd be away from the gossip. When things have calmed down, I'll see what can be done about arranging a marriage for you. Perhaps with a colonial." She studied her carefully, and Emerald found herself flushing, thinking she knew what Geneva was wondering.

"You are not pregnant? If you are, you will tell me now."

"I did not marry Jamie," she said breathlessly and lifted her head a little higher.

"I did not ask you that."

Emerald lifted her chin. "Then I would not be with child, madam."

Geneva watched her.

In the silence Emerald heard the French clock ticking. She did not lower her gaze.

Geneva sighed, satisfied. "Thank God. Then I will be able to gain you a respectable husband in due time. There is no more to be said on the matter. We'll talk again in a day or two. In the meantime, I'll have a room prepared for you for the night."

Emerald was surprised that she was willing to aid her, having thought the worst. Obviously Geneva did not know that her cousin Karlton was being detained by the High Admiralty—or that Baret Buckington had dueled Levasseur on Tortuga and vowed to marry Emerald!

Emerald walked slowly toward her cousin until she stood in the lantern light closer to the chair. She could see the careworn lines in the once flawless face and the look of unhappiness in her eyes that could not be covered by her dignity. Emerald knelt beside her, her gaze anxiously searching Geneva's.

"I think you do not understand the entire story, madam. Or what has recently happened here in Port Royal. I fear it is not good news, and what I have to say will shock you."

Geneva was watching her, heedful. "Can anything shock me?"

Emerald hastened to cover the awkwardness by saying quietly, "Zunsia told me of your illness, and naturally his lordship would wish to keep back from you anything to cause alarm."

A cynical smile formed on Geneva's mouth. "I'm certain that would be his reason for silence. He has proven a thoughtful husband and is overly concerned about me."

Emerald thought she detected slight irony in her voice, and wondered, but Geneva went on casually enough.

"If you have news I'm not aware of, then I wish to know what it is at once. I am not so ill that I cannot deal with it. I only wonder that Lavender has said nothing to me."

"I am sure, madam, it's because she cares too much for you to worry you now," said Emerald stiffly, for she didn't believe her own words. "There is much to explain. Where shall I begin?"

"You can start at the beginning. And I would like a cup of that tea first, if you'd pour."

Minutes later, while Geneva drank from her cup and watched her, Emerald paced the lush rug and told her cousin everything that had happened, including her abduction from the wharf at Baret's orders. Once or twice she glanced at her, expecting to see shock and was surprised to see only a calm expression and alert interest. She told of the death of Jamie and the pirate Sloane, and how Baret had entered Maracaibo to locate Lucca, the one man who could bear witness to the innocence of his father. And then Geneva interrupted her tale for the first time.

"And Baret continues to think Royce may be alive?"

"He is certain of it. He believes that—" She stopped, catching herself from mentioning Felix in her haste to explain. She must never forget that Felix Buckington was now Geneva's husband. It must be left to Baret to tell Geneva of his involvement, if it proved true.

"Yes? Go on," Geneva said.

"Lucca is dead, but Captain Buckington believes he knows where his father is being held and that he can free him on the next expedition with Henry Morgan."

Geneva leaned forward, anxious. "Who else in the family knows of this beside you and your father?"

Emerald looked down at her. Did Geneva herself wonder about Felix? Could she have rethought Lady Sophie's warnings?

Emerald felt a tightening of her spine, and she glanced toward the closed door. Had she heard quiet footsteps? Evidently Geneva had not heard anything, for she pressed for more information.

"No one else knows," said Emerald.

"It is best they do not."

Emerald felt the moment pass in uncertainty as they looked at each other.

"After you arrived at Tortuga, what happened? Were you reconciled with your mother's family there?"

"No, I saw no one," she said hesitantly. She must tell her about the duel . . .

"How did you arrive here? I was under the impression from Lavender that you and the girl Minette arrived on a hired schooner."

Emerald stiffened. It was like Lavender to imply the worst. "I came safely aboard the *Madeleine.* The vessel is anchored now in the bay. I was to go to England for schooling, but the war has put an end to that."

175

"England?" She looked surprised but went on. "Then Karlton is in Port Royal? Does he know you came to see me?"

Emerald knelt beside her, her anguish revealed. "No, madam, they've arrested him for piracy! He's innocent, I know he is! And if you could convince Lord Felix of this, my father would soon be released!"

"Karlton's been arrested?" breathed Geneva. "When?"

"This morning, soon after we docked. He came ashore to arrange my passage to England and to call on Governor Modyford. He was held for questioning, then indefinitely detained. Now the Admiralty is insisting he was involved with Viscount Royce Buckington several years ago in taking the Spanish galleon the *Prince Philip.*"

Geneva stood, pale and angry, but her voice was restrained. "Karlton had nothing to do with the *Prince Philip.* Governor Modyford knows that. So does Felix."

Emerald got up too. *But Father* was *involved,* she thought uneasily. She could not bring herself to admit this now.

"Felix will return late tonight, but I shall speak with him first thing in the morning. Karlton must be released at once. Imagine the scandal of this! First Royce and now Karlton, and with the earl at Foxemoore—he will be furious over this. Whatever could Felix have had in mind?"

Yes, what did he have in mind?

"Then you'll do something to help my father?"

"Of course, Emerald. Karlton is my cousin, and I'm very fond of him even if we do not see eye-to-eye on some important matters. So that is why you came. And I thought it had to do with your running away. Emerald," she said kindly, "I've misjudged you, I think. The tale of your running off with the indentured servant isn't as dreadful as Lavender seems to think. She too will be pleased to learn the truth. I'll inform her first thing tomorrow."

"She knows the truth but refuses to accept it," said Emerald quietly. "I spoke with her this afternoon at my father's house on Fishers Row."

"Lavender was there?"

"Yes. She—she knows everything, as does most everyone else, but there are few who will as readily believe me as you. I'm grateful for your trust, madam."

Geneva smiled crookedly. "You needn't keep addressing me as 'madam.' I'd prefer it if you'd call me Geneva. And what do you mean, Lavender knows everything? There is more?"

Emerald drew in a breath and touched her hair as if to make certain it was in place. "Lavender has heard about a duel on Tortuga, and she is angry with me, although I had nothing to do with it. Lady Sophie already knows, and I suppose you are the only one who doesn't."

Geneva's thoughts seemed to irritate her. "Evidently there are a good many things kept from me. And I shall need to begin doing something about it." That she was thinking of Felix or Lavender, Emerald could only guess.

"What about this duel?" Geneva asked. "Was it fought over you?"

"Yes," she said quietly.

Geneva's brow lifted, and she studied her face until Emerald blushed. "Well, you are a very pretty girl. Who fought this scandalous duel over your affections. Do I know them?"

"Baret Buckington and Rafael Levasseur."

"*Baret*—" began Geneva and didn't finish. She sat down again, staring at her as though completely overwhelmed.

Emerald bit her lip and turned quietly away, waiting for the storm to break.

"Well," said Geneva after a long silence. "I must say this is most interesting. No wonder Lavender is upset. She informed me just this afternoon that she does not love Grayford and wants to break their betrothal as soon as the earl returns to England. The war has interfered with that, and I see we've a pretty mess of affairs on our hands."

Emerald remained silent, her back turned. "I am certain Lavender won't be the only one who will wish to annul a betrothal. Captain Buckington had thought Lavender already married to Lord Grayford when he agreed to marry me. He will naturally wish to change his mind when he learns the truth."

"When he . . . agreed to marry you."

"Yes," Emerald said quietly, feeling ashamed. "I spent a month aboard his ship. The crew of the *Regale* was informed that he bought me from Jamie Bradford for twenty thousand pieces of eight." Her nails dug into her clenched palms. "And—and my father demanded he marry me because he'd ruined my reputation. He demanded the viscount duel him to the death. The viscount refused and agreed to marry me."

She did not mention Levasseur further. The scandal was embarrassing enough, especially when it appeared that she and her father had forced Baret into an agreement.

What Geneva was thinking, or what her expression might have been, Emerald did not see, for she kept her back turned as the tense silence grew and the clock ticked louder.

"I see," Geneva said at last.

Emerald didn't think she did understand everything, but there was little else she could say to ease matters.

"And this betrothal of yours to a blooded viscount, you are willing to hold him to it? You will never be accepted in London. You know that. Regardless of Karlton's plans."

"Yes. I understand I'd never be accepted, nor do I wish to be a countess. I am willing for him to break the betrothal, and it's what Lavender wants and expects. It will be what he wants too, of course. I've no mistake of that. That he chose to go along with it to begin with was an error on his part."

"If Karlton demanded a duel to the death to defend your honor, I can see why Baret may have felt the need to pretend for a time. We both know Karlton is a stubborn man when it comes to his plans. I'm pleased to hear you've not let this incident go to your head, Emerald. Many girls in your unique position would deceive themselves into thinking such a marriage could work."

Emerald felt the pain of her words, made even more sharp because Geneva was being kind and meant no insult. They were spoken as though Emerald would surely understand that she was not suitable to be Baret's wife.

"Yes," she said tonelessly. "I understand he was doing it to keep from killing my father."

"And what did you expect to do about this betrothal once you arrived in Jamaica?"

"I was to go to England for several years for schooling. The viscount wanted it, and so did my father. I, too, wanted to go very badly. All that has changed now," she said miserably and turned around for the first time. "I've no choice but stay in Port Royal. I won't go back to Foxemoore. I'll stay with Minette in the lookout house."

Geneva looked distressed. "If it wasn't for this odious war! I was to bring Jette to Buckington House to be placed under the tutorage of Sir Cecil Chaderton. Now I suppose we'll all need return to Foxemoore. Doubtless, I'll wish to retain Sir Cecil to see to his education there." She sighed. "More's the pity, I'll need to explain your betrothal to the family. I don't fancy doing so, I can tell you that. Aunt Sophie will swoon when she hears. And Karlton arrested for piracy!"

"You need not tell her of the betrothal," said Emerald, her voice stiff. "There's only what happened on Tortuga. A promise to a den of pirates holds no authority in the Harwick or Buckington family. I've no ring, and I'm sure his lordship will think up some reason to save face."

Geneva looked at her thoughtfully, as if she guessed her emotional injury.

"I'm sorry this had to happen to you, Emerald. It was unfair of Karlton and Baret. I'm also certain Baret will do what he can to shield you from further shame. In the meantime you must put all this from your mind. I'll do what I can to have Karlton released, and I'm sure he'll want you to return to the bungalow at Foxemoore."

She couldn't tell Geneva yet that she would never return to Foxemoore. She could not bear to face the family or live with the knowing looks that would be sure to come her way from both gentry and indentured servant. Somehow she'd live with Minette at the lookout house until her father could send her to England.

"You cannot go back out in that storm. Did you come here alone?"

"No, Zeddie drove me, but I can't leave Minette by herself at the house. I'll be all right. Now that I know you'll do what you can to have my father released, I can endure anything. Good night—and thank you."

Emerald knew Geneva was watching with a slight frown as she retrieved her parasol, wet cloak, and slippers from the chair. She crossed the room and opened the door to leave, again thinking she heard stealthy footsteps.

But there was no sign of anyone's having been in the hall when Emerald stepped out. Not even Zunsia was there. Emerald closed the door behind her and was about to leave by way of the front door when she heard a whisper behind her. Turning toward the stairs, she saw Jette crouching behind the banister, holding a lantern.

"Jette!"

Already regal with his birth, he placed a small finger across his lips and motioned her to silence. He came down quietly, watching the parlor door to make certain Geneva did not appear. He was a delightfully handsome boy with dark hair and olive eyes, reminding her with a strange pang of the rogue that was his older brother.

He came up to her breathlessly, his eyes wide. Taking her arm, he tugged at her to follow him. "In here, Emerald, hurry. Shh! They won't look in here."

The room was an office, and Emerald had the uneasy feeling that this was the last place in which either of them should take even brief refuge. He shut the door silently and set the lantern down on the desk, his eyes gleaming as brightly as a cat's.

"You'll stay, Emerald?" he pleaded, whispering. "I heard her ask you. I don't like it here. Felix wouldn't let me bring Timothy and Titus." His frown told her at once there was already a deep wedge between him and his guardian. "And he said the hound couldn't come indoors. I don't like Felix."

His abrupt honesty reminded her that Jette, even as a child, had not forgotten that he was the grandson of Earl Nigel Buckington.

"I'm sure he has his reasons for not wishing the hound indoors," she said with a smile.

"No, he doesn't. He's mean, that's all. Doesn't like any of us, especially me. Oh, Emerald, I'm glad you're back. Geneva's been sick. And I've been afraid."

The emotion behind his words was not lost on her, and neither was the genuine glimmer of childish fear in his eyes. She remembered her own suspicions, and her concerns grew. She didn't wish to alarm him more by saying she agreed with him.

"Oh, I'm sure Felix likes you, Jette. He's a very busy man, and—like you said—Geneva's been ill. He's been worried about her, and his mind taken up with the coming war."

"Maybe. I still don't like him. And I don't like this house either. There's nothing to do all day but read, and he won't let me go outside. At Foxemoore I could ride Royal with the twins, and the hound would run with us."

"Who is Royal?"

"My new horse," he said proudly. "Geneva got him for me. And she let Timothy and Titus ride a horse with me, double. I heard what he said about my brother, so I don't like him."

Alert, Emerald knelt, searching his face. "What did he say about Baret?" she asked, keeping her voice as calm as possible.

Jette frowned. "He told Sir Jasper Baret would hang."

Emerald restrained herself from showing any expression. She wondered just how Felix had meant those words to the odious Sir Jasper: that Baret's present life would inevitably lead to his arrest for piracy, or that Jasper himself would see to his death? That Jasper had come to the town house was odd.

"You heard them? Sir Jasper was here?"

"He doesn't come much, 'cause I heard Felix get mad at him once. He came once soon after we got here. That's when I heard Felix say Baret would hang."

She squeezed his shoulders. "Don't worry about Baret. He's wise enough to avoid any traps."

"Emerald? I haven't told anybody about Baret looking for our father. I've kept it a secret like you told me. Timothy and Titus too."

"You must be sure to do so."

"Where's Baret now? Do you know?"

"He's safe," she assured him.

He looked hopeful. "You're coming to Foxemoore? Maybe I'll go back too. The war made it so I don't have to go to Buckington House. I'm glad Holland is fighting us. Maybe they'll take Jamaica! Geneva said Baret's mother was from Holland! Are you going to help Sir Cecil with my schooling?"

She had not heard footsteps, but the door opened abruptly. Jette whirled from her grasp. Emerald turned, trying to shield her dismay over being caught uninvited in a private office chamber.

13

THE SURPRISING SCHEME
OF EARL NIGEL BUCKINGTON

From beneath a wide-brimmed hat adorned with a gem-sprinkled ostrich feather, Earl Nigel Buckington looked down upon his grandson Jette. The earl's wealth of silvery hair was drawn back from his tanned face, making a striking contrast with his dark eyes, reflecting as cool and hard as gems in the lantern light. They swerved to rivet upon Emerald. Under that regal, withering stare she felt herself wilting like a plucked flower in the noon sun.

For a measureless moment he stood in the doorway, a commanding presence, who, despite the heat, was immaculately garbed in a dark blue satin doublet and thigh-length jacket. Black leggings encased his legs.

Jette rushed toward him, his relief spilling over. It was perhaps to the earl's credit, thought Emerald, that his presence evoked so little fear in the child. In the months that the earl had been in Jamaica, it seemed he had won the affection of his grandson even if Lord Felix had not.

"Grandfather, it's you. I thought it was—" He stopped.

There was a flash of a sapphire ring, and lace spilled from his cuff as the earl laid a hand on Jette's dark head. "You thought it was your Uncle Felix, and no wonder you look as if you've swallowed a frog. What are you doing in his office?"

A rebuke for me, not Jette, she thought, embarrassed, but the earl's full attention was fixed upon his grandson.

"I wanted to talk to Emerald alone," Jette told him with blunt honesty. "I didn't think we'd get caught in here 'cause Felix is out again."

"It is well for you that he is. He will not take kindly to your snooping about his office, Jette."

"Oh, I wasn't snooping, Grandfather. I already did that."

His grandfather's mouth turned upward with amusement. "Already a spy for King Charles, are you?"

"Me and Emerald are both spies," he said with a secretive tone.

Emerald didn't move.

The earl turned his head and looked pointedly at her. "Indeed?"

She managed a curtsy. "Only a game he likes to play, my lord Buckington. If you will pardon me," she continued breathlessly. "I'll be leaving at once."

"Don't go, Emerald!" cried Jette, coming between her and the door. "We can stay up late and have hot cocoa with Grandfather. The cocoa comes from our plantation, doesn't it, Grandfather?" he stated proudly, looking up at him.

Cocoa with the Earl of Buckington? Jette simply didn't realize what he was saying.

"And that scoundrel brother of yours would fare better if he'd own up to caring for its future instead of marauding the Caribbean."

"You'll stay, Emerald?" Jette pleaded again.

"It appears you've captured the hearts of both my grandsons," came the earl's sardonic voice.

Emerald flushed, her eyes avoiding his and centering instead on Jette's smiling face. "I taught Jette at Mathias's singing school," she explained, half apologizing. "He and I became friends." She smiled at Jette. "Thank you for the invitation, but the storm is worsening. Zeddie and I must get home."

"You will not leave yet," the earl said firmly. "Since you're here, you and I have something to discuss. We might as well begin. Jette, you may leave us now."

She knew what he wished to speak to her about and prayed that the Lord would bring courage and peace to calm the ceaseless thudding of her heart.

"Emerald's going to help Sir Cecil be my tutor at Foxemoore," Jette told him, and his eyes seemed to plead silently with his grandfather.

"Is she now?"

What dreadful things he must think of her, believing she had been out to entrap the viscount into a marriage he didn't want and now, having accomplished that, out to woo Jette over to her side by including herself in his schooling. It didn't matter that Baret had requested her involvement; the earl wouldn't likely accept that.

"Are you of the opinion the master from Cambridge will be needing your expertise?" asked the earl with a cynical glimmer in his eyes. He could not have made his estimation of her qualifications any clearer.

"My qualifications are limited to music, your lordship," she confessed. "But like Lavender, I too had a skilled tutor while growing up. She and I were both pupils of my father's uncle, Master of Arts Mathias Harwick. He taught at Cambridge before deciding to come to Jamaica during the Civil War. However, your grandson Jette does enjoy making plans without taking into consideration what his family may wish."

"In that he is much like his older brother," he said dryly.

Emerald's gaze lowered.

"You may go to your room now, Jette, and wait for me. You will be pleased to know I've come to take you back to Foxemoore in the morning."

"Foxemoore! And can I ride Royal? And can Timothy and Titus ride double on Sugar?"

"I think so."

Jette turned to her, his olive-green eyes shining. "And you can ride with us too, Emerald! Honey is still there."

"Off with you now," his grandfather told him. "I'll be up to say good night soon."

"Yes, Grandfather."

Jette hurried out, and Emerald stood without moving as the earl shut the door firmly and faced her, no smile remaining.

Now the terrible scourging of her emotions was coming. How could she defend herself against his charges? Should she even try? What good to draw her rags of dignity about her and insist she was a lady? The earl would never accept her self-defense.

"So, you are Karlton's daughter."

So much said in so few words. She felt the hotness rise to her cheeks, for, though he did not say it, "Karlton's wench" would have sufficed.

As he stood taking her in, she imagined that he was measuring her by what he had already heard about her mother. The fact

184

that Baret had been called out in a duel over her ruined reputation would be considered humorous. Neither side of the family believed she had a reputation worth defending. Did the earl think her father would ask for money in order to slip silently away and leave the titled family in peace?

She felt ashamed as he stood dissecting her as though she were guilty of a grand scheme. She swallowed, holding back the tears that suddenly wanted to spill over. He'd only take her tears as proof of guilt and think she was appealing to his sympathies, afraid of his authority to cast her into Brideswell for a month for trying to coerce the family into payment.

Emerald managed a stiff curtsy. "My lord Buckington—" her voice oddly was low and calm but breathless "—I can explain everything."

"So you have said. There is no need. I quite understand what is on your mind and, I might add, on the mind of your father."

"May I be so bold, sir, as to say you do not. At least not where I'm concerned."

"You underestimate yourself, Emerald. Your father's schemes I know well enough, but Mathias wrote of you while I was still at Buckington House, just before his death. He claims you are a young woman of high Christian ideals. Now that I've seen you for myself, I'm inclined to accept his sound judgment."

Stunned, she stared at him. "Mathias wrote you about me?"

"I've met enough women in my lifetime to recognize innocence when I see it. That you are a victim rather than the instigator shows in your blush and in your eyes. You may relax, my dear. I've no intention of throwing you to the bears to defend Baret's reputation. He is perhaps little better off than you at the moment. The scamp is wanted for piracy and could easily hang!"

In a gesture of impatience that must have stemmed from anger that matters had turned out this way for his grandson, he removed his hat and dropped it on Felix's desk. "Maracaibo," he said with disgust. "The Spanish ambassador is likely to register an angry complaint in the court of King Charles."

Emerald remained silent, watching him warily, unsure whether or not she could believe his estimation of her. She was relieved that Mathias had written to him, though, and accepted this act of providence as coming beforehand by the mercies of the Lord, who had known the direction of her future. A good word had been passed to the earl about her character. *Thank You, Lord.*

"I've no reason to doubt that my grandson abducted you as you claim. Sophie and Lavender have their own reasons why they wish to question your story, but I do not." He looked at her. *"Why* the scoundrel would abduct you aboard the *Regale,* however, is what piqued my curiosity. Now that I've seen you, I can guess. You are a most striking young woman. Baret has always been a rake when it comes to women."

Her fluster only increased, and she loathed herself for it. She wished to be demure, as elegant and poised as Lavender. Instead, she stammered and blushed like a child. She also found it strange that he would say Baret was a "rake." She had not found him anything like Sir Jasper.

A small breath escaped her lips, and she fumbled with her hair, too aware that it was still wet and misplaced. She must appear to him as a bright-eyed wench, despite his complimentary words. His sophistication and title embarrassed her, and she began to feel the room cramped and airless.

He smiled, and his dark eyes were much like Baret's. "Have you nothing to say for yourself?" he asked when she remained silent.

The rain beat against the glazed window, loud and demanding. "Your understanding, my lord Buckington, brings me profound relief."

"Does it indeed?"

Yes, he was too much like his grandson.

"I've already explained to Lady Geneva that I'll not go along with my father's wishes to become . . ." She paused.

"To become Countess Buckington?" he finished for her, using the words she would never dare speak to him.

Her gaze lowered. He did have a malicious teasing streak after all, just like Baret. Or had Baret inherited it from the earl?

"The title has a rather pleasant ring to it, does it not? 'Countess Emerald.' The things lacking, of course, could be supplied—customary jewelry, polished manners, the confidence that comes from being a lady of the blood. Ah! That is another matter. And in that lies the difficulty, do you agree? The bloodline of a countess is rather important in Whitechapel, although there is the scoundrel in each of us, including His Majesty."

186

Baret had said some of these same things about the nobility but in a much more direct way. Baret often seemed to scorn nobility as though he didn't want it. The earl, she knew, held titles in high esteem.

She made no reply to his rhetorical question. She was not suitable, no.

"I'll not keep you longer than necessary." He briefly motioned her to a hardwood chair with an imposing back that fanned out over her head.

"Your lordship, there is no need for this. You need not try to explain. If I pride myself on anything, it's in being realistic. I'm aware of my unacceptability as countess. And despite your anger with your grandson now, I am certain the two of you will come to peace eventually—at least I hope you do—and Baret will be an earl. Nor do I fancy myself as a countess in London. May I please go?"

"Baret has evidently decided otherwise. He must believe you acceptable, or he wouldn't have agreed to marry you."

"It is not exactly so. What happened on Tortuga was a mistake."

"A mistake," he repeated with mild unbelief. "Baret was a prey of circumstance, I suppose."

"Perhaps not," she agreed quickly, remembering his strength of purpose. "But my father took advantage. The viscount went along with his demands to avoid killing him in a duel. My father knew he could rely on his honor and deliberately forced him to the point where he couldn't refuse before the buccaneers."

"And saving face before this brotherhood of thieves and rogues was of great import to my grandson."

"Because he believes his father is alive, and he needs their cooperation."

"You are quick to defend him."

"I do not defend all he does, your lordship. I also believe he sails close to being a pirate and a scoundrel."

Her words gave him pause. "If you admit this to the High Admiralty, you may see him arrested and brought to England to stand trial. Is that what you wish, after all? It is hardly the role of his betrothed, unless Mathias was wrong. Perhaps I have misread you. You may have plans to inherit as a wealthy young widow."

She flushed, offended, and stood. "You have not misread

187

me. I do not wish his arrest, nor will I testify to his doing wrong in Maracaibo. Even so," she confessed, "I will not deny he is a buccaneer with questionable ways. He is motivated, however, by the high ideals of his father."

"My son is dead," he stated, but his eyes softened for the first time. "If Royce lives, he lives on in Baret's heart. Unwisely, he risks his life and reputation on a goal that cannot succeed."

She remained cautiously silent. If the earl was to learn of Lucca and why Baret was convinced that his father yet lived, it must be left to Baret to explain, including any involvement of Felix.

The earl appeared satisfied with the explanation of her intentions, but he watched her thoughtfully as though she had proven more complex than he had expected. Whether this pleased him or not, she couldn't guess. What did he want of her where Baret was concerned?

"As for Baret being taken advantage of," he said at last, "I'm hardly able to see him in that position. He knows what he wants and usually gets it, one way or the other."

She wouldn't stop to consider why those words should have ignited a small flame of expectation in her heart, providing a safe haven for her fomenting emotions.

"I'm confident the viscount will be the first to admit he was unfairly taken advantage of when he sees you again."

He smiled thinly. "It appears you are admitting to more than your share of blame for this unfortunate incident. Unfortunate, because now that I've met you, I see you are a young woman of rather rare character, considering your upbringing. Mathias is to be commended."

"Your compliment brings me pleasure, Lord Buckington, the more so because it comes from you. And you are right about Mathias. I owe him so much. God was gracious to bring him into my life when I needed him so desperately. My father was away at sea for long periods, and I was left alone at the bungalow on Foxemoore."

"Not a pleasant situation, I suspect."

She sat again. "Mathias taught me to rely on the watchful eye of the Lord. It's been an adventure—and one not lacking its problems."

"Nor its divine reasons for being, if you believe as did Mathias in Calvin's theology. God is working all things together for a high and good purpose in the lives of His foreknown children! However, Tortuga was unfortunate for you, as I see it. And Karlton is responsible. Had he married according to the family's wishes, his daughter would find matters more to her favor at this stage of life. And yet here you are! The one woman my grandson was willing to duel a French pirate to claim! An incident not altogether without its romantic flare in the minds of the women who had earlier designs on him. There are, despite his ways, more titled ladies anxious to marry my grandson than he deserves."

"I do not see my position in so favorable a light, my lord Buckington. These ladies in England have little to fear from me, since I will not hold him to a vow given under duress."

"It seems to me you take Baret's betrothal more lightly than does he. Am I to assume, then, that you do not wish to marry Captain Baret 'Foxworth'?"

Her throat tightened. She lifted her head with dignity, aware of the amusement in his eyes. He didn't believe her, and she wasn't so certain she believed herself.

"Perhaps the roguish buccaneer-turned-pirate is not good enough for so fine a Christian young woman?"

Was he mocking her?

"I think you know better than that, your lordship. He—is a fine enough catch for any woman—as Lady Thaxton will tell you, if you ask her."

At the mention of Lavender, she noticed a flicker of irritation. Was it displayed against Lavender or Baret?

"I am told by Karlton that my grandson has fallen in love with you."

Taken off guard, she could have laughed with the cynicism she felt. Baret in love with *her*?

"My father exaggerates," she said gravely.

His keen gaze regarded her, and to her frustration she felt the blush creeping back into her face.

"Baret made no mention of being in love with you?"

"No, m'lord, nor would he," and she added with an indifference she didn't feel, "I think you're already aware that he's in love with Lady Thaxton."

"This upsets you?"

She moved uncomfortably in the chair. "I don't see that I

189

am entitled to question his feelings in the matter, your lordship."

"You are quick to deny. Should I believe you? You do not care for him then?"

She sat stiffly. "I did not say so."

Why would he ask such questions? He was weighing her responses like a barrister. What was he trying to find out? She had already told him that she didn't share the grand plans of her father for winning a position in the family, but she must not allow herself to forget the earl had his own purposes. What motivated him now remained unclear.

"So you know about the long betrothal he has had with Lavender?"

"I am well aware, m'lord," she said simply.

He mused on her answer. "And are you also aware I do not wish Baret and Lavender to marry?"

She sat, hands folded in her lap. She might tell him of Lavender's plans, but she remained silent, not wishing to betray her, in spite of the contempt with which her cousin often treated her. "Yes. Lavender—Lady Thaxton—told me. His reputation as a buccaneer is a grief to you and the family."

His dark eyes flashed with sudden temper. "I warned him before he left Jamaica. The scamp ignored my warnings and entered Spanish territorial waters. He drew sword against soldiers of the ambassador! You are aware of that, of course, since you were aboard his ship."

"Yes, m'lord. I'm sure he'll be able to explain."

"Oh, no doubt. He always does. But he's gone too far this time."

Too far? Wait until he hears about the San Pedro!

"Baret will never settle down and become the heir I wish him to be. So I've chosen Jette. Until he grows up, should anything happen to me, Felix will manage Jette's estate. As for Baret, I haven't decided . . . though I've doubled his shares in Foxemoore sugar and consigned him a cacao plantation. Baret has shown no real interest in sugar."

Her mind had stumbled over the news that Felix would become Jette's guardian should anything happen to the earl. She was still contemplating this when the earl reached across his son's desk and, lifting the lid on the silver *cigarillo* box, removed a slim Cuban *seegar*. He proceeded to light it, his temper unabated.

"Because of Baret's rebellion, Lavender is now betrothed to the stepson of Felix. She will marry him not because she loves Grayford but because she is a delightful child, far too good for Baret. She's suffered years of illness and deserves a much better life in England than she has had here in Jamaica. Now Beatrice is dead, adding to her sorrow."

Emerald was careful to keep her expression unreadable. What would the earl do if he knew that Lavender had already let it be known she intended to get Baret back? She believed that Lavender was as ambitious and strong-willed as the earl. What was it about Lavender that had convinced both Baret and the earl that she was delicate and of a sweet submissive spirit?

She's deceptive, she thought, irritated. The earl might think she would marry Grayford to please him, but Emerald wasn't as confident. Lavender would thwart him if she could—and harvest both Baret and the inheritance.

"I want to keep them apart. That is where you come in," he was saying.

She blinked. "M'lord?"

He looked at her. "If you were the little strumpet I first thought you to be, I'd be packing you off on the first ship I could find and be done with you. Fortunately, I can see I need not worry about making a pet of an adder and getting bitten. With that settled, I've decided to stand behind Karlton's demands. You will insist my grandson carry through on his vow to marry you. I will see there is a public betrothal at Foxemoore when Baret arrives."

She stared at him, not trusting herself to speak. She must have misunderstood. Had she heard correctly when he said, "When Baret arrives?" Did he really expect Baret to come back to Port Royal and face piracy charges?

She remembered her last meeting with the viscount. He had intimated a reconciliation with his grandfather over fighting the Dutch. She wondered whether the earl intended to get his grandson back with his cooperation or without it?

He appeared calm. "I have my reasons for doing this. Only a woman of your character could prove useful to me. I could not trust a more ambitious woman with what I have in mind, whereas I have confidence in you to play the role."

Play the role. She stood to her feet, holding her voice steady.

191

"I'm in no position to question your prerogatives or your judgment, m'lord. And I suppose it's a common thing for the family patriarch of your titled position to decide what each member of your family may or may not do. But tonight I've already told Lady Geneva I'll not marry a man who doesn't love me. Especially one who carries a torch in his heart for another woman."

"Oh . . . *that.*" He waved a hand. "You misunderstand my intentions. Let us say that as long as you are his betrothed, Lavender will go through with her marriage. Once she and Grayford have married—well, then your betrothal to Baret will end, and you will return the Buckington family ring. I may be angry with Baret, but he remains a blooded viscount, and he will eventually marry accordingly."

Her heart swelled painfully. "You wish me to play theater. To pretend. Is that it?"

"Something of that nature, yes. I must not take the chance of Baret's coming between Lavender and Grayford. I warned him I'd favor Grayford if he proceeded with his shameless conduct. His wanderlust and refusal to return to England and assume his family responsibility as heir to title and estate will lead to disinheritance. Like his father, Baret is arrogantly indifferent to public opinion or the family wishes, and this time he'll pay. His obligation to you puts a pretty end to any notions he or Lavender may have to renew their engagement. In return, you will live at Foxemoore in the Great House, and you will be treated with the respect a future countess deserves. In the end, I will see to an appropriately arranged marriage for you in England or—if you prefer—a comfortable inheritance either here on Jamaica or in London with your father."

So. He wanted to use her as a wedge between Baret and Lavender. The unflattering notion that she was worth no more than that brought her disappointment.

"You mean, once my usefulness is over, you'll no longer have any cause to keep me in the family. You only want to use me to hold Baret to the bargain until Lavender and Lord Grayford are married."

"You will be rewarded amply enough. I believe Karlton wishes to send you to school in England."

"I—I won't be used for anything so ignoble."

"Ignoble? Rubbish! I'm offering you the opportunity to

become the future countess for as long as it's necessary. And in the end, your reputation will be enhanced by having been the betrothed of a Buckington viscount."

"What you ask of me disregards my own dignity as a woman," she said, her voice shaking.

"A matter of feminine ego, is it? We shall soon see it coddled and flattered."

"I do not refuse because of pride!"

"I offer you the honor of becoming the betrothed of my grandson, not at the point of your father's sword but with my approval, a matter of some reputation in England! I offer you the privilege of wearing the Buckington jewels, of having beautiful gowns made for you. Despite your upbringing and that scandalous duel, your reputation will become such that I shall be able to arrange for you a genuine marriage with a man of title. And do you jerk your chin at that, madam?"

Tears stung her eyes. "Please try to understand. I cannot receive a betrothal and a public commitment of his love so lightly. Do you think I have no feelings?"

"I do not doubt you are a woman of deep feelings."

"The viscount will think me small and possessive, deliberately holding onto him when he would prefer otherwise!"

"We ultimately come back to your father's wishes. And mine. And whatever you may think of them, you will need to accept the circumstances and to adjust."

She stood, holding back tears. Her protests meant nothing to him. Now she knew what Baret must have felt in his younger years when denied the right to choose his path. The earl had his plans, and no one would thwart them without reaping a bitter harvest.

"And if your grandson chooses to disregard your plans, no matter that I seek to hold him to them?"

"I have urged upon Governor Modyford a plan that will involve Baret and Henry Morgan. The matter is sure to please, and Baret will cooperate. It will not please my son Felix, so he must not know. Not yet. But in the end, even Felix will see it was a wise thing I've done."

Her interest was tantalized, and she hoped he would explain more, but he did not. "If I refuse?"

"You will cooperate to free your father."

Her eyes darted anxiously to his.

He smiled thinly. "Yes," he said, "I know about his being held by the Admiralty. Felix was involved in his arrest, and I am aware of that too. I suspect you came to see Geneva tonight to plead for her to intervene. Believe me, there is no one who holds more power over Felix than I. No matter what Geneva may do, if I choose to thwart her, there is nothing she can do to help Karlton."

"But you wouldn't thwart her," she pleaded. "He's innocent. I know he is."

"A debatable issue. One that is beside the point. We are not discussing the piracy of the *Prince Philip* or whether there is treasure buried somewhere in the West Indies. I will see Karlton freed on one condition—that you remain the betrothed of my grandson until such time as I decide to end the betrothal. If not, I have authority over the governor and influence with King Charles. I could write to His Majesty tonight and have Modyford removed as governor. I could have your father sent to England to the Tower. And if I chose, my dear, I could send him to Execution Dock. But you need not look pale; that is not my plan, nor my wish. I like Karlton, scamp that he is. And now that I've met his daughter, I can see why Baret would risk a duel to save you from a French pirate."

And she had almost thought the earl actually wanted her to marry Baret. She'd been foolish to even permit herself to think so. He was, and always would be, the blooded Earl Nigel Buckington received at Whitehall in intimate friendship with King Charles. And Baret, too, would remain the future earl. Not all his exploits and scandalous ways on the Caribbean would change that in England, nor with his grandfather, despite his words to the contrary. It was only Emerald Harwick who remained unsuitable.

"I feel certain Karlton will also agree to my wishes," he said, and his voice was so firm that she believed her father indeed could not refuse, no more than she could. She wondered that she felt so tired.

He crossed the chamber and opened the door. He smiled, and for an instant she looked into the face of Baret Buckington.

Emerald curtsied and walked past him into the hall, feeling dazed.

He followed, on his way to the steps to Jette's room. "I will have a talk with Geneva. In a few days, someone will be sent to Fishers Row to bring you to Foxemoore." He climbed the steps. "Good night, Emerald."

14

A CALL FOR THE BUCCANEERS

Expecting the arrival of her father with Zeddie, Emerald felt her taut nerves become more unsettled as the hours dragged on. From far away, a low, dull booming might have passed for thunder.

"Cannon from Fort Charles?" she wondered aloud to Minette.

Minette joined her on the porch of the lookout house. "Maybe Zeddie was wrong about that Dutch ship not shooting at us."

Emerald shaded her eyes against the afternoon sunshine and gazed down Fishers Row, hoping to glimpse the buggy bringing her father. The booming grew louder, followed by shouting voices.

"Why, the sound we hear is beating drums," Minette said.

"And look—way down the street. Those are Governor Modyford's criers. I wonder what's happening?"

"Maybe Zeddie knows. He's coming now."

Emerald peered anxiously to see Zeddie turning onto the crowded street.

"Uncle Karlton's not with him," said Minette worriedly.

Emerald hurried to wait for him on the steps. As soon as he was within earshot, she called, "Zeddie, what happened? Is he still being held by the governor?"

"He's released him," he called up. "I've other news."

That her father had not been held was enough to restore hope. "Where is he now? Is he coming?" she asked as Zeddie climbed the steps.

"Aye, he's coming. He's out to buy your passage to England—if there's any ship."

Minette let out an excited squeal. "Then we're leaving soon, Emerald! All our worst fears were for nothing."

Remembering the words of Earl Nigel Buckington, she

196

wondered if matters were that easy to unravel. Beside trying to sail during war time, had he not said the betrothal must take place first?

Zeddie did not look as optimistic as Minette. "Ye'll both sail, to be sure, just as soon as Emerald meets with the governor and answers his questions. I heard say the Admiralty official will be there too—some dour-faced Earl Cunningham, an acquaintance of Lord Felix."

The reminder of the ordeal ahead sobered any enthusiasm Emerald had over her father's release. And just what sort of fellow was Earl Cunningham? She shuddered. How could she possibly tell all the truth as she knew it and at the same time protect Baret and her father?

"When do I appear?" she asked cautiously.

"I'm not knowin', m'gal, but Sir Karlton will explain when he comes. He'll be havin' supper here. I wouldn't worry none, seein' as how he parted on friendly terms with Modyford. Seems a few pearls baited the governor's generous mood. An' I didn't see his lordship Felix anywheres about."

She turned her attention to what the approaching drums might mean.

"They be the governor's criers making an announcement."

"About the Dutch ship?"

"Sink me, not the ship—the war!"

Yes, the war. And how would this complication add to their difficulties? Would Baret yet decide to fight for Holland?

Zeddie told them the governor's criers were spreading throughout the streets of Port Royal, St. Jago, and Passage Fort, calling any and all privateers to gather for the reading of an important announcement from Governor Modyford and the Jamaican Council.

"I listened to 'em. As soon as the drummers finished their ruffles, the crier clambered on top of stacked rum barrels announcin' how England's at war with Holland. An' Governor Modyford is willing to sell commissions again to any privateer who will attack the Dutch."

"Can he do that? Will the king approve of the buccaneers returning to Jamaica?"

"Approve! Why it was His Majesty who sent a letter to the governor advisin' him to recall 'em. I suspect Lord Felix won't be

197

none pleased with this turn, but the governor and planters is worried aplenty. They're using the war to appease the buccaneers, saying English territory must be safeguarded for King Charles."

"Does the governor think Jamaica will be attacked?" Emerald asked.

"Seems the planters think so. An' with the buccaneers takin' to Tortuga, they're a mite worried. The turn will serve Lord Felix right enough. Let him and his London Peace Party stew in their own turtle juice. They done hanged one pirate too many to lure 'em back now."

"Will the buccaneers come back?" asked Minette hopefully.

Emerald knew the reason for her interest. But if there was any chance that Sir Erik's ship, the *Warspite,* might dock, Minette had false hopes of seeing him again. She was looking to get hurt by the cool and reckless Farrow.

"I doubt the buccaneers will leave Tortuga," Emerald said quickly, trying to keep her voice from betraying the pounding of her heart. What was it the earl had said? Something about "when Baret arrives"?

"There are few privateers in town, an' the ones I saw showed about as much interest over a commission to attack the Dutch as a dead fish would show over live bait. Sink me sails! There ain't more'n a dozen sea rovers remainin' anyhow. And they're more fishermen than they are true buccaneers. The buccaneers are elsewhere. Some say the captain of the Brotherhood—Mansfield—is around the cays of Cuba or Panama. The word will have a time reaching 'em. And so Modyford is sending his man Bennett to bring em' word and lure em' back to Port Royal. Now, the French governor on Tortuga is another thing. He's determined to keep the Brethren there, seeing he gets a share of their booty."

Zeddie slipped the leather sling containing his pistol over his head, knocking off his golden periwig as he did so. His shaven head was covered with a blue bandana. Walking to hang his pistol on a hook on the wall, he said, "The governor knows Jamaica's safety is dependent on his private navy of buccaneers. He's also smart enough to know there's no love for attackin' the Dutch—*or* the French. So I'm wonderin' what he has up his sleeve. I'm thinking he'll send a trusty man to Tortuga to ask for a meetin' with the buccaneer captains, all unknown to his lordship Felix."

"Can he do that?" asked Minette hopefully. "Call for the captains, I mean?"

"Sure now, since he has the authority to issue marques against the one enemy the buccaneers hate, Spain. If it's only the Dutch? They'll stay on Tortuga, to be sure."

Minette grew silent, and Emerald said too casually, "We'll be leaving for England anyway. It doesn't matter to us."

"Yes, and I'm plenty glad too." Minette walked over to the mirror and looked at her image, taking her honey-colored ringlets and piling them high on her head. "Why, I look all of seventeen this way. Emerald, don't you think so? Do you have any hairpins?"

"I just hope our ship sails before real war breaks out on the Caribbean," mused Emerald worriedly.

Minette turned from the mirror, her amber eyes wide, and let her hair fall. "What if we get caught at sea between Dutch and French warships? Oh, I don't think I could stand another sea battle. They'll sink us, for sure."

"It's a risk I'm willing to take. Anything to reach England."

The sun was setting like a burning jewel over the sea when Sir Karlton arrived at the lookout house. The supper table was set and waiting his arrival, with hot platters of his favorite recipe of fried fish, baked plantains in their yellow-brown leaves, and bowls of sweet fresh mangoes, guavas, and melons drizzled with honey.

Emerald ran to embrace him. "Papa."

"Now, now little one, 'tis all right. It could have been worse. I'm alive at least, and free."

At once he was pummeled with questions. "When will I see the governor? What about Lord Felix—will he be there? When does the ship leave for England, Papa?"

He shed his black periwig with distaste. "Looks like a dead dog," he jested, handing it to her between thumb and forefinger. "Style, *bah*. 'Twas the trouble of having to meet with Earl Nigel at Geneva's town house. The man is as much for propriety on a hot humid day as the governor."

So he had met and talked with the earl. Had Nigel informed him of his plans to go through with the betrothal? Her stomach felt queasy as she briefly searched his rugged face, wondering. What would Baret have to say about it? She thought she knew. She let the moment slip past, for as yet she hadn't even told Minette what had happened, perhaps because she was still in a daze over the turn of events.

She looped her arm through his and walked toward the table. "Come and have supper. We've made all your favorite things, and Zeddie fried the fish in coconut oil the way you like it."

Because of the tropical heat, men often shaved their heads and wore pirate scarfs or, like her father, had their hair clipped short about the ears. He took the clean blue scarf that Zeddie handed him and tied it on in preparation for taking his seat at the table. As she pressed for answers, her father proceeded to calmly remove his camlet jacket and cravat and hand them to Emerald, who ran to hang them in the closet and hurry back, afraid she'd miss some of his news.

"Don't run, lass. You're a lady. Nae forget you'll be a countess one day." His eyes twinkled.

So the earl had told him. Naturally, her father would be pleased.

"Yes, Papa, of course." She gestured to Minette, who brought a bowl of warm water and set it on a stool beside his chair, where he was wont to wash his hands before commencing supper.

Emerald took her chair with a rustle of skirts, and Minette wrinkled her nose at her, for it was her duty to wait on the table with Zeddie. Before her grandfather Jonah had died, he and Minette had both waited on table while Zeddie had helped with the cooking. Sir Karlton insisted that only Zeddie knew how to make his coffee and fry his flour-dipped fish in a crackling two inches of oil.

Sir Karlton towered a good six feet, with broad shoulders. His rough suntanned hands displayed several pirated rings, one showing a black bull with ruby eyes. "Taken from a don," he had said. "The man stole it first. I simply collected a due to England." His deep-set eyes bore a silvery hue in the light from the lanterns and candles. He fixed them on his daughter with thoughtful pride.

Emerald sat poised and quiet now, wondering whether to tell him about Cousin Lavender's visit and her intention to

200

marry Baret, despite either his plans or the earl's. It would save them all a great deal of turmoil if she did not explain yet.

His gaze softened with fatherly affection. "You look as becoming as your mother," he said. "She wore her raven tresses piled at the back of her head too. A lady she was. None could outdo her when she wanted to prove it." He chuckled, as though enjoying some entertaining memory.

Emerald did not share his pleasure. She picked up her fork and flicked at the fish fillet. She had no appetite, and the smell of fish was so strong she asked Zeddie to open the door and let the evening breeze flow through the house.

"Baret should see you now," said Karlton. "He'd be impatient for that wedding."

Emerald tried to keep her expression unreadable. She picked up her cup and sipped the lime water sweetened with honey. Then she smoothly changed the subject. "What did the governor ask you? Does he think I know anything about the voyage to Maracaibo? Of the *San Pedro*?"

His expression turned mellow but secretive. "He's satisfied, so you needn't worry none."

She wondered why he was satisfied. The pearls? Something else she was not yet privy to? "Zeddie said I would be called to Kings House to answer for myself soon."

"Nigel won't want more scandal. He'll be sure to pressure Felix to drop the issue," was all he said.

Emerald tensely watched him as he ate his supper and the breeze flickered the candle flames. As yet, she had not met Felix, though she had seen him from a distance at the wedding.

"There's fine news, daughter. Earl Nigel has made it clear there will be a public betrothal on Foxemoore in a few weeks."

A few weeks! Emerald clutched the fork. She swallowed. "Did he? That's rather shocking, isn't it? Does he think the viscount will submit? Will Lady Thaxton simply smile and agree? She didn't marry Lord Grayford after all, you know." Her heart thudded ridiculously.

Minette danced about in the background as though celebrating, her antics unseen by Karlton. Emerald ignored her.

"*Bah,* if the captain of the H.M.S. *Royale* is smart, he'll postpone that wedding indefinitely. She'll make a man a flighty wife. Drive the poor fellow to indigestion, to be sure."

"Papa—" she began uneasily, but he lifted a hand, his eyes meeting hers evenly.

"Pass the honey, lass."

She drew in a breath and watched as he poured a heavy layer on his buttered biscuit.

"When you'll speak with the governor is uncertain. You may not see him at all until the official dinner and ball at Government House."

She stiffened in the hardbacked chair. "What dinner?"

He smiled. "The one you'll be attending, looking like the countess you'll be one day. And sporting the Buckington ring."

"I don't care for official dinners. They're full of stuffy people who stare at me. And I can imagine the stares I'd receive now if I went!"

"Nonsense. With the Buckington ring in display, they'll be congratulating you."

"There is no ring—and there won't be."

He looked at her, holding out his empty coffee cup toward Zeddie, who refilled it with style, one ear turned to the conversation. "Baret will give you the ring at Foxemoore before the dinner at Government House takes place. Nigel is on our side, daughter."

"As if Baret Buckington will marry just because his grandfather expects it! He's in love with Lady Thaxton! And he's man enough to get what he wants, no matter how much you or the earl manipulate him. Oh, Papa, it's gone far enough. Let's leave here at once aboard the *Madeleine*. We'll sail for England and visit your cousin at Berrymeade and forget all about Port Royal."

"Tsk, listen to her, Zeddie! She's captured the heart of Viscount Baret Buckington, even my lord Buckington says he'll stand behind us, and my daughter continues to insist on cowering like a wilted flower. Now, lass, there'll be no more of this kind of chatter. Baret will give you the ring, and the betrothal will be decently announced as family custom demands. It's the way it's always been done, and Geneva and Sophie will say nothing now that Nigel agrees."

Her personal objections seemed to be getting nowhere. She would try another approach. "Baret doesn't dare show himself in Port Royal! He's wanted for illegal entry in Maracaibo. If you insist, you'll see him arrested and put in Brideswell until Lord Felix has him hanged."

"So that's the flurry behind your unreasonable spirit, is it?" His eyes narrowed thoughtfully. "Felix wants him hanged, all right—and me to boot, if he can, but for different reasons. It's to my benefit that Nigel and the governor have plans Felix doesn't know about yet," he said with satisfaction. "The rascally mouthed spy!"

Felix a spy? Now she recalled that the earl too had mentioned a plan that would please Baret but not Felix.

"Plans about the war?" she asked anxiously. "The drums today—the governor expects the buccaneers to return?"

Minette drew near the table and watched him, her heart in her eyes.

His satisfied smile vanished at his thoughts, and he didn't seem to notice her. "He can beat the drums all he wants. Neither Morgan nor Mansfield will fight the Dutch. Nor will any true-hearted buccaneer."

"What then, Papa? Can you tell me?"

"I can tell you Modyford doesn't trust Felix as much as he pretends. Trouble is, he's in a hard position to keep Felix's Peace Party satisfied on the one hand and the buccaneers and planters on the other. With Nigel's secret support, Modyford's willing to sanction an expedition against Spain under Henry Morgan. And I'm to bring the news from Morgan to Baret."

So that's what the earl meant when he told me Baret would return.

"And all this with the governor's permission?" she whispered.

He smiled. "Aye, daughter—and the earl's. It's the sort of venture Baret will relish."

She was not pleased with the thought. "What about the *San Pedro*? What of his entry into Maracaibo? What of Lucca, and what about you, Papa?"

"You needn't fret over me." And his secretive look of pleasure returned, as though he had some plan of his own. "I've made terms with the governor. It's why he released me when Nigel requested it. A wise man, Modyford."

She worried about the glint in his eyes as he gazed thoughtfully at the candle. She recalled what Geneva had said about her father's having had nothing to do with the *Prince Philip*. Emerald, of course, knew better.

"What kind of terms?" she asked, thinking of the *Prince*

Philip's treasure. "Has Baret gone to Margarita yet? Do you plan to go with him after all? Oh, Papa, I wish you wouldn't."

"Now, now, none of that. We'll not discuss the treasure now. Your father is an honorable man, to be sure, and so is Buckington. We're neither one pirates. We'll be doing a bit of business with Modyford is all, since the man isn't above a bit of pocket-padding himself when it comes to Spanish pieces of eight. And now we have Earl Nigel on our side as well."

She watched him. "What kind of business?"

"Enough questions. The less you, Minette, and Zeddie know, the better off you'll be. But there's no need for alarm, daughter. The governor is privy to the information now and is expecting a trifle in exchange for my release. And it's quite a different cause which brings me to see Baret on Tortuga. Enough now," he repeated.

He stood, pushing back his chair. "And now for the news I've not been wanting to tell. It's about your voyage to England."

Emerald tensed, unsure whether her unease came from his smooth change of topic or from his sudden frown. What she saw flickering in his expression set her on the edge of her chair.

"About England," he said. "There's been a change of plans, daughter."

She stared at him, and Minette watched with expectant eyes. "Papa, don't tell me you've changed your mind about my going away to school?"

Sir Karlton cleared his throat. "It wasn't me, little one. I've done my best to convince Modyford—"

"Modyford? The *governor's* going to detain me?"

"No, and do you think I'd sail to Tortuga and Porto Bello and leave you here if I thought you'd be detained at that filthy Brideswell? Why, I'd shoot the first cullion who'd dare to bring you there! Nay—" he calmed himself "—nay. Nor would Nigel allow such a dastardly thing. Just as soon as the war is over and the Atlantic is safe to cross, you'll be going to school. You too, Minette." He turned his head and gave her a nod. "You're getting prettier with each passing month, and I aim to see you marry above your station. You look quite French. That scoundrel Erik Farrow—"

Emerald stood, pushing back her chair. "You mean we're

204

not sailing until after the war? That—that could be a year. Even longer."

"Aye . . ." He sighed, sat down again, and cut into a melon with a sharp dagger. "I did my best. There are no ships leaving for England, and the governor informs me none will. It's his ruling, daughter. I'm sorry. I tried to convince him. Nigel also seems to think you should stay. You'll be going to Foxemoore."

"Not going . . ." Minette groaned.

Emerald stood, a thousand thoughts racing through her mind. This meant she must face the family after all. Even with the earl wishing it of her, she recoiled at the possibilities. No wonder he could say there would be an announcement of her betrothal on Foxemoore. He had known that she would not be able to go to London.

Emerald leaned with dismay across the table. "The war hasn't happened yet—not the fighting anyway. The Atlantic is surely still safe for voyaging. It can't be worse than meeting Thorpe and the *Black Dragon!*"

"I wouldn't count on it, lass. If the Dutch from the American New Amsterdam colony decide to send a man-o'-war down to the Caribbean, it won't take 'em long. And there are ships at Curaço. And the French have ships at St. Kitts."

"What about English Harbor? What about Lord Grayford's ship?" she argued desperately. "What about Barbados?"

"Grayford's ship was hit and is undergoing repairs at Antigua. Grayford seems a wee untested, if you ask me. The king should have given that sweet ship to Baret. Now there's a scoundrel who could teach 'em a few lessons."

She sank slowly back into her chair. She saw him watching her with a flicker of sympathy in his eyes.

"I'm truly sorry, daughter. I know how you were looking forward to England, and so was I. Even so, matters for you have changed for the better here in Port Royal, and your time in England will come one day. And in the meantime, I hear Baret's old tutor, Sir Cecil Chaderton, is also delayed here. Now there's a scholar if there ever was one. You can learn more from Sir Cecil than you could ever learn at St. Paul's in London. Your day at Buckington House will come."

Will it? Emerald wondered dully. Would she ever escape the cockatrice den of Port Royal?

"I promised Baret you'd be sent there," he said with a frown of remembrance. "It was the bargain we made for the marriage, and we better keep it. If not—"

His voice went on, but she was no longer listening. Her dreams were slowly dying. From outside, as the evening deepened, she could hear the carousing beginning as the kill-devil rum began to flow in the taverns and gambling dens.

Minette had walked to the door and was looking out in silence. Emerald imagined her thinking that all her hopes of becoming a lady and snagging Erik Farrow were as doomed as her own. At Port Royal she would always be known as a half-caste slave.

Return to Foxemoore. All happy expectations of tomorrow vanished like mist in the morning sun.

"A traitor, that's what Felix and the Peace Party is. An' all the while, Felix is engaged in the king's colonies smuggling slaves, rum, and other goods to the Spaniards. If I could prove it, I'd hear no more from him, I tell you. And I *will* prove it. I've much to tell Baret when I see him."

He pushed his plate back and pulled out his pipe, stretching out his booted legs. "It should be a satisfying consolation for Baret to be called by Modyford. It's almost amusing that even Felix and his London officials must treat him more kindly. He will be forced to soften his stance. Though Baret is wise enough to not trust him. Aye, it would be amusing to see Felix when he learns of the deal I've made with Modyford. Felix is a dangerous man, little one, nae forget that." He looked at her across the candle lighted table.

Emerald saw concern in his eyes, and at that moment genuine fear was rekindled in her heart. "Will you go alone to Tortuga to see Baret? Does the governor intend to send some militia with you?"

He smiled tolerantly. "I have all the Brethren of the Coast behind me. There's only a few rats to worry me—Sir Jasper and that roguish French nephew of mine. Rafael will answer to me for his betrayal. Now, I'll be getting some rest. I'll be leaving far before dawn to bring Baret the news. Morgan will be expecting us both."

He stood. "Zeddie, I'm trusting my two lassies to you while I'm gone. Keep 'em safe until Captain Buckington arrives."

"Sure now, Karlton, I'll see to it. Ye've nothing to worry about except yourself. I'll be seein' you to the *Madeleine* come morning. Speakin' of that cur Sir Jasper, I'm thinkin' that Dutch ship in Chocolata Hole is his work, his and maybe Lord Felix's. An' there's slaves aboard."

"Slaves, is it? The bounty will yet be the seaweed to drag him below the black depths," growled Sir Karlton. "Maybe I'll have a look at that mysterious ship, Zeddie. Tonight, before I set sail for Tortuga."

Emerald sat lost in her own thoughts, vaguely aware that her father now peered at her worriedly.

"Now, Emerald, enough of your disappointment. You've got the whole world ahead of you now that the Earl Nigel's behind your marriage. You'll soon be wearing fancy gowns and tinkling with family jewels. And Baret's enough man to turn any woman's head. You've exciting socials to look forward to, including your official betrothal. Enough moping now. You've much to thank the Almighty for."

"Yes, Papa." She stood, walked to where he was, and threw her arms around him tightly.

"'Tis not a long good-bye," he said with rough tenderness. "I shall be back."

She kissed his cheek and nodded, then climbed the steep steps to the crow's nest.

A minute later Minette followed her, and Emerald saw she was pale and despondent.

Emerald glanced down the stairway. Her father and Zeddie were talking in mysterious, quiet tones. Then she went to their room and lighted the small lantern.

Minette sank to the quilts on the floor, head in hands. "We'll never get out of here."

Emerald said nothing. She walked to the round window and stood looking out. The sun had long since set, and rain clouds were quickly blocking out the moon. A storm was blowing up.

Be Thou our guide, our guard, our shield, she prayed.

The freebooters may have abandoned Chocolata Hole for French Tortuga, but Emerald discovered the next morning that smuggling continued to flourish under the guise of respectability worn by certain members of the governor's own council.

"That Dutch ship transferred its bounty of human cargo onto a second ship. We saw it all," said Zeddie with loathing. "Leastways we did till your father left for the *Madeleine* and I was hit on the noggin'. Getting clobbered seems my ill fate," he complained, groaning as he took a cup of coffee from Minette.

Emerald dabbed turtle oil and rum on the bloodied bruise and secured a clean bandage in place. "I have my notions about Sir Jasper being involved. If I could convince the governor, I would."

"Not much chance of that. Jasper has friends on the council. Him and his cockleburs were out doin' their mischief, to be sure, and they knew I saw 'em too. In the dark hours of the wee midnight, the ship slipped away beneath the sleeping guns of Fort Charles. Got friends there, too, is my guess."

Emerald brushed a dark wisp of hair from her forehead, and her winged brows formed a scowl. "If anyone ought to be hanged on Gallows Point, it's the vile-hearted slavers. Did you see the ship they were transferred to?"

"Aye, I saw it," he murmured darkly. "It's bound for the Main to sell to the Spaniards is my guess. And who did I see a-talking with the captain, some newcomer to these waters, but that foppish bloke Sir Jasper. An' stab me if'n I didn't also see the big barracuda himself, Lord Felix Buckington, loiterin' farther back on the wharf. Then somebody clobbered me."

She remembered what both Zunsia and Jette had said about smuggling. That Felix might be involved did not surprise her, but it was curious that a man in his position would risk showing himself near the ship. "You're sure it was Felix?"

"My good eye is as sharp as a bat's. I saw him."

Minette produced a crooked smile. "We say 'as blind as a bat,' Zeddie."

"No matter, m'gal, 'twas the same thing. I saw his lordship Felix Buckington. I'd recognize that dandy anywhere."

Emerald had no cause to doubt him. "Yet he and his officials have the gall to hang pirates," she fumed. "They find piracy an embarrassment to their own noble cause of smuggling to the colonists against Madrid's wishes. Governor Modyford should be informed, even if they don't believe us."

"And have our own necks stretched? Sink me if'n you think *I'll* chatter. Lord Felix is a powerful man, m'gal. In London he dines with His Majesty, and here on Jamaica he sups with Governor Modyford." He touched his bump. "I've been warned. A titled man is to be left alone."

"They didn't leave Viscount Royce Buckington alone," she said thoughtfully. "And I doubt if Felix plans to leave Baret free to sail the Caribbean either—if he can stop him."

Zeddie turned his head away, straightening his black eyepatch. "Nonetheless, I've my orders from Karlton to keep an eye on you, and that's job enough for a man with new aches in his old joints. I seen the carrion still roosting on the crossbar at Gallows Point, just waiting for the next rogue to dangle, and it ain't going to be me if I can help it."

"If the governor suspected Lord Felix of smuggling," she said quietly, more to herself than to Zeddie or Minette, "it might give him the leverage he needs to keep Felix from running things in the council. When it comes to Spain, I happen to know the governor would prefer to issue commissions to the buccaneers. It's Felix that puts a curb on the governor."

"Vapors," said Minette. "You're right. Having something like smuggling to hold over his lordship might even make a difference when it comes to the way the Admiralty Court treats Captain Buckington. Do you suppose it was this that Uncle Karlton was secretly musing about?"

"But who'd take our word against Lord Felix, if it came to that?" He cocked his eye toward them. "You want to take on the likes of Felix? Earl Nigel has complaints enough that his son Royce was a pirate. Do you think he'll let loose of Felix too? With Baret followin' the ways of his father, the earl doesn't have anyone left except Felix and little Jette."

He emptied his cup of coffee and added, when Emerald mused in silence, "I wouldn't worry none about Captain Buckington. The man's as smart as they come. It's my guess he knows his uncle through and through. And he's probably already knowing about smuggling—among other things just as black and odorous, like Lord Felix betraying his father to the Spaniards. To be sure, if Captain Buckington shows up to see the governor, it'll likely be because he has know-how enough to dodge any plans Felix has for his dangling."

Emerald wasn't as confident as Zeddie. The thought of Baret's death left her cold.

15

IN DARKNESS AND
THE SHADOW OF DEATH

Emerald listened, eyes and ears straining for the sound that had jarred her awake. She sat up, peering into the moonlit darkness toward the small door that faced the steep flight of steps.

Hearing little more than the familiar, raucous noises coming from Port Royal's gaming and bawdy houses, she decided there was nothing to disturb her. By now Zeddie would be asleep in the chair near the front door. The knowledge that he slept with pistol at hand gave her a sense of security.

"Gamblers and rum drinkers," she murmured wearily and prepared to turn over and go back to sleep. Returning to Foxemoore would at least mean pleasant summer nights, she thought, fluffing her pillow. Oh, for the comforting trill of songbirds and the bright morning chatter of parrots instead of pistol shots!

The humidity made her restless. Unable to return to sleep, she arose from the lumpy bed, quietly, so as not to awaken Minette, and went to the window. The wind was pleasant, and she lingered there, letting it cool her moist skin.

Watching the moon reflect on the shiny, dark swells of the bay brought the *Madeleine* to mind. She felt a pang when she thought of her father's departure. By now he would be well out at sea on his mysterious voyage to meet with Baret. Just what did the governor's call for a reconnaissance expedition along the Main entail?

She mused over the extent of Baret's dangerous mission with Henry Morgan, and a frown touched her brow. What would be involved in that? How far into Spanish territorial waters were they expecting to venture? And what of his previous buccaneering undertakings on the Venezuelan coast? Was the governor expecting to overlook this, or was this matter about Morgan some sort of trap to lure him here to arrest him?

A pistol shot rang out, reminding her of the danger that

encircled them all. Then the late night closed in, hot, humid, saturating the cramped crow's nest. High atop the lookout house, a gust of wind thrashed the outer wall facing the Caribbean.

Then Emerald saw a man moving away from the outside steps below. She took a small step back. There was something familiar about his walk, something that caused her to skin to crawl. *Mr. Pitt?* What was *he* doing here this hour of the night? The hair on the back of her neck prickled.

He was dragging something—a body?—toward the sand! Her heart leaped to her throat. Awareness of what had awakened her dawned, bringing terror.

It had not been rum-sodden revelers on the beach but some struggle downstairs. Her subconscious had reacted by looking toward the door because in her sleep that was where the awful sound had come from. And now the man who looked like Mr. Pitt was striding toward the house.

She turned from the window, her face pale. A ribbon of moonlight across the wooden floor seemed to point toward Minette's pallet. It was empty.

"Lord, protect us," she prayed desperately, her knees going weak. She sped to where she kept the new pistol Baret had given her. She lighted a candle with shaking hand and then struggled with clumsy fingers to load the gun with powder. From below, she heard heavy boots boldly coming up the outer steps.

Emerald cast aside thought for her own safety and came out the crow's nest door, the wood beneath her bare feet still warm from the day's heat. Below the shadowed stairs, a glowing lantern cast swaying shadows on the bare wall.

"So you had to investigate, did you?" Mr. Pitt's gravelly voice sounded from downstairs. "I should send you to work cane with the rest of the slaves. You'd learn a thing or two, fast! But no, you and Karlton's brat parade Port Royal like you're both high-flung ladies. You'll tell me what she's done with her cousin's jewels, or I'll go up and force it out of her."

"We have no jewels, Mr. Pitt. No jewels at all. They—they was taken."

"Taken, eh? Sure they were. By Emerald. From Levasseur's ship. She has 'em. I heard that French pirate raging against her thievery at the Red Goose last night."

"He's lying. We have nothing—"

"She comes back sporting silks and lace. She has the jewels all right, and you both expect to slip away to London with 'em. You're coming with me to Foxemoore!"

"No! I won't go with you, Mr. Pitt, and you can't make me."

"No?"

Minette cried out.

Emerald heard him slap her and then the sound of a body falling to the floor. Her fear turned to anger. The odious brute! She started down the stairs, holding the pistol ready at her side, surprised at how well it fit her grip. She paused halfway down the steps, seeing Pitt towering over Minette, who lay sprawled at the bottom.

"So pleasing me is too good for you, eh?"

"You dare touch my cousin?" Emerald demanded in a too-calm voice. "I'll have you arrested for breaking into my father's house."

Pitt turned to look up, his full attention now on Emerald. His eyes hardened. "So. Li'l Saint Emerald's finally awake," he slurred. "Been sayin' your prayers and readin' the Book, 'ave you? Get down here, m'lady. We have us a matter to talk about."

His sweating face was flushed with rum. His lank, reddish hair stuck to his forehead. His stained shirt was open, and his chest heaved. He walked around the banister and stopped at the foot of the stair, one foot on the bottom step and a leer across his leathery face.

"You've forgotten something, m'lady," he jeered. "We had us a li'l bargain before you upped and ran away on Foxworth's ship with my share of jewels. I'm wantin' them now, as my patience has come to its end."

Don't panic, she thought. She had handled Mr. Pitt before, and with the Lord's help she could do it again. She was disturbed, however, that he'd suddenly turned so bold. Did he know her father was gone? Still, Papa had sailed from Jamaica many times, leaving her alone on Foxemoore, and Mr. Pitt had never been this impudent before. But perhaps on those occasions he'd not been lusting for Spanish treasure that he supposed she had taken from Levasseur's ship.

Minette had taken those jewels, but Baret had them now. Would Pitt believe her?

She decided to buy time, hoping against hope that Zeddie—where was Zeddie?—would return in time to help her. "You're drunk," she told him flatly. "If Lady Sophie knew, she'd remove you from being overseer at once. As an indentured servant, you'd go straight back to work in the boiling house."

"Indentured servant, eh? *Hah!* Not for long, m'lady. My time at Foxemoore ends come January, an' Governor Modyford is issuing grants. I've some money set aside for working on the side of Sir Jasper, an' with my share of the jewels I'm buying Jamaica land."

"Work on the side for Sir Jasper!" she scoffed. "Doing what? Smuggling slaves and rum to Spanish colonists? And what will Governor Modyford do if he should find out you and Sir Jasper were involved in smuggling human beings from that Dutch slaving ship?"

His eyes studied her. "I wouldn't go talking like that if I was you, m'lady. It ain't just Sir Jasper whose neck is at stake but a few big barracuda too. It may be you'll find yourself locked away in Brideswell for piracy along with Foxworth."

"You won't frighten me, Mr. Pitt. My father's working for Governor Modyford now. And Earl Nigel's grandson isn't likely to be arrested—not when the governor's calling for his return to Port Royal on business for His Majesty."

He smiled. "For His Majesty, eh? Is that what he told you? If the 'earl's grandson,' as you want to call Foxworth, unwisely shows himself, it will be because it's part of the plan to arrest him. Lord Felix and Sir Jasper is more clever than that, m'lady. And now, the jewels you owe me."

Had her father been deceived, then? Had Lord Felix only used Governor Modyford as a trap? What if the governor was not even aware of Henry Morgan's expedition? But that wasn't possible, for Earl Nigel was involved as well.

"They have plans," he said. "And I have some of my own. If Jasper can climb to the planter gentry, then so can I. Aye, m'lady, and have myself a fine miss in my chamber too."

"Jasper's sugar holdings don't make him a gentleman. And no matter that you buy land—you'll remain a smuggler just like him."

"Fine chatter coming from a pirate's brat. Levasseur's jewels . . ." he reminded her impatiently. "I spared Ty's life with only a branding when I might've hanged him. You went slipping off with the jewels on Foxworth's ship, but your little scheme didn't end well, now, did it? Jamie's dead, and Foxworth don't dare show his face or he'll be arrested and hanged. So suppose you just hand over what you owe me."

"I don't have any jewels. As for the 'bargain,' you didn't keep it. You vowed you wouldn't have Ty branded, and you blamed the slave rebellion on him and Jamie. Neither were involved. Jamie may be dead, but Ty is still wanted by Lord Felix. If there's a bargain to be kept, it's left to you to tell him Ty is innocent."

"Ty will hang for sure if he shows himself in Port Royal, same as Foxworth. A bargain is a bargain. He's alive, ain't he? That's more'n can be said for your father. What are you squawking about? I've plans to do you well enough—and Minette too, if you cooperate."

She tensed. "What are you saying? Not that I have any reason to believe you. You'd lie just to frighten me."

He grinned up at her. "I don't need to frighten you, m'lady. Lord Felix will do that when he puts you in Brideswell to lure Foxworth back. What I say is the truth. I was always a gentleman, now, wasn't I? And I aim to become more of a gentleman, just as soon as you keep your part of our bargain made that afternoon on the road at Foxemoore."

Her heart was thudding, for something in his eyes told her he was not lying this time. "What about my father?" she pursued warily.

"Don't listen to him, Emerald," cried Minette suddenly. "He's already told me, and it can't be true. It just can't be."

Minette's cry only caused Emerald's fear to spiral out of control. Except for Geneva, there were few in the family she trusted, including her own pirate cousin, Rafael Levasseur.

Pitt started up the steps.

Emerald raised the pistol so that he could see it. "Get out."

He halted, eying the weapon, but then looked at her long and steadily. "Oh, I'm leavin' all right, but *with* the jewels, an' you an' the African wench is comin' with me. I'm claimin' you both, and who's to stop me now, eh?"

Whatever would make him entertain such ideas? The kill-devil rum?

"A li'l saint wouldn't go splattering the brains outa poor Mr.

Pitt, now, would she? Not the saint who wants to turn the babble of the Africans into the music of angels!"

She held the pistol aimed and steady. "I don't need to kill you. I'd be justified in wounding you if you intend to harm me or Minette. There are no jewels here. If you want them, you can go to Tortuga and threaten Captain Buckington, seeing as how he took them from me for safekeeping. But I doubt you have the courage to face Baret Buckington. Now get out of here before I'm forced to maim you."

His teeth showed in an ugly smile. "Big talk from a li'l saint. Your poor papa is dead, m'lady, an' if you wish to do some crying, my shoulder is more willing than even Foxworth's. I don't see him here to protect you."

Her mind reeled.

"You and the slave wench is alone now," he said, slowly coming up the steps. "An' you need me to take care of you, m'lady. Best give me that pistol before you hurt somebody."

"You're out of your senses," she said, her voice shaking. "He's not dead. He left for Tortuga to find Captain Buckington. Rum has fevered your brain."

"Outa my mind, am I? I saw the whole thing. But I ain't tellin' what I know to the militiamen until you divvy up like we bargained. I'm telling you there isn't anything going to keep me from buying land Modyford is willing to sell. This is my chance, and nobody's going to ruin things."

"He's not dead," she whispered.

"That one-eyed nape Zeddie nearly got himself killed spying on Sir Jasper and his lordship. They was taking no more chances, with your father prowling about and ready to report everything to the governor. I was trailing Zeddie tonight, at Jasper's orders. Soon as him and Karlton parted company, someone shot your father in the back. I heard the pistol shot, m'lady. An' I went back to see what happened. He was shot straight through the heart. Last I seen, about an hour ago, militiamen were hauling his body away."

She stared down at him, her mind's eye envisioning her beloved father lying breathless and bloodstained. Her protector, friend, and strength had been taken from her. As swiftly as a hurricane could leave a house a bundle of scattered sticks, her hopes, once thought secure in the love of her one parent, had been ripped from her.

The confident face of Mr. Pitt stared back, reminding her of a vulture, waiting.

The cause for his impudent boldness made sense now. He would never say these things about Sir Jasper and Lord Felix if he didn't feel certain he could protect himself and make good his plans. If her father were alive, he would fear to threaten her like this. He believed he could get away with it. The gleam in his eyes convinced her that he spoke the truth about her father's death.

He took another step upward. "M'lady, you're all alone now, you and the wench both. You need me, and I'm willing to be a friend. I can use an African wench for a maid, and I'm willing to marry you and give you a home. Foxworth will hang. But even if he don't, he won't keep that dueling bargain. He has himself a hankering for Miss Lavender."

All alone. Shock held her unable to move, staring into his face, the hand holding the pistol gone limp. Not even his words of marriage jarred her with their absurdity. Her father was dead.

Below them, Minette hovered in terror, now gripping the banister. "Emerald, he's got no mind to marry you, but make you his mistress. Fire the pistol!"

Her father was dead . . .

Pitt struck the weapon from her lifeless hand, and the metal clattered cold and hard onto the steps. Emerald came awake as his bearlike arms clamped about her and his sweaty face came down on hers, smothering her cry of horror. She clawed at him, struggling to free herself.

"I got nothing to lose to kill you!" Minette's voice was oddly calm. Pistol in hand, she gazed up at Pitt with eyes gleaming like slits of burning amber. "I'd soon be hanged as see you have Emerald and me be your slaves!"

Sobered, Pitt jerked away, and Emerald sank onto a step.

"You're an evil man, Mr. Pitt. You blamed my brother for something he didn't do. You branded him on the forehead like a man does his cattle. And now you think to have Emerald and me?"

"Put that away, you little fool." He lunged downward, but Emerald threw herself against his arm. He lost his footing and went stumbling against the wall.

216

A shot rang out, and Emerald heard a gasping intake of air.

Pitt stiffened, then quivered with spasms and slumped down on the steps. The smell of gunpowder and a small puff of whitish-gray smoke hung ominously over the stairway.

Emerald drew back, leaning against the banister, her eyes wide. A foreboding silence clutched at the room. Then she became aware of the wind, sending the front door creaking to and fro.

Pitt was conscious. He sat looking at Minette, blood seeping from a wound above his right collarbone.

Minette still clutched the pistol with both hands, her face white, her gaze transfixed. A moment later she took to weeping and shaking.

Emerald could not weep, though her heart swelled with hot pain. Her beloved father was dead. The words echoed and reechoed. *Gone. Gone.*

She sidled past Pitt and went slowly down the steps on legs that wanted to buckle. She took the pistol from Minette's hands. Their eyes met, frightened, dazed. Emerald looked back at the overseer. A rivulet of blood stained his faded shirt. She must save his life—for Minette's sake.

And then footsteps sounded from outside, slow, cautious.

Emerald turned and stared at the gaping darkness beyond the door. Zeddie?

Sir Jasper emerged from the darkness and stood in the doorway. His fine velvet jacket shimmered with jewels. His trousers were bloused inside his Spanish leather boots, and a wide-brimmed hat shadowed his swarthy, bearded face. His thick black hair was waved Cavalier-style above his shoulders.

He eyed the sprawling Pitt, then the pistol in Emerald's hand. Like a fox quick to survey the unguarded henhouse, he appeared to reach a conclusion befitting himself. With a gleam in his eyes, he doffed his hat.

"Well, now, darlin', it appears you're in trouble up to your pretty neck. Port Royal officials are wanting you to testify against that pirate Foxworth. Now you've gone and shot the honorable overseer of Lord Felix, a judge on the High Admiralty Court. 'Tis in your favor I came to check out the pistol shot instead of the governor's militia."

The suggestion that he could do something to help her

brought a flicker of light into Emerald's darkened mind. On the other hand, the man was as troubling as Mr. Pitt.

Militiamen seldom came to check out pistol shots in Port Royal at this time of night. What was Sir Jasper doing so nearby that he could arrive at the opportune moment? Had he been returning from the wharf where Zeddie had seen him with Lord Felix just before her father was shot?

Minette was now on her feet but was trembling with shock. "Mr. Pitt broke in and threatened me, then Emerald. He hit Zeddie too—and might have killed him, he struck his head so hard. Go and see if you represent decent authority!"

"Zeddie?" he inquired with mock disbelief, glancing about the room. "Then where is he?"

"Mr. Pitt carried him away. Please—won't you look for him? He will need help."

"Sure, we'll look for him, but it's Foxemoore's overseer you best worry about. If he dies, Miss Emerald will face charges of murder."

Emerald's eyes met his satisfied gaze.

Minette gasped. "It was *me* who fired the pistol, not Emerald."

Sir Jasper lifted a hand, his wrist sprinkled with lace, as though her words were only an annoyance. "Is that your pistol, Minette?"

"No . . . but . . ."

"Whose pistol is it?"

"It's mine," stated Emerald, and her voice sounded steady. "You know it's mine. Viscount Baret Buckington gave it to me."

"You mean the pirate Foxworth," he corrected. "That is the name under which he'll be tried and hanged, darlin'."

Mr. Pitt stirred from his stupor. His eyes were glazed, and a look of hatred mottled his face as he looked down the stairs at Emerald.

"She did it all right. Karlton's brat tried to kill me!"

Emerald's head jerked toward him. Though weak, pale, and holding a hand to his wound, he leered, apparently satisfied at the trouble he was bringing upon her.

"You're lying," Emerald said.

"I'll swear to it," he rasped.

"I'll tell the truth!" cried Minette.

218

Sir Jasper remained unmoved. "A woman who deliberately shoots the overseer of Lord Felix is called a murderess."

Pitt pointed a shaking finger toward Emerald. "Arrest the pirate's strumpet, Sir Jasper. I demand it."

Emerald looked helplessly from Mr. Pitt to Sir Jasper, and what she saw in Jasper's swarthy face added to her despair. He wanted this!

"Say now, darlin', this is a serious matter," Sir Jasper drawled. "With Karlton arrested for sailing with that blackguard Foxworth—"

"No," cried Emerald, "that isn't true, and you know it. My father was released. And now—"

"Whoever told you so, darlin'? Why, some equally black-hearted pirate helped him escape the island. The governor's looking for him even now. Lord Felix will need tell him the dark news of his death. He was shot trying to get away to the *Madeleine.*"

"No," she breathed and now feared that somehow his release had been a trap. "Earl Nigel arranged his release."

"I'm afraid not, sweetheart. And you, too, are wanted to answer to the Admiralty officials. Now, trying to murder Mr. Pitt will see you arrested for sure. Lord Felix knows well enough how you ran away with Bradford, a man wanted along with your cousin for starting a slave rebellion. You blamed Mr. Pitt for what happened to Ty and shot him."

She could see where his suggestions were leading.

He smiled. "You'd best cooperate with us, unless you want to be sent to Brideswell tonight. I can't say how long you'd be there until Lord Felix arranges for your trial. Maybe months. A dreadful place, darlin'."

Her cold hands gripped the banister. "You were with Mr. Pitt tonight when you murdered my father. You won't get by with it. You'll answer, if it's the last thing I do."

"*I* killed Karlton? Absurd, indeed. For what cause? I'm a sugar planter, a respected member of Governor Modyford's council."

"Smugglers, that's what you all are—and he secretly works for you," she said, pointing at Pitt. "You're both evil slavers. I'll send word to Captain Buckington. He'll see you pay for this."

"Suppose you call him, darlin'. The Admiralty officials are

219

just waiting for him to enter Jamaican waters. And as soon as he does, he'll be clamped into irons and sent to England, where he'll hang in keeping with the piracy charges of his father, that scoundrel Royce Buckington."

Her breath came rapidly. Zeddie had been right. He had feared she was bait to lure Baret back to Port Royal. With her father dead and her arrested, they were certain they could entice him to return.

Then all her father's words about a legal expedition with Morgan—and the governor's recalling Baret to meet with him about service to King Charles—had been a lie? Had he been deliberately set free without the governor's knowledge? Why then had he been killed before he could lure Baret back?

Something had gone wrong. Had her father learned the truth and perhaps refused to cooperate with Felix and Jasper? So they had killed him?

Then the governor would go on believing that her father had broken out of gaol and was seeking to escape to the buccaneers on Tortuga when someone in the militia shot him in the line of duty. And what of her? This meant the governor or the Admiralty officials were still intent upon hauling her up for questioning about Maracaibo.

"Brideswell's no place for a pretty woman without a father. The news will soon spread you're alone," said Sir Jasper. "If you cooperate with me, sweetheart, I'm sure I can smooth matters over. Isn't that right, Pitt?"

Pitt's pale face dripped sweat. "Sure," he breathed, "as long as I get the African wench."

Minette backed away. "I won't go anywhere with you."

Emerald's throat was dry, and her heart thudded in her chest. "I'm not alone. Neither is my cousin. I've seen Lady Geneva. And the Earl Nigel Buckington met with me too. I'm the betrothed of Viscount Baret Buckington."

Sir Jasper smiled an unbelieving smile. "Sure, sweetheart, have your dreams. But before either Geneva or the earl finds out where you are—should they care—months will have passed. Brideswell is the last place they'll look for you. And if I inform Lord Felix that you ran away again—this time to Foxworth in Tortuga—do you think the Harwicks or Buckingtons will doubt it? No need to look so despairing. There's always me."

Minette came forward, trembling. "You can't arrest her! It wasn't her," she repeated. "It was me."

"She's lying," growled Pitt. "It was Emerald all right. She's hated me ever since the branding. Back then, she threatened to get even with me. Running away with Jamie tells you what kind of wench she is. I tell you, Sir Jasper, she belongs in Brideswell with the rest of the murderous women. Was only God's mercy spared me to live."

Emerald could see that, between Mr. Pitt and Sir Jasper, she didn't have a chance to convince anyone of the truth until either Geneva or the earl came to her rescue. She must get word to them.

Sir Jasper looked at the empty pistol. "Now, don't be lying to save your cousin," he told Minette. "The pistol's in her hand. An' despite the pretty words coming from both of you, I saw what happened."

Emerald's eyes met his.

"You shot him, darlin'."

"I'll tell 'em the truth!" choked Minette.

"Think they'll take the word of an African slave against mine? A member of the council? One of the biggest sugar planters in Jamaica? You be a good girl, Minette, and take care of your new master, Mr. Pitt. Me and Miss Emerald have a few things to discuss."

Emerald stood transfixed. She saw him focus on the useless pistol in her hand. "Get out," she whispered. "And take him with you."

Jasper hesitated. "You wouldn't shoot me, darlin', if you could. I'm the one hope you have left. I can save you from Brideswell, or I can call for the authorities and have them take you away tonight. Instead, I'll take you to Jasper Hall," he said. "There is much there to amuse you, including trunks of silks and boxes of gems and pearls, all just waiting for you."

This could not be happening to her.

"When Captain Baret Buckington learns of this, he'll be calling on you at Jasper Hall."

"And until the pirate shows up for his lady, I'll take my chances. I've heard about your sharing his cabin on the *Regale*. And how Karlton wanted to kill him if he didn't marry you. Well, now! I always knew you weren't the angel you pretended, so there's no use putting on airs for me. Cooperate, darlin', and you won't need to worry about anything. Isn't that right, Pitt?"

"As long as I get my share, Sir Jasper. There's the matter of the jewels she stole from Levasseur's cabin two months ago. I want the acres you promised me, and some of those slaves from the Dutch ship."

"Your mouth, Pitt, will one day see your own neck stretch. You'll get your acres—and a few slaves. That Jew will pose no problem. He can't do much but complain to Modyford. When you've served your remaining year at Foxemoore, you can ride out and claim Hoffman's acres. By then he'll have worked the land for you and improved the cottage."

Even in Emerald's own anguish she was furious over this calmly proposed injustice. "Get out. And may God reward you for your cruelty to the man! And I'll go to Brideswell before I have anything to do with you!" She whirled on Pitt. "That goes for you too. Minette is no one's slave, do you hear? She's my cousin!"

"Like Ty," he slurred. He leaned forward, coughing, hand pressed to his wound. "I'm still trackin' him with hounds, m'lady. Almost had him once. I'll find him yet. He's not in the Blue Mountains. Has plans to take to sea with pirates. But Lord Felix is watching the water too. We'll get him yet, an' when we do, I'll see him skinned alive. Better yet, I'll take him as my slave."

Sir Jasper walked to Emerald and removed the pistol from her hand. "Shall we go, m'dear? 'Tis a long but pleasant ride in my carriage to Jasper Hall. All you need do is write a letter telling Governor Modyford about Foxworth's voyage into Maracaibo. Two of his crew were murdered. Levasseur's already sworn to Foxworth's guilt. If you back him up, there'll be no more trouble for either you or Minette."

"Now wait a minute," began Pitt. "I'm not through with the African wench yet. And the jewels—"

Emerald jerked free of Jasper's hand, watching him with loathing. "Baret had nothing to do with the death of Jamie or the pirate Sloane either. Levasseur knows that. It was he who killed them both. And I won't betray Captain Buckington with a letter of lies to satisfy either you or Lord Felix. If the earl knew you were trying to get his grandson hanged, you'd soon be swinging from Gallows Point yourself."

His eyes hardened. "Foxworth will be arrested and tried for piracy whether you cooperate or not, darlin'. He'll show himself to the governor when he hears Karlton's dead and you've been arrested. By offering to bring you to the comforts of Jasper Hall instead of the horrors of Brideswell, I was trying to make matters easier on you."

"On me or yourself?"

"His lordship Felix is adamant about your writing that letter. He will let you sit in Brideswell for as long as it takes to convince you. Foxworth will not learn where you are until Felix is prepared with evidence to make sure the piracy charges will stand."

She drew in a breath. "Well, he won't get what he wants from me."

"You speak bravely, but unwisely. You're in no situation to stand against Felix Buckington. At least at Jasper Hall you'll be treated kindly." He smiled. "Come now, sweetheart, what's a wee letter agreein' to being abducted by Foxworth and forced to sail to Maracaibo? He tried to rescue Lucca, didn't he?"

"You mean you don't know?" she taunted. "You and Felix who've planned his downfall so well? And my father's death?"

"How harshly you indict me. I, who had nothing to do with Karlton's shooting."

"Are you so certain Baret breached Spanish territorial waters? Whose word do you have except my cousin Rafael's, a known pirate! Do you think His Majesty will take his word against the viscount's?"

"It's not what I know Foxworth to have done but what Lord Felix wishes to learn."

"I know what his lordship wants. He wishes to see his own blood nephew hang, even as he betrayed his half brother Royce. I know nothing about Maracaibo. And if I did, I wouldn't tell you."

"Then you'll end up telling Lord Felix himself, darlin'. And he doesn't have the interest in your case that I do."

"I know full well your interest in my case, Sir Jasper. And I should rather sit in Brideswell than become your mistress."

"A pity. Perhaps a few months keeping company with rats and lice will convince you of my charming company."

Her emotions recoiled, and in a panic she watched as he

223

walked to the outside door and called below, "Wooton, summon the militiamen. Foxworth's little sweetheart is willing to risk her own neck to save his. She tried to kill the overseer of Lord Felix Buckington. I'm a witness."

Emerald tried in vain to keep her alarm under control. Minette rushed to her side, trembling, her eyes wide with help-lessness.

Pitt coughed and choked, still sprawling against the wall. "You wench," he breathed to Minette. "You best get yourself over here and attend me."

Minette looked hopelessly at Emerald. Their gazes held in desperation. Minette's eyes filled with tears.

Emerald took firm hold of her arm. "We'll get out of this, you'll see," she whispered as they clutched each other. "You'll be on Foxemoore. See if you can get a message to the Great House."

"He won't let me out of his sight. I've never been so fright-ened in my life."

"You blubbering wench, get your body over here," snarled Pitt. "Can't you see I'm bleeding to death?"

"The Lord is our high tower," Emerald was able to whisper as loud footsteps sounded up the steps and several militiamen entered.

As Minette gingerly neared Mr. Pitt, who latched onto her wrist and jerked her down toward his feet, Emerald met the eyes of a big, strapping youth wearing the faded red coat of the Jamaican militia. She searched his sullen face for sanity, but he refused to meet her gaze.

"Come along, miss."

"I'm innocent," she stated firmly. "You've no cause to arrest me. I want to be brought to Lady Geneva's town house on Queen Street."

"Take her to Brideswell," Sir Jasper told him with the wave of a hand. "The strumpet tried to murder this man. 'Tis a merci-ful thing for her that he lives."

The militiaman remained sullen. "The chief turnkey is asleep," he said. "He's in a foul mood. He warned us not to waken him tonight. What'll I do with her—put her in one of the doxy cages?"

Emerald fought down her horror. The cages were located near the turtle market and were used to lock up for the night all manner of troublemakers and drunken doxies to wait trial by dunking or whipping at the pillory in the square. In the past she had looked upon the poor wretches in the filthy cages as objects either for her pity or loathing, depending on their crimes. Now she was to be one of them? Suddenly the matter took on an entirely new face. Now she knew what it felt like to be abandoned, held up to ridicule and mistreatment.

If I ever get out of this, she thought, *I'll remember prisoners as real people who need a friend. O God, help me, and I'll try to help others.* And a Scripture verse flashed to mind: "The God of all comfort; who comforteth us in all our tribulation, that we may be able to comfort them which are in any trouble, by the comfort wherewith we ourselves are comforted of God."

Sir Jasper interrupted her thoughts, staring at her with cocked brow. "Have you reconsidered, m'dear? You can always come to Jasper Hall, where the bed is dressed in satin."

"Your nefarious plotting will fall on your own head one day. It's you who should be arrested and sent to the gallows, not the buccaneers! Even Captain Levasseur, loathsome pirate as he is, would not treat me like this."

"No? And where would you be today if Foxworth hadn't come to your aid? Jamie would be dead, and Rafael would have forced you at pistol point to marry him."

"So you do know the truth after all, when it's not to your advantage to lie about Baret."

Sir Jasper sighed. "A pity you hold to your rags of decency. Foxworth would surely forgive you for coming with me a few weeks, seeing as how he's already had what he wanted."

Her eyes flashed, and her palm struck the side of his face.

Sir Jasper turned white with rage. "Away with the strumpet! She'll not be put in the cages—put her in confinement! Tell the turnkey he'll be hearing from the governor's officials at the Bailey in a few days."

"Aye, I'll tell him. With two killings tonight, and now this one accused of attempted murder, ol' Braxden will be in a sour mood when we waken him again. Come along, miss." He took firm hold of her arm and led her out the door.

"I'm innocent," she pleaded as he led her down the steps into the humid darkness. "You must listen to me!"

"They all say that."

"Please—have you ever seen me before at Brideswell? If I was a doxy, you should recognize me. You've never arrested me before tonight—and you can tell I haven't the smell of rum on me."

"True enough about the rum. But seein' as how I've only been at this a week, I wouldn't be knowin' how many times you've been hauled to the cages. Anyway, that man was bloodied up all right, and Sir Jasper has your pistol. He's an important man on the council . . ."

"He's a smuggler and a pirate, and he ought to hang! Please —I must get a message to Lady Geneva Buckington."

"Come along, miss, an' don't give me any trouble."

"But I'm innocent. Sir Jasper is lying, and I can prove it."

He stopped by a cart drawn by two horses and called to a fellow guard. "We've been ordered by a member of the governor's council to bring this one to the detention hold."

"What do we got this time? A woman?"

"Aye, a murderess."

Emerald wanted to faint. *Lord,* she prayed, fighting back her tears. *Help me. I commit myself to You.*

The outer door of the gaol swung open, and a lantern was thrust rudely into Emerald's face. She blinked several times before she could see the guard on duty.

"Aye, what 'ave we here, gents? Ain't seen a doxy this pert of face and figure before."

"She tried to kill a man. Hold her till morning. Sir Jasper says he'll be in touch." The militiamen went out, and Emerald was left with the turnkey.

"A murderess, eh?"

"Lies. I'm the daughter of Sir Karlton Harwick—" Her voice broke. "It was my father who was killed tonight . . ."

"Aye, we heard of Sir Karlton turning pirate. He escaped, but the authorities at Fort Charles caught him. He was killed putting up a fight." He looked at her slyly. "So you're alone now?"

She swallowed her fear. "No, I'm not alone. I'm the betrothed of Earl Nigel Buckington's grandson. And I wish to send a message at once to the Buckington residence on Queen Street."

There was a chortle of laughter from another guard who appeared from a back chamber.

"Well, now, imagine this," the turnkey said with a wink at his fellow jailer. "We've a countess in our midst. What say, shall we bow a bit and kiss the lady's sweet hand?"

Emerald pulled her arm away and stepped back.

"There ain't no ring," he said. "Say now—you wouldn't be fooling us now, would you?"

"Maybe the earl's grandson can't afford one," mocked the other guard.

"Or maybe she's got it hidden on her?"

The turnkey grabbed her, and Emerald screamed hysterically, fighting him off.

A voice interrupted angrily from a darkened doorway. "Clyde! What goes here? You waken me again, you blundering cocklebur?"

"Pardon, Your Honor," said the turnkey. "We've a murderess with us. She's a mite hysterical, seeing as how her conscience is darkened by the thoughts of hell. Shall we put her in manacles?"

"Do you think she'll sprout wings and escape?" came the sarcastic retort. "No, you fop, put her in solitary hold."

The door banged shut behind him, and he presumably returned to his bed.

"See what you've done, you feisty strumpet? Your hysterics have me in trouble again."

Impatiently he pulled her down a foul-smelling passageway to a chained wooden door. She tried to break away, but he seized her roughly and drew back the bolt, then shoved her into the odorous blackness.

"Sleep well, me cantankerous countess."

The door banged shut behind her, and the sound of the bolts and locks wrapped about her soul as certain as iron chains.

Emerald stood transfixed in the thick darkness. Sudden hysteria reached out its mad fingers to drive her to endless screaming. Her hands formed fists against her mouth, and she squeezed her eyes tightly shut. The putrefying stench gagged her.

There was a tiny patter—rats' feet?—and for a moment she thought she would faint. She backed away and bumped into a stone wall, crying out in terror when her fingers touched slime.

An odd itching soon overtook her ankles and began to creep up her legs. Lice! Thousands of them! In panic she did scream and stamped her bare feet until, in a frenzy of horror, her knees gave way and she fell to the floor, weeping mindlessly.

There was no one to turn to. She was abandoned. If only Baret would come and suddenly and daringly rescue her. If only Geneva would come. The earl. Anyone. What if no one ever came?

With a stricken sob she remembered, like a child waking from a nightmare, and cried out, "Father God, where are you? I can't stand it! You wouldn't just leave me here. I know You wouldn't! Help me!"

16

BOUND IN AFFLICTION AND IRON

The broiling sun beat upon Minette, huddling in the back of the open wagon on its way inland from Port Royal to Foxemoore. Devastated, her emotions had withdrawn into a world of silence where she tried to shield herself from the cruel words of Mr. Pitt. She was beyond tears now, and a merciful dullness had settled in on her heart. Nevertheless, questions arose to which she could find no answers from the brazen heavens above. Had she been saved from Spanish slavery for this?

For a short time after leaving the lookout house, she had succeeded in blocking out Pitt's boasting voice but not the jackals of doubt that encircled her faith. Her confidence in the Lord had been shaken with the harshness of new circumstances. Had God forgotten to be gracious? Did He not see what had befallen her and Emerald? Her cries for deliverance uttered through the night had gone unanswered.

She envisioned God as far removed from her isolated world of pain, even indifferent to her plight. While she was a small sparrow caught in the trapper's snare, the evil man was victorious and boasting of his cleverness. Yet the merciful Lord of whom Great-uncle Mathias had taught seemed to do nothing about it. How could this be?

"Fret not thyself because of evildoers . . . for they shall soon be cut down," she had read in the Psalms. But what if she met her doom before the Lord dealt with Mr. Pitt? What if Pitt forced her to defile the sanctity of her body by making her his mistress? Would God allow such a hideous thing to happen?

There was no hope. She was now seen as just an African slave. She had no rights, no dignity, no say in what her owner might do to her. She was property. There were no laws in Jamaica to protect her. Even if Mr. Pitt killed her, no one would accuse him of murder! To kill a slave was little more than killing a sick mule. Her safety with her master rested in her value as a worker or in pleasing his sinful flesh.

"'The Lord is my shepherd; I shall not want,'" she said aloud. "'Though I walk through the valley of the shadow of death, I will fear no evil: for thou art with me.'" *With* me—through it all?

"Shut up," said Pitt over his shoulder. "You mention His name one more time, and I'll box your ears good. I had my fill of religion when old Mathias lectured me. It's a relief the man's dead and gone."

The wagon bumped along. And now she realized they were not heading in the direction of Foxemoore but toward the small cacao plantation belonging to the newcomer Reuben Hoffman. What had that no-good Sir Jasper said? Something about Pitt taking Hoffman's acres and cottage? Anyone of Jewish descent fared little better in Jamaica than an indentured servant or a slave, when it came to acceptance and rights.

Pitt drew up near Hoffman's cottage and sat easing the reins as he gazed about with satisfaction. The woods had already been cleared. Hoffman and his son had one ox that they used to till the land. Cacao had already been planted by Spaniards who long ago had turned their backs on that crop and gone to Havana to raise tobacco.

The door opened, and Hoffman came out on the porch with a boy who looked to be thirteen or fourteen. Like the Jews of Barbados, those in Jamaica had migrated from Brazil, Surinam, and other sugar colonies. Mathias had said they lived apart, congregated in the Middle Precinct of Port Royal in a tiny ghetto on what was named "Jew Street." Minette felt sure they'd been forced to name it so.

Although, by the standards of the day, Jamaica was considered a haven for those persecuted, the Jews did not fare as well as most and were looked upon with suspicion. Some were wretchedly poor, others were shopkeepers with goods but very little property. Mathias, who had tried to engage in friendly dialogue with the local rabbi had said they kept their wealth fluid and shipped much of it to colleagues elsewhere. "They are grudgingly tolerated by the Jamaican government and forced to pay a special Jew tax," he had said.

"Afternoon," Hoffman called, curiosity in his tone. He obviously wondered what Pitt was doing looking over his small acreage.

"A nice piece of land," said Pitt.

"We think so, don't we, Isaac?" he said to his son.

Minette glanced at the boy. He had a black curl on either side of his head. The lad made no response and watched Mr. Pitt uneasily.

"You have papers proving this land is legally yours?" demanded Pitt, not favoring them with eye contact but taking in the neat little cottage.

Minette's eyes drifted to a mother cat by a newly planted flower patch. She was contentedly licking her kittens. An empty dish sat nearby. *They* had found a home. Minette's head lowered, and she plucked at the tear in her skirt.

"I bought it a year and eight months ago," Hoffman said cautiously.

"Where did you buy it?"

"Spanish Town—seat of Jamaican government."

"From who? A rabbi?" Pitt asked with a leer.

"No, from the previous governor."

"You got papers?"

"No . . . but it's on record in Spanish Town."

"No, the council says it ain't on record. And if you ain't got legal papers proving it, you've got to leave."

"I won't leave! I bought this cacao plantation when there was nothing here but a few trees—the rest I've put in myself. Isaac and I have worked from sunrise to sunset and—"

"Without papers you got no proof. I got papers. Issued to me by the new governor, Thomas Modyford."

"But—what about the papers issued to me by the previous governor?"

"Guess His Majesty decided Roundheads loyal to Cromwell were traitors, unfit to issue papers. Especially to Jews."

"I'll get those papers. I won't leave."

"You try. You won't get 'em, Hoffman. Now look, I got no quarrel with you. I'll even let you and the boy stay and work my land till I come claim it next year. That's all I got to say. If you want to argue, you go see Sir Jasper in the Parliament." He snapped the reins, and horse and wagon jolted forward at a quick trot.

231

Sitting in back, Minette saw Hoffman place an arm around his son's shoulders. The boy's gaze faltered, and then he looked over at the cat and kittens.

As Pitt drove on toward Foxemoore, Minette could find no solace in the familiar dirt road. It was now a strange road, a frightening road, for she traveled not as Emerald's cousin but as a slave. Hedged with palm trees, it reeked of heat-sodden earth and shrubbery. After the rain, the stinging insects were at their worst, but today she did not bother to slap them away. She was a sacrifice for a pagan idol, and no amount of fighting would deliver her.

The creaking wheels and the horse's steady plodding reminded her of biblical Samson, blind, mistreated, chained like an ox going round and round, pulling a bitter load. *If I was Samson,* she thought, *I'd bring Mr. Pitt down to utter ruin!*

Tears did not flow, but she wondered with hopeless resignation where her Lord was now, when she needed Him most. She was a small sparrow caught in the trapper's snare, but had not Uncle Mathias taught her that the Lord watches over the sparrow?

"A sadist," Emerald had called Mr. Pitt. Now she understood what her cousin had meant.

Where are You? she prayed.

He was all-powerful. With one word He could cause Mr. Pitt to slump over dead. She stole a glance over her shoulder, and the sight of the man flooded her with burning hatred. *I wish you were dead.*

And then she loathed herself for feeling hate.

Her eyes lifted then to the cane field, where she saw slaves—hundreds of them. She saw the women first, shamefully unclothed from the waist up, crawling on their knees through the cane with hoe knives in their hands. Some had newborns strapped to their backs.

Minette began to weep, unable to silence the sobs in her throat as her eyes flooded over and blinded her vision. *I see, Lord. It's not only my sorrow but the anguish of a human family. Yet each is an individual with a face, a different face. No face is exactly the same, no heart responds to the hot blue sky above in the same way. But what can I do? I'm helpless too.*

"Cease your blubbering, you cursed wench," said Mr. Pitt,

232

flicking the reins. "I've enough of your squalling. You tried to kill me, and I ain't forgettin'."

He sat ahead on the driver's seat, a matchlock beside him and a whip on his lap. Sir Jasper had sent a man to attend his wound after the militiamen took Emerald off to Brideswell, and now Pitt was bandaged and presumably recovering, although she noticed with satisfaction that his complexion looked pasty and his eyes had a yellowish tinge. He had coughing spells that would immobilize him for several minutes, and then he'd pop open a flask he carried under his shirt. The rum did little for his brain, but it did seem to ease his coughing spasms.

Next time he falls into a spell, I'll jump wagon and run for it. But his coughing had eased during the hours on the road. He also kept turning his head to glance back at her, as though he expected her to try to escape and was just waiting to lay his whip on her back. His countenance intimidated her.

"You'll pay a high price for shooting me," he repeated. "So you think yourself too good for the likes of me, do you?"

Minette remained silent. She wrapped her arms around herself and buried her head on her knees.

"Look at you, like some turtle sticking its head in its shell. An' I even was going to give you a pretty frock. An' one of them feather bands with beads to wear."

Minette's mind carried her to the coast of Africa, where she imagined the slave traders rounding up her mother. She would have been prodded with a sharp pole onto a waiting vessel and headed with others down into the cramped, dark hold to stay without food or water, sometimes for days. Then she would arrive in the West Indies to be paraded before thoughtless and greedy planters and merchants, to be bought as one bought a pig, a milk cow, a horse.

Her mother's fate had been slightly better than those brought to Spanish colonists. She'd been taken to St. Kitts, bought by a French pirate in a gambling game, and then brought to Tortuga. There Minette had been born and, through her French father, became a cousin of Emerald.

Mr. Pitt's voice shook her awake. "Are you listening, girl? I said you've ruined any chance you had. Do you hear me right?"

"Yes, Mr. Pitt, I hear you."

When they arrived at Foxemoore, he stopped the wagon on

233

the narrow road between the cane fields. He climbed down and came around to the back, where he stood mopping his brow. His canvas shirt was stained with dried brown blood.

He gestured with his good arm toward the field where the women worked. "Ain't a one of 'em who wouldn't come running to take what I offered you. You ruined your opportunity, girl," he repeated bitterly. "Now I wouldn't trust you in my bed, lest you put a dagger in me. You'll go to the cane fields. An' you'll use a hoe. You'll soon learn what it's like to work. You'll work from dawn to dark. Seven days a week, you'll work. If you don't, I'll be lookin' for the chance to lay you before my whip."

"Yes, Mr. Pitt."

"An' if I catch you tryin' to escape like your brother did, I'll teach you a lesson you'll long remember. Now, out with you." He took her arm and jerked her from the wagon.

Minette, frail and small, tripped and fell into the hot dust.

He smiled cruelly. His face dripped perspiration, and he pushed back his stained Panama hat. "Up with you," he ordered. "Get your body to the field where you belong."

Minette got to her feet, feeling a twinge in her ankle. She was aware of her torn frock—and her missing shoes, still with the rest of her things at the lookout house. Her tangled hair hung like wild-honey ringlets, sticking to her face and neck.

"I need shoes to walk," she said.

"You'll walk like the rest of your kind. Always whining. Grateful for nothing." He turned his broad back and gazed off in the direction of the cane workers. "Big Boy!" he hollered. "Get yourself over here."

A handsome, bare-chested African, wearing cotton britches cut off at the knees and a hat of dried woven cane leaves, came at a trot, whip in hand.

Minette tensed when she saw him. It was Sempala, but Mr. Pitt had changed his name to show authority. He was now Big Boy, the muscular chief taskmaster on the field. If a slave was strong, outwardly obedient, and considered loyal, a European overseer gave him authority over the other slaves, sometimes even making him a personal bodyguard. Africans such as Sempala, however, were usually hated by their own who cut the cane and worked in the sugar mills, where molasses and rum were the chief by-products. For a slave such as Sempala to rise from the field, he must prove his willingness to use the whip on rebellious workers. For this ugly task, he had served Mr. Pitt well.

Sempala glanced at Minette, then looked away, but she noted his surprise when he recognized her. The year before, Sempala had gone to Sir Karlton to plead for Minette in marriage. Her uncle had refused. But when Sempala had solicited Mr. Pitt's help, Karlton reconsidered, telling Minette how handsome and upcoming the African was.

Minette had used Emerald to intercede with Great-uncle Mathias.

"He shows no promise toward the true God but holds to his tribal worship in secret," Mathias said. "Whereas Minette has confessed faith in Christ."

The matter had ended badly, with Sempala turning bitter toward her. She had avoided him after that when walking the narrow cane roads on her errands for Mathias.

Sempala noticed Mr. Pitt's stained shirt and the visible bandage about his upper chest. "Someone hurt you, Boss Man? You want me to break him in two?"

Minette stared at the rust-colored dirt beneath her feet and felt the hair lift on the back of her neck.

"Was a wench who shot me. Emerald Harwick. She's in the gaol now waiting to hang, with fit company of rats and lice."

Sempala must have been shocked, but he wore his face like a tribal mask. Only Minette, who knew him better, could see the amazement in his eyes.

"Harwick's dead," Pitt said, as if to hint of why he could get by with his present actions. "I'll be taking over the Harwick bungalow myself." He nodded toward Minette. "She's just another slave now. Gets no special treatment 'cause her uncle was Harwick. She'll work the fields on the far end."

Minette tried to show no emotion as she stood between them, a small waif and two giants discussing her fate. How indignant Emerald would be if she knew Mr. Pitt was moving into her father's house.

The soles of her feet were burning from the hot soil, and the twinge in her ankle was growing more painful.

"An' if she gets better treatment," Pitt was saying, "I'll whip *you.*"

"Yes, Boss Man, no special treatment." Sempala turned and

gloated, his eyes mocking. "Move, you black wench!" He shoved her forward.

Minette stumbled.

The cane grew high and green on either side of the path. Minette walked ahead, and Sempala strode behind her like an African chieftain. The sky was royal blue, the earth beneath her feet a rich brown, but she saw no beauty and found the intense sunlight sapping her strength and leaving her exhausted.

"How come you let him catch you, huh?"

"Leave me alone, Sempala."

"An' you was goin' to marry yourself a handsome white man!" He laughed loudly, slapping his knee, and looking up into the bright sky.

"I said leave me alone." Tears welled up.

"A mighty warrior, a buccaneer named Farrow, huh? Look at you, gal. You is as bad off as me." He yanked on her tangled ringlets. "An' just 'cause your hair is faded don't mean I'm going to treat you nicer than Yolanda's wench."

Tears ran through the dust on her face, leaving little trails.

"Sempala will look a little more like a man to you now," he said, whistling, as he sauntered along behind her, whip over his shoulder. "My skin is black, and I like it. You're gonna like it too. 'Cause you is just as African as me."

He took his prod and gave her a gentle shove. "Move, **gal**. You is too slow for me."

Minette winced and tried to quicken her steps.

"I has me a hut. You'll be moving in soon maybe."

"Please leave me alone, Sempala. Can't you see I'm in sorrow?"

"I can see. Can't go squalling to brother Ty again either, like you always did when I come near."

"I wish he was here!"

"Bet you do. There's talk. He's not in the Blue Mountain anymore. If he's caught here, Pitt will kill him. So if you want kindness, gal, you best give Sempala the smiles he wants when he wants 'em. I'm second to Boss Man Pitt."

"And a traitor to your people," she snapped.

"*You* is talking? Why, you used to live in the white bungalow and walk past us like we wasn't good enough for you. You didn't wanna be black like us."

"My mother was African, and I'm proud of it, but can you blame me because I didn't want to be a slave? If I'd married you, you'd never be a free man and our children too would be slaves. Don't hate me for wanting to escape, just like Emerald."

"I don't hate you. But you think like a white woman. You'll learn the white men won't want you. That warrior Farrow should see you now. You is finally in your place. *Stop.*"

She stopped, her heart throbbing.

He snatched a hoe from a woman. "Go to the boiling house." He handed the hoe to Minette and pointed. "See that circle? You keep hoeing till the sun goes down. Orders from Boss Man Pitt."

The other slaves glanced at her and Sempala, their eyes showing spirits beaten down and without hope. Then they returned to their work.

Minette began to hoe and found the instrument too big for her small hands. As the hour wore on, her soft palms, unused to hard labor, formed blisters that soon broke and stung as sweat ran into them.

The afternoon wore on endlessly. The sun grew hotter. Without hat or parasol, she thought the unbearable heat would bring on a faint. Her skin was burning, and her lips grew dry and cracked. Sweat ran down her face and blurred her vision.

Once she slumped to her knees, her brain overcome with dizziness. The other slaves glanced in her direction, but none came to aid her. She knew they dared not.

I don't care if Pitt does whip me, she thought. *I want to die.*

She heard someone come up behind her then. She felt strong arms lifting her from the hot ground and carrying her between two rows of cane to where there was shade. Whoever it was placed her on some dried cane leaves. Then he removed his shirt, folded it, and placed it under her head. Her eyelids were swollen, and her face burned. She tried to see who it was, but it hurt too much to look.

"You rest," he said in a low voice. "I know who you are. Miss Emerald's cousin. I'm Ngozi. She saved me from Pitt during the uprising. She saved me from hanging. I'm not forgetting. Here, drink."

She grabbed the water skin and brought it to her mouth. Her lips cracked and bled as she gulped the warm drink, and her thirst was such that it might have been sweetened lime water.

He pulled it back. "Not much—it will make you more sick."

"Ngozi." She wept with relief, her eyelids stinging from the salty tears. "I must get to the Great House. My cousin is in Brideswell, arrested for trying to murder Mr. Pitt. It isn't true— I'm the one who shot him, but Mr. Pitt won't listen. I've got to do something to help Emerald—"

He looked at her with pity but shook his graying head, half-covered with a bright orange scarf. His dark eyes were weary pools that reflected his own suffering.

"Pitt and Sempala watch us night and day. We cannot take chance now. You must wait. But there is hope—" He stopped. "Someone comes."

The stalks rustled, and Sempala pushed his way through. Seeing her, he frowned.

"I *said* you was white. Look at you. Roasted like a skinless rabbit."

"What you do to the girl, Sempala? You got a serpent's heart of cruelty."

"Can I stop Boss Man? Is he not the big chief now? Harwick is dead. Work must be done. Pitt will whip me if I help her. Will my raw back free her? Free any of us?"

"We do her work for her today. If he finds out, he whips us, not you."

"If you wasn't an old man, Ngozi, I'd think you has a heart for Minette."

"You talk foolish. I have a heart for God. An' He told me to help her."

"Your white God don't help you none that I can see. How come you isn't Boss Man, huh?"

"If my Savior could suffer, I can suffer until He says, 'Enough now, it is over.' The girl is sick and full of sorrow. Do not stop us. You know you like her."

Sempala frowned at Minette. "Who else will help?"

"The indentured servant, Danny."

A moment later there was another rustle of leaves, and an Irishman stepped out, the one called "the papist" by Mr. Pitt. "Hoot! I'm no' afraid of Pitt's whip. I'll help ye, lassie."

"If Boss Man finds out, I know nothing," said Sempala. "I won't defend you."

"We'll take any whipping."

Sempala looked down at Minette, then at Ngozi and the Irishman. He nodded, turned his back, and walked to the next row.

If Mr. Pitt wondered that she hadn't been brought to the bungalow ill, he said nothing when he came daily on his gray gelding to look over the slaves and the work done. Always her share was completed. He said nothing after demanding to see her palms. Satisfied with her blisters and sunburned skin, he rode on.

One night Minette awoke in the slave hut where she slept on the floor with other women and girls, hearing men's voices outside. Fear gripped her, thinking it could be Pitt or even Sempala, but then she recognized Ngozi's voice.

"Run! It's Pitt," Ngozi said to the men. And then she heard the sound of fleeing feet.

The next noon, Mr. Pitt rode up with Sempala walking beside his horse. Minette saw Pitt glance at her, but his attention was fixed on Ngozi. He reined in, fingering his whip.

"Where were you last night?"

Ngozi remained calm and dignified. "Sleeping in the hut, Boss Man. My body grows old and tired."

"You lie. I went to the hut, and you was gone."

"I was there, Boss Man. Ask the Irishman."

Pitt turned in his saddle. "Well, papist?"

"Hoot, Mr. Pitt, he was there. His snoring kept me awake."

Pitt looked at each man, then around at the other slaves, who stood in somber silence. He fingered the whip handle, his jaw flexing.

Sempala appeared nervous.

"You're all in this together, a rat pack of liars. I know someone's been bringing food to a runaway in the woods. I'll find out who. And when I do, there'll be more hangings. The first to dangle will be you, Ngozi."

Pitt turned his horse and rode away, Sempala running after him.

"One more year and he'll be gone," said Ngozi.

"So what?" said a slave. "Somebody else will take his place."

17

THROUGH
THORNY WAYS

Emerald heard no voice and saw no angel as she prayed, "Father God, where are You?" but a drenching peace as sweet as the dawn flooded her spirit. Her circumstances had not been altered, yet she knew beyond human ability to see that though the conditions binding her seemed dark and hopeless, she was not abandoned. The God of all comfort was faithful. She was living in the very presence of the God of Light. *He* was here. With her. He was strengthening her, taking away her hysteria, bringing courage where minutes before it had fled.

"Jesus," she whispered, delighting in the name that had made her a child of the heavenly Father.

Gradually her thudding heart slowed. She was no longer in a panic. The itching was bearable. The darkness remained but was not as terrifying. They could do nothing to her except what He permitted. And whatever God permitted in suffering would not go beyond what she could endure, for He had promised that His grace was sufficient.

Outside the gaol the chief turnkey sat at his unkempt desk. A dirty lantern glowed on the piece of paper delivered to him a minute ago by a liveried slave. The turnkey squinted and read the brief message:

> *If Emerald Harwick is physically accosted while in Brideswell, you're a dead man.*
>
> Sir Jasper R.

How many days had passed, or had it only been one? The bolt was thrown back, and the door creaked open, letting in a stream of light. Emerald blinked and turned her head away from the painful glare.

"So be it, countess," came a familiar, mocking voice. "A good day to you, and out you come. Make haste, little bird."

Emerald hesitated, and the turnkey lifted both heavy brows. "What's this? Ye be wanting to stay, do you?"

"You—you mean I'm free to go?"

He brayed like a donkey. "Like a birdie with clipped wings, my lovely. You can hop about the outside all you want, but you ain't be flyin' high any times soon."

Disappointment fell. She'd been foolish to even think matters could work out so quickly. Jasper had said "months." She ejected the word from her mind and refused to let it add to her alarm. One day at a time.

The guard gestured her down the smelly passageway without so much as laying a hand on her arm, and she wondered about the cautious change that had come over him. But she gratefully accepted the answer to her prayers.

With the help of daylight, she could see her new holding place. It was perhaps not much larger than the small front chamber in the lookout house. She winced at the hideous sight of women covered with sores, their hair matted and their clothes torn and dirty. Most were half-castes or Africans and Caribs. There was one Spanish woman with disheveled hair, who cursed the turnkey, showing him her fist.

Emerald's first reaction was to pull back in horror, but for some reason she held her ground.

"Well, look at her," mumbled one of the European doxies. "An angel, from the looks of her."

"Careful, you minx," called the turnkey. "She's a cold-blooded murderess, that one."

The woman cocked her head. "A murderess, eh? And who'd you do in, the gov'nor's fancy mistress?"

"I'm not a murderess. You've nothing to fear from me."

"Innocent, she says," cackled one. "Blimey, so am I, ain't I, Maria?"

The Spanish woman spat and tossed her tangles.

"It makes no mind to us," said another. "The bloke had it comin' is my guess. They all do."

One of the women walked up to her with a smirk. "Gimme that bonnet. Sun's hot when we're put out to exercise."

241

Emerald hesitated, then handed it to her. "I'm giving it to you out of kindness, not because you demand it."

Another, with cold, glassy eyes, walked up next. "Yeah, angel? Then your sweet kindness will give me that necklace." She reached a gnarled hand with blackened nails to pull the Huguenot cross from her throat.

Emerald stepped back, covering the necklace with her hand. "It's a French Protestant cross, and it means too much to me. It belonged to my mother."

"Well it's gonna belong to me now. Hand it over. I'll take your dress too!"

"No. I'll not give it up."

The other women grew silent and stared, clearly waiting to see what would happen. The showdown didn't delay long. Emerald expected it and was waiting when the doxy sprang, fingers grabbing for her throat.

They fell together to the floor, struggling, but Emerald was fighting for more than her mother's cross. She knew she must show herself strong, or the others too would turn on her. Although a fighter, the doxy was perhaps in ailing health, for Emerald realized she was strong enough to match her. And then the woman produced a small knife.

Emerald caught her wrist and wrested the knife away. Having the advantage now, she rose to her feet.

The woman, lying on her back, raised herself on both elbows. "Well? Go on with you. Use it! Or call the dirty turnkey!"

"I've no wish to use it," said Emerald, pushing her hair from her face. "All I want is the right to keep what's precious to me. You can have it back if you promise to leave me alone."

The woman stared at her belligerently for what, to Emerald, seemed minutes. Then she grumbled something and nodded.

Emerald hesitated, wondering if she could trust her. She decided there would be nothing gained if she did not, nor could she survive long among these vicious women unless they accepted her enough to at least leave her in peace. Cautiously, she reached down a hand to help her attacker to her feet.

The woman stared at her hand as though she pointed a pistol, then cautiously took hold, and Emerald pulled her up. They looked at each other steadily.

Emerald handed her the knife, and the doxy took it.

242

"I'm Faith," she grumbled, "and don't laugh, or I'll box your ears. I didn't ask to be named that."

"I think it a fine name, but perhaps a little out of place on you."

Faith smirked. "Yeah . . . well . . ." She shrugged her bony shoulders and nodded toward the door. "There's a chapel here—down the hall—just before the door to the courtyard. Nobody goes though, least of all the stinking turnkeys and His Honor. They're as wicked as we are."

The very word *chapel* washed against Emerald's soul like a sweet sea breeze.

"Yeah, how'd *you* know?" asked one of the others.

"'Cause I went in there once," snapped Faith, putting her weapon away. "I was curious. There ain't nothing there 'cept some pews and candles and podium."

"When was the last Sunday a minister came to hold services?" asked Emerald.

Faith gave a laugh. "Here? They don't ever come here. Nobody does, leastways no angel—male or female."

"Ain't so," spoke up an African girl. "We has us an angel now. An' she beat you good."

When the girl smiled at her, Emerald saw that her face bore several deep scars and a memorable mark on her forehead similar to Ty's.

Thereafter Emerald was called "Angel," and the women left her alone. They continued fighting among themselves, however, over food or the best places to sleep.

Emerald thought of the chapel. She would await an opportunity to slip inside when the guards let them out into the open courtyard for exercise.

When exercise time came, however, she saw to her horror that the male prisoners were let into the courtyard at the same time. She lingered behind, hoping to go unnoticed and steal into the chapel instead, but the chief turnkey seemed to constantly watch her, though he too left her alone.

"All's well, countess. Out with ye now. I'll be on guard in the courtyard so them napes can't get ideas."

"I'd prefer to visit the chapel instead."

He gawked at her, then scratched his head. "The chapel, you say?"

"Yes, the women tell me there's one here that's always open."

"Aye, but none of them cackling birds go there. It's full of mice too."

Mice were the last varmints that now troubled her. "It's fine with me. I don't care. May I go?"

He looked confused, then shrugged. "'Spect so. That's what it's there for."

She thanked him, and even her thanks seemed to bewilder him.

"Sure, countess," he mumbled.

During the grim weeks that followed, Emerald looked forward to her daily hours of peace and quiet in the musty chapel. The pews were in shadows, and it was deserted, but she didn't mind. She spent her time in prayer and meditation on the Scriptures that Mathias had had her memorize through the years, for there was no copy of the King James Bible chained to the podium.

Here she interceded for Minette and Zeddie—was he dead or alive?—and asked that one of them might somehow contact Geneva or Earl Nigel and inform them of her fate. By now the earl would have sent a carriage to the lookout house to bring her to Foxemoore. He would know that she was no longer there and would wonder what had happened. What had Sir Jasper and Lord Felix told him, if anything?

The days crept by with no word from outside. The nights were the worst, for her sleep was troubled by the moans of the sick and the cursing of the other prisoners. She wondered again that there was no minister to call even one Sunday a month. The inmates seemed condemned to their fate and forgotten.

When I'm free again, she told herself, for she would not allow herself to think otherwise, *I will do something about it. I shall see acts of mercy extended toward the prisoners—Scripture teaching and Psalm singing. I'll ask the women of St. Paul's to send their discarded clothing and bars of lye soap!*

Her hands would form fists as she lay on the filthy straw. *And I'll do something to stop the guards from violating the women. Maybe I could even ask the governor for women, instead, to be on duty at night at the front desk.*

But who would ever listen to her? Again she grieved over

the loss of her father and what his death meant to her and Minette. There was no one now, not even faithful Zeddie.

But there was God.

She often wondered about Baret. In the night, when the moaning of the sick and dying from the other wards filled her ears, she longed for his presence as she never would have admitted to herself before coming to Brideswell. She relived the voyage on the *Regale*. She found herself remembering only the pleasant times, the sound of his resonant voice, his handsome appearance that grew clearer in her memory with the passing days.

I must look a fright, she thought one day, for though she was permitted to wash, her clothes were torn and soiled beyond cleaning, and the vermin had become a horrid fact of life.

How long would it prove beneficial to Jasper to keep her here? Or was it Lord Felix whom she could blame for her fate? Had he ordered her father's death? How could she bring him to justice if he were guilty? How could she ever prove it? She could not, of course, even as Baret could not prove that Felix had betrayed his father. Felix was too cautious to stain his own hands. Someone else would accomplish his work—perhaps not even Jasper but a hired assassin. She must not dwell on her dismay, for it turned easily to hatred that embittered her soul.

One night she made the deliberate decision to choose young Joseph in Egypt as her encourager. Joseph too had been lied about, thrown into prison, and forgotten. Yet the Lord was with him, the book of Genesis said, and gave him favor in the jailer's sight. She was safe and permitted to visit the chapel each day. For this she was grateful, viewing it as a mercy and a reminder that her Shepherd had not forgotten her, even as He had not forgotten Joseph.

A wistful smile touched her lips as she dozed off. "Maybe I'll be made a ruler," she murmured.

Perhaps another week had passed before the chief turnkey brought her news she'd been anticipating.

"Sir Jasper is here to see you."

He was waiting in the keeper's cramped office, and even Emerald had to admit that, after a depressing month in the ward, Sir Jasper was a fine sight to behold in his expensive finery and meticulous black periwig. His maroon taffetas were spotless, and his wide, linen shirt lapels boasted a flashy peacock pin clustered with sapphires, rubies, and Margarita pearls.

Questions rose immediately to her tongue, but she bit them back. He might look pleased to see her, but he was no friend. On his account she was here. Bitterness and resentment hardened her face, for although she knew that the Scriptures told her to forgive her enemies, she did not have that grace now. Her hands clenched.

"So you've remembered where your lies have put me."

He stepped back and took her in. "My, but you look the vile urchin, sweetheart. 'Tis a good thing the gallant Foxworth can't see you now, or he might sail for worlds unknown!"

His remark was thoughtlessly cruel, and her anger burned. "You have the gall, Jasper! What have you come for—to torment me further? If that's all you have to say—"

"By the king, it's not all I have to say. I've kept up with your fate fairly well. I dare say, darlin', you have me to thank you've survived as well as you have. None of the mongrel guards have touched you, have they? I thought not. I warned that the man who did would be hanged. So there, now give me a wee smile of gratitude and pack your bag. My coach is waiting."

As though the matter were settled and she had nothing to say about it, he settled back in the keeper's chair and put his boots on the paper-cluttered desk.

"I'm free?"

He smoothed his collars, rings flashing. "You have me to thank, m'dear. Pitt has withdrawn all complaints and signed papers I had drawn up by my barrister, attesting to your . . . er . . . mistaken identity."

Emerald stared at him. She could also remind him she had him to thank for putting her here to begin with. And now, having treated her this way, did he think he could so lightly dismiss this month of dark despair?

"Then you've gotten what you wanted from this debacle, or you wouldn't have convinced Pitt to sign papers. Has Captain Buckington arrived? Does Felix have him?"

"More's the pity, no." He looked at her, musing. "Felix's plan to lure him here hasn't worked. He's a cautious and clever fox. Using you as enticement was an error."

So. Baret hadn't concerned himself enough with her fate in

Brideswell to take the risk of coming to Port Royal. She tried not to let Jasper's barb cause pain. It would have been reckless of Baret to come, she thought. What good would his arrest be to either of them? Exchanging himself for her might have been gallant, but his arrest and trial wouldn't have safeguarded her future.

Still, though she knew this, her feminine feelings were slighted by his negligence. *I'm being foolish and sentimental. I'm glad he didn't come—that he's safe.*

Her silence seemed to bring Sir Jasper satisfaction. "I always did say you wasted yourself on him." He stood. "There is one condition for your release."

Her anxious eyes darted to his, and the old loathing was rekindled. "I should have known—"

"His lordship Felix wishes to speak with you. He waits now at Jasper Hall."

She stiffened. "I'm sure he doesn't wish Geneva or Earl Nigel to learn from me of his treachery against me and Captain Buckington! Does he think he can beg my forgiveness so lightly?"

He went to the door and opened it, obviously anxious to depart. "He'll speak for himself."

She knew she was foolish to put any confidence in his words. Trusting Jasper was like swimming with a shark. Her eyes turned hard and cold. "And who will speak of my father's murder? Or am I to forget that also and go on my merry way?"

"Sure now, darlin', you don't think either myself or Felix would go so far as to kill him?"

Her icy silence brought a cruel smile to his lips. "And after I've gone to such pains to see you released to my care."

"*Your* care?"

He shrugged. "I'm an officer in the militia as well as a council member. You've few other friends in Port Royal who'd come to your aid."

"Thanks to you and Felix, there are none who know. What did you tell Lady Geneva and the earl? That I'd traipsed off again with another pirate?"

"You'll need to ask Felix. I may be a member of the council, but I don't hobnob with the earl or Lady Geneva. Shall we go, or do you want to extend your stay here in Brideswell?"

Her hands shook with the expectation of leaving, even if it meant going with Sir Jasper. If Felix did want to speak with her, there'd be no avoiding it, and she had a good many questions of her own to ask. Besides, Jasper was a rake, but she had more chance of escape from Jasper Hall than from here. And if she refused to leave with him now, he might withdraw his support.

She could take no more of Brideswell. At the moment she was willing to take her chances at Jasper Hall.

"I've no bag to pack," she reminded him coolly. "My personal things are at the lookout house. If I recall, you were in a hurry to see me arrested and taken away."

"A hasty action I'll be sure to make amends for, m'dear. Forget your meager frocks. Everything you will need to emerge for your tête-à-tête with Felix is waiting for you. I am always a generous host."

Emerald scanned his smiling face with caution but walked past him out the door. The chief turnkey was waiting for them, release papers in hand and a sheepish look on his face. She reached for them, but Sir Jasper plucked them from the guard's hand.

"Thank you, Clyde, old friend, an' a cheery day to you."

"Aye, Sir Jasper." And his beady eyes returned to Emerald. He offered a half grin and a duck of his head . "An' a fair day to you, Miss Emerald."

"I'll be in touch with you one day again," she said, and when his eyes opened wide, she added, "About the chapel, remember? I hope to find a servant of God who will come to hold Sunday services."

"Er . . . aye, sure, miss. I'd forgotten."

"I hope I won't," she said wearily.

"Most do, soon as they leave," he said, suggesting by his tone that he expected the same of her good intentions.

"Then I'd lose sight of the lessons I've learned here," she told him. "They were too painful to cast aside at the first smell of summer flowers. Would you do me a last favor, Mr. Clyde?"

He scratched his head. "Sure now, if it ain't too hard."

She slipped off her shawl and handed it to him.

He took the wrap, looking puzzled and uncomfortable.

"See that Faith gets that. And tell her the women will be hearing from me one of these days."

He held the article awkwardly, as though ashamed of his past actions. "I'll . . . er . . . tell her, miss."

The carriage jolted and lurched as it raced from Port Royal toward Spanish Town and farther inland, where the sugar plantation called Jasper Hall was located. The tropical countryside flashed past the window like the plumage of a flock of colorful birds.

Emerald drank in deep breaths of fresh air, and, despite the presence of the odious Sir Jasper seated opposite, she savored the sweet smell of freedom's flowers. How blue the sky and brown the earth. How precious the gifts of God, too often taken for granted. Jamaica, for all its reckless ways and the dangers that threatened a young woman of her circumstances, was worth the spiritual struggle to set the prisoners free in Christ.

Was it possible that the Lord had not called her to go away to England after all but to remain and fight for those weaker than she?

A glance at Sir Jasper reminded her of how little she could accomplish without the strength of position and power to confront those who wielded the whips of selfish authority. And yet, if God was calling her to a task greater than her highest human potential, then would He not supply the means to accomplish His purpose?

"At this speed we'll be there in another hour," he commented. "I'm sure you'll be pleased to shed those vile clothes and prepare yourself for a luxurious stay."

She pretended not to notice the glint in his drowsy gaze. "And you're certain Lord Felix Buckington is there also and wishes to meet with me?"

"Would I mislead you, sweetheart?"

"Why, Sir Jasper, whatever gave you the notion I'd suspect such a thing of you?"

He smiled sadly. "Unfortunately for me, Felix *is* there, waiting. We'll both dine with him tonight. You'll find him charming company but a most determined man."

Emerald lapsed into silence. Had Jasper lied when he said Felix no longer sought his nephew? What if the original plans to lure him back to Port Royal remained intact? What if Felix still expected to use her in some way?

249

18

THE DUTCH SHIP

Where did his loyalties belong? To England or to Holland? Baret mused over his quandary as he walked to the quarterdeck railing, feeling the warm wind tugging at his hat.

Cayona Bay lay languid today, surrounded by miles of hot, white sand and slim, straight palms. This was Tortuga, pirate stronghold belonging to France and under the jurisdiction of a governor sympathetic to the buccaneers' concerns. Unlike the new British governor of Jamaica, Modyford, French Tortuga welcomed the Brethren of the Coast with a friendly camaraderie rooted in the governor's craving for Spanish treasure.

Baret looked over the ship's side. A longboat and several of his crew were waiting. They would row him across Cayona's small but excellent harbor to board the rendezvous ship where he expected to meet with other captains of the Brotherhood. And with Henry Morgan.

Morgan. Baret hesitated as he stared at the ship, actually studying its lines for the first time. He lifted his telescope and focused on the vessel.

Shuffling footsteps sounded behind him as Hob walked up. *"Har,* me lordship, so ye be noticing yon difference same as me. Was a shock it were."

"Yes, a mistake, all right. I shouldn't have taken Captain Farrow's word for it. Never trust an enemy-turned-friend, Hob. You'll find yourself like a turtle on its back, just waiting to be snatched up and dumped into your own soup pot."

"Not a pert thought. Yet 'twould sooner be picked up by Lord Felix than raise me pistol against a good Protestant from Holland. Ye know whose smart ship that be?"

"I'm knowing, old friend."

"A piece of eight says the Brethren knew it weren't Morgan's ship. A piece of eight also says it will be gone by sunset and explodin' a few cannon on English Antigua."

Baret had already switched his interest from the so-called rendezvous ship of Morgan to a nearing longboat bringing Erik Farrow. Baret waited for him, his intense dark eyes reflecting restrained impatience for what he perceived a careless misjudgment on the part of the Brotherhood.

"That isn't Morgan's ship." Baret gestured with his head toward the supposed rendezvous vessel as Farrow boarded.

Erik, in keeping with his style, remained unconcerned as he joined him. Taking the telescope, he fixed it on the mysterious ship.

Baret watched him. He usually found Erik's impassiveness amusing, and he enjoyed goading him into an emotional response. He leaned on the rail and affected the role of viscount. "I am disappointed, Erik. You are no admirable watchman for His Majesty. Your rum-eyed crew ought to be flogged."

"Your lordship?"

"That's a Dutch warship."

"It is?"

Baret smirked. "You know it is. For your silence you could be arrested by my noble uncle and dangled at Gallows Point."

Erik apparently missed Baret's intended irony, for they were both Dutch sympathizers, although Baret had promised his grandfather he would fight for England.

"It was not I, your lordship, who informed the Brotherhood that it was Morgan's ship."

"Ah?" said Baret, disbelieving.

Erik's smile offered pretentious apology. "A thousand pardons plus one. I suppose it is Dutch, after all."

Baret offered a bored gesture as though it no longer mattered. Then he frowned, his thoughts turning elsewhere.

Erik removed his hat. His golden hair was tied back with a leather thong. Then he, too, suddenly frowned, gazing out toward Cayona Bay toward a second ship making for Tortuga's harbor. "That's Captain Mandsveldt. I hear he comes from a prosperous raid on De La Vacha."

He had pronounced the old Dutchman's name correctly, whereas Baret had noticed that both English and French called the captain "Mansfield."

"Maybe he has news of Morgan." Baret turned his glass onto Mansfield's ship.

"That's the reason I came." Erik lifted a piece of paper from inside his frilled shirt. "This is for you. From Morgan."

"What news?"

"He's not coming to Tortuga. He's staying on at Port Royal."

"Not *coming*—" Baret plucked the message from his hand and scanned the single line. "'Campaign delayed,'" he read aloud, "'H. Morgan.'"

Seeing his one golden opportunity for entering Porto Bello to search for his father lost, Baret crushed the paper into a wad. "Delayed! Again! I must see him. We *must* attack Porto Bello! I cannot hold Miguel captive forever. And if I release him, he'll be quick to bring warning to the officials of our plans."

"Har!" said Hob, pouring coffee into a cup and handing it to Erik. "I was right, Cap'n Foxworth. Ol' Governor Modyford be wantin' an attack on the Dutch, not them yellow-livered papists! Ye do owe me three pieces of eight, Cap'n Foxworth!"

Baret tossed him the coins and looked at Erik. "Morgan won't attack the Dutch—neither will Mansfield. So why, I'm wondering, would Morgan stay grounded in Port Royal instead of joining the Brotherhood here? It's a curious thing."

Erik showed nothing of his own disappointment at the delayed expedition, but Baret guessed it was as stark as his own.

"Forget Morgan. We have two of the best ships on the Caribbean. We can make an expedition of our own," Erik said.

Baret considered him, tapping his chin. "You'd risk Porto Bello?"

"I risked Coro and Puerto Cabello."

"For Porto Bello we'd need at least one more ship."

"Pierre LaMonte might join us again."

"Ask about, but be discreet. Even here, there are few I trust. The French buccaneers may have cheered my defeat of Levasseur in the duel, but they are first loyal to their own blood. And with England now at war with both Holland and France, they will be sure to side with them."

He lifted the glass again toward Mansfield's ship. The stalwart Dutchman would be a good man to join, but he was getting old, and having just come from a raid he wouldn't be anxious for another so soon, least of all on the queen of Spanish strong-holds, Porto Bello.

"So Morgan's stayed in Port Royal," mused Baret again. "Odd, don't you think? What would Morgan have in common with Modyford, when he's ejected the Brotherhood from Jamaica?"

"More than you may think. And he's not gulping rum in a bawdy house but sipping sophisticated Madeira in the governor's residence. In the company of the new lieutenant governor—and his daughter."

Baret lowered the spyglass.

"The lieutenant governor has a name you're sure to find of interest—Colonel Sir Edward Morgan."

Baret squinted at him sharply. "You mean Morgan's uncle from Wales?"

"His choleric uncle is now second to Modyford, appointed by His Majesty."

Baret leaned on the rail, pondering. Morgan had cause to stay in Port Royal all right, and if he knew the mind of the tough buccaneer, the cause would be something big. But what could be bigger than sacking Porto Bello?

Baret recalled that Colonel Sir Edward Morgan had been a staunch Royalist who had fought long and bitterly for the king against the Roundheads under Cromwell. When Charles Stuart had been forced into exile, Sir Edward and his wife and several daughters also went into exile, forfeiting his land holdings. He was a poor man now, for the king lacked money to repay his loyal cavaliers for their losses. The king must have awarded the post of lieutenant governor to him for his past service.

"Henry Morgan is courting his cousin, Mary Elizabeth," Erik said. "It may be we've lost the best captain the Tortuga Brother-hood is likely to have for some time."

"I can't see him nibbling crumpets and sipping tea in a par-lor for long. Not while Spanish treasure waits to be gathered like fat eggs from a sleeping hen. Morgan must have plans. And with his uncle as lieutenant governor, we may have run into luck, Erik."

Erik seemed to ponder also. "Unless we underestimate his secret ambitions, your lordship. He may not be content to re-main a freebooter after all. Notice how cautious he is when it comes to an expedition without a commission."

"You're right. And so far his luck holds. On the Gran Grana-da raid, he convinced the governor he hadn't realized all English commissions were called in. So far, he can say he's strictly the king's privateer. Which is more than either of us can do," Baret said. "I wonder what his uncle may think of Jamaica's private navy."

"Jackman seems to think the wind may be blowing in our favor again. The planters are worried about an attack from Spain. They're complaining to the governor for sending us packing."

Baret's interest grew. Jackman. Morgan's lead captain. Then Morgan *must* have an expedition on his mind. Was he waiting for the well-wishes of the governor in the form of legal commissions? "Jackman is *here?*"

"Arrived this morning. There's another man too—the one who brought this message from Morgan. He's a friend of Mody-ford and is asking to see you."

"Asking to see me. Now this is interesting. Where is he?"

"With the French governor. There's to be a meeting later on the beach. Mansfield's men will be reporting their booty. But take heed if you go there, Baret. Yves Montieth will be present also. He's heard about your duel with Levasseur. They're related."

"A chance I must take. Either Jackman or Mansfield may know what Morgan is up to. And I wish to see this 'friend' of Modyford's bold enough to come here to see me!"

"With Gallows Point waiting, you best be on guard."

Mansfield's arriving ship fired a greeting to Tortuga's fort, high on the bluff. The French governor's militia answered with a welcoming volley. The old buccaneer headed into Cayona Bay with flags flying and drums beating.

Hob laughed. "*Har.* Cap'n Mansfield carries a sweet haul this time. Look how low she sits in the water."

Baret and Erik went down the quarterdeck steps.

"Need I remind you there is the unresolved matter of the treasure of the *Prince Philip* on Margarita?" Erik said. "Each day we delay gives Levasseur more time to find it on his own."

"You need not remind me. I await the return of Karlton. Do not worry about Levasseur. He's not clever enough to guess its place of concealment. That information remains with me—and Karlton. Margarita will wait until we attack Porto Bello."

Since 1660, the white-and-gold lily-dotted banner of the

254

Bourbon dynasty of Louis XIV, king of France, had been flying not only over Tortuga but above ports Margot and de Paix on Hispaniola. Tortuga—French for "turtle"—had a fort built high on the bluff overlooking Cayona beach. It bristled with guns taken through the years by the buccaneers from captured Spanish vessels.

The fort had been built by an early self-imposed governor, a French Huguenot by the name of Levasseur. His hatred for Spain and its persistent persecution of Protestants who had escaped to the West Indies had eventually turned that Levasseur into a raving pirate.

Baret heard that he eventually went mad and was murdered by a fellow pirate. Since then, the freebooters had managed to drive off further attacks on Tortuga by the *guarda costa,* and governors more respectable than Levasseur were sent out from France in an attempt to govern the turtle-shaped island and its defiant pirates.

Unlike the English governor of Jamaica, the new French administator, Bernard Deschamps, Chevalier du Rausset, welcomed the buccaneers and worked with them by secretly granting marques to attack Spain's shipping and her colonies. This he did by granting commissions not from the king of France—who, like King Charles, was at peace with Spain—but from Portugal.

Portugal had been at war with Spain since the 1640s. By his selling Portuguese commissions, the buccaneers were able to legally sail as privateers under Portugal's flag and defend themselves from arrest by France for piracy. Henry Morgan had sailed under a Portuguese commission on his last raid.

Captain Edward Mansfield was returning now with just such a commission.

Clear and calm, Cayona Bay reflected the overhead sun. By the time the longboat from the *Regale* arrived, the captains and their officers were already gathering on the beach beneath an awning of dried palm branches.

Baret and Erik, with members of their separate crews, stepped onto the glittering white sand. Baret settled his hat against the glare and looked up at the governor's fort. Cannon stared sightlessly at the Dutch ship, resting unobtrusively at anchor without flag, before what he suspected was a secret voyage to attack Barbados. His cousin Grayford, commanding the H.M.S. *Royale*, was also anchored in the harbor, unsuspecting.

If Baret wished to gain the favor of King Charles, he might sail tonight to warn the English. The noble deed would also win the graces of his cantankerous grandfather. But somehow Baret felt no driving passion to betray the Dutch. He debated with himself without coming to a decision.

His boots sank into soft, dry sand as he walked up the beach with his lieutenant, the big redheaded Scot, Yorke. Erik followed just behind with his own officer, Jeb, who sported a gold ring in his left earlobe.

Baret wore a gaping white shirt of cool cotton and dark breeches, in the belt of which he carried a brace of pistols, since only a fool or a novice would meet with the pirate captains without weapons. The Brotherhood might entertain mutual respect for one another, but that could swiftly turn to temper and a duel.

Yorke carried his machete and a broad-bladed cutlass, and Baret's serving-man, Hob, insisted on bearing his captain's baldric with style, a delighted grin on his leathery old face.

Baret paused on the beach before joining the parley under the awning, his gaze flickering over the ruthless breed. Among the pirates of the West Indies, they represented some of the most brutal men that the Spaniards had yet confronted. Nevertheless, their costumes were as fine and varied as any in the courts of England, France, or Spain, since what they wore was the rich fruit of plunder. Still, for the most part, the taffetas, velvets, Mechlin and Bruges lace was soiled, torn in spots, and sometimes stained with brine and blood-spattered.

Some disdained fashion, and these wore calico shirts and loose breeches of rawhide, or baggy cotton pantaloons bloused at the knee. All wore long, rat-tailed mustaches. Because of the sweltering heat, many had shaved their heads and wore scarves to protect their scalps.

"Seems the hardest barnacles of 'em all be gatherin' for the divvyin' up," mused Hob.

Baret agreed, and then his gaze unexpectedly fell upon Captain Rafael Levasseur. So. He was back. Baret's anger slowly heated. "He's managed a swift voyage from Port Royal," he said over his shoulder. "Cecil informed me he met with Felix."

"Trouble," said Erik, nothing in his voice.

"Traitorous scum," grumbled Yorke. "Ye shoulda sunk his ship when ye had the time, Captain. I wonder what he wants besides trouble?"

"Rest assured we'll soon find out. He appears to anxiously await our arrival."

Beneath the sailcloth were a wide carved table and several chairs, the chief seat waiting for the governor. Some wooden chests sat on the sand, guarded by several buccaneers with pistols.

In the two years that he'd searched for his father, Baret had allowed himself to become acquainted with them all, hoping to win their confidence as one among them and so to discover any news of Royce Buckington. One of those pirates was the black-browed Pierre LaMonte, who now sat sprawled in a low chair, scanning the others in silence. His reputation along the Mosquito Coast brought terror to the Spaniard colonists. But not nearly as much as did that of Jean David Nau, better known on the Main as Captain l'Olonnaise. Tales of his crew and their horrendous expeditions beneath the skull and crossbones had convinced Baret the man was a sadist as hopelessly evil as the Inquisitors.

There was also Captain Michael le Basque, a deadly man with the rapier, and the blond, blue-eyed Dutchman Roche. Beside him, sprawled on the sand, was Captain de Montbars, known to the Spaniards as the "Exterminator." Cream lace spilled from his cuffs and embroidered his wide collar, magnificently arranged over an emerald-green velvet jacket. A ruby glowed hotly on his pistol belt.

"There are few Englishmen," Baret commented to Erik, noticing several hard glances from the French.

In light of the war, his presence might be looked upon with less favor than usual, although they knew of his loyalty to Holland—there were few who would not have heard about the martyrdom of his mother. But as Erik had already warned him, the duel with Rafael Levasseur had not set well with many of the Frenchmen.

"And look who comes now," said Erik in a low voice.

Baret followed his gaze. Yves Montieth was cutting his way through the other captains, who grudgingly moved aside to allow him berth. Then Yves stood with booted feet apart in the hot sand, looking about with belligerent curiosity as if to see who among the Brotherhood was there to match his own grand presence.

Baret felt the fierce black eyes measure him, and it was clear from Yves's expression that Erik was right. He knew about the duel with his relative Rafael.

Baret returned the even stare. From experience he knew that the one way to avoid trouble was to not flinch in the presence of cutthroats. Pirates and buccaneers alike respected little else other than courage and skill with weaponry and ship. A man who backed away from an insult did not live long, unless he surrendered to the position of a lackey.

Levasseur said something to Yves, who nodded and, turning, spoke in sharp French to his lieutenant. The officer primped his oiled mustache and looked over at Baret, then at Erik. The three pirates doffed their plumed hats, a sign they wished no confrontation.

Baret and Erik exchanged glances.

"Don't believe them," Baret murmured but smiled in their direction and removed his own hat with fanfare, bowing low from the waist. Then he walked toward the meeting.

A murmur broke out among the pirates when several men were seen approaching from the direction of the governor's fort.

One of the captains stretched out his legs in the sand, glaring as he watched them come. "So the stinking governor's finally decided to keep the meeting. About time, I say. Who does he think he is, to keep good men waiting?"

"He comes for his divvy," said another.

"Where's Jackman and Mansfield?" inquired Baret.

Heads turned slowly in his direction and he sensed again their resistance to his presence.

But the Dutchman Roche eased the moment. "Mansfield's sick. Stayed aboard his vessel. Jackman went to see him."

Odd, thought Baret. "When the booty's to be divided? You mean he trusts you sharks?" he asked lightly.

"Are you suggesting, Monsieur Foxworth, that I, Jean David Nau, cannot be trusted?" asked a black-browed pirate with lofty disdain.

"Monsieur, no! Why, we all know how well *you* can be trusted, my captain!"

Roche chuckled, and several others smiled briefly, but the rest wore hot-tempered scowls.

"Behold, the gallant and noble French governor arrives," announced Baret. "Arise, Brethren, in the company of thrilling excellence and integrity!"

"*Har,*" chuckled Hob. "Seen more excellence in a squalling Spaniard danglin' by his thumbs."

The captains grumbled, but those sprawled on the sand pushed themselves up and stood in slouching stances. "Greetings, Monsieur Governor," they mumbled, pulling off their hats, then pushing them back on.

Two militiamen, bearing the soiled fleur-de-lis, escorted the governor under the canopy.

Baret was taken by surprise when he caught sight of the Englishman with him. James Warwick was a member of Modyford's council.

After Charles had been anointed king, he rewarded the English islands in the Caribbean for their loyalty, granting several baronets and knighthoods on Barbados and Jamaica. One of those receiving the title of baronet was the pompous Warwick, sugar planter and friend of Felix.

Warwick, looking out of place in a hat with a withered brown turkey feather and a yellow coat sporting large wooden buttons, came to stand under the canopy. He was supported by a brawny militiaman, who looked ill at ease as he eyed the captains he knew well from better days at Port Royal.

"Well, gentlemen, Port Royal has sorely missed you. Modyford sends his toast for what ails ye, and a hearty summons back to your home port," the baronet said.

The buccaneers exchanged glances.

"Monsieur Captains!" mocked Pierre LaMonte. "We are honored! It is the English governor's friend Warwick." He bowed. "Monsieur. You have not come to Tortuga to arrest us law-abiding Frenchmen, then?"

"I am certain, Captain LaMonte, that will not be necessary," Warwick said in a firm voice, ignoring the laughter.

"*Oui,* monsieur? Is it so?" Pierre good-naturedly gestured toward Baret. "Not even this half-caste Englishman and Dutch pirate, fit for Execution Dock?"

Baret smiled. "Not Execution Dock, Pierre. It is too far. Gallows Point will suffice." And he doffed his hat toward Warwick. "A pleasant afternoon to you, Baronet Warwick. You're in time to witness the biggest pirate of them all, the governor of Tortuga, divvying up the booty the fair citizens of his island have recently borrowed from a Spanish merchant ship on its way to Cádiz. On with it, Pierre! What have you brought the governor? Pearls from Margarita Island, perhaps?"

The French governor smiled unpleasantly, his eyes unblinking beneath folds of fat. "Monsieur Foxworth has a questionable sense of humor, Baronet." He cleared his throat and gestured to Warwick. "Be seated, please."

Pierre grinned at Baret and smoothed his curled mustache. "Perhaps we should give a share to Monsieur Warwick to bring back to his darling wife at Port Royal, eh?"

Warwick cleared his throat, for it was known that his wife decked herself with Spanish jewelry. "You may keep your pearls, Captain LaMonte." He looked toward Baret. "It is you, Captain Foxworth, whom our beloved Governor Modyford wishes to entertain."

Laughter erupted.

"How generous of him, Baronet. You won't mind if I decline the invitation? But are you sure it's the goodly Jamaican governor who wishes to entertain me and not my warmhearted uncle?"

Again there was a chuckle. "You're naught but gallows bait for him, Foxworth," a pirate said. "He'll sleep well knowin' you're dangling in the salty breeze a'right."

Warwick held up a hand. "On the contrary, Captain Foxworth, Lord Buckington didn't send me, nor does he know I'm here. It's the governor himself who wishes your presence—and Henry Morgan."

At the mention of Morgan, Baret's interest sharpened, but he did not trust Warwick or the governor. "You've brought me a letter from Morgan?"

Warwick smiled. "Well, no, but I've been commissioned to be his spokesman."

"You'll forgive any affront to your well-known honor, Baronet, if I question your legal commission."

"Now look here, Baret—" he began, but Levasseur interrupted him. "Monsieur Foxworth, it is I who have the letter—not from Morgan but from Demoiselle Emerald Harwick." His black eyes glinted with malicious good humor. "You wish to see this letter from a damsel in harm's way, monsieur, yes?"

A tense silence descended on the gathering. Levasseur now had Baret's full and unamused attention.

Warwick looked angry. "You stay out of this, Captain Levasseur. I've been sent by Modyford."

"And I, Baronet, have been sent by a woman of grave importance to both myself and Captain Foxworth," snapped Levasseur.

Baret watched him intently. He did not like this unlikely turn of events.

"I wish to speak with you, monsieur."

"In private," Baret rejoined. "You and I, alone." He looked directly at Levasseur's relative Montieth.

"Of course, monsieur, alone," said Levasseur. "What else?" And he spread his arms wide. "The beach?"

"After you, my captain."

Levasseur bowed, pushed his way through the musing captains, and sauntered on ahead toward the shore, while the remaining pirates listened and watched with a new caution of their own.

"Captain Foxworth," called Warwick as Baret turned to follow. "I am most serious about meeting with you. When can we talk?"

"Tonight, at the Sweet Turtle. Captain Farrow and my lieutenant will make arrangements with you."

"Very well," he said disconsolately. "I had hoped to get this over with and return to Jamaica."

"What, monsieur!" mocked the French governor. "You do not appreciate the company and climate of Tortuga?"

"No offense, Governor," Warwick hastened to add and cast a knowing glance toward the flagless ship at anchor in the bay.

The French governor was foxy enough to notice his look, as did Baret.

"Then you will stay, monsieur," he stated quietly. "Not one day only, but several days at least. *Oui, oui,* I insist!" He held up a big hand when Warwick protested. "In the name of His Majesty of France, would you insult me?"

"Well no, naturally not, Governor—"

"Good, else the Brotherhood would need to insist otherwise." The warning was disguised with a smile. "You see, we must entertain you at the fort. Yes, and my wife and daughters too. They will make you most comfortable."

"Well—if you insist."

"We insist, monsieur. Most definitely."

His voice ebbed away on the breeze as Baret walked across the sand with Erik. *So the baronet recognized the Dutch war vessel.*

"I do not like any of what is going on," Erik said. "Knowing Felix, he may have sent Levasseur to try to trap you."

"My thoughts as well. Nevertheless, let us see what he has to say about Emerald. Wait for me at the Turtle after the govenor's meeting. The baronet, too, is to be considered with caution. We'll see what message he claims to bring from Modyford."

Baret parted from Erik and walked alone toward the beach, the wind blowing against his hat and shirt. The mention of Emerald had sobered him. If more than her voyage to England had gone awry, why hadn't Karlton come to tell him? Levasseur had just arrived from Port Royal and would know what was happening there, but trusting any information from the wily Frenchman was always a risk. He could not forget that Levasseur had met with Felix. Whatever information he now brought might indeed be the makings of a trap.

Levasseur stood waiting, his face hidden beneath his cocked hat, one lean, wiry hand tapping his baldric. Behind him the sun glittered on the water, and the bay shimmered with silvery ripples.

Baret paused a few feet away from him, hand resting on his own baldric.

"I bring news, captain."

"As friend, or enemy?"

"Monsieur! You hurt Rafael's heart. You speak of the duel?" He waved a hand. "Ah, that. It is nothing. You let me live. What peasant would argue with the withdrawing of the rapier!"

Baret smiled crookedly. "You would, Rafael. On with it. Where is the letter from Captain Harwick's daughter?"

"There is no letter."

Baret's expression did not change, but his eyes flickered.

"I shall explain," Levasseur said.

"See that you do."

"My beloved English uncle, Karlton, was arrested for piracy

and accused also of working with you, monsieur, in the Maracaibo incident that took poor Lucca's life. I, a blood kin and friend, used all my skill to help him escape. But, alas—"

"Where is he?"

Levasseur sighed and lifted a helpless hand. "Dead, monsieur. Shot in the back on the wharf while seeking escape to a longboat. It is most sad."

Baret watched him, restraining his shock and dismay. Dare he believe him?

"How do you know he's dead?"

Levasseur laid a hand to his heart. "Me? I too was in Port Royal, where I waited to set sail aboard the *Venture*. I was expecting Karlton to follow aboard the *Madeleine*. He was coming here, so he said, to find you, to warn you of Monsieur Felix. But, alas! A boat arrived late with a member of Karlton's crew, a man you know and trust—Monsieur Tom is his name—and he told me the monstrous news of my uncle's death. I came here at once, bringing with me Monsieur Tom so that you would trust me, for there is yet more to this sad tale."

He watched Levasseur, searching for evidence that he was lying, but there was nothing in the man's face to convince him the story was fabrication. Tom, a friend of Karlton's, was a man Baret knew to be trustworthy because of his Christian testimony. If he was here with Levasseur, then the news must be true.

"Tom waits in the Turtle," said Levasseur, as though reading his mind.

Then Karlton is dead.

He thought of Emerald.

"What other news?"

"Demoiselle Emerald used a pistol to shoot an innocent man. Now she is being held in Brideswell as a murderess."

Baret stared at him. *Murderess? Impossible!* He cast that notion aside and concerned himself instead with the fact that she was locked up in Brideswell. He knew it was a foul and filthy place and that the guards could not be trusted.

Levasseur appeared pleased at his shock.

"When?" Baret demanded.

Levasseur spread a hand. "Two weeks, maybe three."

"And you only *now* come to inform me!"

"Monsieur captain! I only now learned of it!"

263

"And the man they claim she's murdered?" asked Baret.

"The overseer of Foxemoore. She may hang, monsieur."

The overseer. Baret tried to place him. Had she not warned him about the man? What was his name? Pitt? He had arranged for her cousin Ty to be branded as a runaway. If she had shot the man, he thought he knew the reason.

"When did this happen? Before Karlton's death?"

"Afterward. He came to the lookout house to take her to Foxemoore."

"More likely to take advantage of her situation now that her father was dead."

"Perhaps, monsieur," he said agreeably, and Baret measured him, not liking Levasseur's humility or apparent friendliness. Nothing had changed between them. Not even Emerald's incarceration could bridge the dislike they felt for each other. What was Levasseur up to? Had Felix sent him, using Emerald's situation and Karlton's death to lure him back to Port Royal?

"Who else was involved in her arrest beside Felix?"

Levasseur shrugged. "I do not know even that he was involved. I have seen no one, Foxworth."

"Sir Jasper?"

"Who is to say? What will you do, monsieur? If you will do nothing, then I will see to my cousin's rescue from Brideswell."

"Rest assured, my captain, I have every intention of returning to Port Royal. I made a vow to her and Karlton, and I'll keep it in due time."

Levasseur smiled coolly for the first time. "There is no reason now to keep the vow, monsieur. A suspected murderess has no reputation to defend or protect."

"I will be the judge of that."

Levasseur's black eyes snapped with energy. "She should be brought here to Tortuga to live among her relatives—and mine. It is here she belongs, and always has, not on Foxemoore, or in your England. If she goes anywhere else, it should be to France —with me. You will surely change your mind about her now. There is also the matter of Mademoiselle Thaxton."

Baret grew uncomfortable as he always did at the mention of Lavender.

"There is something you must know, monsieur."

"Suppose you tell me what it is about Lady Thaxton I should know."

Levasseur now looked amused. "The marriage, monsieur, has not happened yet. The war has separated the two lovers. Mademoiselle is now vowing she made a rash mistake in breaking off her engagement to you."

This, added to the news of Karlton's death and Emerald's being held in Brideswell, was too much for one day. For a moment Baret felt nothing. Then, the implications of the triangle cut deep. He felt a surge of excitement at the news that Lavender was unmarried and immediately became angry with himself.

Levasseur eyed him, cautious, pleased, evidently guessing the blow his words had delivered. "It is said, monsieur, by men who know you, that Mademoiselle Lavender sent you a letter of her marriage when we rendezvoused with Captain Farrow. Did you think her married before our duel? If so, that changes matters considerably, does it not? Emerald will not be pleased you wished only to marry her because your true love had married another."

Baret's jaw tensed, and he placed his hands on his hips. "Yes, I knew about her plans. I admit I was angry."

Levasseur smiled. "It is expected, monsieur, yes. I quite understand. Women are miserable creatures. We cannot live with them, nor without them. Tell me, Monsieur Foxworth, would you have agreed to marry Emerald and dueled me if Mademoiselle Lavender had not sent you that offending letter?"

Baret looked out at the silvery ripples on the bay. How could he answer? He himself did not know.

"Monsieur, let us put the duel behind us. The woman you love is not married. She longs to break her engagement to your cousin. Mademoiselle is surely fair of reputation and of noble English blood. Whereas the woman I want is more fitting the rogue that I am. She is an accused murderess. Her mother was the daughter of my uncle—a worse pirate than I. Is it not plain which woman should belong to whom?"

Baret continued to stare out at the calm sea, his insides a storm of conflicting emotions. He could, if he wished, give Levasseur more reason to hope. He suspected Emerald of caring for Levasseur more than even she knew.

"What do you intend to do, Monsieur Foxworth?"

Baret looked at him narrowly. "I intend to give myself time to think matters over. Karlton's death is a serious blow. Nor could I live with myself if I did nothing about Emerald's situation."

Levasseur showed his pleasure. "Agreed, we cannot leave her in so filthy and lewd a place. You will go with me to Port Royal to free her by our swords?"

He would be a fool to allow Levasseur to know his plans. Even if what he told him were true, Baret was certain Felix was behind it somewhere. Cecil had seen Levasseur leaving his presence. That Levasseur might be working for Felix, taking the place Erik had once held, seemed feasible. But neither would he let Rafael think he suspected him.

"We will do what we must to see her out of Brideswell."

"A wise decision, Monsieur Foxworth. When do we leave?"

"Soon," he said evasively. "Perhaps tomorrow. Tonight there is the meeting in The Turtle with Modyford's man. I will see what he has to say for himself and the governor."

"A fair arrangement," said Levasseur after a moment, "but whatever happens, I will not leave Cousin Emerald in Port Royal. She is safer here."

"Whatever is decided will be decided by myself and Emerald," corrected Baret. "You can rest assured I'll care for her future now that Karlton is dead."

"As you wish. It is not the answer that pleases me, but I can see it will need do for now, monsieur captain."

Why was Levasseur so obliging?

"Then we will make arrangements to quietly visit Port Royal," Levasseur said. "Our plans, do we make them aboard my ship or yours?"

Baret scanned him. "We will make them at the Sweet Turtle after we hear what Warwick says."

"You will not change your mind?"

"Nothing could keep me away—including Felix—or Gallows Point. I am sure, Captain Levasseur, that is as planned."

"Then we see eye-to-eye, monsieur." He bowed and walked past him to rejoin the meeting underway beneath the sailcloth.

Baret looked after him. He was still standing there when a watchful Erik walked out on the beach to join him.

"Trouble, my lord viscount?"

Baret looked at him grimly. "Karlton is dead."

266

Erik was clearly startled. "A duel?"

"No. Levasseur says he was killed by the militia when trying to escape. I have another notion of how it might have happened."

"Miserable luck. And if you return, you too will be arrested."

"I must take the risk." He looked at Erik. "Emerald is being held for attempted murder of Pitt, the overseer of Foxemoore."

"Impossible, your lordship! She would never do such a thing. It's a trap set for you. You can look no further than Lord Felix."

"And Sir Jasper." Baret's eyes hardened, and he tapped his fingers against his pistol brace. "I will sail for Jamaica tonight."

"A mistake. It is what they expect and wish you to do."

"I'm aware of that."

"And you'll go to Gallows Point?"

"I have a plan . . . you can help by diverting Levasseur and his relative Montieth. I'll need to slip away without his knowledge."

"I'll help, but it is better that I sail with you. If you get caught in Port Royal Bay, you will never get past the guns of Fort Charles without help from the *Venture.*"

Baret smiled thinly. "I know, but I'm not fool enough to sail under the guns of the fort. Not yet. I have another option."

Erik lifted a golden eyebrow. "I can think of no option, your lordship."

"When it comes to a woman, Erik, never take a man's loyalties for granted."

"You have me at a loss."

Baret turned and looked out toward the Dutch ship. "We both know whose ship that is."

Erik followed his gaze, dubiously. "A Dutch captain's."

Baret glanced at him. "You mean, the Dutch Admiral de Ruyter."

Erik's cool silence admitted that he also knew.

"I suspect," said Baret, "he's come to do a good deal of mischief to an English island—what do you think?"

Erik was expressionless.

Baret's mouth turned. "Antigua, do you think? English Harbor will have ships aplenty."

Erik squinted at the vessel. "Or Barbados."

So he did know. "Barbados. I suspect the Dutch admiral has a fleet."

"It is a good thing that you and I are loyal to Holland in this war."

"Yes," Baret agreed. "Because if we were not, we might slip away with our pompous Baronet Warwick, make a daring run to Barbados to warn the English governor, and—" Baret deliberately stopped and waited for Erik's sagacity to catch up with his own. He was taking a risk in letting Erik know his plans. Erik could refuse to cooperate and instead alert the French governor to warn Admiral de Ruyter by firing the fort's guns.

Erik folded his arms. "And having warned Barbados and foiled the Dutch, we could return to Port Royal and most likely find good favor with Modyford, your grandfather, and—"

Baret smiled dryly. "His Majesty King Charles. The very circumstance my grandfather wishes for. Viscount Baret Buckington would at last be viewed as the king's honorable and gallant privateer, rather than a pirate awaiting capture and Gallows Point."

"And in doing so Lord Felix would be defeated in his purpose to have you arrested and tried as a pirate. At least for a time."

"Time enough to rescue Emerald and see her settled safely elsewhere," said Baret casually. "Time enough, perhaps, to even find out who murdered Karlton."

"A cunning plan, my lord Viscount."

"Yes . . ."

"A pity our hearts are not in it." He looked out longingly at the Dutch ship.

"Admiral de Ruyter is a Christian gentleman," said Baret sadly. "An excellent captain."

"Yes, and the English are too arrogant. They need a lesson in humility. If the Dutch took Barbados—"

"The H.M.S. *Royale* is there," said Baret. "And Grayford is a miserable naval captain. If they capture the English ships there, he is likely to go down to defeat. But it's not for him that I turn against Holland."

No more needed to be said. It was for Emerald. A heroic deed would allow him to move to protect her.

"Did you notice Warwick earlier?" he asked.

Erik looked at him. "Yes. He guessed the ship was Dutch and that the governor was giving him refuge until he chose to move against English holdings."

"And Warwick was itching to board and leave at once to warn Modyford, but the Frenchman was too clever and guessed. He's being kept here until the admiral gets away. But you and I don't need to warn Modyford. We can be at Barbados *with* Warwick in time to help Grayford and the H.M.S. *Royale* hold off the Dutch attack." Baret cocked his head, watching him, his dark eyes lively and growing impatient. "Well? Are you with me or not?"

Erik's bored expression remained unchanged. "As you wish, your lordship. Anything for a Stuart king."

Baret thought he might just as well have said, "Anything for Madrid," so slight was Erik's enthusiasm for attacking the admiral's fleet.

"Not a Stuart," said Baret, feeling irritation not with Erik but with himself. "Rather, anything for Harwick's daughter. I won't leave her in the filthy confines of Brideswell. The turnkeys are little better than the pirates here. If anything has happened to her, Felix will wish he'd never been born."

"Your daring may be to set Emerald free, but Lavender may think you do it for her beloved husband. Need I remind you she could soon be a widow?"

Baret eyed him. "I see your mind can be as wretched as mine. True evidence Calvin was right about the total depravity of man. You will be pleased to know you need not wish for the worst—our sweet, fragile rosebud is not yet Lady Grayford. The marriage was postponed until after the war."

Erik stared at him.

Baret frowned at his response. Erik looked as though he'd been pardoned from being a galley slave aboard a Spanish treasure ship. Baret lowered his hat, and the plume danced in the wind. "You don't stand a chance. Forget her. You'd do well to take another look at Emerald's cousin."

Erik's gray eyes turned chill.

"I want to meet with Warwick," Baret said. "It's best he know what we plan to do. If he's in on this from the beginning, he'll be the first to trumpet our heroism to Modyford."

"He'll probably leave for the Sweet Turtle as soon as the

meeting's over. But caution—Captains Montieth and the Dutchman Roche will be with him, selling booty. They had some heavy prizes. Treasures belonging to the *infanta.* "

"All the more reason to join them," said Baret lightly. "I'm in the mood for a pretty piece or two. Have Yorke and Hob pass word to my crew to get the ship ready. We leave, say . . . midnight?"

"Agreed."

"Now back to the governor's meeting."

When Baret and Erik drifted into the Sweet Turtle, Baronet Warwick was shouting with the voice of a Parliamentarian. "Honorable Captains, I again bring you warm greetings from Port Royal, from Governor Thomas Modyford and his new lieutenant governor, Edward Morgan, uncle of one of your own, the daring Henry Morgan."

A few grumbles erupted. l'Olonnaise snapped, "An', monsieur, what does this Modyford want with us now, except bait for sharks?"

"The governor is again offering commissions," Warwick said.

"And where is Morgan?" someone asked doubtfully.

"He's at Spanish Town, meeting with Modyford. He's asking for a special gathering of the Confederacy of the Brotherhood to be held in two weeks at Port Royal."

The buccaneer captains exchanged wary glances.

"And how's we to know, monsieur, that the gallows does not await us?"

"Aye, and why should we forget friends dangled there only weeks ago?"

"If a pirate was hung recently," said Warwick calmly, "it was because of crimes in the Caribbean. You are not pirates but privateers—if you return to Jamaica and receive commissions from His Majesty."

"You mean Modyford is issuing marques against Spain?"

"The governor is offering commissions, yes. And he's willing to grant loans again for ship repairs as well. He sends assurances you will be treated to a warm welcome. And as you all know, there is no port in all the Indies that welcomes privateers like Port Royal."

Baret noticed that Warwick chose his words carefully. The buccaneers exchanged sardonic glances.

"And none so quick to hang us."

Warwick cleared his throat as cold eyes fixed upon him. "Gallows Point will be closed . . . er . . . indefinitely. There's a war to be fought."

"Indeed, monsieur, an' who are we noble Frenchmen to fight?"

"Why, the Dutch, of course and the—" Warwick caught himself from a worse blunder. The word *French* was left unspoken.

He confronted cool Gallic smiles.

"You were saying, monsieur?" breathed l'Olonnaise.

Warwick lifted a hand. "My good Captains, please. I have come to you in good faith. If it's commissions you want, then you'll get them. If it weren't so, would I have ventured to come here?"

"That depends, monsieur, on the real reason for your visit. Perhaps it is one certain pirate that the Admiralty officials seek."

"I am sure, Captain, that you have me at a loss. I was sent by Governor Modyford."

"What kind of commissions? Do you think we've a stomach to attack our own?" asked the Dutchman Roche. "The French governor already offers us marques to fight Spain!"

Ah, thought Baret. He had been counting on the fact that the buccaneers would not agree to attack the Dutch islands even to plunder Dutch goods. That left only the *Regale* and the *Warspite* as fighting ships for King Charles.

Baret walked to a table where several pirates in costumes as garish as peacocks sat in cool shirts and linen pantaloons. Their long, rat-tailed mustaches complemented their King Louis XIV hair length. One threw down three golden doubloons for a single coconut shell of rum, as Baret joined them.

Warwick noticed Baret, and, soon closing his speech, came to the table. "Foxworth, I should like to speak with you alone as soon as possible." He turned back to the pirates. "And now, your wares, my Captains. What have you this time?"

Baret lingered, looking upon the wide and elaborately carved table before which stood a small iron-clasped chest, under guard by three buccaneers, fingering their pistols.

"Here, Your Excellency, is the sweet prize of a don's wench

271

herself, taken from Santo Domingo by me own nimble fingers. Feast your lovin' eyes on what we bring."

A resounding shout arose when one of the bearers threw off the catch and there was spilled onto the table a scintillating, dancing mound of treasure. Necklaces, brooches, finger rings, jeweled crosses, goblets, plates, and altar ornaments became heaped into a small but radiant pile.

Baret glanced at Warwick and saw his eyes bulge and his face flush.

"It's your choice, Foxworth," said the buccaneer in charge. "If it wasn't for the *Regale* comin' to our aid when ye did, we'da been sunk and shark bait by now. Take your share."

At the mention of Baret's aid, Warwick looked at him sharply and quizzically.

Baret smiled faintly. "A mere trifle, Baronet."

Warwick cleared his throat.

Baret inspected the necklaces and brooches and decided they were too heavy and Spanish in taste for his liking, but worth a great deal of money. He plucked several from the pile and dropped them into his pocket. Then a jeweled comb caught his eye. He picked it up and inspected the flashing jade-green emeralds. They were of good quality. He chose some Margarita pearls, several finger rings of gold with emeralds, which looked the right size and matched the comb, and a well-crafted silver hand mirror, encrusted with seed pearls.

Warwick flushed with pleasure when the wily captain suggested that, since he was a very old friend of Foxworth, he should take a few morsels as gifts without paying. He gaped and pawed at the booty.

When they were outside Warwick drew in a deep breath. "Blast me, Foxworth, there's a bit of pirate in me as well."

"You, Baronet? An honorable member of the Jamaican Council? Surely not! It is men of your character, sir, that restore my faith in all that is law-abiding and honorable."

Warwick cocked an eye at him as if trying to decide whether he was serious.

Baret smiled. "Shall we go, Baronet? It seems we each have a fine bargain to make with the other."

"Bargain? Yes . . . er . . . that is, Governor Modyford wishes to speak with you in private about your entry into Maracaibo."

"Maracaibo?" he asked innocently.

"Henry Morgan will be there. He's recommended you to the governor as a steady man."

"The news is intriguing. Before I show myself, however, there is a small matter of some import awaiting our urgent attention. May I suggest that, in the name of King Charles, I, with certain other well-disciplined buccaneer captains, thwart an attack of the Dutch on English ships at Barbados?"

19

WHY ARE MY
WINTERS SO LONG?

Jasper Hall did not live up to the image that the English name had forged within Emerald's mind. As she stepped from the carriage onto the burnt-orange tiled courtyard walled with smooth stone, she was confronted with a sprawling, Spanish-style hacienda unlike any house she had seen in Port Royal.

If the house had been built as a single story dwelling of rambling stucco and wrought iron, a second level had since been added with an attractive red tile roof. There was also a six-foot-wide strollway encircling the second story, kept cool by the speckled shade from overspreading trees.

Expecting to see smugglers such as Jasper loitering about, she was led across a courtyard of serene solitude where pleasant sounds came from a splashing fountain. She noticed somber slaves filling two large *ollas* with water and then suspending them from terrace beams to be cooled by wind and shade.

Several well-armed guards dozed in hammocks strung between pepper trees, where black-and-white roosters and auburn banty hens took refuge from the afternoon heat on low branches. Would there be a way to escape this place and return the three miles to Spanish Town and Government House?

Even so, what good would that do her? she reminded herself. In her situation, Emerald wasn't likely to convince the governor or his officials to take her word above Sir Jasper's. It was Felix who held the key. And she was certain she already knew his asking price for Mr. Pitt's confession of her innocence.

Besides, Sir Jasper held a respectable seat on the very council she must appeal to. And if the powerful Lord Felix were called in to hear her tale of horror, he would gravely side with Jasper and make her appear some strumpet fabricating a story to gain her freedom. With her father dead, Geneva ill, and Earl Nigel unaware of what had befallen her since their meeting in the town house, her hopes were smothered. Reality was her prison, and dreams would not create a door of escape.

And now, if the courtyard had first appeared serene, she thought of it as secretive. Its black and purple shadows, smelling of hot stone, seemed to hide the identity of men and women long dead. Who was the Spanish official who had built the house years before Cromwell's Western Design allowed an English army to capture the sparsely inhabited island from the band of Spanish soldiers guarding it?

This place does not fit the odious Jasper, she found herself thinking uneasily. He was unpleasant enough with all his lustful schemes, but there was evidence of another presence here, perhaps a man who preferred to move within the shadows that veiled his identity?

She walked behind Sir Jasper into a cool and spacious front salon, a prisoner of his whims. She had one small hope: Jasper was in service to Felix Buckington and would do nothing to see his own plans fulfilled until he knew Felix no longer needed her presence in order to arrest Baret.

Her faith was unexpectedly encouraged when a thought flashed into her mind: *From whence comes your help? Why hope in an enemy? Do not look to Felix! Your help comes from the Lord, Maker of heaven and earth.*

Yes! Only God could help her.

The apostle Paul had been in a Roman prison, yet Paul saw himself not a prisoner of Nero but a servant of the Lord. *He who sent an angel to loose Peter's chains when he was in prison, could have done so for Paul, could do so in my situation,* she thought. If He did not, there were reasons why.

The first night in her chamber at Jasper Hall, Emerald's soul cried out without ceasing to the Lord. But fear finally crowded out her prayers. At first she refused to sleep in the fine bed with its clean satin sheets and coverlet. She sat in a chair, straining to hear footsteps with each creak of the wooden beams or rustle of the trumpet vine growing below the second-story strollway. Distraught, she contemplated risking a fall from the terrace to climb down the vine into the courtyard. But flaring torchlight and the bootsteps of the guard on watch soon convinced her that was folly. With loathing she remembered the turnkeys at Brideswell.

She closed her eyes tightly, trying to shut out her fears, and the kindly face of Uncle Mathias came to mind. She saw the humble singing school on Foxemoore, saw the Bible in his hand, heard him reading one of her favorite verses from Psalms—*"I will both lay me down in peace, and sleep: for thou, Lord, only makest me dwell in safety."* David had written those words, and who knew better what it meant to be hunted and hounded and vulnerable? Yet he could sleep, in the open under the watchful stars, because the plans God had for him were good. Again, purposefully, she committed herself to the Lord and then lay down.

She didn't wake until the rooster crowed in the pepper tree below in the courtyard. A new day had begun, bright, hot, bringing her new resolve to remain strong in the Lord.

She did not see Jasper that day, nor was there any indication that Felix had arrived. Had something happened in Port Royal to circumvent his plans? Questioning the hefty and large-boned woman who brought her meals proved futile. It was as if the mulatto were both deaf and dumb. Emerald could see the woman resented her, perhaps suspecting she was a consort of Jasper.

That afternoon the woman brought an armload of satin and taffeta and lace. Her dark eyes were sullen as she spoke for the first time.

"The master says to adorn yo'self."

Emerald had a notion the dresses had been unwillingly confiscated from someone else in the house as young as herself.

"They belong to someone else?"

The woman pursed her lips, refusing to answer.

"I don't want them," Emerald told her. "Take them back to Sir Jasper. What I have on will do," she said of the plain muslin dress she'd selected after shedding her ill-smelling garment worn at Brideswell.

The woman's heavy-lidded eyes drifted over her. "Don't matter what you want, but what master wants."

"He's not my master, and I'm dreadfully sorry he's yours. He's a smuggler of slaves, of rum, a man without honor."

The woman shrugged her heavy shoulders under their yellow wrap. "They all is."

Emerald turned away with a pang. "Not all," she murmured, thinking of Baret.

"These is presents," the woman told her sulkily. "Other girls be dancin' round the room all in a hurry to put 'em on and look pretty."

Emerald folded her arms and glanced morosely toward the terrace where the smell of flowers wafted in on a humid breeze. "Then I'm not like the other girls. The last thing I want is Sir Jasper eyeing me."

The woman watched her curiously. "You don't love Sir Jasper?"

"*Love* him! Believe me, I struggle not to hate him!"

"You love another man?"

Emerald walked toward the terrace and now heard rain pattering on the vines. "Yes," she admitted quietly. *But I'd never tell him. He loves someone else.*

The woman brightened at the news. "These dresses be the senorita's. She'll be happy you don't love Sir Jasper."

Emerald conjured up images of some feisty beauty from Madrid. Then suddenly she again found herself wondering not about Jasper but about the man whose presence permeated the hacienda. She turned to the slave.

"When you say the *master*, do you speak of Jasper or another?"

The woman walked quickly to the divan and laid down the dresses. Emerald waited for an answer, but evidently the woman decided she'd best leave, for she headed for the door.

"Wait, please," begged Emerald. "You can help me. I don't want anything here at Jasper Hall. All I want is to get away as soon as possible. You could help me leave undetected."

The woman considered but shook her head. "He won't let you go."

"If I could get a message to Foxemoore plantation, someone would come for me. My family doesn't know I'm here."

"I heard say they thinks you ran away again. No one is lookin' for you now."

"Please, I know you don't like me being here. I'll leave if you'll help me."

The woman shook her head and left the room.

Emerald confronted a closed door. In dismay, she let out a breath and sank onto the divan beside the senorita's dresses.

Jasper Hall remained silent as the evening broke with another sudden rain squall. There'd been no further mention of Felix

Buckington. She wondered if he would even come. Perhaps Jasper had lied, thinking she would leave Brideswell with less apprehension if she believed Felix was at the plantation. In the two days since her arrival she'd seen no one except the house slave and, from a distance, guards. And occasionally Jasper, who was seeking to woo her with fine gifts and elaborate courtesy.

There was a pretentious knock, the door opened, and Sir Jasper walked in, resplendent in black satin pantaloons, a sash, and a claret-red jacket with silver lace and large silver buttons. His full-bottomed black wig was carefully arranged with royal flair. He carried a wine goblet.

Emerald refused to acknowledge his smile and gesture that complimented her attire. She had decided it was only sensible to wear the clothes provided. The dress was saffron satin with round neckline, full sleeves to the elbows, and a sweeping gathered skirt, over which was a second skirt of black Spanish lace.

"Ah, sweetheart, a fitting frock for one so sweetly charming. You'd put Barbara Palmer to shame," he said lightly of King Charles's mistress in England. "I should take you there for all to see."

She gave him a menacing glare to make sure he knew she rejected his suggestions. "You're so free with your odious compliments, Sir Jasper. Are you not afraid to go to England?"

"Afraid? Whatever for?"

"Seeing as how His Majesty might hang *you* for piracy instead of the viscount!"

He smiled, but the smile grew wearied. "Ah, my charming little serpent. So fair of face, so biting of tongue. What I see in you is a mystery even to me. Come, darlin', you're so tense. Do relax and have a bit of Madeira. It will help you cope."

"You mean it'll turn me into a stupid little wench. Please take your liquor and leave—there's the door, sir."

He sank onto the divan instead and sighed. "How wearisome your religious restraints become. Ah, well . . ." He glanced about at the red flagstone floor. "Such a lovely chamber. It once belonged to the spoiled and lovely Dona Maria Gonzalo." He gestured to the daybed where satin frocks lay in a heap. "Sweetheart, I treat you like pampered royalty, yet you reject my gifts as well as my advances."

"At what price do you offer them, Sir Jasper?"

278

His eyes mocked her. "I suppose Mathias, with his thunderous brow, taught you to deny all fleshly enjoyments as coming from the devil himself."

"He did not, though he would have been wise to warn me about *your* enjoyments."

"How pious you sound."

"And, of course, I'm supposed to apologize for piety? I should be ashamed of it, so I could boast of being sophisticated in things concerning lust and greed?"

"Lust and greed!" He leered and threw back his head. "Sweetheart, you're a fledgling after all, alas! Nothing could be more immature. I thought you wiser to the ways of reality, but all you do is quote little platitudes fit for well-scrubbed faces in the nursery."

His mockery stung, for Baret Buckington had first described her as being a mere fledgling. However, Baret had not spoken in mockery but protectively.

"Grow up, m'dear," he goaded, tasting his wine. "This is Port Royal! Not a convent! The changing times and culture give leeway for young women to loosen their prim and proper ways. The old days are gone. Who's to tell? And should you stay uppity, who'd appreciate your fidelity? Not Baret Buckington. Don't let him fool you. He's the worst of rogues with women."

"He is not!"

"Most surely he is. I see he's pulled the scarf over your eyes. Ask him who Carlotta is."

She looked down at her frock—the "senorita" was Carlotta? She glanced quickly at Jasper. Was he the other man Carlotta had wished to marry? Was this the hacienda in Spanish Town that Baret had told her about?

"I know about Carlotta. She's a cousin of Baret's."

He shrugged and emptied his goblet. "Ask your gallant and noble buccaneer. He probably won't remember either. He collects 'em. And soon forgets 'em."

"I know better than that."

"Do you?" Jasper removed his jacket and laid it across the divan back. "Just what do you know about him except his long betrothal to Lavender Thaxton? Did you ever wonder why that betrothal lasted so long?"

"Because—she's ill. And he's a buccaneer, with business of his own to see to. He's not ready to settle down."

"So he told you—and her." He chuckled. "He likes his freedom. And his entertainments."

She glared, folding her arms. "You're lying."

"So he's an angel, is he?"

"He's a graduate from divinity training at Cambridge, and he's more of a man and a gentleman than you'll ever be."

"Gentleman! He's a rogue, m'dear, and you're deceived. As for you, who are my only interest at the moment, you do yourself an injustice. Your family rejects you anyway; they scorn your reputation. What reason have you to deny yourself? Especially when I'm prepared to offer you ease, comfort, and a good deal of wealth. I'm anything but a poor man, you know."

"Should I be flattered? How easy you make things sound. Simply throw away the rules and live as I want. Who cares? And whose business is it? Truth becomes mere clay to shape as we wish, just as long as it benefits our plans or eases our circumstances. You've turned things inside out, Sir Jasper."

He slouched on the divan, resting the side of his head against his hand. "Your words weary me. If I'd wished to hear a sermon, I'd have made Mathias a crony. He's dead. So is your father. You'd best think of your future. You have nothing."

If she permitted the painful memory of the deaths of the two bulwarks in her life, it would leave her depressed and weakened. "Not all have abandoned me," she said tiredly. "Geneva, for one, has not. If she knew her husband held me here a prisoner—"

"Geneva is an ill woman. She's a broken reed, if you think to lean upon her."

Geneva wasn't well, but Jasper made the situation sound far worse. Had something drastic occurred since Emerald had spoken to her at the town house six weeks ago? Or was he only using the devil's tactics to dishearten her: No use resisting. She couldn't win. Might as well give up.

"Don't misunderstand me, darlin'. I do respect your ideals. They're fine for the cloister, for the parson's daughter, for a rich girl with a strong family to stand behind her, but they won't work in the glare of life as it's truly lived. Port Royal is a ruthless monster that'll swallow you whole if you fight against it. Don't oppose the tide and times. What did Mathias receive for his noble pains?

The old man is dead and gone, with nothing to show for his sacrifices except a burned-down hut and a satchel of scribbled notes. Is not your future here and now worth more than that?"

She'd left the satchel at the lookout when brought to Brideswell. Now she turned toward him, alarmed. "What do you know of those notes?"

He seemed to measure her response thoughtfully. "They mean something to you, do they?"

Wisely, she said nothing more, thinking he might send for them and use them as a bargaining tool. She changed the subject back to her meeting with Felix Buckington.

"I wish to speak with his lordship now. You'll bring me there, please."

"You squawk like a parrot. Will you bite the hand that offers you sweet morsels?" He came toward her dangling a pearl on a gold chain. "Desist, darlin'. Surely you'll allow me to place this pretty thing about your neck," he wheedled.

"Come a step closer, and I'll scream. Where is Felix?"

His eyes snapped. "All right, you snarling little minx, have it your way—for now. Felix waits below. He'll call for you in due time. And don't look relieved," he mocked. "Felix is not as moved by your charms as I am, but you have something he wants even more—a letter he wishes you to write to King Charles."

"I'll not write any incriminating letter to His Majesty. You might as well let me go," she said, knowing it was hopeless to say it.

He laughed. "Sweetheart, having gone to such lengths to lure Buckington into the trap, do you think either of us will remove the bait now?"

"Then it *is* Baret you want," she breathed, "and you think he'll risk arrest to take me away from you? He doesn't know I'm even here!"

"He knows, and you can be sure Levasseur will earn his pieces of eight, as well as satisfy his vengeance over that duel."

So her French cousin was involved. "You're mad. Captain Buckington isn't foolish enough to fall for your scheme. He won't trust Rafael. He knows what a miserable pirate he is."

"He won't trust him, but he'll come."

"So you think. He has his own cause already. He won't risk failure for what you tempt him with."

281

He looked uneasy, as though a thought from the past disturbed him. "Yes, there's his father. He expects to find Royce alive. But he's dead—Foxworth just doesn't know it yet. But he'll come to Port Royal. And when he does, you'll soon change your mind about the letter—or see him below on the rack. Ah, yes, alas, the noble Spanish officer who built this sweet hacienda made sure he had his dungeons furnished with all the instruments used so well in Cádiz."

Her breath tightened. "You're not serious! You'd torture him? That's cowardly. At least Levasseur was willing to fight an open duel for what he wanted."

He was undisturbed. "And he lost and was humiliated. So much for his open duel. I intend to win, whatever the means, cowardly or not. But let me assure you, darlin', there is none better than I with the sword. If I choose to use it, I will not lose."

Her mind was still on his first threat. "You'd resort to such evil, for what? More power, more pieces of eight?"

He sighed. "Life without honor is a sacrifice, I admit, but that is the way of things, m'dear, and there's no use lamenting it. And now, since you are so anxious to confront Lord Felix, see to your appearance. He would find untidy face and hair inappropriate for his refined tastes." He made a gesture of departure and went to the open door. "And see you don't try to escape by way of the terrace when you are called to him. The guards will be posted."

She watched him leave, and a surge of hopelessness swept over her despite her bold words. "Lord, what am I going to do?" she cried in anguish.

There was not only the letter to avoid writing, but Jasper's odious advances to deter. She feared that soon all her talk would be pushed aside as his frustration with her refusals grew.

She was beginning to learn it wasn't always the Lord's purpose to deliver from trial. Others, more obedient than she, had faced suffering, loss, earthly ruin, even death. Yet God was not capricious in what He permitted to befall His own. He was a God of infinite design. His ways could not always be understood by her feeble mind, but she knew enough about His character to trust His perfect love and wisdom.

"In whatever circumstances come," she said aloud, "He'll prove faithful to me."

She walked to the pile of exquisite frocks and snatched up the first one that appeared to fit. "Lord," she prayed, gripping the dress to her pounding heart. "You have taken away my earthly father, and I feel so alone, so abandoned. But You are my heavenly Father. I commit myself to Your faithful care. I choose to trust in Your love toward me, whatever happens."

Emerald stepped hesitantly from her chamber onto the balcony above the wide stairway that led down to the salon. A written message had arrived, informing Emerald that she should join Lord Felix and Jasper there for dinner. It was early, but she would drift in that direction—and explore. It appeared that the guard usually loitering in the upper hall had been called away.

She paused at the balcony rail. Below she could see a door standing ajar and golden light spilling out across the tile floor. Polished dark wood, wine-colored rugs, and wall tapestries smothered her with their Spanish ambience. Paintings hung on the wall beside the door.

Then her heart squeezed into her throat. What was a painting of Viscount Baret Buckington doing on the wall of Jasper Hall? Or was she not at Jasper's plantation after all? Could he have taken her elsewhere? But why?

Tensely, she glanced back over her shoulder to see that the corridor leading to Jasper's suite of rooms was empty. Swiftly, she gathered up her skirts and hurried in the opposite direction to the stairs. She peered over the banister. No one was in view. She descended, heart pounding, casting another glance behind her for Jasper or one of the guards. She reached the salon and breathlessly walked toward the paintings that hung on the dark yellow plaster. Waves of firelight flickered from severely ornate silver lanterns.

Two men, dressed in masculine finery, looked down on her like Cavalier rogues, swords unsheathed, and wearing plumed hats. She would know the young viscount anywhere, for he now haunted her dreams, but who was the older man? Even from the painting she could see the same virile look and strength of will.

"They're both rebels, I assure you, Miss Harwick."

Emerald whirled.

Felix stood there.

Lord Felix was not large-boned or physically powerful, but

the man's forceful personality gave that impression. He was tall and spare with erect shoulders, as swarthy as a Spaniard. His startling blue eyes glanced determinedly, and she detected ruthlessness there. His mouth was thin and strong; his aquiline nose boasted of superior blood. His black camlet coat had bone-colored lace at the wrists, and there were dense ruffles at his cravat along with the glimmering sapphire she had seen him wear before.

She glanced toward the paintings, and he followed her gaze, knowingly. "My half brother, Royce," he said, but his voice harbored no warmth. "As you see, we do not resemble each other. I take after my mother's family. And of course—" he gestured with a slim, brown hand "—my nephew Baret, a troublesome individual and, as you well know, like his father a pirate —but perhaps an even worse scoundrel."

She might have contradicted him but dared not.

So then, *Felix* was the presence she had felt in this house, but why had Jasper led her to think she was at Jasper Hall on his own plantation? More curious perhaps was why Felix had paintings of Royce and Baret on his wall. They were not in display out of family affection. And who was the mother of Felix? She had heard little about her. Perhaps she had been from Spain. If so, that could account for his sympathy for Madrid.

She stared at him, more concerned than ever over his marriage to Geneva. If she had any consolation at all, it rested in the presence of the one man even stronger in will than Felix—his father. Earl Nigel had been at Foxemoore to see to the well-being of Jette and Geneva. Geneva had mentioned returning to the plantation, now that the war made it impossible to sail to England.

Distaste for the man before her surged. Emerald blamed him and his schemes for the death of her father. She wished to accuse him openly, but wisdom forbade such an emotional display. She was now left to his authority, as was Baret. Lord Felix Buckington was not the foppish, odious Sir Jasper, but a coldly ruthless man.

He took command at once. "Come into the den and sit down. We have much to discuss before dinner." And he smiled.

Emerald's skin crawled. He could be charming, but she wondered what Geneva had seen in him, for she detected a cruel streak.

Emerald stood in the cool, shadowed den with its flagstone floor and dark furnishings splashed with warm orange, red, and yellow. She watched Felix go behind a large desk and unlock a drawer. A moment later he straightened, producing a letter.

"Do you ride?" he asked casually.

Emerald stirred. "I beg pardon, your lordship?"

"I asked whether you enjoyed riding horses."

She wondered at the question coming at a time like this.

"Yes, I ride very well."

"The mention of horses has brought the first glimmer of life to your eyes. Jette also enjoys riding, but he's not skilled yet. You learned while with your mother's relatives on—where was it—Tortuga?"

On guard, she hesitated. He was pretending not to be aware of her background. He knew well enough.

"No, I did not learn on Tortuga. I left there as a small child."

"I once visited Lyon, France, and met members of your mother's family. Did she ever tell you of them?"

Startled, she considered. Felix had met her mother's family? She took a moment to measure what might be behind his question, or if he even spoke the truth.

"Yes, she mentioned them, but I was quite small and remember little of what she said. They fled the persecution. She did mention visiting royalty once."

Was it her imagination, or did his eyes glint? *He doesn't believe me.* Yet he appeared to be sympathetic. He walked over to light a second lantern, letting a flood of light into the chamber. As he did, insects entered through the window and made sounds that wore on her nerves.

Emerald turned her head away from the lantern. Lighting it was a purposeful endeavor on his part. He wished to see her more clearly. Why?

The humidity from the rainfall was oppressive.

"My father brought me to Foxemoore, where I grew up," she said to break the silence. She omitted the fact she'd grown up in the bungalow next to the slaves' quarters. He knew all this, so why was he pretending interest?

"Yes, Karlton," he said sadly, "his death was a tragedy," and he turned again to the desk, tapping the letter. "A horrid turn of

285

events. I want you to know I'm doing all in my power to discover what happened and who is to blame for his death. Rest assured, your father's death will not go unpunished."

Her hands clenched. Her eyes drifted to the letter. Why this little meeting when he knew very well she was being held here against her will? It was Felix who had arranged for her arrest. Did that letter have anything to do with Baret?

"I've not told Geneva yet about his death," he said thoughtfully. "She's very ill, and the news may weaken her still."

Her heart lurched, and her eyes darted to his riveting blue gaze. It was all she could do not to blatantly accuse him.

"Then there's this scandal you find yourself in. Geneva must not learn of your incarceration in Brideswell. She's bedridden now and under a physician's care. I sent for him from Barbados."

Geneva had been well enough to be on her feet when she last spoke to Emerald at the town house six weeks ago. What had happened since that fateful night?

"She's a brave woman," he was commenting. "She was ill even when we married but did not wish to delay the wedding."

Geneva ill at the time of the wedding? He was lying!

"I had hoped the voyage to London would change matters, but the war has intervened in more than your schooling."

Did he know she suspected him? His searching look warned her he was trying to learn just how much she did suspect. Had Jasper told him she insisted he was behind her father's death?

It was to her advantage now to make him think she was gullible and trusting.

"Your interest in my father's death brings me peace at last, your lordship. Geneva has told me of your brilliance in the Inns of Court. And how the king himself sent you here to stop the evils of piracy. Jamaica needs a man of your talents."

His lips drew back. "Your confidence encourages me. I shall try all the harder for the sake of justice."

"That is reassuring."

He continued to tap the letter on the edge of the desk, studying her.

Emerald stood casually, she hoped, but sweat trickled down her ribs. She glanced toward the open windows where the rain monotonously beat upon the courtyard. She swished her black lace fan.

"You are a wise young woman, Emerald. Jasper informs me you believe Karlton was innocent of piracy?"

Her face felt stiff from keeping her expression one of friendly pretense. "I'm certain he didn't try to escape Brideswell, as the guards said. My father wasn't a pirate, and he had nothing to do with Maracaibo."

"That is what we intend to find out. The Admiralty officials now believe he may have been innocent after all."

Was this true, or was he merely saying this to take her off guard?

"Sadly, they have another in mind who was behind the entire debacle in Lake Maracaibo."

Baret, of course. She remained silent.

"A man was killed in that pirate raid, a very fine man of the government of Cromwell, named Lucca. You knew him?"

"No," she said truthfully, "I didn't know him."

"Do you know why I've ordered Sir Jasper, a member of the council, to bring you here?"

That he underscored Jasper's position did not go unnoticed. "Yes, he made it clear. However, I know little of your nephew's voyage, since it was Levasseur who first planned to abduct me. The indentured servant you sought for involvement in the uprising on Foxemoore was Jamie Bradford, Levasseur's lieutenant. They were searching for the treasure of the *Prince Philip*. It was your nephew, Captain Buckington, who rescued me."

Clearly, this was not what he wished to hear—or what he intended for her to tell Governor Modyford.

"Baret has long sought for both the treasure and the whereabouts of my brother, Royce, whom he insists is alive. Sadly, it isn't so. He's sought to convince Earl Nigel of the same thing, but the earl wisely refuses to permit false hopes to govern his life. Unfortunately for Baret, he is now a pirate with a warrant on his head. The *Regale* is a pirate ship. Naturally, you already know this, since you sailed on the *Regale* into Lake Maracaibo."

"I know nothing of Maracaibo, Lord Felix. I was transported aboard my father's ship before the incident of Lucca's death."

He ignored the truth. "I can see why a woman of your background would wish to try to shield him from his just fate. The option of marriage to a Buckington, even a Buckington scoundrel, is tempting. I, for one, can no longer shield my nephew. I've done so for the last several years. His Majesty demands justice and an end to piracy in the Caribbean. As a member of the Admiralty court I must act for the king."

She remained mute, his words storming her mind. *"A woman of your background . . . . Act for the king."*

"I can only tell you what I told your father, Earl Nigel. Regardless of my background, or perhaps because of it, I've entertained no false hopes of marriage into the Buckington family. As for the viscount being a pirate, I'm also sure, if he is one, he does not sail by the same articles as does Captain Levasseur."

She looked at him innocently. Levasseur worked for Felix. "It is my dreadful cousin Rafael Levasseur who is one of the worst pirates on the Main, your lordship. Like you, I understand that family blood must sometimes be put aside. And therefore, I can only mildly lament your energetic efforts to locate and hang him at Gallows Point."

His eyes barely flickered. "Rest assured, my dear, he will come to his due reward. However, it's your involvement with my nephew that disturbs the High Admiralty. I'm afraid, you'll either come clean and confess all you know or go up before the officials. Naturally, I had hoped for your cooperation and so wished for your needs to be met, rather than Brideswell."

"I've told you, m'lord, I know nothing of the incident at Maracaibo. I wasn't there. As far as I know, it never happened. Surely you would not wish me to fabricate a tale detrimental to your nephew, the earl's grandson?"

He smiled. "You're a cleverer young woman than I anticipated. Naturally I would not wish my nephew to be arrested and stand trial for something as notorious as piracy."

"Of course, you wouldn't, m'lord."

He lifted the letter, eyeing her thoughtfully. "I have here the statement of my overseer, Mr. Pitt. Mr. Hiram Walker Pitt, I believe is his whole name. In this letter he admits his error in accusing you of attempted murder. He realizes now that neither you nor your African cousin were involved. The attack came from a rum-sodden sea merchant who broke into the lookout on Fishers Row."

She tore her eyes from his gaze to stare at the precious document that would set both Minette and her free.

"I'll have a copy made of this letter to be given to you tomorrow. The original I will deliver to the Bailey. Your reputation will be restored, and the matter forgotten."

Her heart pounded as her eyes fixed on the letter.

Baitingly, he laid it on the desk. "You'll be free to leave first thing in the morning."

She stared at him, waiting for the conditions.

"Is . . . there anything else?" she asked.

He smiled. He opened the drawer and took out a piece of parchment. He pushed it across to her, followed by a quill and ink well. "You'll sign and date this official document to be sent to His Majesty. Do you read?"

"Yes," she choked and picked up the document, her hand shaking.

He came around the desk with the lantern and set it down close beside her. Then he walked to the open window and looked out.

A moment later she looked at him, drawing in a breath. "M'lord, I cannot sign this. I would become the witness to see the viscount hanged for murder and piracy."

"It is either him or your own trial for attempted murder."

"But you know I did not try to kill Mr. Pitt! And you know Baret is innocent!"

"I know nothing of the sort. You are both guilty of sordid crimes as far as I'm concerned, but in pity I seek to spare you from hanging for the sake of my wife!"

His sudden anger set her off guard. For an instant she'd nearly believed him. She wanted to mock his concern but did not dare go so far.

She threw down the document on the desk. "I cannot in Christian conscience lie to save myself. The crimes listed here are fanciful and vicious exaggerations—"

"Exaggerations?" he cut in. "Did he not enter Lake Maracaibo?"

"I do not know."

"Of course, you know. You know about Lucca."

"He sought his father—"

"Ah. So you admit you know he entered Maracaibo?"

"I'll not sign this, Lord Felix. I cannot."

"You're being foolish. Is it because of an infatuation with Baret?"

"No—no—"

"Money, then. I can see you set up well in England after the war."

"I cannot sign." She turned away, gripping her fan.

"You will sign, Emerald. And if it's not your own welfare for which you will cooperate, then you will sign to save him."

She looked at him. "I don't understand. My very signing will *destroy* him."

"Save him, yes. From a fate far worse than a trial in London. There is at least a possibility he will be found innocent of piracy and murder. But the fate now at hand will be worse than death."

She paled. "Please explain."

"He was captured by the *guarda costa* on a recent raid in the cays of Cuba. He's being held for the piracy of the Spanish galleon *Valdez*. *Capitán* Espinosa don Diego de Valdez will see him imprisoned in Cádiz."

Emerald gripped the desk, searching his face. His sober countenance convinced her. Then he didn't know yet about the *San Pedro*. Or that it was Baret who aided Carlotta to escape marriage to the don at Margarita. But Cádiz!

"If you sign, the Spanish ambassador will see my nephew released from trial by the inquisitors to stand trial for piracy in London. As you see, I've done my best to help him, despite his unreasonable hatred for me. He blames me for the death of his father, a matter I'm entirely innocent of. And one day I'll prove it."

He pushed the letter from Mr. Pitt across the desk to where her hand gripped the edge. She recognized the sloppy handwriting of the overseer and the official seal of the court.

"You're free, Emerald." He dipped the quill into the ink pot and handed it to her, along with the document to be sent to King Charles.

Cádiz . . . the inquisitors . . . Baret would never recant . . . they'd torture him to death . . . maybe bury him alive . . .

But what if Felix was lying? Why should she trust him now?

Her hand shook as she took the pen. Quickly she signed her name.

Felix did not smile. Instead he laid a sympathetic hand on

her arm. "You've had a trying time. I'll show you to your chamber."

"No," she said weakly. "I shall be all right. I'll find my own way." She picked up the letter from Mr. Pitt, and Felix went to the door and opened it wide.

She walked out and across the tile floor to the stairway. As she slowly went up, her knees nearly buckled. Her heart throbbed painfully as she gripped the letter of her freedom.

What have I done?

But Baret was held a prisoner in Cuba! He was to be sent to the inquisitors!

Did she believe that?

Guilt and sorrow overwhelmed her when she at last entered her chamber and shut the door. She rushed onto the outside balcony and leaned against the rail. The rain wet her face, warm and steamy. She stifled a sob and was seriously contemplating the risk of going over the side by way of the trumpet vine when she noticed that it was already torn and loose.

"Not considering jumping on my account?" A calm, resonant voice shocked her into a gasp.

She whipped about.

He stood back in the shadows, handsomely garbed in black, the doublet embroidered with silver thread and worn over a white shirt.

"Baret!"

"Is it anguish over my fate or yours that tempts you to such disaster?" he asked lightly.

She indeed appeared as though prepared to jump. She gripped the rail.

"But—you can't be here. The *guarda costa* arrested you!"

"Not quite."

She rushed toward him. "You must leave here at once," she whispered. "Felix is below now, so is Jasper, and your uncle has—" A hand went to her aching throat as she remembered the document she'd signed. Baret would never forgive her. He'd never understand why she had believed Felix. The letter from Mr. Pitt dropped to the wet terrace floor. The rain splattered on it.

He stooped and picked it up, looked at it, then at her. A brow lifted. "Not a love letter from your French cousin?"

Her mind flashed back to the scene on the *Regale.* "You don't think I betrayed you?" she had asked.

"No."

"You trust me? You don't think I'm the kind of girl that would be—"

"Unfaithful?"

"Yes, you don't think that about me, do you? Perhaps all the gossip in Port Royal has influenced you even more than you realize."

"No," he had said softly.

Now, as she stood on the terrace staring at him, agony gripped her. Her hands turned cold.

"Give it to me." She reached for the letter, desperate.

Calmly he caught her wrist, searching her eyes. "Why in such a frenzy?"

Her breath came rapidly. "You don't understand," she whispered. "You don't realize what I've been through—" Her voice broke.

His dark eyes softened as he slipped an arm about her waist. "I do know," he said quietly. "Emerald, why do you think I risked coming here? Levasseur told me you were in Brideswell. I went there first. The guard told me you'd left with Jasper for his plantation. When you weren't there, I suspected he'd brought you here."

But where was *here* if not Jasper Hall?

Baret had risked returning to Port Royal to find her. His gallantry, and perhaps even something more, something she dare not contemplate, only deepened her sense of betrayal.

"I've thought about you ever since you left," he whispered. He bent toward her lips, but she pushed both palms against his chest.

"Baret, I've done a dreadful thing," she choked.

He hesitated, searching her face. He stared at her for a long minute, and she thought she would faint under a knowing look that turned angry.

For the first time his gaze dropped to the heavy pearl pendant about her throat. He took in the lace on the sleeve of her elaborate dress. He reached a finger and deftly cupped the pearl, lifting it for inspection, as though weighing it. At that moment Emerald thought it weighed as much as the entire world. Why did he look at her like that? She winced at the sudden pain she saw in his face, then the cynical mockery as his hand dropped from her waist.

"Between you and Lavender, I've been a fool," he said in a low voice. "I thought you were—" He stopped.

How could she explain! Her own misery overrode anything he might think of Jasper, and she brushed past him, tears in her eyes, into the chamber.

He wouldn't believe her innocent, no matter what she said. No one had ever believed her to be anything more than a strumpet. Her eyes brimmed over. Her hands shook as she lowered the lantern light, telling herself nothing mattered now but his safety. The slaves or guards might see his shadow from below the terrace and inform his uncle. How had he gotten inside without being seen?

"Lord Felix—he'll find you. You must go at once. I didn't want you to come."

"But I did. A poor investment in risk. I should have stayed in Tortuga. I now see why you didn't want me."

She whirled, stricken. "No—you don't see. You're wrong! I prayed you wouldn't come because it's a *trap*. It's not me they want, but you."

"Do you think I didn't know that when I came? I knew Felix was here! I know what he wants from you—a confession of piracy to send to the king."

She paled. But he didn't know she had signed that confession.

"Jasper is the least of my worries. Evidently he doesn't worry you either."

"Baret, how can you! I thought you knew me better than this."

"I thought I did too."

His suggestion lashed her. She turned away stiffly, so that he wouldn't see how much his words hurt.

"If your despair comes from what I suspect it does," he said flippantly, "don't let it keep you awake at night. By cutting Jasper into pieces for dog meat, I'll once again save your noble reputation."

She sucked in her breath and turned back to him, her heart pounding so hard that she felt breathless.

He snatched up a taffeta frock and looked about the chamber, taking in the huge satin-covered four-poster bed, the divan.

To her mute horror she noticed that Jasper had left his jacket.

Baret's intense dark eyes came to hers, causing her face to warm from more than anxiety. He laid the dress with the others and walked up to her.

"Baret—"

"Turn around," he ordered.

When she only looked at him, he took hold of her shoulders and wheeled her firmly about. Catching hold of the pendant clasp, he broke it. He dangled the large pearl before her eyes.

"A cheap counterfeit. Your taste needs improvement, dear." He threw it down. "And what did you surrender for his kindness in bringing you here from Brideswell? And to think I offered marriage and twenty thousand pieces of eight! Looks like I've been cheated."

He caught her in his arms and thoroughly kissed her, but there was no respect in his embrace. She had finally met the other Baret Buckington, and she was shocked by his rush to judgment, by his temper. If she didn't know better, she'd think him jealous. She was able to struggle free, but only because he abruptly let her loose. With tears in her eyes she slapped him, more hurt by his mistrust, his belief that she'd behaved cheaply, than by anything Jasper would have said to her.

"How dare you?"

"So indignant, madam!"

She stared at him, her emotions crashing, leaving her so weary she collapsed onto the velvet settee.

He threw aside his plumed hat. "Where's Jasper?" he gritted.

She stared dully at the floor.

His eyes narrowed. "Never mind. I'll find him myself."

She looked up, startled by fear as he threw open the door and walked into the corridor.

Emerald stumbled after him and grasped his arm. "No! It's not what you think, Baret! How could you think so low of me—"

She stopped, unable to go on as memory of her betrayal hotly accused her. She had let Baret down, but in another way—

one that could cost his life in the Tower or destine him to a perpetual career on the Caribbean as a wanted pirate.

Sir Jasper was crossing the salon from the den, where she'd met earlier with Felix. As he neared the stairway, he looked up and saw Baret on the landing. Jasper showed a flicker of alarm, then his gaze darted to Emerald, who stood bracing herself against the wall.

Baret drew his dueling pistol from his baldric.

"You're a dead man, Jasper."

Jasper turned pale beneath his tan. Dots of sweat stood out on his forehead. He was like a trapped animal bent on survival; his eyes darting about the salon for an escape route.

Emerald's gaze swerved to Baret, saw his hand rise and steady the pistol. If he shot Jasper without a proper duel, he could be accused of murder.

"Baret, don't!" She threw herself against his arm.

In the seconds that Baret was off guard, Jasper drew his pistol. Baret pushed her away. Jasper's gun exploded.

Emerald's hands flew to her mouth as she saw the impact and the spreading red stain on Baret's white shirt. He caught himself against the banister and managed to raise the heavy pistol as Jasper cautiously stalked up the stairs, spent weapon in hand, as if a wounded tiger waiting to spring.

Baret aimed. A blast followed, and smoke drifted between them.

Jasper staggered to the side, gripped the rail, then slumped to one knee, his glazed eyes looking up at Emerald with puzzled consternation. "Em . . ." He choked and sank forward, the pistol loosening from his grip. The jewels on his hand caught the lantern light and sparkled.

White-faced, dazed, she stared down at him. Then she spun toward Baret. He was still on his feet but sagging against the banister.

She rushed to him, taking hold of his arm, but his look froze her. It was the look a man of title might give a servant.

He removed her hand, nothing in his touch or in his voice. "I'm well enough, madam." He moved to the stairs and started down.

She feared he might collapse, but he seemed determined

he would not and faltered only once. He paused on the stair beside Jasper's body, looking down at him.

Erik Farrow appeared in the salon entrance below, the lantern light falling on his golden mane. His frosty gaze swiftly took in the scene, slipped over Jasper to Emerald on the landing, then back again to Baret. He frowned at the bright stain on Baret's shirt. Sword in hand, Erik walked toward the stairs, his calf-length boots echoing across the tile floor.

"Where's Felix?" breathed Baret.

Erik's frown deepened, but it wasn't clear if it was because of Felix or because of Baret's wound. "Gone. All his hired help too. Sit down, your lordship. Let me look at that."

Emerald watched, her throat constricting as Baret lowered himself to a step. The sight of blood brought her terror and anguish—terror that she was losing him, anguish because she blamed herself. And because, even if she could explain, he thought she had compromised.

Erik opened Baret's shirt and tore away a section of cloth. He pressed it into the wound to stanch the bleeding. "There may be a doctor on the plantation."

Baret pushed himself to his feet, unsteady but determined. "I'm all right. I won't stay here."

Erik glanced up at Emerald. Did he guess she had something to do with his bitterness? Captain Farrow seemed curious over what might have affected Baret so strongly, but he turned his attention back to him. "The horses wait. The guards are silenced."

"It doesn't matter now."

Emerald swallowed and took several hesitant steps down the stairs, holding onto the banister. She wanted to cry out, *Please, Baret, trust me, believe in me. I dreamed of you every night in Brideswell, as the rats and lice roamed over my filthy bed. I remembered you. You are everything that I want, and I want you now as I've never wanted anything else in my life.*

She loved him, but she would lose him to Lavender. There was no hope now.

"What about her?" she heard Erik ask him in a low voice.

"She's free to do whatever she wishes."

Erik turned and looked up at her, expressionless, taking her measure.

Emerald's gaze faltered.

As they left, Baret paused before the two paintings on the yellow stucco wall. As if seeing his father and himself together were difficult to handle emotionally, he turned away and walked to the door with Erik's support.

Emerald stood on the stair, desolate, hoping that he would look back at her, that the old familiar flicker of emotion would renew itself in his dark eyes, that there would be no disappointment, no misunderstanding of what had happened with Jasper.

But he walked out, and then she heard the sound of horses riding away.

Silence descended upon the hacienda. Emerald clung to the banister, her taut emotions stretched to the point of snapping. As she looked upon Jasper's body, the dazed chill that had gripped her began to shatter. Outside, the squall had intensified, and a tropical storm blew against the front door. Erik had not closed it tightly, and it blew open. Rain fell on the polished tile.

The thought of spending another night here was unthinkable. Regardless of the storm, she must reach the stables, find a horse, ride to Port Royal to the lookout house. She feared that even if her hem brushed against Jasper's body, she would scream and keep on screaming.

Lord, help me!

She eased her way down the stairs, nearing Jasper, who lay sprawled across the steps, the pistol near his clawed hand. Drawing her skirts back, she squeezed past.

She walked swiftly through the salon, flickering with torch light, her steps sounding like castanets on the tile floor. The rainy night stifled her with humidity. She flicked a glance at the painting high on the yellow wall, and the glimpse of Baret brought a renewed pang.

"Murderess! That is what you are!"

She looked up. A young woman of Spanish descent stood above the stairs, glaring. Carlotta? Undoubtedly Carlotta.

"I didn't shoot him," Emerald protested. "He tried to kill Baret Buckington. It was self-defense."

"Murderess," insisted Carlotta bitterly. "I will tell my father!" She broke into tears. "I loved Jasper—" Carlotta started down the stairs to where he lay. "You will pay!" she screamed. She knelt to snatch up Jasper's empty pistol.

Emerald fled through the open door into the warm rain and wind. She ran wildly, soon drenched to the skin and stopping in her mindless flight only when her beating heart felt as if it would burst.

She halted on a wet tile court, gasping, blinking through the rain. Which direction to the stables?

A jungle of green vines crawled along the wall like twining serpents, their coils reaching out to twist about her. Her jaw clamped. She thought of how Baret had abandoned her here on her own, something he would never have done in the past.

She ran again, tears as well as rain wetting her face. She tried to recall the layout of the hacienda from the afternoon she'd arrived with Sir Jasper.

Somehow the man did not seem dead. She imagined she could hear his footsteps following her through the darkness. Or was it Carlotta?

She paused again, this time between two yuccas in large, adobe planters, and glanced behind her. It was only the wind that raced after her, whipping her skirts. She wasted no more time. There was a gate ahead, and she ran through it, coming out into a grassy yard.

Nearing the stables behind the house, she ceased her running and walked cautiously toward the building, wondering if it were possible to saddle a horse without awaking the grooms. Did they sleep near the horses or in quarters behind the stables? She paused to consider her dilemma, glancing behind her to make sure she wasn't being followed.

She wouldn't get far on foot. To reach Port Royal, she must have a horse. She remembered something Erik had mentioned to Baret: "*The guards are silenced.*" Did that include the grooms? Why would no one except Carlotta have responded to the pistol shot?

Halting outside the stables, she heard nothing but wind and rain. The hinges creaked as she opened the door of the low stone building, and she was met by the musky odor of manure and horses drifting from the interior. Her hands trembled as she lit a lantern near the door.

She coaxed the first friendly horse at hand and was relieved to see it was a mare. Carlotta's horse, perhaps? Emerald wasted no time in leading it to the block. The rain continued to beat against the side of the building, drowning out any footsteps.

Her fingers were still shaking, and she shivered uncontrollably, casting glances toward the door. She expected at any moment to see Carlotta standing there with raised pistol and Spanish fury in her eyes.

She saddled the mare and led it through the stable door. The wind drove the rain against her face as she swung into the saddle. She touched the horse's flank with the bone-handled whip and sent the mare running swiftly down the muddy road between the hacienda and the main route to Spanish Town. Moments later they left the ordeal at Jasper Hall far behind.

She'd ridden perhaps a mile when the thud of racing hooves behind her emerged from the night. Emerald brought the whip down hard on the mare's muscular flank.

But the rider was gaining on her. In another minute he came up beside the mare, shouting in the face of the wind and rain. *"I'm a friend!"*

She recognized the voice and turned her head, slowing the mare. It was Erik!

The sign of the Royale Inn swung on squeaking hinges in the wind. The outer courtyard was entirely enclosed with a wall and despite the steamy night an open fire sputtered to stay alive in the slowing rain. Emerald watched the firelight cast weaving images on the stone wall, reminding her of two dancing wolves with pointed ears. Weary, she stood by the open grate where slabs of meat sizzled, their juices splattering onto the coals.

She held a steaming cup of tea between her palms and had grown uncomfortably aware that she was soaked to the skin. The lace on her frock hung limp, and there was a tear in one of her petticoats. Her hair hung down her back in wet ringlets. She was also aware of two scoundrels sitting on the other side of the yard, watching her over their rum, but she ignored them.

Captain Farrow came back with two plates. "You'd better eat," was all he said.

As if she could. But his politeness went a long way to lend ointment to a torn and bruised spirit. She managed a half smile and took the plate.

He looked up at the dark sky, blinking into the rain. "I think we would do best under that ledge."

She nodded and sat down on the bench, holding the plate that seemed to weigh a hundred pounds.

He ate in silence, and she glanced at him curiously. Like Baret and others of the nobility, he wore his golden hair in the masculine style of the king's daring Cavaliers. He had on what reminded her of a French artist's flat cap, tilted stylishly to one side. His features were somberly handsome, sensitive, yet decidedly rugged, and she knew he was a dangerous swordsman, again like Baret. He wore an all-black suit, and a pistol was in his waistband and perhaps a dagger in his boot.

Emerald took a bite of something she knew was nourishing. "I've never had a chance to thank you for rescuing Minette from the *San Pedro*. We are—were both extremely grateful, Captain Farrow."

"Where is she?"

"At Foxemoore. With Pitt."

"Willingly?"

"Oh, no! As a slave! I must free her as soon as I can!"

He picked up a mug and concentrated on a fly as though it were of interest, then swiped it away.

"Captain—about Baret—he will recover?" she asked for perhaps the third time.

"Jasper was a better swordsman than a marksman."

"Thanks to you, Bar—the viscount lives."

He lifted the mug and drank, frowning over some private contemplation. He watched the innkeeper turn the slab of meat on the grate.

"I must speak to the viscount. Please."

He finally spoke. "You should know his lordship isn't likely to forget about finding you with Jasper."

She stood stiffly, anguish clearly written on her weary face. "Captain Farrow, things weren't as they appeared! I loathed Sir Jasper! His lordship rushed to conclusions he had no right to make. Oh, you will tell him the truth for me?"

He looked at her, then studied the mug in his hand. "If he will hear. What do you want me to explain?"

Her eyes pleaded, for Erik was now the only contact between herself and Baret. She pushed her hair back, growing embarrassed under his even look.

"Tell him I must speak with him."

"He's not one to listen. He's already planning his expedition with Morgan. He'll leave in a week or two."

She believed Erik would also be going on that expedition and that the time remaining was short.

"Please, surely you can make him understand he's wrong."

It was the first time she heard him laugh. "One isn't likely to convince him of anything. He makes up his own mind."

"Then I simply must see him to explain. Take me to him now."

"I'll tell him you are here, but I can't promise."

She smiled her relief. "Captain Farrow, you're the only friend I have now. And you're the one man he will trust."

An odd expression showed briefly on his face. She wondered if she'd been too friendly. "If he won't see me," she said, "tell him I'd been at that place only two days! I'd been brought straight from Brideswell. The clothes, the chamber, the jewels— Jasper tried to buy me, but I refused him. How could Baret even think I'd cooperate with that man?"

After a long moment, Erik shrugged. "The viscount is a skilled swordsman, an excellent buccaneer, and, alas, he remains blooded nobility, a viscount. He grew up in the king's company and could have had for wife a number of women who bear titles and family wealth. But if he is all these things and more, he is also as much a rogue as I am, madam. You must ask yourself why he nurses his anger more than he concerns himself with the gunshot wound. I've only two answers to offer. Either he wishes a thing against you that he may marry Lady Thaxton, or he's in love with you. You must answer that for yourself."

The suggestion that he was doing this in order to gain Lavender was a devastating blow. Why hadn't she thought of it before?

"He's not in love with me," she said tiredly and swayed a little from her weariness.

He reached a hand to steady her. "Better sit down. There's a carriage leaving for Port Royal tonight. Have you a place to go if I take you there?"

"Yes, but I wouldn't want to impose further on your kindness, Captain Farrow. The viscount will need you until he's on his feet again. I can ride the carriage safely to my father's lookout house."

Erik watched her, then turned the mug about in his hand. "I'll try to talk to him." He set the mug down. "He should be awake by now. I'll bring him supper and explain what happened."

She smiled for the first time. "You're very kind, Captain Farrow."

"Your words will be remembered. Will you be all right if I leave you here for a time?"

"Yes, I'll be fine," said Emerald, her spirits beginning to rise.

But Erik looked at her optimistic smile and frowned.

Baret grimaced, impatient over the limitations his injury caused him. He could do nothing, when a hundred things needed to be done. He had not ridden far when he had halted his horse in the blinding rain and told Erik to return to the hacienda for Emerald. He'd been wrong to hurt her as he had by walking out. And now he was furious with himself for risking her further. He'd known of this inn and insisted on coming here while Erik went back for her, but he'd made clear to Erik that she wasn't to know he had sent him.

He'd behaved the perfect rogue. He wouldn't admit it was because she had aroused a jealousy within him that he hadn't suspected even existed. He pushed a chair out of his way with his boot and turned as the door opened quietly and Erik entered.

Baret searched his suave face, growing more impatient with his inabilities to handle matters himself. "Well?"

Erik walked to the window and looked below into the courtyard, even though it was surely raining too heavily to see anything.

"Did you find her? Where is she?" Baret asked, beginning to grow alarmed. If anything had happened to Emerald, he'd never forgive himself.

"She's below. She wants to see you—to explain."

Baret remained silent. He tried to get to his feet but swayed and grabbed the bedpost. "No. I'm in no mood. I need time to think."

"She says she's innocent about Jasper."

"She told me the same thing once before," he stated bitterly. "Only then it was about Levasseur."

That Emerald was safe satisfied Baret for the moment, and he eased himself back down against the pillow.

"Rest, or you won't be sailing with Morgan." Erik poured coffee from a pot and calmly handed him the cup. "You're certain you won't see her now? Let her explain?"

"No. See that she gets back safely is all." Baret looked at him. "You spoke to Carlotta?"

"Yes."

Baret smothered his unease. "What did she say?"

"She says the death of Sir Karlton and six weeks in Brideswell weakened Emerald to succumb to Jasper. They'd been together for several weeks."

Baret's jaw flexed as he stared at his cup. His insides ached worse than his injury. He tried to push the tormenting thoughts from his mind, but the more he did, the more vivid became the image of Emerald in Jasper's arms, and he smashed the cup across the room.

Erik watched him. "Perhaps your cousin has reason to lie."

"She has no reason to lie. We're friends. It was I who saw that she arrived at the hacienda—where she wished to go. There's nothing between us. She doesn't know about the betrothal. She knows only about Lavender."

Erik shrugged. "Any daughter of Lord Felix should be looked upon with suspicion. I didn't think you cared this much for Karlton's daughter."

Baret leaned back, his good arm behind his head. He stared up at the ceiling. The rain pounded against the window.

Erik sighed. "Rest. By the time you heal and the expedition with Morgan is over, you'll see matters with a clearer eye."

20

EDGE OF LIGHT

The morning star rose in the eastern sky, its light pulsating with the promise of bright, new hope. Looking out from the crow's nest, Emerald saw it as a glimmer of God's watchful care throughout the long journey her soul had taken in darkness. She had ridden up Fishers Row on the mare, exhausted—Erik had been mistaken about the availability of a carriage—but the long night of trial was fading. The sun would soon break forth, rejoicing like a strong man to run its race across the heavens.

"Even here amid my sorrows, Your hand has led me," she murmured. "Even in my night, You have been a light about me. You have not forsaken me. You will not forget me, even when my hopes turn to nightmares. You have a noble purpose as sure as Your faithfulness."

A name came to her mind as if written there by the finger of God. *Sir Cecil Chaderton. A friend loves at all times.*

Excitement flared like torch light. The beloved Sir Cecil, a true servant of God! On board the *Regale,* had he not led her in devotional reading of the Scriptures and in prayer to consecrate her years on earth to God's purposes? She could turn to him now.

Sir Cecil was at Foxemoore, seeing to the education of Jette. She would write to him at once.

"Oh, God, thank You for showing me the pathway of hope."

Morning sunlight filtered through the round window of the crow's nest in the lookout house. She sat at her father's desk with a pot of tea, her eyes burning from lack of sleep, and completed the letter to Sir Cecil. She explained briefly all the evils that had befallen her since arriving at Port Royal. She told him of her father's being shot and killed on the wharf and her experience at the hacienda in Spanish Town.

She went on. Minette, as far as she knew, was a house slave to the overseer, and Emerald feared for her safety. With Geneva now too ill to burden, there was no one she could turn to on behalf of Minette. Emerald told him of the death of Sir Jasper the night before, and shuddered as she relived that ordeal. Added to all this, she wrote, was the viscount's misunderstanding of her presence at the hacienda.

Emerald paused, holding the quill. She thought of the document she'd signed for Lord Felix, and she winced. She could not yet explain that to Sir Cecil, who was closely allied with Baret. And just how *would* she explain it? And what of Baret? Was he even in Port Royal now? What if the Admiralty officials had managed to locate and arrest him before he could escape to the *Regale*?

She rejected the desire to pick up the spyglass and look out the window to see if she could glimpse either his ship or Captain Farrow's *Warspite*. She knew Baret was too much the buccaneer to anchor within view of the guns of Fort Charles.

Was he recovering well from his gunshot wound?

The morning grew late, the sun hotter. She hastened to draw the letter to a close, sealed it, and addressed it to the scholar. Then she dug a coin from the small money pouch she and Minette kept in the desk drawer. She would find a half-caste at the turtle crawl near the market to bring the letter inland to Foxemoore.

If the Lord blessed her efforts, perhaps within a day or two she would have the company of Sir Cecil Chaderton at the lookout house to aid her in the matter of Minette.

It was Friday, and the fish market would be busy. The sky was blue with a few clouds left over from yesterday's storm, and the humidity was not as noticeable. In order to get her mind off her cares, she tied the mare a block from her destination, having decided to walk the rest of the way. The locale for shopping was visited by the gentry and was safe during the day.

Walking alone without Minette and Zeddie reinforced her loss, and a sudden pang of sorrow over Zeddie filled her heart. In the past he'd been close at hand, sauntering behind her with his purple-leather bandolier slung over his shoulder, sporting his huge pistol. What evil had befallen him that dreadful night Pitt and Jasper had come to the lookout house? According to

305

Minette's brief account, poor Zeddie had been knocked unconscious. And Emerald had seen him carried away toward the beach. Had they dumped him into the bay?

She assumed him to be dead. Had he survived, he would have found her soon after she'd been locked up at Brideswell and would have gone for help to the town house on Queen Street or Foxemoore. By now, Geneva or Earl Nigel would have known of her plight and the death of her father. Instead, they'd been told the tale circulated by Sir Jasper and Lord Felix that she'd evidently "run away again with another buccaneer."

Zeddie's silence meant the worst had happened. *I won't think about all this now, or I'll become so morbid I'll be good for nothing but weeping parties.* She would take one day at a time and leave tomorrow with the Lord.

Holding tightly the letter addressed to Sir Cecil, Emerald quickened her steps past the familiar markets, grog shops, and businesses belonging to rich merchants only too willing to scoop in the loot and contraband that the buccaneers harvested.

The fort guarded the entrance to the harbor, and cannons bristled between the crenels. She noted King's House and the private residence of the governor, sitting dominantly on a green slope facing the Caribbean at a prime location for receiving the cooler trade winds.

The market was near the northwest corner of the harbor. There fishermen and turtle harvesters did their nightly business in small boats with lanterns. As she drew near the open stalls, she found herself close to the fenced-in turtle run that belonged to Hob. Again she fondly remembered him and hesitated by the fence before walking on. If by chance Baret had slipped out of the harbor on his way back to Tortuga, Hob might have once again joined him.

Not that it mattered about Baret any longer, she thought numbly. After what happened at the hacienda, she doubted if she would ever see the viscount again. The betrothal, a precarious entity even at its best, was now once for all out of the question.

She tensed, remembering the document Felix had in his possession. What would Baret and Earl Nigel do when they discovered that she was the "witness" who had signed it?

Then there was the official letter affirming her innocence

in the matter of Mr. Pitt. Felix had gotten what he wanted and wasn't likely to bother her again. But Pitt was another matter. And Pitt had Minette. But Baret had taken her copy of the letter! Without it, she would remain vulnerable to any new threat that might come her way, especially after the shooting at the hacienda. What if Carlotta swore to the authorities that she had been involved?

A hundred desperate thoughts ran through her mind, renewing her fears as she stared blankly at the turtle run, thick with olive-green shells partially buried in the white sand.

"Emerald! Emerald!"

Surprised, she turned and saw a fine carriage parked on the cobbled space near Kings House. *Why, that's Lavender's carriage,* she thought, seeing Jette seated inside. He'd lifted the window sash and leaned out, waving and grinning.

Emerald hesitated, not wishing any contact with Lavender, but she did not see her inside the carriage. A guard of red-coated militia was also on the square. Emerald wondered what might be going on and why Lavender would be there at all—and with Jette.

"Emerald, come here!" he called anxiously.

The carriage driver turned in his seat to lean down and see what the new heir of Earl Nigel was up to.

Emerald recognized the driver as Percy, the head groom at Foxemoore, a friendly Irishman who had thought well of her father. She saw the perfect opportunity to have her letter delivered to Sir Cecil, and, glancing quickly down the street, she darted out into traffic, lifting her skirt hem.

Percy had once sailed with her father to the Virginia colony to buy horses when Karlton ran Foxemoore for Lady Sophie. Eventually, Karlton made him trainer of the fine line on Foxemoore. In an arbitrary fit over Karlton's "buccaneering," Lady Sophie dismissed Percy from his position and contracted for the indentured servant Mr. Pitt, whom Sir Jasper had convinced her came from England with an exceptional record. Her father had managed to keep Percy on as head trainer, despite Mr. Pitt's wish to get rid of him.

Emerald rushed up to where the carriage was parked beneath several palms. "Wait, Jette," she called to the boy, "I need to speak to Percy," and she ran to the driver's side.

"Percy!"

The brawny Irishman had thick black hair, bristling with gray, and wore an oil-stained jerkin. He turned at her voice. "Why, Miss Emerald, they're saying you was living wi' your mother's family on Tortuga."

"I never went there, but I've no time to explain now." She lowered her voice. "Is Lady Thaxton in town with Jette?"

"Aye, she is," he said. "And so is—"

"She mustn't see me. Here—" she pushed the letter at him "—please take this and see it reaches no one except Sir Cecil Chaderton. He's at Foxemoore?"

"Aye, and so's his lordship the earl himself, and Lady Geneva. But she's sick, so I've heard, and in a weak way."

The news was disturbing. "Will you see that Sir Cecil gets this as soon as you return?"

"Sure, Miss Emerald, and all the serving folk heard about Sir Karlton. 'Tis a sad day for all of us, and our prayers be wi' ye."

"Thank you, Percy. Do—do you know if a proper burial was ever arranged?"

He shaded his piercing dark eyes with a gnarled hand and looked at her, troubled. "Far as I know, he's buried at sea."

Her anguish must have been visible—she had wanted a Christian burial. He looked at her kindly. "It was a sorrowful thing that happened to him, getting arrested like that. No one can convince me he was guilty of piracy, or that he escaped the gaol."

"Did the militia tell Lady Sophie about me—about my going to Tortuga?"

"I'm not rightly knowing that. The news came through a groom whose sweetheart is Lady Thaxton's serving girl."

"Oh, I see well enough. The story of my running away to Tortuga makes sense if it came by way of Lavender."

"You mean you didn't go on the *Madeleine* to Tortuga?"

"On my father's ship?" she asked, bewildered. "No, not since we returned nearly two months ago! But there are few who'd believe me, any more than they believe my father was innocent. Anyway, what happened since I arrived is worse, so I'll not be making an issue of the tale where Lavender is concerned."

"'Tis none of my business, Miss Emerald, but does anyone at Foxemoore know you're here in town alone?"

"The letter to Sir Cecil will explain everything."

His bronzed face softened, and he touched his cap. "I be sympathizin'. No need tellin' you how to be careful till you hear from him. Is Zeddie with you now?"

Her eyes filled with tears. "Zeddie is missing—and may be dead too."

"Why, how can that be?"

"It happened the night my father was killed."

He frowned. "Now, miss, that can't be, seeing as how he was seen weeks ago boarding the *Madeleine* and going with the new sailing master to Tortuga."

"What!" Joy flooded her heart. "Zeddie is aboard the *Madeleine?*"

"Aye, I'm sure of it. It was said you were aboard too—with its new captain, that buccaneer friend of your father."

She knew of no such buccaneer, nor did she care at the moment how he'd gotten control of her father's ship. Zeddie was alive! And that meant he'd eventually be returning to Port Royal in search of her. Had he been led to believe she and Minette had been abducted to Tortuga, perhaps by smugglers serving Sir Jasper? She was sure he would have an explanation for leaving her forgotten in Brideswell. Only his own death or an outright lie would have lured him away from her side.

"If Zeddie's on Tortuga, he'll soon be coming back with the rest of the buccaneers and pirates," said Percy, nodding toward the militia and the Kings House. "It'll be a fine gathering, I'm told, all vowing allegiance to the king and Henry Morgan."

She wondered what he meant. "The buccaneers are returning to Port Royal? What about Gallows Point?"

"That'll all be done away with, so I heard Lady Thaxton saying."

"Percy! Would you mind telling me what's going on in King's House to bring Lavender here? And what is the militia doing?"

"You mean you don't know? Why, it's all over Port Royal. The earl's grandson—Captain Buckington—is being commissioned by the king."

She stared at him, dumbfounded.

"You mean arrested!" she corrected.

"No, not arrested. Commissioned as the king's agent."

Still she stared, completely bewildered.

Percy laughed. "After him and that other buccaneer Farrow saved English Barbados from the Dutch, the earl's grandson won't likely be arrested. Hardly, miss!"

Surely Percy had his facts in error, but before she could ask, Jette called, "Emerald, are you coming back with us in the carriage?"

She looked at Jette, her mind in confusion.

Percy placed the envelope inside his jerkin and nodded toward Kings House. "Captain Buckington and Lady Thaxton is coming now. She'll be telling you all about his heroics, if you give her half a chance. I'm wondering what Lord Grayford will be saying about them. Heard her tell the viscount he was coming to the governor's house with the rest of the buccaneers."

"I must go now, Percy. Don't forget the letter to Sir Cecil." She turned to leave, taking only a moment to grasp Jette's extended hand. "I'll talk with you later, Jette."

His olive-green eyes searched her face anxiously. "Where've you been, Emerald? When Grandfather sent the carriage to Uncle Karlton's lookout, you were gone. Some say you ran away with a pirate."

Her heart squeezed with pain. Somehow the speculation hurt even worse coming from a child. Jette's affection and respect meant a great deal to her.

"I didn't run away," she assured him. "I wanted to come and help with your schooling. I've been here all along, but I can't explain now."

"But why not? Baret will be glad to have you ride back with us."

The longing in his eyes tugged at her heart. "No, your brother wants to be alone with Cousin Lavender now."

"I don't know why," he mumbled crossly. "They don't say much."

"I'll talk to you again," she said. "Just as soon as I meet with Sir Cecil."

"He's coming to see you at Karlton's old house?"

"I hope so. Good-bye, Jette."

"But, Emerald—"

Percy's warning voice alerted her: "They're coming, lass."

She must get away before Baret saw her! It would never do for him to think she was trying to use Jette as a wedge to come between him and Lavender. Not answering the boy's childish protest of disappointment, she hurried away, crossing the street to the turtle crawl as though bent on shopping for supper.

A minute later, with her back toward the square and the Buckington carriage, she glanced cautiously over her shoulder, her emotions unable to resist a fleeting look at Baret. Was he recovering?

He did not look wounded, she thought, sizing him up, and decided his jacket still covered a bandage. He was handsomely dressed in green and black, a white ostrich feather in his wide-brimmed hat. He appeared to be on his best behavior for Lavender's sake. Even so, there was no misinterpreting the spirit of the buccaneer about him. Well, she had lost him now.

A dart of jealousy burned its way through her heart. *He thinks the very worst of me, and I'm innocent. Whereas Lavender wears the betrothal ring of Lord Grayford! So what's she doing being escorted about by the viscount? As if I didn't know well enough her plans to get him back!*

She knew it was wrong, but a well of self-pity bubbled up in her heart. Her fingers clutched the front of her dress, ruined by the rain of the night before, and her eyes narrowed as she watched him being attentive to her cousin.

Baret escorted Lavender by the arm as though she were a duchess entering a carriage to visit the king. Perhaps in future years they would be doing just that.

Lavender was, as always, the image of sweetness and gentleness garbed like a fragrant spring blossom in frothy pink and white lace and frills. Her golden hair gleamed like a halo. She gazed up at him, a smile on her heart-shaped face.

In a moment the goose will be in a swoon, Emerald thought.

She watched how carefully he handed her into the carriage. Yet he had left Emerald alone at the hacienda to make her own way back to Port Royal on a borrowed horse in a squall. He hadn't even cared! It was Erik Farrow who had returned to help her.

Lavender's no more a real lady than I, she thought bitterly. She fed her frustration by staring, trying to see Baret's expression.

Was he as mesmerized by Lavender as she was with him? But his cocky hunter-green hat was in the way.

I hate her, she thought, her nails digging into her sweating palms. *O God, forgive me. I don't hate her, not really. I don't want to feel this way, so full of jealousy and resentment—*

Scalding tears spilled down her cheeks, and she was help-less to stop them. *Emerald, you're a silly fool to feel so broken about this. You're only hurting yourself.*

Baret turned her way, but she saw no smile on his face. Then Jette took hold of his arm and said something, pointing anxiously. He saw Emerald then, but if there'd been no smile on his face when he'd turned from Lavender, neither was there a hint of interest now upon seeing her at the turtle run. Emerald found the cool, restrained expression of a stranger more devas-tating than any outright scowl. It was as if he did not even recog-nize her. He entered the carriage and closed the door.

Emerald walked briskly back to where she'd tied the horse.

A moment later the Buckington carriage drove past her. She ventured a glance and saw Percy touch his hat in her direc-tion. Jette was watching, bewildered, but the one who mattered most did not favor her with a glance. She swallowed hard as the carriage moved down the street and turned toward the town house on Queen Street.

So then. It was over, once and for all. And Lavender had him back.

Mercifully, her feelings had withdrawn into a shelter of self-preservation, and she felt numb. It had to end, she told herself. Buccaneer or not, he was a viscount. But did it have to end this way?

I won't think about it.

She would wait for Sir Cecil and anticipate a plan by which she could gain Minette's release. After that, she didn't know. Her father owned shares in Foxemoore, and the bungalow would have been left to her, so the possibility of returning remained viable. But the strength to enforce her rights was lacking.

There was some legal document her father insisted had come from the elder Earl Buckington, proving his right to the sugar shares. Now, if the document truly existed, those shares were hers. She would need to go to her father's chamber in the bungalow and search through his trunk. Perhaps she could find it. She could not think of doing so now.

At least there was the lookout house, she told herself. Humble though it was, it was a roof over her head, and she could count on the fact that it wasn't worth the conniving of Lord Felix to snatch away. There was reward in the humble state of things after all. The ambitious usually left one alone among rats and cockroaches!

She mounted the mare and rode to Fishers Row. She would need to have the horse returned soon lest she also be accused of being a horse thief as well as a murderess and a strumpet!

How bitter she was beginning to sound. *Please, Lord, do not let me become hard and cynical over the injustices of life. Keep my heart tender, my faith young and brave.*

She turned her thoughts away from negative things to her blessings. As much as she found fault with life in Port Royal, she could at least manage to live here on her own, especially if her beloved Zeddie returned. For the foreseeable future she felt more comfortable with just trying to make ends meet.

Perhaps she could go into the turtle business. Who was to say that Emerald Harwick couldn't develop the humility needed to sell turtles herself? A few times when younger, she had gone to Chocolata Hole with Great-uncle Mathias to buy turtles from Hob. She could catch her own and sell them on the better streets. That way she could avoid going inside the taverns, brothels, and gambling dens. She could make the rounds of the back doors of the gentry instead.

When she arrived back at the lookout house, her weariness from lack of sleep and the long ordeal of the past weeks hit her all at once. Wearily she climbed down from her mount and led the mare safely to the back where there was shade and grass.

"Oh, I know you're spoiled and used to sweet hay, but we're together in this for now. If I can sell turtles, you can eat sea grass." She gave a few pats to the strong, glistening neck as the soft brown eyes looked at her. "Cheer up. I'll send you home as soon as Zeddie can take you."

Emerald removed her hat and shook out her damp, dark tresses. The scorching sun beat down upon her as she walked around the narrow house to the front steps. The glitter of the bay jabbed painfully bright at her eyes. She climbed the stairs to the door, entered, and, too tired to worry whether some rogue had entered during her absence, went up the steps to the crow's nest. She ducked through the small round door and, tossing her hat to the desk, fell across her father's bed.

If Percy was right, Zeddie would be coming home. There was a glimmer of light after all. The morning star of hope continued to shine.

21

A VIRTUOUS WOMAN,
WHO CAN FIND?

The trade wind was blowing through the open window. It lifted the lace hem of her skirt, awakening her. Emerald's eyes fluttered open to see the setting sun. She'd slept for hours! Feeling rested, she got up from the bed and reached for her brush. She gave her hair generous strokes, but her hand became still when she smelled the enticing waft of coffee blowing in through the window from the cook shack.

She looked toward the door leading downstairs. Strange, she thought. Who would be brewing coffee? She walked quietly to the window and glanced below to the causeway built on stilts, and to the pile of wood used for the outdoor oven. But she saw nothing stirring in the ebbing blue twilight.

She heard the mare moving about below, and her soft whinny as if greeting a friend. Cautiously, Emerald turned away to glance once more toward the open door. Then she heard footsteps.

Someone is downstairs.

Unlike the terrifying night when Mr. Pitt had broken in, she felt no alarm—yet. Perhaps Zeddie had returned from Tortuga sooner than Percy had expected. Was it possible that Sir Cecil had been at the town house and Percy had already delivered the letter?

Leaving the crow's nest, she stepped to the upper railing and peered directly below. But the room was asleep with evening shadows, and she saw no one. As she came silently down the flight of steep steps, the aroma of freshly brewed coffee grew more enticing.

She halted mid-stair to look again over the railing, and her heart caught with alarm and excitement when her eyes fell on a hunter-green hat with a white plume. A jacket lay on the chair, one she had seen him wearing hours ago when he was with Lavender.

He wouldn't come here, she thought, her tension growing. Nevertheless, the hat and jacket belonged to Baret, and somehow she could imagine his brewing coffee while she slept the afternoon away!

She glanced down at her soiled dress and turned to quietly retrace her steps to change into a more suitable frock. She hated this dress anyway because Jasper had given it to her. Its cost and flair represented everything that had maligned her virtuous reputation and had brought suspicion between her and Baret.

The unmistakable squeak of leather boots halted her, and she stiffened on the steps, her hand closing tightly about the railing.

"I see you've added horse thievery to your list of offenses. There's no telling what Carlotta will say about it. You take her lover, and now her prized mare."

Her cheeks flamed. It was like him to enjoy making a horrid matter even worse.

But she turned slowly in the direction of his voice. She spotted him now, stretched out leisurely in the chair in a shadowed corner, his high leather boots crossed, one arm behind his dark head as if he didn't have a care in all Jamaica. Nor did it seem to bother him that his presence contradicted the fact they were not on speaking terms.

At the moment, how he'd managed to make coffee without affecting her sleep escaped her, but here he was, as if the incident at the hacienda had been a dark illusion.

If only it were so, she thought desperately, but when he stood, a rugged and handsome Cavalier out of place in the crookedly built room, she saw that he was no illusion—and neither was the shooting incident. A bandage showed through his laced shirt.

She resisted the absurd pounding of her heart, caused by a motley mixture of anxiety and longing for him. Her feelings were all the more troubling when he retained a poise that was imperturbable. Perhaps his restraint was best. The one time she had witnessed a crack in his composure had been when he believed she had compromised her Christian virtue. She folded her arms, watching him through lowered lashes.

316

He came to the steps.

"What do you want?" she asked stiffly.

His half smile was cynical. "The wrong question, madam. What do *you* want?"

"Not your rudeness, I assure you."

"I've come with news. I thought you'd like to know that your darlin' Jasper, unlike sweet Jamie Boy, has escaped the Grim Reaper. You won't need to search your trunk for Puritan black after all. Lament no longer, m'lady, Jasper has avoided passing on to his everlasting abode!"

"He's alive?"

"Unfortunately. Ah—the color of youthful vibrancy returns to your wan cheeks. Please, don't faint away with heart-stopping relief. I've no smelling salts."

"Leave here at once!" she cried.

He folded his arms. "Not yet. We've important matters to discuss. Enough of Jasper. I'm sick of his name. And I didn't come here to browbeat you. I came to forgive you."

"Forgive me!"

He placed a hand on his chest and offered a slight bow. "From the heart, of course."

"So I see, m'lord."

He walked to the table and grabbed the coffee pot, then poured coffee into her father's mug.

She held back frustrated tears and gripped the banister tightly.

Jasper was alive. She remembered Carlotta's hiss: *"Murderess!"*

"If there is any relief, sir, it's from a far different cause, since I find Jasper an odious wretch. But I can see that any explanation would meet your immediate rejection. Your mind is made up about me. Just like all Port Royal."

He said nothing but glanced at her, a slight frown on his face.

"There's no undoing of prejudice, nor any use in defending one's character once a mind is made up. I've always been Karlton's 'little brat.'"

"Maybe, but then again, perhaps not. We'll settle for horse thief," he said lightly, his smile cynical. He looked at her throat. "But you are still too fair for Gallows Point. Looks like we'll need to consider other remedies and what I can do to save you from the stone throwers."

"Do they include you?"

"I've come with terms of conditional peace, if you'll cooperate."

She was curious and scanned him, wondering. "And if I don't submit to your terms to save me from my 'branding'?"

"You've no choice after all. I did buy you, remember?" A flicker of irony came to his smile—and something else. Disappointment? Regret?

Whatever it was brought pain to her heart. *Oh, Baret, if only you trusted me.*

"I bought you twice, actually—from Jamie with rubies, from Levasseur with a duel. "'Who can find a virtuous woman?'" he quoted softly from Proverbs. "'Her price is above rubies. The heart of her husband doth safely trust in her.'"

Emerald turned her head so that he wouldn't see the welling tears. The silence lingered. It was on her tongue to cry again, "I'm innocent." Something dreadful had happened to convince him of her guilt, but what? Who or what had so turned him into believing a lie? Her eyes narrowed. She plucked at the torn lace on her sleeve. "I won't need to burden you, m'lord. I intend to start a turtle business."

"A turtle business?"

"It's respectable."

"Yes, a little wet and sandy, however." He looked down at her bare feet. "You're prepared to haul out your calico drawers again from your trunk and wade knee-deep in water and sand? Hob will appreciate your company."

"You make it sound foolish!"

"Not foolish at all. Just not what I have in mind."

"What *you* have in mind! I no longer thought you had anything in mind except misunderstanding the facts. As for the horse, I intend to send her back. There was no carriage from Spanish Town as Captain Farrow thought, so we rode back together most of the way. He left me outside Port Royal."

"No matter. I've decided to be generous with you. Keep the mare."

He owned the horse? But how, unless that painting of himself and Royce on the hacienda wall was more meaningful than she knew. She thought of the document she'd signed and looked at him nervously. Did he know? He couldn't. He was being too pleasant, despite the cynicism in his manner.

"You'll hang for your generosity if you stay in Port Royal much longer," she warned uneasily. "Your uncle is a powerful man."

"So you've discovered. He drives a hard bargain, doesn't he?"

She glanced at him, but he showed nothing but a half smile. "He was working with Jasper in smuggling."

"Smuggling is the least of his sins. But why warn me? Don't tell me your conscience bothers you? You're worried about that document you signed?"

Her face flushed meekly. "Like other things, I can explain the document."

"I've no doubt. And you will. To Governor Modyford in a few days. There'll be a meeting of the Jamaican Council at Kings House."

"The governor—" She clutched the rail tightly, thinking the worst.

He walked back to the table, caught up what looked to her to be a leg of something that on a better occasion might have been able to fly, and ate while he watched her, not bothering to sit.

"Why would Governor Modyford wish to see me about it? Would they arrest you?"

"Do you intend to come to the hanging?"

"Signing that was a dreadful mistake," she pleaded. "But it was a mistake. I'll tell him so. I thought you had been . . . Lord Felix told me . . . and about the smuggling, Zeddie saw Jasper and Felix on the beach dealing with a Dutch slave ship. The slaves were bound for the Spanish colonies."

He sobered. "That doesn't surprise me. I knew about the smuggling. I wouldn't mention it to the governor yet. I'm still working on your father's death and wish to keep Felix unaware of what I'm up to."

That brought her a measure of peace. If anyone could find out who was involved in his death and why, it would be Baret.

"The meeting will be safe enough for me," he was saying. "Modyford's calling the buccaneers back from Tortuga. There's a gathering with the planters and merchants, but it's rather a sham since he's already agreed with Henry Morgan on an expedition. But first, Modyford will want to ask you a few questions. The High Admiralty official will be there as well—Earl Cunningham. *He'd* like to arrest me. Cheer up—it's my neck dear Uncle Felix wants stretched, not yours." His eyes hardened. "For whatever reason, you've already given Felix the ammunition he wanted. Fortunately, circumstances do not permit him to use it."

"He *lied* to me. You must believe me. I can explain."

"You don't need to."

"At least give me the chance!"

He pulled a familiar envelope from his shirt. "This is all the explanation I need. Your freedom from Brideswell—in exchange for my arrest."

"That isn't true."

"But I don't blame you for signing, dear. Pitt and Felix both had you chained to the rack. I'm only disappointed that you cooperated with Jasper so easily."

"I didn't cooperate. I refused him," she choked.

He waved a hand. "It doesn't matter anymore. I've spent one sleepless night too many over this. I've decided to pardon you." He tossed the bone onto the platter and wiped his hand on a cloth. He frowned at her, his dark eyes intense. "I've had time to think over my rather crude behavior in saying what I did at the hacienda. I had no right to hurt you with my cutting remarks." He watched her, expressionless. "I've decided you're very young. And a girl in your predicament, under the emotional stress of having just lost your father deserves understanding. At least— that's what I told myself when I came here. But I haven't handled it well, have I? You will understand however," he said flatly, "that any notion of marriage between us is over. The betrothal will be temporary."

Temporary! Her mind flashed back to her meeting with Earl Nigel at the town house. Could Baret know about his grandfather's plans? Did he expect to carry them out even though he believed she "cooperated" with Sir Jasper?

"There will be *no* betrothal," she choked. "How can you even suggest it? I never believed I could take it seriously, even when my father was alive. And it was your grandfather who insisted we go through with it for purposes of his own."

"Yes, I know."

"Then you know about my meeting with him at the town house?"

"It's all part of a bargain I have with him that concerns Henry Morgan, but you needn't understand it all now. I saw him this morning, and we settled matters. I didn't go to him when I first arrived. I went to the hacienda, thinking you might need me. "

She winced. *I did need you*, she wanted to cry. *Desperately I needed you.* But something in his face stopped her from admitting this. Despite his casual kindness, there remained a subdued burning anger in his eyes that now and then sparked as he looked at her.

"If I've compromised, as you believe, I should rather be dead than stand here and endure your tolerance! My conscience is clear."

"That's what I've come about. To ease your conscience." He folded his arms. "You're forgiven for signing the document. Perhaps because it poses no real threat to me at the present. By the time it does, I will have had audience with the king. Felix, however, doesn't know that yet. He'll learn tomorrow night. The moment will be sweet."

"Why not a threat? I don't understand."

"You will. I've also decided to forget your other mistake. But I have to admit it's a pity you wasted yourself on that daw cock Jasper."

She flushed. "I wouldn't have Jasper on a silver platter to save my neck—or yours."

"You spent six weeks in Brideswell. That's enough trial for any young girl to handle. Your father was killed, and you had no one to turn to. I can see why you might succumb. But while I wish to protect you, I won't take you to London."

He picked up the pot and refilled his cup.

She came down the remaining steps, clutching the rags of her dignity.

He lifted the cup, drinking as he watched her.

"I did *not* succumb to Jasper." She came toward him. "You told me he was alive—ask him. Ask Carlotta. She'll tell you."

"I did ask her."

She tensed. "What did she tell you?"

His jaw flexed, but he made no response to her question. "I brought you the letter you went to such extremes to get." He dropped it casually on the table.

Her gaze came to his and, despite his indifferent tone, she saw anger smoldering in the depths of his eyes.

"You should have known I'd come for you. That I'd defend you from Pitt. You might have held out a little longer until I arrived. But I didn't come here to accuse you. I wanted you to have the letter and let you know the document you signed won't matter all that much where my arrest is concerned. I have plans that may thwart Felix when it's all over."

She tried to piece together the jumble of confusing facts.

His gaze softened. "You looked so miserable today when I saw you that my conscience began to trouble me again." He cupped her chin as though she were a small child. He smiled wryly. "For old times' sake, I wanted to call on you. We'll forget the past. Sit down and eat. You look half-starved."

He pulled out a handkerchief and handed it to her. "And dry your eyes. Too many tears have been shed already. Lavender and I have agreed on how to help you."

At the mention of Lavender a dreadful suspicion arose, and she stepped back. She imagined the things her cousin would have said to him, pitying words, pretending concern for her future after the scandal of Brideswell and the hacienda.

He frowned when she simply lowered herself slowly onto a dining chair.

"Emerald," he said gently. "I'm sorry about this."

White and shaking, she breathed, "I don't want your pity."

I want your love, she wanted to say. *I want your highest regard. I want you to look at me the way you used to—the way you looked when you spoke of the virtuous woman of Proverbs.*

"I shouldn't have dealt with you so harshly," he gritted. "I don't know why I did."

"Don't you?" she whispered. "Oh, Baret—it's not because you cared that you were hurt, because you wouldn't ever allow yourself to fall in love with me. That would be unthinkable. You love Lavender, because she's such a wonderful saint, a lady, and you've always thought badly of me even when you pretended you didn't—"

"Emerald, don't." He set down his cup.

"Well, I don't want your help," she choked. "Least of all Lavender's hypocritical acts of mercy. I don't need her—or you."

"On the contrary, you do. And you're behaving as a spoiled child, instead of admitting your weakness and accepting help."

"You dare accuse me of being spoiled? Put your precious Lavender in Brideswell for a day and see her whimper and scream to get out! If anyone would compromise her honor to sleep in a bed of satin, it would be her!"

He pulled her from the chair, his eyes like dark burning coals. "Emerald—"

She struggled, beating against his chest with her fists, sobbing. "I didn't give Jasper what he wanted!" she screamed. "Why won't you believe me! Why!"

"Darling—" He grasped both of her hands, stilling them hard against his chest and drawing her head against him. He soothed her, stroking her hair as she wept.

"I've decided to take you away from here. I wasn't going to say anything yet. I was going to wait until after the expedition with Morgan. But I think we'd better discuss it now."

She looked up at him, astonished. "And where am I to go? The war makes leaving impossible, and I've Minette to think of. And anyway, I can't leave with you. I'm staying, and I'll make it on my own."

"You can't stay unless we're publicly betrothed. I'll be gone on the expedition for months. What will you do?"

"I've this house. I will do just fine."

"You'll get eaten alive if left here. Jasper was only the beginning."

"I told you, I'll sell turtles!"

"Until the first pirate decides to claim you. Who's to stop him if I don't?"

"I've survived before. You owe me nothing. You've only made my life more complicated and—and miserable."

"I can avow to the same, madam. Nevertheless, I've no choice in all this. I can't leave you here without Karlton unless everyone expects me to marry you. Not after what's happened."

She pulled away. "And just where were you going to take me after this pretended betrothal? Tortuga?" she asked with a trace of bitterness.

His eyes narrowed under dark lashes. "I was thinking of the American colonies."

She looked up, surprised. "Oh—so now it's Massachusetts to raise piglets like Jamie Bradford. Is that what Lavender asked you to do with me?"

"I do as I wish. This is my idea. It's the best I can come up with, considering. And I was thinking of the Carolinas. I've thought of buying a plantation. I could set you up there. Zeddie can go with you, and Ty too, if he wishes. I've money enough to take care of you and Minette once my own future is settled."

She searched his face, moved more than she had expected to be. "You're serious."

"Of course, I'm serious. It's the least I can do for friendship's sake," he said flatly. "But don't rush to the conclusion that I care beyond friendship. The moment you gave yourself to Jasper was the end of anything between us."

Stung, she caught her breath.

He too seemed to consider the harshness of his words, then in frustration he walked to his hat and jacket and snatched them up impatiently. He looked back at her.

Pale and shaken, Emerald stood holding the back of the chair.

"We'll talk again later," he said. He walked to the door.

She went after him and grabbed his arm. She spoke impulsively. "And where are you going now? To *her*, of course. She wraps you around her finger. You may own me, but she owns you."

Her outburst was a foolish mistake. She saw a faint scowl and the flicker in his eyes. She had only worsened matters. The more she accused Lavender, the worse she portrayed herself. The harder she tried, the faster she would drive him toward her cousin.

I'm sorry, she wanted to say. After all, he had come. He seemed to care enough about her to want to involve himself in her future. Even when he believed the worst, he had been moved by compassion to try to make amends.

"Oh, Baret, I shouldn't have said that. You have every right to go to her." Emerald's heart burned in her eyes. "But the least thing you can do is speak with Carlotta."

"I said I have." He frowned. "Emerald, why prolong this? I don't want to hurt you more than I have to."

"Did she also lie about me? Who *is* she?"

"A cousin," he said. "She's one of Felix's daughters. I once told you he was in sympathy with Spain. Well, now you know one of the reasons why. He was married to a Spanish ambassador's daughter."

Struck to silence, she stared at him.

"She and I have little in common. But she has no reason to lie to me about you and Jasper."

"She *is* lying, Baret. She was angry and jealous. Go to her again. She'll tell you. She has to."

He put his hat on. "We'll go through with the betrothal, because I won't leave you here without protection. You need someone behind you that men like Jasper fear to cross. If it hadn't been for Felix and Jasper believing I'd be arrested on my return, he wouldn't have dared to misuse you. That goes for Pitt too. I've a score to settle with him."

She heard little of what he said for her heart ached with turmoil. "Then you intend to marry Lavender?"

"Emerald, I don't want to discuss it with either of you."

Did that mean Lavender too had been "discussing it"?

"Lavender came to see me before my father was killed. She wants you back," she said quietly. "She made clear she'll do whatever she must. She, too, lies about me. I suppose that's why you were with her this morning—because you both intend to inform your cousin Grayford about how the two of you feel when he returns."

He threw open the door. "I'll come back."

"I don't know what you're so upset about, Baret Buckington. You've gotten what you wanted."

He looked at her, infuriatingly unreadable. "Have I? Pack your trunk. We're leaving tomorrow for Foxemoore."

"No. I won't go there. I only agreed to cooperate with Earl Nigel's wishes about the betrothal because he threatened to send my father to the Tower. It no longer matters," she said reflectively.

"Nevertheless, I don't see how we can avoid carrying out the bargain."

How tasteless he made it sound, and of course it was.

"My grandfather fears my presence in Port Royal will come

between Lavender and Grayford, and I want this expedition on the Spanish Main. So if he wants a public betrothal, he'll get one."

"To sail with Henry Morgan, you must agree to your grandfather's rules."

"And so I shall."

"You think nothing of a public betrothal to me as long as you get this legal expedition."

"Perhaps better than anyone else, you know why it's so important to me. I'm willing to publicly claim you, despite everything that's gone before. Does that not say anything of honor?"

"You do so because it affords you the right to sail to Porto Bello."

"Better to sail under commission of the king than hang, don't you think? You've no cause to scorn the gesture, madam," he said dryly. "As the betrothed of the viscount you will have a cloak for your reputation."

"Is that all it means to you—a cloak to shield me from what you wrongly think happened?"

"Not just Jasper. You've also forgotten your illustrious cousin Rafael. I see no cause for you to be angry with me about a temporary engagement. The situation will suit both our causes well."

She turned her back. "And when your expedition with Morgan is over, and you return with your father, then what?"

"You know the answer," he said quietly. "I'll take you to the Carolinas."

"And then you'll decide you were in love with Lady Thaxton after all."

He folded his arms. "I've decided I'm not in love with her or anyone else."

"Your commitment to your freedom suits you well," she said coolly.

"I am bound to you for as long as it is mutually agreeable."

"I do not vow so lightly, m'lord Buckington."

"Oh?" He walked back to her, took her arm, and turned her around to face him. His dark eyes glinted. "You have already vowed to me on Tortuga, and I to you. Remember? I made a promise to your father, and I intend to keep it."

"Until it satisfies your purpose, or Lavender's, to break it?"

"Lavender can do nothing I do not agree to. Look, Emerald, I want this expedition with Morgan to Porto Bello, and I intend for nothing to stop me, including your reluctance. You've already been unfaithful to me. Do not speak so self-righteously of honor and vows!"

"I was not unfaithful!"

"Do we need go through this again?"

"Very well, Lord Buckington. You shall have your pseudo-engagement to appease the earl, since it suits you. It will also suit my purpose. I will go to Foxemoore, as you ask. But in going, I shall expect to take full advantage of being your betrothed. I'll pursue the causes on my heart even as you pursue your Spanish dons for revenge."

A brow lifted, and his eyes flickered over her face. "You shall have my wholehearted support, madam—especially for your new-found courage to stare down the foxes."

"You best hear what I have in mind before you so readily agree."

"I think I know what you have in mind."

"I won't return as Karlton's little daughter, prepared to slink away to the bungalow upon the first instance of conflict. I'll live in the Great House—and Minette will live there with me. I'll let everyone know I expect to be Lady Buckington. Are you sure you want Lavender to endure my eminent presence?"

A faint smile touched his mouth. "Return to Foxemoore and do all that is on your heart."

"I will," she said boldly. "But you may end up being sorry you ever decided to go through with our temporary betrothal."

"I'll back you up," he promised.

"Mr. Pitt will be fired and sent to the boiling house where he belongs."

"As you wish."

"And a friend of mine—a slave named Ngozi—will be made overseer."

He scanned her. "Why not?"

"And I shall start Mathias's singing school. I'll change the hopeless African chants into Christian music—and teach them to any who will listen."

She thought she saw a spark of approval in his eyes. He kept watching her, musing, as though he were uncertain about something and growing troubled.

"Well, have you changed your mind?" she asked bluntly.

"No . . . not about the betrothal. Or the expedition. I just can't see why a woman willing to risk so much for the slaves would trade away her honor for satins and jewels—cheap ones at that."

Her heart throbbed. "I haven't," she said in a whisper. "I've not compromised. I was only there two days!"

He came alert. "Carlotta said weeks."

"Impossible! Ask the turnkey at Brideswell. And if she is prone to lie about the length of time, why not about Jasper?"

He looked at her for a long moment. She couldn't tell what he was thinking, but he did not appear content with things as they were.

"I'll leave one of my crew on guard for the night. I'll be in touch."

He shut the door behind him. She heard him leave, then sank into her father's chair.

If she did as he wished and allowed him to bring her to the Carolinas—but he was doing so only because he felt responsibility for her safety, not because he was in love with her.

Emptiness stalked her spirits. Again the words from Proverbs walked through her soul. "Who can find a virtuous woman . . . her price is far above rubies." Remembering the jewels that Baret had paid to Jamie and Levasseur for her brought tears to her eyes. He no longer thought she was worth them. He was helping her out of honor.

Perhaps an hour passed. Emerald still sat in her father's chair. Then there were footsteps outside the door—unsteady footsteps that rekindled memories of the night Mr. Pitt had come. Cold fear broke out. She told herself there was no chance of that happening again. It must be the crewman that Baret promised to send. She now thanked God for Baret's concern.

She opened the door and stepped out onto the landing, and a cry of joy broke from her lips.

"Aye, m'gal, 'tis me. You're not seeing a ghost."

"Zeddie!" she cried as he came to her, tears in his eyes. "Oh, thank God you're alive and well. I thought they'd killed you too."

He held her awkwardly, patting her head. "So the napes must've thought, and so did I, for a week. Ol' Hannibal found me wandering about dazed and took me aboard the *Madeleine.*"

"Who is Hannibal?"

"A freebooter, an' a friend of your father. I told him what happened, and he searched for you but was told you'd gone to Tortuga with Levasseur."

"Rafael! As if I'd go with him."

"So I thought, but there were supposed to be witnesses enough. Lyin' ones, so I see now. But I thought you might've went with the rascal in hopes of finding Captain Foxworth. Then I heard you was in Brideswell. But the turnkey said you was with that Jasper at Spanish Town. Then when I got there, they said you wasn't and that he was sick in bed. I stayed at an inn in the storm, then came here."

They went inside, and she told him all that had happened.

He shook his head gravely. "These has been dark and evil days, m'gal, an' it looks like for you at least they ain't over yet. The loss of Sir Karlton ain't a light thing."

She walked to a chair and sat down. "Zeddie, I still can't believe he's actually gone."

"Nor me, m'gal."

"We both shall miss him dreadfully."

There was a knock on the door. He scowled, but Emerald stood to reassure him. "It's all right, Zeddie. That should be the crewman Baret sent to guard us tonight."

Nevertheless, he opened the door cautiously.

But a moment later a young and capable buccaneer politely identified himself as Tom, then took up his position outside the door for the night.

Alone in the crow's nest later that night, Emerald tossed restlessly in her father's bed, unable to sleep. The precious letter confirming her innocence in the matter of Mr. Pitt lay safely in the desk drawer. *Baret,* she thought with a pang, *I can never tell you I love you now. It would only make you feel more obligated toward me.*

She looked out toward the moon, shining brightly in the dark sky. A word from the Psalms came to mind: *And He shall bring forth thy righteousness as the light, and thy judgment as the noonday. Rest in the Lord, and wait patiently for him.*

She would do that.

22

CALLED TO
KING'S HOUSE

Zeddie hadn't driven the buggy very far down Fishers Row when he had to slow the horse and pull over to the side.

"Drums? Again?" Emerald stared ahead. "Another of the governor's announcements?"

The booming grew louder, combined with shouts of the governor's criers sounding through the streets.

"They're calling for the freebooters to gather for an announcement. I heard about it at Tortuga. Modyford and the council is offering commissions to fight the Dutch."

Remembering Baret's refusal to involve himself in a war against his mother's people, she wondered how many other buccaneers would oblige the governor.

The crier clambered on top of stacked rum barrels. "Hear ye! Hear ye! His Royal Majesty's Governor Thomas Modyford is granting marques to any and all private ships to attack the enemy in the Caribbean waters to strengthen, preserve, enrich, and advance the safety of the English-held territory of Jamaica for His Majesty King Charles!"

"Gutter scrapings," mumbled Zeddie. "It's Spain who remains the enemy of England and all the king's colonies in the Indies."

So that was the reason for the meeting at King's House, thought Emerald. Then why had she been called to this extravaganza? While the freebooters met with the governor's officials and received their commissions, the planters, Port Royal merchants, and members of their families were to be entertained by the governor. Nervously, Emerald touched her gloved hand to her meticulous hairdo, wondering that she even had the nerve to show herself.

If she hadn't, Baret would have come for her and insisted. Still, it seemed an odd thing to her to answer the governor's questions in the library, while the officials and their wives and daughters waltzed about the green. What if everyone knew she'd been at the hacienda when Sir Jasper was shot by Captain Buckington? Another scandal involving her!

If the governor's criers expected the freebooters to show excitement over the issuing of commissions, they must have been disappointed. The dozen remaining privateer captains congregating on the wharf lounged about, bored and sullen.

A pirate shouted, "Who among us cares about attacking Hollanders and Frenchies?"

"The governor is meeting with the chief captains of the Brotherhood tonight! And Henry Morgan is the first to sign!"

"What's the pay?"

"Governor Modyford will see loans given to resupply your ships. All booty taken from England's enemies on the Dutch-held islands of St. Eustatius and Curaço is in your hand!"

The privateers exchanged glances, but it was clear even to Emerald that enthusiasm was low. The Dutch colonies were not deemed to be as rich as the Spanish galleons.

"We'll wait and see what Morgan has to say."

When the crowd dispersed, Zeddie, wearing a scowl, drove the buggy toward King's House.

"The governor knows Jamaica is dependent on the buccaneers for safety. He also knows there's no love for attackin' the Dutch or French, and so I'm wonderin' what he has up his sleeve to bait 'em. A few meager cups and bales of cloth taken from the Dutch colonists won't whet their appetites. It's vengeance on the Spaniards they want, and doubloons aplenty. You saw there was no excitement for his marques, not when the French governor is wantin' to keep the Brethren on Tortuga—an' offering commissions against Spain to do it."

"Surely there won't be fighting with the Dutch so quickly," said Emerald, trying to hold back her concern.

"I wouldn't count on it, m'gal. I heard a strange tale about Barbados while I was on Tortuga. Seemed the Dutch admiral came calling. That's why the governor is a mite worried. If the Dutch from New Amsterdam decides to send a man-o'-war to Jamaica, it won't take 'em long. And the French too has warships at Martinique. An' now you know why Modyford is sharing his Madeira with Morgan."

331

In Emerald's mind she could see no reason for concern for the island. Her father had often said that Port Royal harbor was the best natural seaport in the Western Hemisphere and that it was defendable. She told Zeddie so.

He straightened his periwig. "Aye, the harbor is capable of holdin' all the ships of Christendom is my guess, but the king's ships ain't anchored here, as ye see. Commodore Mings was already called to England when the war looked nigh—so Jamaica is left with only the buccaneers. An' what of the king's ships is left in the Caribbean will sail the waters of the Hudson Bay now that war is announced for sure."

She must have shown her concern, for Zeddie hastened to add, "To be sure now, ye've no cause to worry. Any Dutch or French ship poking about Jamaica will find the buccaneers more'n enough to turn 'em all to flames if it comes to it."

"If Governor Modyford can promise them booty," said Emerald, not at all certain he could. "And what of the king's navy?"

"Ain't enough of 'em, m'gal. An' since Mings was called home to fight the Dutch, how many warships have ye seen sitting in the harbor? None, save Lord Grayford's. An' he was at Barbados till a week ago." He gestured toward the harbor. "That's the *Royale* there. She took a hard hit, from the looks of her. See them timbers boarded on her side? Sure now, she must have suffered a beating."

Emerald noticed raw planks nailed over holes in the ship's hull. She wondered if Lord Grayford had been injured, but Zeddie didn't seem to know. She thought of Lavender. What would she do about keeping company with Baret now that her fiancé was home from the war?

"Then," said Emerald thoughtfully, trying to piece together any part Baret might have in all this. "Even if the Dutch and French don't attack, Spain could . . ."

"Aye, an' I 'spect your concern is what's troublin' the governor. There was two attacks on the other side of the island this month alone. Some Spanish captain left his credential on one of the trees. Said he was coming back—and that he wanted to meet some particular captain in a duel at sea."

She moved uneasily. Was Baret Buckington that captain?

"Then what good is the king's navy at Antigua if they're

leaving the island vulnerable to attack? What can Lord Grayford do alone?"

"Aye, an' that's the whole thing of the matter botherin' the planters. So they've been complainin' to Modyford to call the buccaneers. Which is unusual, seein' as how they were behind Lord Felix in kickin' 'em out to begin with. I wonder what his lordship will have to say about their return? The shindig the governor's posing tonight is a warm welcome. The Spanish sympathizers in the council have the short end of things for now. Traitors, that's what the Peace Party is. An' all the while, men like Lord Felix is engaged in smuggling goods to the Spanish dons."

The governor's Port Royal residence was built near the batteries that controlled the entrance to the harbor. Emerald arrived by buggy, and Zeddie showed his displeasure as he helped her down.

"I'd feel a mite better, m'gal, if I was permitted to go in with you to see the governor."

Emerald clutched her bag. "Don't worry. With Captain Buckington in Port Royal, I won't be carted off to Brideswell. And he's returned Mr. Pitt's letter stating my innocence."

"Pitt," he growled. "That rotting morsel of odorous fish bait. We ain't seen the end of his treachery against you, to be sure. I'm thinkin' Captain Buckington will be calling on him before all this rolls out to sea an' is forgotten."

"It's Minette I'm concerned for. By now I should have heard from Sir Cecil Chaderton. Percy was certain he could get the letter to him, but then maybe Sir Cecil isn't there after all. Go to Foxmoore, Zeddie. See what you can find out."

"And leave you here unguarded?" he complained. "If that Sir Jasper shows, I'd as soon cast him to the sharks."

"It isn't me they're interested in now. It's Captain Buckington. Jasper will have learned a hard lesson when it comes to him. He's always been cautious of the viscount, and a coward. He'll avoid me from now on. Anyway, I don't think he'll show tonight."

"If he has to bear witness to what happened between him and the viscount, he'll come," said Zeddie unhappily. "And I ain't as convinced he'll leave you alone or has learned his lesson yet. A coward he is, to be sure, but he has himself enough slimy snakes to do his bidding for him when it comes to Captain Foxworth."

Emerald believed Zeddie was right and wondered that Baret would continue to boldly show himself in Jamaica. Would he be here to see the governor?

"Find Percy and see if he delivered my letter to Sir Cecil. And ask around the slave huts about Minette. I'll wait for your return at the lookout house."

She watched him climb up to the buggy seat and reluctantly drive away. Then she turned toward King's House. Pearl-like oyster shells lined the walkway up to the residence. Groupings of palm trees were here and there on the lawn, their branches alive and noisy with parrots, while crimson roses crawled along the lattice and swayed in tropical dance as the breeze blew.

Drawing in a breath and lifting her chin, she walked forward. She wore the comely burgundy dress with burgess lace that she had borrowed several months earlier from the stored trunk in the lookout house—the trunk that had turned out to belong to Baret, and a dress that was intended for Lavender.

Her eyes cautiously took in the file of soldiers belonging to the Port Royal militia, wearing yellow-and-red uniforms and carrying pistols and cutlasses. Her heart skipped a beat. Their presence evoked ugly memories of being hauled off to Brideswell. Now, however, it wasn't Emerald that Lord Felix expected to threaten with arrest. She was no longer needed to establish Baret's guilt. The incriminating document she had foolishly signed was enough to stand in court.

She soon discovered she was wrong about the seriousness of the gathering. As she approached the residence, she could hear voices arguing beneath the canopy.

"Accursed Spaniards. Only a buffoon or Madrid's sympathizers can't see how they aim to retake Jamaica. The dons will never be satisfied till they see us all dunked and drowned like sea rats. And what does His Majesty do for us in time of war? Recall the Royal Navy to the Atlantic! And here Jamaica sits unguarded in the midst of a Spanish sea."

Emerald walked past the disgruntled planter only to confront a militia officer with pistol bristling in his belt.

"Your name, madam, before I can allow ye entry."

"Miss Harwick," she said quietly, expecting the name to be followed by a leer in his beady eyes, but his blank, sun-leathered face showed that she was nothing more to him except some unknown planter's daughter. Not even her father's recent death seemed to dawn on him.

"Governor Modyford has requested my presence," she told him as he checked a list in his roughened hand.

He scratched his wavy eyebrow. "Spell it."

"I'm not a party guest, sir. I've been called by Lord Felix Buckington. I wouldn't be on that list."

He grunted agreement, reached into his pocket and drew out a scrap of paper. "Aye, ye're right." He turned, shouting in a flat, harsh voice, "Willoughby! Bring the girl inside! There's going to be a meeting in the garden!"

The soldier escorted her into the mansion and across a salon toward a garden area on the opposite side.

"Miss Harwick's here to see you, sir."

"Good. Send her out," said Governor Thomas Modyford.

Emerald passed through double veranda doors into a cobbled courtyard of humid fragrance and tobacco. Several men stood from their chairs, setting their goblets down on tables.

Sir Thomas towered above her. He had a wide but thin mouth that bore a twisted smile of perpetual boredom beneath a curling dark-brown mustache. His head had been shaved due to the heat, and he wore a scarf, thus appearing not so different from the pirates he had previously hanged. His heavy hand, sporting a number of bejeweled silver and gold rings, gestured her toward a chair opposite him and the two Admiralty officials.

"Miss Harwick, be seated, won't you? I believe we've met before. Foxemoore, wasn't it? The wedding supper of Geneva and Felix."

"Yes." She took her seat, her skirts rustling with an elegance she did not feel. She checked for indecision in the governor's wide jaw, wondering how well Felix managed to control him. She found not weakness but the resolve of experience in the West Indies, the brute strength of a bull, the cunning of a diplomat wise to the ways of his opponents in Madrid and London. He did not look not like a man who would simply indulge himself while ambitious men such as Felix and Jasper ran the island. Knowing this gave her more confidence.

His sharp gray eyes twinkled ruefully over his new post as Jamaica's governor. Except for a brassy complexion that was all too typical of many of the gentry in Jamaica and Barbados who downed too many rum toddies, he seemed an exemplary English official representing His Majesty.

A swift glance about the immediate garden informed her that Felix had not yet arrived, and for that reprieve she was grateful. Two other gentlemen stood near the governor. One was a fleshy, red-faced choleric clad in heavy taffeta and gold lace, a silk handkerchief wound turbanlike about his shaven skull, revealing himself a man accustomed to the Indies. His counterpart was gaunt and grim-faced. She could imagine his silver goblet filled with vinegar. He wore a heavy white periwig and severe black, and he peered down at her with the sobriety of a judge.

"M'dear," he said, pulling a lace kerchief from his wrist and dabbing his pale forehead. "I hope you understand the trouble you are in, along with your pirate . . . er . . . friend Captain Foxworth. I am Lord Winston Carberry, second Earl of Cunningham, member of the High Admiralty Court."

Emerald stood and curtsied. "M'lord of Cunningham!"

"And he's a crotchety old scoundrel beside," interrupted a brittle voice from behind her. "He's in a dour mood because he misses his bone-chilling London fog. Don't let him frighten you with his icy title."

Emerald turned, shocked, as did the others.

Governor Modyford chuckled. "Come and sit, Nigel. We've been expecting you. Felix with you?"

Emerald stared at the newcomer. Earl Nigel walked into the courtyard from the house in immaculate velvet and gold braid. She saw his sharp, dark eyes laugh in the direction of his fellow earl, Winston Cunningham.

Cunningham smiled grimly and blotted his forehead again. "How you have survived this heat, Nigel, is a tale Charles will be interested to hear," he said of the king.

"We both had best learn to survive, Winston. It seems the blasted Dutch intend to keep us here indefinitely. Unless my nephew returns us both to Whitehall."

"You speak of Grayford?"

"I speak of Baret," said Nigel with a hint of victory in his voice.

A casual listener would not have noticed that inflection of pride in his voice, but Emerald, knowing of the tension between Baret and his grandfather, came alert. She looked at the earl, wondering. Then a movement farther away in the garden drew her attention from the earl to Baret himself.

How long had he been there? He was lying in a hammock strung between two palms, a table at hand with tall glasses of honeyed lime water, perhaps, and a bowl of fruit. A bright-eyed mulatto boy waited on him, grinning as Baret held a blue parrot on a rounded perch and fed it bits of banana and mango.

"Good evening, Grandfather," Baret said in Nigel's direction.

Earl Cunningham turned to look at him, proving he too had not known of his presence, but Governor Modyford showed no surprise and had already motioned for his servant to refill the goblets.

Emerald wondered what was going on but wisely just stood waiting, wishing she could fade into the shadows.

Baret gave the parrot perch to the boy and rose from the hammock. He deliberately bowed in the direction of Earl Cunningham. "My lord Cunningham, I understand you've been searching for me."

Emerald heard quick, urgent footsteps sounding from the lighted salon. A moment later Lord Felix appeared, three swordsmen belonging to his personal bodyguard behind him. His eyes darted about the courtyard until they fell on Baret. Felix walked toward him, followed by his men. He pointed.

"Arrest that man. He's alias Captain Foxworth of the *Regale,* a ship that sails under no commission except the skull and crossbones! I am ashamed to say my nephew is a pirate, a man who has entered Spanish territorial waters, landed with his murderous crew at Lake Maracaibo, and fought a battle with the soldiers serving Don Miguel, ambassador to the court of King Charles."

Emerald tensed, watching to see what would happen next.

Felix drew from under his jacket a document she recognized as the one she had signed at the hacienda. He handed it to Governor Modyford.

"This is proof from an eyewitness, Thomas. You've no choice now but to arrest him."

Emerald held the side of her skirts, turning her head away to look down at the cobbled court, unable to look in Baret's direction. *I've done this to him,* she thought.

Then Felix walked up to her as though a protective friend.

"I'm sorry, my dear. We all know you were friends with my nephew. You've done what you had to do in the name of His Majesty. There'll be few in Jamaica or in the family who will not appreciate your cooperation in catching the pirate Foxworth."

He laid a hand on her shoulder as though they were affectionately related as uncle and niece.

Emerald drew away from him.

"Geneva understands," he was saying. "She has good plans for you, my dear."

Governor Modyford handed Earl Winston Cunningham the document. "Much ado over nothing, Winston. It doesn't even mention the Venezuelan Main or the *San Pedro.*"

His words must have surprised more than Emerald, for Felix straightened and looked at them.

The official of the High Admiralty lifted an eyeglass and read with a dour look.

Emerald's heart thudded.

A minute later he looked up over his eyeglass at Emerald. "Is this your signature?"

Aware that Baret had walked up and was leaning against the tree, she felt her face flush. "Yes, m'lord," she said quietly. "But it was signed under duress."

"Ah?"

"Nonsense," said Felix impatiently.

"I was told Captain Buckington had already been arrested and was being held in Havana in a torture chamber. If I signed, Lord Felix promised he could intervene with the Spanish ambassador and protect Captain Buckington from further suffering."

"Of course, I promised her this!" Felix said impatiently. "At the time I was told my nephew's ship had been captured by Captain Valdez. Enough of this, Winston. We all know Baret is a pirate. And you, Thomas, you are under authority of the king to put an end to the buccaneers in Port Royal. It's your duty to arrest him."

Earl Nigel stirred, and Felix appeared not to have realized he was present.

Nigel's face was hard. "One would think, my son, that you desire my grandson's arrest on such charges."

"Father, what are you doing—" He stopped.

Baret spoke for the first time. "I asked him to come."

Felix looked at Baret sharply. "It will do you no good."

Baret smiled at him coolly. "Would you arrest the king's agent?"

Felix stared at him, uncertain, like a trapped fox with the hounds moving in. "What are you talking about?"

Baret gestured to Modyford. "Perhaps you'd better explain, Thomas. My beloved uncle seems a bit behind the times. We wouldn't want him kept in the dark too long, lest he make an utter fool of himself." Baret folded his arms and smiled, as Felix's quick nervous gaze left him to look first at his father, then the governor.

Both men appeared calm, but the earl looked angry.

"We can hardly arrest Captain Buckington when His Majesty will be certain to excuse any past infringements on the laws of the Admiralty and will knight him in London."

Felix floundered. "What? That's impossible," he snapped, flushing for the first time. "There's the document proving his guilt."

"And I," said Modyford, "have a second document." He reached out a hand toward the corpulent official who stood between him and Earl Cunningham. "This is Baronet Warwick. You know him, Felix?"

"Of course, I know him," said Felix impatiently. "I sent him to Tortuga—" He stopped, as though he began to understand that something was happening over which he had no control, something that was ruining all his hard-laid plans.

"As the baronet can testify, he was on Tortuga when the Dutch Admiral de Ruyter was hidden and protected by the French governor. Plans were being made for an attack on Barbados and the destruction of all of His Majesty's ships, including your son Grayford's, the *Royale.*"

Felix looked stunned. "Grayford was attacked by the Dutch admiral?"

"No," said Modyford, handing him the document. "As you will see, this letter was dictated and signed by the governor of Barbados to King Charles, recommending Captain Buckington and Captain Farrow for honors. Along with Baronet Warwick, they slipped away from Tortuga, unknown by the French governor, and alerted Barbados to the planned attack. They also fought for His Majesty under the Union Jack and sank several Dutch ships.

The governor of Barbados plainly states that the island would have been overrun except for the heroics of your nephew."

There was silence.

Earl Cunningham cleared his throat and handed the document back to the governor. "Well, I hardly think His Majesty will be wanting to hang your nephew for treason or piracy, Felix. With this letter, I consider the matter closed until I meet with the king—and that, as Nigel has sourly reminded me, won't be until after the war." He replaced his eyeglass, drew in a breath, and turned toward Baret, who still lounged against the tree.

"It seems," said Governor Modyford, "that Admiral de Ruyter arrived off Barbados in April, but failing to capture the ships in the harbor or those anchored offshore, he sailed up to Martinique. There, with the help of the French, he repaired damage inflicted by the *Regale*. Captain Buckington believes he then sailed off to attack the American colonies, probably Virginia and New England."

"By the cock's eye, young man," Earl Cunningham said to Baret, "my wholehearted congratulations! You have both honored King Charles and England. It was a daring and commendable thing you and this Captain Farrow have accomplished."

Baret offered a slight bow and said, "Thank you, sir. It was the least I could do for His Majesty."

Earl Nigel said flatly, "I hope, now, all talk of my grandson's disloyalty to the king will be laid to rest once for all."

"I see no reason why it shouldn't," said Cunningham. He looked back at Baret. "You will need to appear before him in London one day soon, of course, but that will prove no trouble, I am sure. And now, what might you have on your mind for the rest of the war?"

"We'll be discussing that later with the council members and planters," said Modyford.

Earl Nigel walked past Felix without a glance and came up to Cunningham and Baret. "To fight for England, Winston. What else? I always did say Baret was the best man to command the royal naval vessel. This proves it. Three Dutch ships sunk! Barbados saved from England's enemies, and all British ships in Antigua spared capture by Admiral de Ruyter! Wait till Charles hears of this! He'll be calling Baret home to Whitehall at once."

Emerald, dazed, stole a victorious glance at Felix, but the

expression on his white face sobered her at once. Anger and hatred gleamed in his eyes.

"You, at least, do not appear won over, Felix," Modyford said. "You're not still determined to place the label of pirate about your nephew's neck?"

"Naturally, this esteemed victory for His Majesty has come as a shock to me. Nevertheless, it's a pleasant one if the turn about is true. You can be sure that as a member of the Admiralty court this brings me relief. My father and Baret both know how hard I've worked to steer Baret away from his father's exploits on the Main."

Emerald half expected a sharp comeback by Baret, and it appeared that Felix too expected him to open a debate about Royce. When he did not, Felix gave him a measured glance.

How could Felix get by with such a bold-faced lie? she wondered, remembering the anguish he and Jasper had put her through. She marveled at Baret's restraint in the face of his uncle's aggression. Evidently there was much more that Baret wanted, and intended to gain, by refusing to confront him now.

Felix turned toward Baret. "My congratulations, Baret. Grayford, too, will be pleased and quick to offer his gratitude for your victory for the king. He's here tonight with Lavender."

"Your favor, Felix, is accepted gratefully," said Baret. "Am I to assume you no longer wish to pursue the issue of Maracaibo?"

"The matter of Lucca remains troublesome to the Spanish viceroy. But after Barbados, the king will find a way to soothe the Spanish ire. Lucca is dead. The matter of your father ends with him, since there are no witnesses to attest to Royce's innocence in the unfortunate matter of the *Prince Philip.*"

Emerald's thoughts went to her own father. *He* had been a witness. Had Felix known this and moved to silence him even as he had Lucca and the pirate Maynerd? A glance at Baret told her nothing.

"Let the past die that the future might live," Felix was commenting. "If this means you've decided at long last to throw your privilege as the heir of your father behind His Majesty, I can only rejoice you've at last come home." He walked over to Earl Nigel and laid a hand on his shoulder. "My father has longed for this moment. As his son and your uncle, I can enter into that joy."

341

Emerald looked at Baret. He seemed grave, but she knew him too well not to notice the flicker in the depths of his eyes.

"I'm glad you see it this way, Felix," he said. "It's a pity it took a war with the Dutch to bring the family together. You might as well know I met with Lucca in Maracaibo before his death."

"Oh?"

"He assured me my father is dead. And now, as you say, the past must die that the future may live."

Emerald stirred uneasily. He didn't believe this! Lucca had assured him Royce was alive!

Felix studied him, growing more relaxed with the passing moments. "As I have often told you, the sooner you accepted this and proceeded with your own life, the wiser and happier we would all be."

"Yes," said Earl Nigel quietly to both son and grandson as the three Buckingtons stood in public camaraderie. "What's important is the Buckington name and our service to the king. You have that foolish document, Felix?"

As if to end any question of his willingness to cover his tracks and build on what could not be changed—Baret's new role and place in the family—Felix took the document and held it up to a torch until it burst into flame, dancing in the evening breeze.

Emerald watched, relieved, as it burned away her signature that Felix had so cleverly obtained.

The document fell to the courtyard, turning to ashes.

Governor Modyford joined them. "Well, gentlemen, with that settled, the council members wait impatiently to discuss the perceived danger to Jamaica."

Emerald held back, keeping to the courtyard shadows. If Baret was aware of her, he did not let on. The men had all evidently forgotten her and the part she'd played in Felix's ruse. And she now believed that Baret had known all along what the outcome would be, or he'd never have permitted himself to be in this precarious situation. His grandfather, perhaps even the governor as well, had known what to expect. The only oblivious ones had been Felix, Earl Winston Cunningham, and herself. No wonder Baret hadn't seemed worried about her appearance before the governor.

They walked past her toward the lighted salon, talking among themselves of the war.

She took pleasure in watching Earl Nigel throw an arm about his grandson's shoulder. He had waited long to win Baret back to the respectable role of viscount.

It dawned on her that the earl and Baret were fully reconciled. That would mean that his grandfather no longer saw Baret as a scamp who couldn't be trusted with the family title, inheritance, and lands. It would also mean that he no longer viewed Baret's wish to marry the future duchess Lavender Thaxton as a menace to his plans for the family.

Emerald felt pride in his interception of the Dutch attack on Barbados, but she still wondered what could have motivated him, since he was sympathetic to the cause of Holland. It wasn't lost on her that his decision had been made after learning that Lavender's marriage to Grayford had not been consummated— and after thinking the very worst about herself. Had he decided to please Earl Nigel to win Lavender?

Emerald picked up the hem of her burgundy flounces and walked from the courtyard toward the lighted salon. Her business here was over now. She might as well find her way on foot back to the lookout house and wait for Zeddie to return.

Would Baret still insist that she leave with him to begin a new life in the Carolinas? He had said he wished to help her. Maybe she should accept his help. Between him and Sir Cecil, she might at least get Minette back. However, the more she thought of running from the smug faces and knowing eyes, the more she was determined to stay to prove them all wrong about her. No matter that she cringed at the idea of returning to Foxemoore. Why should she slink away in shame when God knew her to be innocent?

I have many sins the Savior must forgive, she thought. *But immoral conduct isn't one of them. And I'm going to stay and prove it.*

After all, what would her beloved father have thought of her slinking away? She could hear his voice now: *You listen to me. I'll not have you hiding yourself like some frightened kitten, too afraid to show her face to important people. I expect my daughter to conduct herself with pride.*

Her eyes moistened. *I'll do it for him, if not for myself.* He had loved Foxemoore, and he worked as hard as any man could to keep their shares in the sugar. The bungalow was hers, even if she never set foot again in the Great House. *And I'll fight for my shares of Foxemoore just the way my father would have me do.*

Peace settled over her heart as now she stood alone in the courtyard. The gentry with their wives and daughters would be gathering in the salon and on the front lawn. She believed she had found the path marked out for her by the Lord and that He had answered her prayers for guidance and help. He wanted her to stay in Jamaica and seek her father's inheritance on Foxemoore. What would become of her, what else He might have for her as time moved forward, she did not know. Faith told her it was enough that *He* knew and that He would make the daily provision she needed.

One day at a time was sufficient. One answered prayer at a time for help and sustenance, followed mercifully by another, would be her portion. The future would unfold day by day. Because her heavenly Father was trustworthy, she would believe that when she reached the end of the hot and dusty road, a well of spiritual water would be there waiting. Like Hagar, "Thou God seest me."

23

PIRATE OR
KING'S AGENT?

Emerald left the courtyard with a rustle of skirts, anxious to be gone before any of the catty women noticed her presence and began their whispering. She was not just the offspring of a pirate's daughter who had run away with Jamie and slept in Captain Buckington's cabin, but now she had since spent weeks in Brideswell for attempted murder. And Baret and Jasper had fought over her at the hacienda!

There's no use in even trying anymore, she thought dully. *All I want is to avoid people and live quietly at the bungalow. If I can have Minette back safe, we'll be able to endure their buzzing tongues.*

Her dark brows puckered as she stood on the yellow tile floor, glancing about the salon, wondering which door would lead her out to the front lawn.

Insects fluttered and buzzed about the saffron light radiating from sconces that looped like honey pots about the wall. Ahead, the double doors leading into the parlor stood wide open for the assembly of Jamaica's ruling class to catch the evening breeze from the bay.

Members of the council and at least a dozen sugar and cacao planters had gathered with Governor Modyford to discuss the safety of the island. An attack by the Dutch or French was on everyone's mind, and an unending rumble of arguing voices cut through the warm evening, punctuated now and then by an impatient outburst.

"Forget the Dutch! It's an attack by Spain we best keep in mind."

A chorus of voices joined in agreement, but the mocking voice of Lord Felix rose above the others. "An unwise excuse to appease the pirates on Tortuga. If His Majesty hears of it, the governor will be called into question."

"Maybe not," came Governor Modyford's voice, and the air of confidence in his tone brought a lull in the discussion.

Emerald's attention was caught away when new guests arrived in the salon. Lavender entered, appearing angelic in shimmering white silk. Her golden hair was arranged in a cascade with tiny pale blue stones catching the light. Walking beside her was Lord Grayford and the staunch Puritan Cambridge scholar, Sir Cecil Chaderton.

A wave of relief enveloped Emerald as though her father had suddenly returned to draw sword against her enemies.

Sir Cecil was conservatively dressed in dark clothing with a wide-brimmed scholar hat absent the plume of the king's dashing Cavaliers. His jaw-length silver hair was neatly paged against a lean, hawklike face, toughened and browned by the Jamaican sun, and he wore a well-groomed, short, pointed Sir Walter Raleigh beard.

At this moment he seemed like a messenger of the Lord, and she hurried toward him, a hind with a wolf at her heels.

"Sir Cecil," she said jubilantly, "you came!"

She had a fleeting glimpse of Cousin Lavender turning her back and giving Grayford no opportunity to acknowledge Emerald. The couple left toward the parlor.

Cecil threw a fatherly arm about her shoulders and walked her toward the other end of the salon, where they could speak in private while guests continued to arrive for the governor's grand dinner.

"My dear child, I came as soon as I received your correspondence. My condolences, where Sir Karlton is concerned. Baret assures me he is searching into the vile matter and won't rest until he knows the truth."

This was encouraging. Baret might hold no serious interest in her, but he had been fond of her father.

"He was murdered," she told him. "I'm sure of it."

"So Baret has said." He shook his head. "Smugglers and piracy. Karlton must have known and perhaps saw more that night than his enemies were willing to allow."

She told him of Zeddie and the Dutch slave ship. "He vows Lord Felix was on Fisher's Row waiting near a carriage."

"Have you mentioned any of this to Baret?"

She looked away, her eyes turning cool. "No. He's been too busy accusing me of surrendering to that vile Sir Jasper."

"Ah, that." His mouth turned wryly. "Don't let that disturb you a moment more. Rare is the case when mindless jealousy does a man good. You'll need to forgive the scoundrel for making matters more bitter for you. I'm sure he has an apt apology at hand, and you'll yet be satisfied."

She looked at him, masking her doubt. She couldn't understand why Cecil would nurture such confidence. She supposed he knew about Baret's call at the lookout house the day before. The viscount's suave dismissal of the matter was as close to an apology as she was likely to receive from him, but Emerald's wounded spirit was far from satisfied. There had remained that burning flicker of anger in his dark eyes. Sir Cecil had called it jealousy. Was it? But how could that be? A man didn't become jealous unless he loved a woman.

Cecil's piercing eyes glinted. "Instead of in a pirate's lair like Port Royal, you should be living safely in England, but, alas, this absurd war with Holland has interrupted all our fair plans. Still, it has accommodated at least one answered prayer where Baret is concerned. You've heard of his victory at Barbados?"

She saw the sudden sparkle of pleasure in his eyes. Lavender and Lord Grayford came to mind. "Yes. The king will knight him."

"And Erik Farrow too. It was a wise move on Baret's part. He saw an opportunity to assist England and made a difficult decision. His loyalty has long been divided between his mother's ancestry and Royce's."

He sacrificed for Lavender, she could have told him but kept silent. She knew why he had fought for the king, even if Cecil did not. She also wondered if Baret hadn't just wanted to excel over Lord Grayford, commander of the H.M.S. *Royale.* Well, he had certainly appeared the better commander this time. Lavender must be exceedingly proud of him.

Cecil must have mistaken her expression, for he frowned. "Poor child, you've been through more than your share of muck and mire recently, but we're optimistic that matters will soon turn for your best interest."

We? she wondered. Was he referring to Geneva?

"Baret, too, wrote me about Brideswell and the house in

Spanish Town," he continued. "He won't rest until these matters are resolved and your reputation is defended and those responsible pay dearly for their abuse. When it comes to protecting those he loves, he has a wretched temper. I pity the overseer when the time comes." He sighed. "I suppose I will need to try to restrain him a little."

So Baret wished to handle Mr. Pitt. What had he told Sir Cecil? She looked at him, alert now and intensely interested in anything Baret would write about her to the one man he respected above all others.

"I wasn't aware the viscount wrote you," she said, hoping for information.

"We are both in agreement where your watchful care is concerned. Baret has asked me to look into the extent of your father's debts to the family and see they're paid in full. There's also the curious concern that Lord Felix has seen to bring up again recently to Earl Nigel and Lady Sophie."

Now it was coming, she thought uneasily—her father's share in Foxemoore was in dispute.

"What might you know of his relationship with Baret's great-grandfather?"

She sighed. "Earl Esmond?"

"Um . . . yes. He died at Buckington House, I believe, soon after he'd changed his will, leaving Karlton a certain share of West Indies land that Felix seems to think should have been his."

"My father told me that before, but he always disputed Lord Felix's claims. I know very little about the legal document." Her voice confessed her own doubt. "He brought me to his office once at the bungalow and showed it to me as proof, but as a child it meant nothing more to me than an official-looking paper with a shiny seal. He always claimed Felix was trying to have it annulled."

"So Baret said. We would both like to see that document, to safeguard it for your inheritance."

"Unfortunately my father didn't keep it at the house on Fishers Row but locked away in the bungalow at Foxemoore."

"I wouldn't wish to add to your alarm, but the groom informed me before I left this afternoon that Lady Sophie's overseer has moved into the bungalow. Why he'd presume to do so, or whether he had your great-aunt's permission, I wouldn't know."

Her hands clenched. Of all the gall! Mr. Pitt in her father's house, sleeping in her beloved father's bed, and rummaging through his personal belongings! She must get him out at once. How could he even dare? After all the sorrow he had caused her. This was the last assault he could make on all that she held dear.

"I see by your expression this causes you bitter grief." He patted her hand soothingly. "I'm sorry to have told you. I'll speak to Baret about it, or you may mention it tonight when you meet with him. Have you any notion why he'd move in?"

"Mr. Pitt has the vain hope of becoming a great planter one day," she said wearily, struggling against bitterness when she thought of him. "Since Jasper has managed to become an important man in the West Indies, then he can as well—so he believes. His time as indentured servant to Lady Sophie ends shortly, and he expects to receive a grant of land from Governor Modyford through Sir Jasper. I'm afraid Mr. Pitt would do most anything to accomplish his goals. He even entertains the notion of finding information about the treasure of the *Prince Philip*."

"Ah. So he expects to search Karlton's trunk."

"The night he broke into the lookout house, he'd come about the jewels he insisted I had."

"Yes, I recall that sordid incident aboard the *Regale*." His expression turned displeased. "Captain Levasseur claimed you had taken them from his ship."

"It wasn't I that took them, but Minette. The viscount retrieved them from my cabin later. As far as I know, he still has them."

A brow shot up. "Indeed? A matter to inquire about at the appropriate time."

"Mr. Pitt must have decided my father had them at the bungalow."

"I doubt the viscount knows this. He's meeting with Governor Modyford now, but I think you should speak with him later tonight." His expression lightened. "He'll want to discuss another matter as well."

Sir Cecil's suggestion that she meet with Baret brought special apprehension because of Lavender's presence. Emerald glanced toward the parlor door, certain that every eye would turn her direction with a knowing glance as she entered. Being

349

in the dignified and Christian company of Sir Cecil would help shield her, but she was anxious to leave.

Remembering that Mr. Pitt was even now in the bungalow, and that Minette was a slave, strengthened her resolve to endure the situation. "Well, if you think it's appropriate," she told him.

With an arm about her shoulder, he led her through the salon to the open doorway of the large and handsomely furnished parlor.

Lanterns burned bold and hot on the walls, dispersing light onto the maroon brocade draperies, French paintings, and golden bowls and vases. An intricately woven Spanish rug with thick golden tassels, pirated during a raid on Santo Domingo, was flaunted in the center of the room. Surrounding it sat an assortment of velvet chairs, divans, and ottomans. At the far end of the parlor was an open terrace with black wrought iron, overlooking the sloping front lawn. A welcome breeze ruffled the drapes and caused the torchlight to flutter.

Emerald tensed and avoided looking into the florid faces of the well-fed planters and councilmen who turned to see who had arrived late.

Seated beside a table on which was placed a crystal lamp, Lady Lavender Thaxton, pale and looking more miserable than Emerald remembered ever seeing her, showed surprise at her entry.

Lord Grayford stood behind her chair, tall and elegant and almost as fair as she. His tanned face reflected none of the turmoil that must surely be going on in his heart, Emerald thought. He knew all about the past relationship between Lavender and Baret and must wonder if she ever regretted breaking their engagement. Now he found himself in the intolerable position of having to wait to marry her until the war ended. Wait, while Baret unexpectedly arrived in Jamaica, not as a pirate wanted by Admiralty officials but as a privateer destined to receive honor in London. Matters had certainly changed.

Yes, Grayford must be unhappy, she thought, but no more so than Lavender. *Why, she looks as though she's been crying.*

Then Emerald saw Baret, in handsome royal blue and a ruffled shirt. He was perhaps the one man in the parlor who looked undisturbed either by news of the war or the presence of Lavender. He was silently listening to a heated debate between Modyford's council members—some of whom represented the king's Spanish Peace Party—and certain powerful planters and merchants who wanted the buccaneers received freely back in Port Royal, even if it meant attacking Spain's shipping.

He appeared oblivious to Lavender. Her tears were probably for him. Did he care? *But I shouldn't feel gleeful,* she rebuked herself with irony. *I, too, am hopelessly infatuated.*

With practiced poise, Emerald sat on the hardwood chair nearest the door. She folded her hands quietly in her lap, becoming aware of Baret's gaze shifting in her direction. For the first time she wished ardently that she hadn't worn the burgundy gown.

She felt her face warm, and, as though willed, her eyes strayed to where he stood, surprised by the interest she found in his gaze. *If I didn't know better, I'd think I was the one he was in love with instead of Lavender,* she thought. Snapping open her black lace fan, she swished it rapidly.

The parlor was crowded, and Baret decided to take refuge from the heat by stepping out onto the small terrace. He folded his arms and glanced over the railing onto the front lawn.

Officials and their wives and families were still arriving for the dinner, but more than a succulent meal was on the minds of the men gathered with Governor Modyford. He well knew that Modyford had called the meeting to convince his council of the need to appease the buccaneers by granting them marques against Spanish shipping.

Baret mused over the delectable thought of attacking Spain, impatiently removing a moth from his glass and flicking it away. Little did the officials know that the decision had already been made in an earlier meeting with himself and Henry Morgan. Even now a letter was on its way to King Charles. But Modyford needed a cover to authorize an attack when England was at peace with Madrid.

The secret plans sanctioned by Modyford and Earl Nigel Buckington to attack the Main had already been discussed in private with Henry Morgan and Baret. Nothing Felix would say now would change that, but the danger remained that Felix would alert the Spanish governors of an attack. For that reason alone, Baret had been against any public meeting discussing an attack.

But Modyford had insisted. If he cooperated secretly with the buccaneers, he had informed them, then he must have a cover to protect him from Spanish sympathizers in the king's court. Valid reasons must be given to His Majesty for allowing commissions, or his enemies would see the governor called to answer before the king.

Modyford had even sent off a letter through the pro-Spanish secretary of state in London to the Spanish governor of Hispaniola, informing him he had orders from King Charles to restrain the buccaneers from attacking Spanish ships in the Caribbean. So he must have excellent cause for calling the buccaneers back.

"Gentleman, I've called this council together for a serious reason. With good cause, Jamaica worries about her safety now that Commodore Mings has been called back to England to fight with Holland. We are in danger, and not only from the Dutch and French. There's reason to suspect a secret attack by Spain." He held out his *seegar* for a half-caste boy to light.

As Baret had expected, Uncle Felix jumped to his feet. "I say, Thomas, this is outlandish! Spain, attack Jamaica? You know very well Spain's ships are woefully undermanned at this time—a credit to the buccaneers." He looked toward Baret.

Baret pretended the scorn was a compliment and, smiling, offered a bow in his direction.

Felix looked around the room at the faces that became suddenly masked at the mention of Spain.

"None of you believe an attack ordered by Madrid is imminent. This is a ruse to reward the buccaneers with commissions."

The governor appeared unconcerned. He was stretched out in a chair with a goblet of wine and his *seegar*, tobacco smoke adding to the closeness of the room. "I, for one, admit nothing, except a dire emergency on this island for protection, for which reason His Majesty has sent me here. You are aware, Felix, that Spain has attacked us thrice with the intention of driving the English off Jamaica?"

"That may be so," he agreed reluctantly, "however—"

"The privateers from Tortuga happen to be the only source of capable defense at my disposal."

Felix gave a laugh. "These privateers, as you call them, are better termed *pirates.*"

Modyford bit the end of his *seegar*. "Semantics mean nothing to me, Felix. If you've another solution for giving me fighting men and ships in time of war, then come forth with it. Or do you think the *Royale* is sufficient?" He turned in his chair and looked across the parlor toward Grayford. "No offense intended."

Grayford smiled thinly, and his cool gray eyes turned on Baret, who lifted his glass and watched Modyford. Baret knew Grayford must feel as though he had been outperformed at Barbados.

"Look here, Thomas," said Felix. "I'll warn you now. Any attack permitted upon Spanish shipping will bring His Majesty's wrath upon your head!" He glanced at the grave expressions of the councilmen. "Need I remind you of England's peace treaty with Madrid?"

Baret listened to Felix with restrained contempt. This was one discussion on Spain he would wisely stay out of, lest he give himself away. He was now deemed an agent of the king.

He knew that the reason Felix wanted to appease Spain was to benefit the Royal African Company. Governor Modyford also leaned toward appeasement but was realistic enough to understand his dependence on the buccaneers. And so he played a conflicting game: conciliation with the Peace Party in London and secret aggression against the Main. The buccaneers, despite their prickly ways, remained his double-edged sword.

"As Captain Buckington will tell you," said Modyford, "the French governor on Tortuga incurs no shame in luring the buccaneers to his port by offering marques against Spain. But in so doing he's left Jamaica with an empty harbor. I've less than a hundred and fifty men in the Port Royal militia. Thankfully, Henry Morgan has agreed to be placed in charge," said Modyford smoothly. "He is now Admiral Morgan."

"Admiral!" Felix banged his fist on the table. "I'll have you in the Tower for this!"

Modyford drew on his *seegar.*

Baret recognized that between the support now coming from Earl Nigel and Modyford's own politically powerful cousin in London, the Duke of Abermarle, the governor need not worry—not yet. Modyford had only to write Abermarle his reasons, and the duke would quietly intercede on his behalf before the king.

"Henry Morgan or not," said a councilman, "the only way

you'll strengthen the militia, Thomas, is to call in the buccaneers with marques against Spain."

"Has the king authorized this?" demanded Felix. "Most assuredly not. I tell you, Lord Arlington has written plainly enough of the king's wishes. Commissions are granted only to privateers who will fall upon the Dutch fleet trading at St. Christopher. They are to capture Curaço, Saba, and St. Eustatius." He turned to an old colonel who thus far had sat mopping his brow, saying nothing. "Colonel Edward Morgan has his orders."

Henry Morgan's uncle, Colonel Edward, was a big, overweight Welshman who suffered from gout. He looked anything but a colonel to Baret, but he was a fighting man who was not to be treated lightly. He was a staunch Royalist and had won honors for Charles in the Civil War. Modyford had recently placed him in command of the planned expedition to attack the Dutch.

"If I am able to get a fleet of privateers," said Colonel Morgan. "The buccaneers have no heart for fighting Hollanders."

"I've word that there are some who will sail to the place of rendezvous," said Modyford. "What's your report, Warwick?"

Baronet Warwick frowned. "I spoke to them on Tortuga, as Captain Buckington will tell you. And Captains Mansfield, Jackman, and a host of others made it clear—the pickings aren't fat enough to bring them out against the Dutch. And the Frenchies are also as disinclined. It's Spain, fellows." He looked about dourly. "Or they'll stay on Tortuga. There are only a few privateers who will fight the Dutch. These are making plans now to meet with Colonel Morgan."

The colonel turned to the governor. "Then let it be known that I'll encourage any of the buccaneers to sail with me, and we'll hit the Dutch islands hard."

"What do you say, Lord Thaxton?"

Grayford smiled wearily. "I have little choice in the matter. I must do as His Majesty requested. I need every vessel I can get, and I'm not looking to see if the *joli rouge* is hidden in the hold. I want guns, fighting men, men with a will to attack. Every privateer is needed, including—" and he toasted Baret with a crooked smile "—my cousin, who has since emerged as the king's agent."

Baret smiled in return. "With so warm an endorsement, does this mean you wish me to command His Majesty's vessel?"

Grayford shrugged and emptied his goblet. "You know the

answer to that, Baret. I never really wanted the responsibility to begin with."

Lord Felix faced his stepson impatiently. "Be careful how you speak of your commission. And if I were you, I would abhor sailing with a fleet of pirates."

Grayford straightened from his position behind Lavender's chair, his lean face hard. "If Colonel Edward Morgan intends to attack Curaço and Eustatius, then I will sail with him and the privateers. The governor has no choice. The king has used them before. Why not now?"

"He's right, Felix," said Baret. "And the more buccaneers you enlist, the less cause you will have to worry about Spanish shipping."

Felix looked at him as though he felt threatened. "And will you also rally to the cause?" he asked.

Baret had no intention of sailing with Colonel Edward to attack the island. He would sail with Morgan, but secretly. "I've already proved my loyalty to the king and will continue to do so."

"You might as well sign the document to be sent to Charles with the rest of us," Modyford told Felix.

"I'll never sign asking the pirates to return to Jamaica in exchange for commissions against Spain. Before this is over, Thomas, you'll have the king recalling you to England."

"It's my opinion we should be grateful we have the buccaneers on our side," said a disgruntled merchant who had lost business recently. "Consider what your nephew recently accomplished at Barbados," he challenged.

"The viscount, we have all agreed, gentlemen, is not a pirate but an agent of King Charles."

And Baret watched Felix smoothly slip out of that noose.

"The sooner commissions are offered against Spain, the better off Port Royal will be," stated a councilman, several other councilmen, planters, and merchants agreeing. "Get on with it, Thomas. Skeletons twistin' in the breeze won't improve the pirate mind-set. We must welcome them to this port to bring in their booty for exchange, otherwise they'll simply go to Tortuga, and His Majesty will lose his portion."

Baret knew Modyford had his cover. The governor's agent would sail to England with a letter for Duke Abermarle, who would then meet privately with King Charles. Modyford's letter explained the "urgency" placed upon him: An attack must take place to keep Jamaica from falling victim to a secret expedition by the dons. Admiral Henry Morgan and a host of seasoned buccaneer captains will respond to their threat to capture Jamaica. The best strategy is to keep hitting Spain hard in her most vital parts—the treasure colonies. Cartagena, center of Spanish naval power; Porto Bello, Panama, Maracaibo, Santa Marta, Rio de la Hacha . . .

Finally, thought Baret, his dark eyes glinting, *Porto Bello.*

The meeting ended, and he leaned back against the terrace rail. His gaze moved to Emerald, who was under the watchful care of Sir Cecil. Baret was pleased to see that his old tutor had done as he requested and was keeping her from leaving. Watching, he found the sweetly alluring face and form in rich burgundy satin and lace to be distracting. Her glossy dark hair was parted in the center and lay over the crown of her head in waves. The long curls that hung in the back were pulled up from her neck, then braided and twisted into a high scroll.

He saw that Lavender had stood to her feet and was looking in his direction, probably anticipating that he would join her and Grayford on the lawn for supper. Then Emerald too, though less obviously than Lavender, cast a glance at him as though to see what his intentions were.

Baret caught up his jacket and hat from the terrace table and walked toward Emerald.

Suddenly there was an unexpected disturbance.

"Send for Doctor Wilkinson!" Grayford called. "Lady Thaxton—she's fainted!"

Emerald turned at Grayford's voice to look worriedly in her cousin's direction. She saw Lavender lying on the floor. *She did that on purpose,* she found herself thinking, astounded. *She saw Baret walking over to me instead of her and suddenly 'swooned.'*

Emerald glanced at Baret. The expression on his face was unreadable, but the concern written there could not be hidden. He moved through the small throng of onlookers and bent down beside Lavender and Grayford.

Emerald knew she'd been forgotten. She stepped back, unnoticed now, and watched as a moment later Baret, not Grayford, carried Lavender across the parlor and into the hall, followed by Grayford, Earl Nigel, Lord Felix, and Sir Cecil.

Emerald glanced down at the black lace fan in her hands and saw that her fingers trembled. Lavender would always get her way. She whirled and was bent on quick flight out of the governor's residence when Sir Cecil reappeared.

She paused, not wishing to appear indifferent to Lavender's "illness."

"Is she all right?"

"The doctor will see her when he comes. I've been asked to stay with her."

"Yes, of course." She snapped her fan shut. "I'd best be going, Sir Cecil."

He laid a restraining hand on her arm as though he read her thoughts. "The viscount has asked you wait. He wishes to talk with you. He says he won't be long."

She was surprised and gave him a searching glance, but he smiled reassuringly. "Remember, he's been close to Lavender since they were children. He's bound to care."

She watched him leave, feeling uneasy about the risks of staying. The parlor was now empty, and she walked back to the front salon to wait in the furnished cubicle used as a waiting room for the ladies to deposit their wraps.

I'll wait, she thought, *but not for long. If I know Lavender, she'll soon awake if Baret is with her. There'll be no leaving the duchess tonight. She'll need his encouragement.*

She tapped her fan against her palm. "She'll never let him go—never."

Lavender felt herself being carried up a flight of steps, down a corridor, and into a chamber. Here, she was laid on a four-poster bed, and the room buzzed as a maid and Colonel Edward Morgan's daughter Mary Elizabeth made her comfortable. Grayford drew near and took her hand, his eyes questioning her worriedly.

But it was Baret's response that interested Lavender, and she moaned slightly, glancing about the chamber to see where he was.

Across the room she saw Baret watching her evenly. He looked concerned, and her heart throbbed with satisfaction. He had left Emerald to rush to her side when she needed him. A glimpse of his dark eyes and the restrained energy in his handsome face stirred her passions from slumber. She'd been a fool to settle for Grayford, but she'd get Baret back.

Again, she glanced across the chamber, this time at the one man she feared, Earl Nigel Buckington. He had informed her bluntly in the carriage on the way from the town house that regardless of Baret's restored reputation over the victory at Barbados, he would not permit them to marry. Her betrothal to Grayford was settled; she must—if she expected any inheritance from the earl—be content with her lot.

Earl Nigel was observing her with a cool, cynical twist to his mouth. He saw through her "illness."

She must make her plans carefully—not move too hastily. The best way to see her scheme fulfilled was to make friends with Emerald again . . . to have her at Foxemoore where she could watch her, to make certain she would not marry Baret. Illness was the master key that would unlock Baret's attention.

But she must watch Earl Nigel—and Lord Felix, too, who was adamant that she marry his stepson, Grayford.

Lavender snuggled her small, jeweled hands deeper into the folds of the silk coverlet. Again, she wished that she were home in London at Buckington House with Baret. She glanced through her golden lashes at Earl Nigel, then at Lord Felix, whom she hoped was not her future father-in-law. She must convince Baret she had made a mistake with Grayford.

The silence in the chamber made her uncomfortable, but being a master at poise, she lay quietly, her heart-shaped face pale, her dovelike eyes a tender blue, glancing from the hard-faced Earl Nigel to the dark, sultry looks of Baret. He stayed on the other side of the chamber, leaning back against a dresser, arms folded, watching her.

The trade winds rattled the stiff curtain of wooden beads that divided the chamber from a small open terrace facing the sea. *Baret loves the West Indies,* she found herself thinking. *I shall make myself love it for his sake. He will want to come here often. And we will have our own town house facing the warm, green-blue Caribbean. I won't allow a mistaken marriage with Grayford to ruin our future.*

Unlike her cousin Emerald, whose reputation was now forever stained after the recent incident with Sir Jasper, Lavender told herself that she could wrap herself in pure white. And it was this that drew Baret, not just the fact that Emerald was pretty.

She would be a duchess after the death of her invalid grandmother in London. Her title would influence Earl Nigel.

For Baret, marriage was not only expected in London but inevitable. She was well aware that women other than Emerald hoped to marry the viscount. If the king received him with honors after what happened at Barbados, even more titled ladies would nurture the same hope.

But competition would not distress her. Unlike the other hopeful daughters of London nobility, Lavender's claim on Baret was well established, and she was certain of her plan to get him back. He would not deny her the marriage that was deemed rightfully hers—not if she could free herself from Grayford without appearing to have caused the broken engagement.

If only he would not survive the war, she thought suddenly. *Then I would be honorably free.* Baret had already once promised to marry her. He had vowed that if she would allow him the liberty of a few years to fight Spain and search for his father, he would return to settle down at an appropriate time.

She had kept her side of the bargain—except for the utterly stupid mistake of becoming engaged to Grayford. But in time . . .

She must make certain Baret did not marry Emerald before she was free of Grayford. Her illness could help to accomplish this also, especially if Emerald came to Foxemoore to attend her. *And I'll be very sweet to her. Neither she nor Baret must know.*

Lavender felt secure and hopeful once again. Had he not come running to her side when he thought she had fainted with a relapse of tropical fever? Her condition added to her fragile beauty and to her hold on him. She smiled to herself.

And so, while Earl Nigel watched her suspiciously, and Lord Felix probably worried that her health would not afford a soon-enough marriage to Grayford, Lavender was composed and confident. Her small hands rested sweetly under the coverlet. She opened her eyes again, as though stirring awake.

"Grayford," she whispered, as though he alone were on her heart. "Are you . . . here?"

"Yes, beloved. Are you all right now? The doctor is on his way."

"What happened? Did I faint again? I felt so ill. I suppose it was this dreadful heat and the horrid talk of war. Oh! If only you didn't need to fight. You and Baret both! What if something happens to either of you? What will the family do?"

"Perhaps be better off," came Earl Nigel's sardonic voice. "Or is it you, dear, who would be better off?"

"Father," Felix snapped. "What's gotten into you, speaking to her like this? You know how ill she is."

"Yes," said Nigel. "We do indeed know, do we not, Baret?"

Lavender feared to look at either the earl or Baret, for she read the thick irony in his grandfather's voice. She looked up to Grayford instead, as if she hadn't heard the cutting remark. She reached a small hand toward him. "Grayford?"

"I'm here, Lavender. Unfortunately, I can't stay—"

"Quite unfortunate," Nigel said. "Who arranged for you to be called back to your ship tonight?"

Lavender closed her eyes. She had, but no one knew.

"The Admiralty, Uncle Nigel—something to do with the plans to meet with Morgan aboard the *Royale*. It's important."

"It's quite all right, Grayford," said Lavender weakly. "Do what you must. But if the governor would be kind enough to allow me to rest awhile before I return to Foxemoore . . ."

Governor Modyford was swift to assure her of his hospitality. "Naturally, Lady Thaxton, you're welcome to remain here and rest for as long as you like. If it proves beneficial, perhaps you should stay the night and return to Foxemoore tomorrow morning."

Mary Elizabeth also hurried to put her at ease, fluffing her lace pillow and saying, "If there's anything I can do, m'lady Thaxton, please don't hesitate to call on me or my sisters."

Lavender smiled. "Thank you. You're all so kind. I'm dreadfully sorry and embarrassed. Governor, I hope this won't ruin your dinner plans."

"Not at all, Lady Thaxton. Perhaps we can have something sent up to you. I'll tell one of the servants to see to your needs."

Grayford still held her hand. "I'll return as soon as I can. We can leave for Foxemoore in the morning."

"You mustn't worry about me. Your duty to His Majesty is so important in the war. And I'm proud of you."

Grayford stood from the side of the bed, looking down at her. As he turned to leave the chamber, his gaze shot across the

360

room to where Baret stood. Their eyes met and locked, then Grayford walked briskly to the door and went out.

He's suspicious of Baret, Lavender thought. *But he doesn't suspect me. It's better this way. I'll make everything up to Baret when we're married.*

As the others began to leave the chamber to await the doctor's arrival, Lavender called weakly, "Baret . . . can you stay a moment longer?"

She saw Earl Nigel look at him, but Baret did not seem intimidated by his grandfather. He paused by the doorway.

"Of course. What is it?"

She tried to read his voice, but it was empty of emotion. He might have been a stranger speaking to her.

"It's about Cousin Emerald," she murmured. "I wish her to return to the Great House with me. Do you think she will if you asked her?"

Aware that his grandfather had also paused at the mention of Emerald, Baret turned to look at him. "I'll only be a moment alone with her."

Earl Nigel's dark eyes were sharp. "You know what I expect of you," he said in a low voice. "If you want your plans to go forward smoothly with Morgan, you'll keep them in mind."

Baret smiled faintly. "Don't worry. Would I disappoint you? I know exactly what I want, Grandfather. And I'm not in the mood to toss my plans overboard now."

The earl looked thoughtful. "I'm glad to hear that." He glanced toward Lavender's bed, still looking troubled, then went out, shutting the door.

24

THE MAN IN BLACK

Emerald began to pace as she waited and neither Baret nor Sir Cecil returned. *I knew it,* she told herself. She glanced across the outer salon at the arriving wives and daughters of council members and the planter gentry. Soon they would be coming to leave their wraps.

I can't endure their seeing me now.

As though jinxed by her expectations, she saw several daughters who were Lavender's closest allies making their way to the wrap room where she waited. She must avoid them. Desperately she glanced about and in relief saw a draped doorway, leading perhaps into another chamber.

She slipped through to the other side.

It was a semidark alcove smelling of turpentine and tropical rot. Opposite the draped entrance, a heavy wooden door stood ajar. She supposed it led into one of the mansion's main rooms. She could escape that way, but what would she say if caught wandering about the governor's private rooms?

I'll wait here, she decided. The girls wouldn't stay longer than it would take them to leave their shawls. They'd soon wander out onto the green or into the back garden, where it was cooler. *Then I'll slip out and leave.*

The girls entered—all of them daughters of Government House officials serving Modyford—talking in a rush. One carried a wicker basket of red-and-white flowers to make into nosegays.

Cautiously, Emerald stepped away from the cracked drape. If they found her here hiding, what would they think?

A girl was talking, her voice petulant and resentful. "And even if she *married* him, she'd never be invited to Whitehall."

"She would so! A viscount's wife?" came a second voice. "Why, any woman he'd marry can have anything she wants. Why

362

should the king care about her past? Mother says he himself has a mistress named Barbara."

"Men," came a scornful new voice.

A sigh followed. "I wish the viscount would marry *me.*"

"He doesn't know you're even alive, Marian."

"If you ask me, I don't think he knows *any* woman's alive except Lavender."

"It's no wonder Emerald's father used to keep her locked up at Foxemoore—I'd be ashamed of her too!"

Emerald froze, her fingers tightening against her satin skirts.

"He wasn't much better. The whole lot of 'em are bad seed, so I've been told, including that Lord Felix Buckington. I heard my father tell Mother that Felix is a smuggler."

"A smuggler!"

"But Emerald is the worst of them all. Lavender says . . ."

Emerald felt a sickening flutter in her stomach. She felt a strong impulse to place her palms over her ears. *You've nothing to be ashamed of,* a small voice seemed to say in her ears. *Step out. Let your presence be known. It is they who need to be ashamed for indulging in backbiting.*

Yet her feet remained riveted to the spot, her heart aching.

"We all know who her mother was—some little Frenchie on Tortuga. Her mother always did have a loose reputation, even in France. But that's not all. The madam—for that's what she was— used to be a spy against England for France. And Emerald was born in the room above her mother's gambling den. And she shot a pirate trying to protect her lover, Levasseur!"

Lies! Emerald's cheeks burned. *Lies!* For a moment she thought she might faint in the hot alcove. The smell of mildew and turpentine was nauseating.

"Eventually her mother was hanged—for murder. Just the way they hang pirates at Port Royal. The ravens pecked at her for two days before they buried her."

"Do stop! We'll be eating soon."

Vicious lies, again. How often had she heard the whispers about her mother, like snakes hissing their venom! Yet never had the charges been so ugly as today.

"I don't believe it," another girl scoffed. "They wouldn't let a *woman* hang for two days, even if she *was* a murderess."

"Indeed, well, you are quite wrong. Seems everyone in Jamaica knows the lurid tale except you, Catherine. But you're forgiven, since you've only newly arrived. Why, Emerald herself tried to kill the overseer at Foxemoore. And if it hadn't been for Sir Jasper, she'd still be in Brideswell. I'll wager he's sorry now he brought her to Spanish Town."

"Why is that?"

"Because the viscount found her in his chamber and shot him!"

There came an excited gasp. Then a flurry of whispers.

Emerald stood behind the drape, too humiliated to muster the courage to move. Her eyes shut tightly, as though by closing out the world of Port Royal she could eliminate the past.

With great care, lest they hear her, she felt her way across the alcove to the door standing ajar. She glanced into the room beyond and saw that it appeared to be a study. Books lined one wall, and a sheaf of documents lay on the desk. A private office? She mustn't be caught in here.

She tiptoed to the opposite door and opened it a crack, peeking out. No one was in sight, though she could hear distant, muffled voices coming through the walls. She stepped out into a hallway.

Swiftly Emerald moved past closed doors and still rooms until, at a corner, she unexpectedly came to the end of the corridor. A flight of steps wound to an upper floor. She was going the wrong direction!

She was about to flee, but then the stealthy sound of a door opening behind her—opening as though someone did not wish to be seen—caused her to pause uncertainly and look back the way she had come.

Was someone else trying to hide? The thought was troubling, for she could not imagine that anyone would have a reason as innocent and valid as her own. She noticed that a door she had passed moments earlier now stood open a few inches, as though someone was listening, waiting.

Then suddenly, from far down the hall but growing louder, the angry voice of Lord Felix shouted, "I tell you, Thomas, the king will hold you responsible for any buccaneer attack against the Main!"

There was no escape now, except up the stairs.

Baret stood watching Lavender, feeling his blood pound, not with passion but anger. He wondered that so little stirred in his heart when he saw her except an odd sort of sympathy. Slowly he'd discovered she wasn't the woman he'd been raised to think she was.

They'd both been children in France when they were introduced. Even then, he'd felt responsible for her and protective. Through the years he'd mistaken that sense of duty for something much more exciting.

He was angry with himself as well. His eyes narrowed. They were both to blame where Emerald was concerned, though he held himself more responsible for not trusting her. He had learned this afternoon that there was strong cause to believe Lavender had deliberately lied when she informed him about Emerald and Jasper.

After Emerald had told him that she had been at the hacienda for two days instead of the several weeks Carlotta insisted upon, he had returned to Spanish Town to look more carefully into the matter. There a bulky woman, a house slave, had come forward to confirm Emerald's statement, adding more information. Emerald had indeed withstood Jasper's badgering insults and his bribes. She'd asked the slave for help to escape to the governor's residence. She had even given brave testimony of her Christian faith.

It was Lavender, who, upon learning that Carlotta was Felix's daughter, bribed her to vow that Emerald had been unfaithful in exchange for release from Brideswell.

Now that Baret was certain of the truth, he wondered how he could have been so stupid where Emerald was concerned. His only excuse was that finding her in Jasper's chamber in satin and jewels had fed his jealous fears. And when Lavender, a woman he thought to be of high character, had sadly backed up the sordid tale, he had been in a mood to accept it—at Emerald's expense.

He frowned when he remembered the insult he had lashed her with. She had been brave and noble, and he had added to her suffering by disbelieving her story. First, she had undergone the brutality of Lex Thorpe! And now this! And he had not recognized her qualities!

He walked to the foot of the bed. Their eyes met, and under his level stare, Lavender's faltered.

"You play a hard game for such a sweet frail thing. Anything to win, is that it?"

He saw her wince and wondered if it was real or meant to soften his temper.

"Baret, you mustn't be cruel," she said. "You mustn't hate me when I love you so."

"I don't hate you. I don't feel anything at the moment but a wish to turn you over my knee and give you a good spanking."

She bolted upright, eyes flashing. "You wouldn't dare. I'm a duchess."

"Ah, the real Lavender has regained her determination— and her health and strength," he mocked softly.

She wrung her hands, clasping them against her lace-shrouded bosom.

He took hold of the dark wooden bedpost. "Tell me, m'dear, were you always this conniving in our past relationship, or was I too consumed with finding my father to even notice until recently?"

"Baret!"

"I beg your pardon! I've insulted you, my duchess!"

"Stop it. You're being dreadfully unfair and cruel to me."

"And you, dear heart, lied to me about Emerald and Sir Jasper."

"No—"

"Yes. And now you think nothing of lying again. You bribed Carlotta to destroy Emerald's reputation. And it worked . . . for a time. I believed you instead of her. I've hurt her," he gritted, "but I actually hold myself responsible."

Tears welled in her blue eyes and ran down her pale cheeks.

His gaze smoldered darkly. "Tears will do you no good this time."

"All right—I did lie—so I wouldn't lose you—because I love you, Baret. I can't lose you, I can't."

He frowned. Her emotionalism troubled him. He didn't want to see her plead. For a moment he stood watching her, and then came and sat by the bed. "Lavender, I don't want to hurt you. I do care about you. But not in the way—"

"Oh, Baret, if you do love me, you can't marry—*her!*"

A flicker of impatience crossed his face. "Don't tell me what I can or cannot do, madam."

Her small hands formed fists, and she pounded them against her skirts.

He smiled, his eyes mocking, yet amused. "Temper, duchess. Remember, you're frail and quick to faint when it suits you. As for loving you, there were times in the past, when I was younger, when I thought I loved a girl with your name and face. But, you see, she never existed. I was away so much that I never really knew the real Lavender."

"How can you say that!"

"A gentle word of advice. Treat Grayford well. He truly loves you. You're not likely to find another man who'll be as whole-heartedly devoted to you when he knows how scheming you are."

"You're teasing me. Of course, you are. You've always loved me. You once told me you'd do anything for me."

"Did I? I must have been naive—or else it was all that Latin and Greek prose Sir Cecil boggled my mind with."

"Baret!"

"Seriously, Lavender, it's over between us."

She reached both arms for him, her eyes imploring. "I won't believe it. I can't accept it. I was foolish and, oh, so wrong about Grayford. Do say you'll forgive me and love me again. I promise to make it up to you."

He ignored her arms. "What was it about Emerald you wished to discuss?"

"How I feel about you isn't spoiled . . . and I do feel ill." Her head dropped into her hands.

"Lavender, my dear—please. You're making it harder on yourself and me."

"All right, I need Emerald with me at Foxemoore. When you and Grayford go to war, it will be dreadful. We'll need each other. You will talk to her? You'll ask her to come and stay with me?"

He stared down at her for a long moment without speaking.

"Please, Baret. I'll need her desperately now that my mother is dead. And Sir Karlton is gone. And Aunt Geneva is ill." Tears welled again. "Oh, this dreadful war! If only we could have sailed to England first."

He stood. "I'll speak to her," was all he said.

367

"Baret—it's not too late for us. My heart is betrothed to you, even if I wear Grayford's ring."

He frowned. "It's over, Lavender. I'm going to marry Emerald."

He was walking to the door when she called: "I'll make you change your mind one day. You'll see. You don't love her."

He opened the door, pausing to look back, and felt an odd pity at the stricken look on her face.

"You're wrong," he said clearly. "I haven't told her yet, but I will." He turned away and walked out into the hall.

Emerald sped up the flight of steps to avoid the governor and Lord Felix at all cost. But as she rounded the corner into the upper hall, a door was abruptly thrown open in front of her, and a clear, strong, familiar voice said, "You're wrong. I haven't told her yet, but I will."

And Baret came through the door.

Seeing Emerald, he stopped short. They stared at each other, equally surprised.

Emerald knew she must appear pale and disheveled by all of tonight's madness that stalked her fleeing steps, and now had she walked headfirst into an emotional scene between Baret and Lavender? She could endure no more! She turned and fled to the stairs.

"Emerald—wait!"

She raced down the steps, her feet flying as swiftly as a hind's, her heart racing. She darted by the cracked door and back through the governor's office, past a startled governor and Lord Felix, out through the drape partition into the wrap room, the salon, and outdoors onto the rolling front lawn facing the Caribbean.

Her breathing came painfully and stabbed her side. But she ran on through the twilight, past gaily clad mulatto slaves carrying trays of citrus-rum coolers. The heads of loitering guests turned toward her. Female brows probably arched, but she was past caring.

Escape! Escape! she thought, feeling the sod sink beneath her feet. On she ran.

A blue-gold star blazed above the bay, yet visible in the twilight. The wind blew in from the harbor, ruffling the water's surface and cooling her skin. She ran until, finally, she could run no more.

She was, she thought, a safe distance away from the lawn guests. She grasped hold of a tree with both arms and sank against it, resting her head against the rough bark. Her breath came in ragged gasps.

As Baret sprinted down the steps in pursuit, something far different from romance arrested his attention. He noticed that one door on the corridor ahead stood slightly ajar, and his instincts halted him. Whereas an ordinary guest would not have noticed—or, if he had, would have paid no attention—a life surrounded with danger kept Baret's suspicions on guard. When he stopped, he heard a faint sound from behind the door, as though a breath drew in with the realization that the advantage of surprise was lost.

Then the door flung open. Baret glimpsed a gloved hand and ducked below the trajectory of a silvery glint of steel as it whispered past his head and solidly impacted the wall. In the next second, Baret whipped his pistol from beneath his jacket belt. The assassin at the Bailey had escaped, but this one would not be so lucky.

He approached the darkened chamber and pushed the door back with a foot, anticipating an explosion of gunpowder to greet him. Silence bade him enter. A trap?

He hesitated only a moment, then stepped inside with caution, prepared to be jumped from either direction. Nothing stirred except the curtains in the muggy breeze. Moonlight flooded in by way of a railed balcony that looked down upon the governor's garden. Had the man gone over the balcony? He looked. But the wisteria had not been damaged, and no one could have climbed down and disappeared so quickly. *Then the man was still inside.*

Baret surveyed the large chamber. It offered numerous hiding places. A heavy brocade drape moved, or was it the breeze? Then, from behind it a door hastily opened and shut. Baret leaped over a divan, swept aside the drape, and grabbed the knob just as a bolt slid into place. Clattering footsteps bounded down some stairs. Then this door led down onto the garden.

He returned swiftly to the balcony, swung one leg over the

369

railing, and grabbed the woody, meandering vine. Three arm-sized branches twisted together to form a trunk. He swung his other leg over the rail and, after testing the giant wisteria for strength, eased himself down, using his feet to brace himself in the descent.

He landed in the courtyard a moment before a man wearing a black mask emerged from around the side of the house.

"Halt, assassin! You will unmask yourself and the man who hired you, or die in your own blood!"

The man, as lean and muscular as a trained acrobat, was clothed all in black and wore a scarf concealing his hair. He sprang, his sword glinting like a silver ribbon in the moonlight.

Baret sensed his assassin's power and confidence. His own blade met the aggressive attack, but it was clear that he was in for the fight of his life. This was a swordsman with fencing abilities equal to . . . Sir Erik Farrow's.

For a moment Baret felt his stomach lurch with sickening disappointment. *Erik?*

No, impossible! Erik would not betray him to death—but how could he know for sure, since the man's face and hair were completely masked? They fought in the shadows as distant laughter and music came from the front lawn, the guests of Governor Modyford unaware of the death-fight in the solitude of the back garden.

The assassin turned his blade and lunged, narrowly missing Baret's throat and nicking his shoulder instead. Baret fought off the attack but could not gain the offensive as up and down the courtyard their steel blades rang.

Then, finally, all Baret's training came to his aid like emotional reinforcements. His Toledo blade found an opening and bit hard, making contact. His sword swept a circle before him, and the assassin fell back with a slash across his forearm. Baret came at him powerfully now, beating back his enemy's blade.

The blood streaming toward the man's wrist threatened his grip. He was unsure now, and his cool confidence appeared to wane as Baret smashed a ringing blow. The stranger staggered, then recovered. Baret pressed him harder. The man sprang like a wounded tiger fighting for his life, lunging in a last desperate attempt to run him through. Baret shook the sweat from his eyes and savagely beat down the blade, feinted back, lured the man in. He took the bait, leaned in to take advantage, but Baret was prepared and met him with a direct thrust. The assassin stumbled, fell, and the hired sword clattered to the cobbles.

Baret approached his fallen foe, reluctant to discover who the killer might be. He stooped and pulled away the mask. Their eyes locked. And relief poured through Baret's soul. *Not Erik.*

"Who hired you?" he breathed. "My uncle?"

He didn't expect the man to answer and was surprised when he did.

"Jasper," he whispered bitterly. "At the order of Felix."

So . . .

"At the Bailey too?"

"Yes."

"Who are you? Where do you come from?"

"Doesn't matter . . . Harwick alive . . ."

"Karlton?"

"Galley slave . . . slave ship . . . on way to Spanish colonies . . ."

Karlton was alive?

The attempted assassin stared up at Baret, trying to speak again, but his words ended in strangled silence.

25

PROMISE ME FOREVER

The sun had long ago set. A blue-gold star, blazing its glory above the bay, was yet visible in the twilight. How long Emerald had simply leaned there against the tree, resting before the long walk back to the lookout house, she did not know. She saw that the moon was now making its way across the ebony sky to dip into the Caribbean.

She now wished she hadn't sent Zeddie off to Foxemoore, for the walk ahead seemed a horrendous task. Still, she must get home. And she couldn't remain here much longer without detection by some meandering couple enjoying the last of the moonlight.

She left the tree, walking slowly now through the shadows, away from the guests, away from Baret.

Palm trees became shivering silhouettes in the purple twilight that enveloped the smooth lawn and towering trees of the garden. Long beds of red hibiscus, peonies, and roses, growing in profusion, scented the breeze.

Raising her eyes, Emerald looked ahead and then stopped, tensing. Baret leaned against a palm, arms folded, his buccaneer shirt showing white in the semidarkness.

"You can run all you want," he said. "You won't get away from me. I won't let you. I would have come sooner, but a small incident delayed me."

The irony in his voice alerted her. She doubted it had been a small incident.

Still, she didn't want to risk her emotions further. She darted away.

He caught her and turned her around to face him, enclosing her in his embrace. "Will you surrender peaceably, madam, or do you encourage me to use other means?"

"Let go of me, please."

372

"No." His brow lifted, and his mouth showed a hint of smile. "One other time you ran away from me and jumped ship. This time, I'm not about to let you escape."

Emerald stared up into warm, intense dark eyes and felt herself weakening. She noticed a silver pendant about his throat, saw that for the first time he wore the family coat of arms, showing he was heir to an earldom. And then she saw the fresh bloodstain on his shirt.

"You're hurt! But how? In the governor's meeting tonight Felix admitted you were the king's agent—you were to be safe!"

"It's all right. The wound is minor. I have much to explain, and I have some wonderful news for you, but now I want to talk to you about us," he said softly.

Could there be such a thing as wonderful news after all she'd undergone, after what both of them had been through? It hurt too much to hope again.

"I must go now, please!"

"I have so much to say. Will you listen?"

A weighty silence settled between them.

"Perhaps this will partially explain . . . I have something I want to give you." He reached into his shirt and handed her a small, ornate silver box that danced with brightness in the moonlight. Then he took her hand, opened it gently, and set the box on her palm. "This is for you. With my deepest apologies, and my heart's devotion."

Her own heart bounced to her stomach then back to her throat. Her eyes closed to hold back the tears. She knew what it was, and she was afraid to open the box, for her emotions were ready to burst. "I can't," she whispered, her throat dry. "Not now, not tonight—"

"Open it."

She swallowed. Her trembling fingers fumbled with the catch, lifted the lid. What lay inside was not the Buckington ring that would vow their public betrothal, but she was far from disappointed.

"It belonged to my mother. In giving it to you, I compare you with all that is fine, noble, and pure."

Her breath caught. A single ruby pendant glimmered like a wine-colored rose, drenching with sweetness and dew. "Oh, Baret . . ." Her voice failed.

He lifted her face. "'Who can find a virtuous woman? For her price is far above rubies.'" He kissed away the tears welling in her eyes. "My beloved is undefiled. 'Thou art all fair, my love; there is no spot in thee.'" His arms enclosed her in a heart-stopping embrace, secure, and wonderful.

"Baret, you can't mean that you're actually in love with me?"

"My love is unquenchable. Is that strongly worded enough, or would you like more?"

Joy that was strong and blessed swelled in her heart. "Yes," she said softly, hoping her voice wouldn't tremble. "It is enough."

He reached for her hand and brought it to his lips. "I need to ask your forgiveness."

"No," she whispered, her heart in her eyes. "You do not."

"I've finally allowed reason to prevail and took time to look into the matter—something I should have done at the start. You never gave me reason to mistrust you, but 'love is strong as death; jealousy is cruel as the grave: the coals thereof are coals of fire, which hath a most vehement flame,'" he quoted Solomon. "When you told me you were at the hacienda for just two days, I went back. The house slave explained the truth. I confronted Carlotta, and she admitted she lied for reasons of her own."

"Because of Jasper?"

He hesitated. "I'd prefer you didn't ask me her reason, since it will cause more pain for everyone involved, especially you. Can you be satisfied with my knowing the truth?"

She suspected Lavender, but anger and jealousy toward her conniving cousin no longer seemed to matter. No longer did Lavender stand between them. Baret believed in her again. What else mattered beneath the sweetly rising amber moon? *He's in love with me.*

"I would like our public betrothal settled and out in the open before I sail in three weeks," he said. "I'm fully convinced of what I have felt from the beginning. Convinced enough to ask you to marry me, not because of a duel, or my grandfather's expectations, but because I want you for my own. And I'm willing and anxious to prove it. Tonight, if you like. There's no reason to wait, is there?"

No reason to wait, her mind repeated in a dazed fluster. "Here?" Her voice failed in a whisper. "Tonight?"

"Cecil is here to marry us. Tonight I would honor my beloved before all. The governor is giving a celebration. Why not make use of it? Anyone of importance in Jamaica is here, including my grandfather. And you," he said, giving her a little squeeze, "look delectable enough to be a bride."

Emerald gave a nervous laugh. "But we mustn't. We can't. I mean, we couldn't—I couldn't marry you tonight—not *yet!*"

He persisted with a kiss that left her breathless. "Why not?"

She tried to pull away. "It wouldn't be decent after all the things said about me. I—there must be at least a year's wait . . ."

"A year!"

"You know what they'll think, what they'll say, if you suddenly marry me now—tonight!" she blurted out.

His mouth curved with irony. "As long as I know the truth, what does it matter?" Then he laughed, seeing her expression. "Very well. I see your point, and it's well taken, especially if you wish to start that Christian singing school. Your pristine reputation we shall guard to the very end! But we'll have the betrothal at least. How and where do you want it?"

She tried to calm the pounding of her heart. "Foxemoore. In—the Great House, with candles burning and everyone there, including—" She paused.

"Lavender?" His dark eyes bore a malicious twinkle. "So you do have a villainous streak after all."

"I was going to say Minette," she said with a laugh.

"Whatever you want. Foxemoore it is. But it will need to take place before I sail with Morgan."

She was still troubled by another thought. "But—how can I marry you when your reputation is restored with Earl Nigel? You're a *viscount!*"

His eyes laughed at her. "Then I'll become a pirate," he said glibly. "And if my reputation is 'restored,' as you put it, I restored it so as to come back to Port Royal to find you. To storm Brideswell if I had to."

"For me! It wasn't for Lavender, then?"

"For you. And from now on I will do everything for us. And now . . ." His eyes held hers. "There's something you're forgetting, something I want from you and have waited to hear. So far I've done all the committing. I've spoken all the words of love. Don't you have anything to commit to me before God?"

She smiled, tears softening her eyes. "I have much to say to you. I have set you as a seal upon my heart, for 'many waters cannot quench love.'" She wrapped her arms about him, taking pride in him, gazing up at him fervently. "My heart, I commit to you forever. Oh, yes, I shall confess. I love you, my lord viscount."

Thoughtfully he wrapped about his finger one of her lustrous curls that had come undone. "Well said. And what of that blackguard pirate Foxworth? Could you love him too?"

"Well . . . if you promise not to tell."

"Your dark secret is safe."

"I confess I love him equally."

"Well enough. He may resort to his old habits. And if he does, you may yet need to be swept away on a pirate's ship. With your endeavors at Foxemoore, and mine with Morgan, we may both end up fleeing for our lives to the Carolinas after all." He smiled. "And now, there is something else. Happy news. Perhaps you should sit down on the grass. I don't want you to faint."

Faint? How could anything bring her more happiness than the words she had just heard him speak? What could mean more to her than his love, than his wish to make her his beloved?

"I'm not the fainting kind," she said breathlessly. "What is it?"

He drew her close, his eyes holding hers. "First, that unknown assassin from the Bailey—I faced him tonight. He's dead."

"Your wound," she said shakily, "Oh, Baret, you are truly all right?"

"Before the man died, he told me who had hired him. As I always suspected, it was Jasper, and behind him, my uncle. I can do nothing about them yet, not until I free my father. But he also told me the good news that—Emerald, your father is alive. He's a galley slave aboard the Dutch slave ship on its way to the Main."

She gasped, stunned, unable to speak, staring at him.

Alive! Her beloved father was not dead as Jasper and Pitt insisted, but alive! Tears of happiness filled her eyes, and she didn't know whether she would laugh or sob.

Baret held her tightly as she cried softly into his chest. "Don't worry, darling. I'll be sailing soon, Erik with me. Between us, we'll take the slave ship just as we did the *San Pedro*. With God's help I'll bring your father back safe. And my father as well."

She believed him.

The aromatic scent of orange and lemon trees in bloom laced the tropical air. The sweetness was heady, and the white blossoms flitted down like snowflakes that refused to melt on the warm grass.

Baret took the ruby pendant, placed it around her throat, and secured the clasp. She looked up at him. In silence he drew her toward him. Their lips sealed their promise.